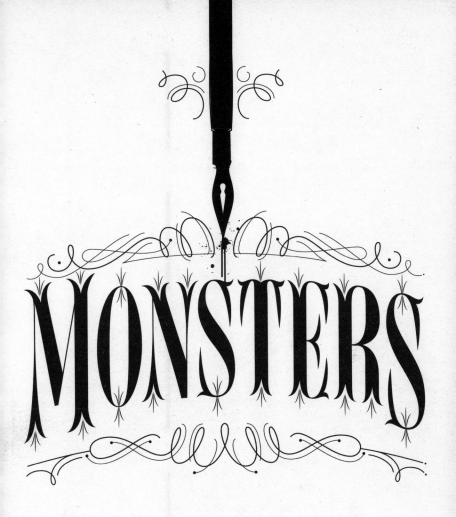

MONSTERS

A NOVEL BY
SHARON DOGAR

ANDERSEN PRESS

Also by Sharon Dogar

Annexed

First published in 2019 by
Andersen Press Limited
20 Vauxhall Bridge Road
London SW1V 2SA
www.andersenpress.co.uk

2 4 6 8 10 9 7 5 3 1

British Library Cataloguing in Publication Data available.

Hardback ISBN 978 1 78344 802 9
Trade paperback ISBN 978 1 78344 803 6

This book is printed on FSC accredited paper from responsible sources

Printed and bound in Great Britain
by Clays Ltd, Elcograf S.p.A.

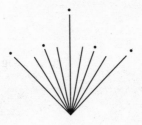

This book owes its existence to Charlie Sheppard, who commissioned me to write it. If you hadn't asked, the book wouldn't exist.

With special love to my father Miraj din Dogar, who, like Mary and her mother, as well as Bysshe and Claire, knows all about exile.

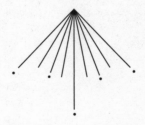

Each man kills the thing he loves . . .
The coward does it with a kiss,
The brave man with a sword!

Oscar Wilde

Did I request thee, Maker, from my clay
To mould me Man, did I solicit thee
From darkness to promote me?

John Milton, **Paradise Lost**

PART

ONE

2ND JUNE 1812: 41 SKINNER STREET, LONDON

Mary stands at the top of the stairs seething with the unfairness of it all. Her stepmother has sent her to her bedchamber – again. Mrs Godwin says it's for refusing to do as she's told, when really they both know it is because Mary refuses to call her Mamma. Mrs Godwin is not her mamma. Mary has managed to avoid calling her Mamma for the last ten years and is not about to break that vow to herself – and her real mamma – now.

Mary hovers at the top of the long flight of narrow stairs waiting for the sound of her papa's study door opening and then closing. Once he's inside she can creep down the stairs. She hears him cross the room and sit in his chair but still she waits. If he hears her open the kitchen door he will get up and ask where she is going – and once she tells him he will want to come. She couldn't bear that; she wants to visit Mamma alone.

Below her, Mary can hear her stepsister Jane and Mrs Godwin laughing together. The sound grates. Papa would not mind if Jane decided to call him Mr Godwin rather than Papa. He would not send her to her room. Or make such a silly fuss about it. That's the problem with her stepfamily, thinks Mary – they have no capacity for reason. And that is why they do not understand her decision never to call Mrs Godwin Mamma. It is not a mere fancy, but based upon the sound principles that her father has taught her. All feelings must be studied before being acted upon. Nothing must be done in haste or without prolonged thought. Mary has thought about what it means to have a stepmother and come to a reasoned decision. It is clearly true that a girl cannot have more than one mamma. And she already has one.

Mary takes a deep breath, it would not be reasonable to do what she wishes, which is to rush down the stairs and confront Mrs Godwin and Jane. Their laughter feels deliberate. Look, it seems to say, how happy we are, without you. If there is a God then she does not understand why he allows people like Mrs Godwin to survive. She would like to run down the stairs and scream at the pair of them: it's MY HOUSE, MY FATHER. But she is fourteen now and far too old to behave in such a childish manner. She closes her eyes, visualising her mother's face in the portrait above Papa's desk. If only she can keep quiet and wait a little longer, then she might creep out of the door and be gone.

'Mary?'

'Oh!' She stifles a cry as she turns, but it's only Fanny, her older sister. Fanny is as quiet as a mouse. She can sit in the corner of a room for hours without anyone noticing, and then she moves and they jump at her presence – as though she has appeared out of nowhere – a ghost.

'What are you doing, Mary?'

'What are *you* doing?' Mary hisses back. 'Creeping up on me!'

Fanny sighs; it is obvious from the expression on Mary's face that she is planning something. She has that look in her eyes, a look of determination and fury that is peculiarly Mary – and that usually means trouble. 'I wasn't creeping up on you,' Fanny says mildly. 'I was simply coming down the stairs!'

Mary is immediately contrite. 'I'm sorry,' she whispers. 'I'm trying to get out without anyone noticing.'

'Why?' Fanny whispers back.

'Because I want to visit Mamma.'

'But—' begins Fanny.

'Alone,' Mary says quickly.

'Why can't you just ask Papa if you might go alone?' says Fanny. 'I'm sure he would let you.'

'Are you?' spits Mary. 'You don't think SHE would make him say no just to spite me, and that Papa would agree with her as he always does, and then SHE would make sure to arrange that he was busy as soon we are about to visit Mamma?'

'You deliberately irritate her, Mary. Why can't you agree to call her Mamma – if you could only do that then everything would be easier!'

'But I can't,' Mary says, scratching the inner elbow of her arm. The skin is already raw and bleeding but she does not notice until Fanny gently holds her fingers back to stop her. 'If I were to call her Mamma it would feel like I was betraying our own mother. Our real mother,' she says staring pointedly, at Fanny.

'Shall I go downstairs and distract HER for you?' Fanny suggests, feeling guilty.

'Thank you!' Mary clutches Fanny's arm, grateful for her offer of help because she knows how much her sister hates to do anything that might cause trouble.

She waits until she hears Fanny's voice guiding Mrs Godwin further down the stairs and into the bookshop below the house. She hears the heavy door between the house and the shop swing shut; her stepmother will be in there for a while now. The juvenile bookshop is her pride and joy, despite the fact that it fails to make them any money. Mary starts off down the stairs. Her father coughs as she creeps past his door, but she carries on into the kitchen. She opens the back door, carefully sliding back the bolt and slipping through before closing it silently behind her, making sure the latch catches. Once she is through the yard and out she begins to run. She meant to walk quietly and confidently away from the house but she cannot help herself. The feel of the breeze in her face releasing all the pent-up fury.

The sight of a young woman running makes people stare. Young women should be calm and considered. Young women should be able to manage themselves, and young women should not allow their own desires to overcome convention. But Mary doesn't care. Whenever she is angry she forgets her shyness, enjoying the looks of surprise, the knowledge that she is different. She was not born to be like other girls; she was born to be like her mother. An outlaw. A radical. She runs until she can feel her heart pumping and her breath coming short and sharp. She runs until she crosses over the bridge into the churchyard, and it is only the thought that she does not want to arrive at her mamma's grave perspiring and breathless that slows her down as she makes her way up the short hill to where Mamma lies buried.

At the sight of the square gravestone standing beneath two tall willows she feels her heartbeat slow, and the usual calm that being near her mother brings begin to embrace her. She sits on the damp grass beside the stone. This is where her papa taught her to read, lifting her small fingers to follow the letters bitten deep into the stone. She lifts her hand now, tracing the letters of her mamma's name:

MARY WOLLSTONECRAFT GODWIN
AUTHOR OF A VINDICATION OF THE RIGHTS OF WOMAN

'Papa's sending me away, Mamma!' she cries out as she presses her hand over her mother's name. 'To Scotland!' She leans her head against the stone. Today it is cool and damp. In the summer it is warm and soothing. Mary knows the feel of it intimately. It is the touch of her mother. The only one she has ever known.

The stone accepts the weight of her thoughts as she rests against it. She does not want to go to Scotland, to leave Papa. What if the family she is to stay with do not like her? Silently the stone relieves her of her fears. 'After all,' she imagines Mamma saying, 'it might be an adventure. Something to write about.'

'Thank you,' she whispers, brushing the hair from her face. 'I'm sorry I won't be able to visit you for a while, Mamma!' The wind lifts the branches of the willow. 'But I'll think of you,' promises Mary, 'and I will have your books with me.'

The stone remains silent.

'Goodbye.' Mary touches the stone with her lips, sweeping the fingers of her hand one last time over the letters of her mother's name before she turns to go.

'Where's Mary?' Jane asks Fanny. 'I can't find her anywhere!'

Fanny does not move from her position by the nursery window, where she is watching anxiously for Mary's return, ready to wave her in when it is safe. She shrugs her shoulders at Jane and holds her tongue, but she is hopeless at lying, can already feel a dreadful blush beginning to creep across her cheeks.

'I won't tell,' says Jane, stepping closer. 'You know I won't. I just want to ask her something.'

'What?'

'Whether or not she's going to take the brown pelisse to Scotland.'

'Why?'

'I look so nice in it! And it's a shame not to be able to wear it.' Jane imagines herself stepping down from a carriage in the coat they each share; it has a high fur collar and a matching hat. It is very *soignée*. Jane's mamma speaks French and has taught Jane the language. She would like to look *soignée*.

'But it's far too smart just to wear!' says Fanny. 'And Scotland can be cold even in summer. I think Mary should take it,' she says firmly.

'But she might not want it,' insists Jane. 'She doesn't care very much for clothes. She says women should focus more upon the quality of their minds – and less upon the cut of their cloth!' Jane mimics Mary's prim voice so exactly that it is hard for Fanny not to smile, but she manages to resist, despite Jane's infectious laughter. It is hard to believe, sometimes, that the two girls could almost be twins, there is only eight months between them but Mary is by far the more grown-up.

'Is your mamma really making Papa send Mary to Scotland?' Fanny asks.

Jane stops laughing at once. 'Mary blames my mother for everything,' she snaps. 'It's not Mamma's fault that your father fell in love with her.'

'Of course it isn't her fault!' agrees Fanny soothingly, although she and Mary most definitely have their doubts about that. When they are alone together Mary often cruelly imitates their stepmother: '*Oh! Is this the famous Mr Godwin I see before me!*' she says in a sickly sweet, cloying voice of feminine flattery, before pretending to faint upon the bed. Fanny is both horrified and amused by Mary's performance. 'She looks after us very well!' she often says in her stepmother's defence. But Mary will not be swayed.

'Why are you smiling?' asks Jane.

'No reason,' says Fanny quickly, 'but Jane, I can't understand why Papa would send Mary away. Without her here who will help him entertain his philosophers and poets?'

'I could sing for them,' says Jane. There is a short silence as both girls try to imagine it.

'I think Papa's friends prefer talking and thinking to singing and dancing,' says Fanny eventually.

'Well, perhaps with Mary away they might learn to like it!' suggests Jane.

'Is that what your mamma says?'

'No!'

'Then why *is* Mary being sent away?' Fanny persists.

'Perhaps,' snaps Jane finally, 'it's because she's unbearable.'

'Jane!'

'Well, she is sometimes – even you must be able to see that.'

Fanny says nothing. She does not want to be disloyal, and yet she does not want to lie. She cannot bear to admit that at times the thought of a house free of Mary's furious feuding with their stepmother fills her with relief.

'Mamma says it will be good for Mary to get out of London,' says Jane. She does not repeat what her mother has really said, which is that it might do Mary some good to listen less to the sound of her own voice and to have the experience of having her nose put out of joint occasionally. Jane is both thrilled and a little disturbed by her mamma's dislike of Mary. At times she imagines what it might be like to be her stepsister, to have grown men pay such serious attention to her and to feel that whatever she had to say would be listened to and approved of, simply because she was the daughter of the great Mary Wollstonecraft and the philosopher Godwin. '*She has the mind of her mother!*' Papa's guests exclaim of Mary, whilst Jane and Fanny sit quietly in the background, listening.

'Well, I can't say what's *really* happening because Mamma's asked me not to!' Jane tells Fanny.

'Well then, I don't want to know,' agrees Fanny properly. 'Not if it would betray a trust.'

'Mamma says that Papa is in such debt,' Jane continues without hesitation, 'that he is sending Mary away to save her from the shame of it – should he be sent to prison!'

'Oh!'

'What is it, Fanny?' Jane runs to her stepsister, for the colour has leached from Fanny's face, and she is swaying where she stands.

'Nothing,' says Fanny, 'it is nothing at all.' But it is not nothing. It is *everything*; for the truth of the matter is that it hurts to know that once again she has been forgotten. As usual Papa has made provision for Mary, and Mrs Godwin has looked after Jane, but no one has thought about Fanny. She does not know why it is always so, but assumes it must be because she is not as clever as Mary. Or as bold.

For a moment Fanny is tempted to turn away from the window. She imagines Mary looking up and finding the space behind the panes empty. But she can't do it. And Mary would probably just walk into the house boldly and take whatever punishment was meted out anyway – arguing that she has a perfect right to be disobedient if she is being treated unfairly. And then Papa, although he never stops Mrs Godwin punishing Mary, will smile at her proud disobedience. But if Papa is really sent to prison, what will happen to *her*? Where would she go? Will she be left here with her stepmother and Jane and Charles, her stepbrother? Perhaps they are keeping her here because they need her to help her stepmother look after little William? Yes, that makes sense, thinks Fanny, for it will save them the extra cost of a servant.

'Mary's waving at you!' says Jane. 'From across the square. Where *has* she been?'

'To visit our mamma,' says Fanny. 'Will you listen at the door and tell me when the coast is clear?'

Jane runs to the door, happy to be a part of the sisters' intrigue. She peers over the bannisters. 'I can't hear anything – I think Mamma's still in the bookshop, and I can't hear Papa!'

Fanny watches Mary as she stands waiting across the square,

her black silk cloak making her a dark shadow in the afternoon light.

Jane rushes back into the room. 'Coast clear!' she whispers.

Fanny lifts her hand and waves.

7TH JUNE 1812: GRAVESEND TO BROUGHTY FERRY, SCOTLAND

'You're sending me away,' blurts Mary, unable to stop herself.

'Mr Baxter is a good man,' Papa says awkwardly, 'and perhaps Isobel and Christine will make better companions for you than Charles and Jane – or Fanny?' he adds quickly. He always forgets Fanny.

Mary stares up at the boat; she hopes she won't be sick. She has a strange lost feeling inside, as though a part of her is already somewhere else across the sea.

'Mamma believes the Scottish air might help to heal your skin,' says Papa.

'No! She simply wants to be rid of me!' declares Mary.

Papa sighs. 'Mary, we both think it is for the best.'

'Do you?' asks Mary coldly. 'Or are you simply agreeing with her, the way you always do, with no thought for me?' She swallows, hard. She must not cry; only girls like Jane use tears to express themselves. Her mamma would not cry. She would hold her head up and stride on to the boat, then write a book about it. Sometimes Mary wonders if she can ever really live up to her mother. She begins to scratch.

'Stop it!' snaps Papa.

Mary wraps her fingers over the sore skin, longing for the moment when she is alone on the boat and can scratch as freely as she likes. The boat's horn sounds. 'Goodbye, Papa.' She would like to reach out and touch him, to be able to show that she is sad to be leaving. 'Do I eat my meals in my cabin?' she asks suddenly. 'Or should I go somewhere else?' She has never been alone on a boat overnight before.

'Excuse me!' her father calls at a passing woman.

The woman turns and stares at them. She is wearing an elaborate hat and travelling coat with a wide expensive fur collar. 'I am in a hurry,' the woman says. It is clear that she does not wish to be detained. Mary shrinks back a little as her papa continues regardless.

'My name is William Godwin,' he says loudly, as though the woman might recognise his name, but she does not. 'My daughter,' her father goes on, 'is fourteen, and travelling alone. Perhaps you might be so kind as to chaperone her?'

'Come, come!' the woman says, sweeping away up the busy gangplank. Mary turns and looks at Papa. 'Go on, quickly!' he says, shooing her forward. She does as she is told, running after the woman and turning briefly at the railings to spot her father's back already walking away. Oh, she thinks, we did not really say goodbye . . .

She would like to call out to him as some of the children next to her are doing; to shout his name and wave gaily, but the very thought of behaving with such abandon makes her blush. Papa would not want her to behave like that. She stands at the rails and waits; perhaps he might turn and wave at *her*. But he does not. She watches until he disappears, swallowed up by the crowd. When she turns back the woman has gone. Mary walks the deck, searching everywhere for her, but she is nowhere to be seen.

Slowly Mary makes her way to her small cabin. She sits on the narrow, hard bed. The boat journey is for two days and one night, and then she will be in Dundee, where she is to be picked up by her father's friend William Baxter, and driven by carriage to Broughty Ferry. He has three daughters, two at home – Christine and Isobel – and another called Margaret, who is married and living nearby. *Christine and Isobel.* She says the names slowly to herself so that she does not forget them. *Christine. Isobel.* She hopes they will be more like herself and less like Jane, who would rather play at pretending to be married than discuss why marriage is a shackle that makes women nothing but a man's property. And yet, if she's being honest with herself, she knows she'll miss Jane's admiration – the way her stepsister sometimes parrots a phrase of Mary's, or repeats an argument, pretending that it is her own.

Mary unpacks her books and puts them by the bed, stroking each one before she puts it down. Books do not alter. They do not remarry like Papa or suddenly sprout, like her own body, changing shape and bleeding each month. The pages of books remain reassuringly the same, the words unchanging. She opens her mother's most famous work: *A Vindication of the Rights of Woman.* Perhaps she could just stay in the cabin and read for the whole of the journey. The thought makes her feel a little less anxious.

She is deep in the book when the motion of the boat changes as it enters the open sea, beginning to heave in rhythm with the waves. At first Mary merely feels a little dizzy, but then the real sickness begins. She rushes for the door, desperate for air.

Up on the deck she clings to the ship's rails hoping her chaperone might reappear.

'Hello!' says a man. He is her father's age and dressed in much the same manner. Mary smiles weakly, afraid of being thought impolite. 'Feel sick, do you?' he asks kindly. She nods, holding on tight to the rail, her stomach rising and falling with the waves. 'Try putting your head down,' he suggests. Grateful, she rests her head upon the cold rails, frightened she might be sick in front of this stranger. When she looks up he is gone.

13

Slowly she stumbles back to her cabin. She cannot move, but only lie and groan in between bouts of the heaving, gut-wrenching sickness, longing for the familiar feel of her own bed and the safety of home. She empties her stomach and for a while feels well enough to sit up. Perhaps she might go up on deck and try to get help. The thought is excruciating. She does not know who to ask and her profound shyness outside of home makes her awkward.

'My own mamma took a boat to France to bear witness to the Revolution, so surely I can go up on deck and find help,' she whispers firmly to herself. She stands up. Good; she can stand without feeling too faint. She reaches for her purse, perhaps she might be able to purchase some medicine to help.

Her fingers find empty space. Her purse is not there. For a moment all sickness is forgotten. Perhaps she put it down? No, it is not on the tiny bedside table. Or tangled up in the bed. It is nowhere in the cabin. She searches her clothes, hoping against hope that it will be caught up in the folds of her skirt. She has no more money. All of it was tied to her, and if she cannot find it then she has nothing.

It takes half an hour of frantic searching before she can bring herself to believe that it is truly gone. She sinks to the bed, a dreadful understanding coming to her: it must have been the man she thought so kind; he must have taken it when he suggested she put her head down. What a fool she is. What a little idiot. How can she ever hope to match her mother who travelled alone across a whole continent when she cannot even successfully catch a ferry to Dundee? Again the sickness overtakes her. It is almost a relief to give in to it, to be too ill to think.

The sickness lasts until the *Osnaburgh* enters the harbour at Dundee. Mary hears a fierce knocking on the cabin door.

'We've arrived, miss!'

Groaning, she gathers up her things. Will someone come and help her? Should she wait? What if the Baxters arrive and enter this small space, full of the stench of her sickness. The very thought of it drives her up and into the corridor, where she is standing, leaning against the wall surrounded by her cases, when Mr Baxter appears.

'Mary?' he asks.

She nods, holding out her hand. 'I'm afraid—' she begins.

'Will you look at you!' From behind Mr Baxter, a small woman appears. 'Seasick!' she declares. 'Your father said so. William, take the wee lassie's bags, and you,' she says to Mary, 'lean against me and we'll struggle up together!'

Gratefully Mary does as she's told. 'I . . .' she tries again to explain that her money is gone..

'Not now, lovey,' the woman whispers. 'Rest first, explanations later.'

For a brief moment Mary closes her eyes and allows herself to lean against Mrs Baxter, enjoying the brush of her hand over her forehead. She is entranced. So this is what it might feel like to have a mother.

When Mary wakes the next morning she's in a small bedroom with light and air pouring through the windows. Beyond the glass the view stretches all the way down to a deep blue loch. She closes her eyes, stunned by the quiet. Instead of street hawkers calling their wares, she can hear the sound of birds and the breeze in the leaves of a tree that hovers over the house.

'Hello!' says a voice at the bedroom door. 'I'm Izy. Are you feeling better?'

Mary looks up into a pair of bright blue, curious eyes surrounded by a shock of thick gold hair.

'Yes, thank you,' says Mary. The two girls stare at each other; Izy Baxter overwhelmed by the fact that she is in the presence of the real Mary Wollstonecraft's daughter. And Mary simply feeling shy. Izy waits for Mary to say something. She has been told of how intelligent she is, of how she is likely to supercede even her mother. But Mary is simply looking at her, saying nothing.

'Oh,' says Izy eventually, spying the pamphlet lying by Mary's side, 'you're reading Byron! He's a Scot, you know! We do actually have some of our own poets up here in the wilderness!' she adds, sitting down on the edge of Mary's bed.

'I read it as soon as it was published,' says Mary gratefully. 'Did you know, he sold fourteen thousand copies in one day!'

'My ma says grown women send letters to him – asking for a lock of his hair!'

'Fourteen thousand locks of hair,' says Mary. 'He'd have no hair left on his head if he agreed to send them all a lock each!'

'A bald Byron!' Izy laughs so much the bed shakes.

Mary stares at her. People usually admire Mary for her intellect not her humour. She has never really made anyone laugh like that before.

'Will you get dressed and come for a walk?' asks Izy.

Soon the girls walk out together every day, often disappearing at breakfast and failing to return until supper.

'Do you ever imagine travelling alone like your mother? Is it true that she walked through Paris and the streets flowed with blood!' Izy can never ask one question where two will do.

Mary nods. 'She truly stepped in a puddle of blood once,' she tells Izy proudly. The girls grimace with glee. 'She might have lost her head!' claims Mary.

'And then you would never have been born!'

Mary says nothing. She does not like to think of her birth, or of her mother dying so soon after.

'Let's run up the hill, turn three times and see who we'll

marry, will we?' shouts Izy, noticing the pain in Mary's eyes and thinking to distract her.

'But why? It's just superstitious nonsense!' says Mary.

'For fun!' says Izy. 'Do you never do anything just for fun, Mary Wollstonecraft Godwin?'

'No!' says Mary.'

'Oh!' says Izy, stunned by the idea of eternal seriousness. 'Would you like to try it?'

'I might,' agrees Mary.

Izy takes her arm. Mary feels silly. 'One, two, three, go!' Izy sets off up Law hill, pulling Mary along beside her. 'C'mon, Mary, you have to run hard or the witch won't tell ye!'

Mary presses her feet into the rough turf; the wind comes up over the crest of the hill almost knocking them over.

'Turn!' Izy shouts, pushing her hard. 'Turn three times, widdershins!'

'What's that?' shouts Mary.

'Anti-clockwise!'

Mary spins around, her cloak flying in the wind and a breathless laughter rising up in her. The girls fall to the ground, up above, the clouds race across the sky. Not a trace of grey. Mary's cheeks pulse with the effort and every time she looks at Izy their laughter begins again.

'Ask, then,' Izy says after a while. 'Ask in your mind who it is that you'll marry!'

Mary closes her eyes. Who will I marry? she thinks to herself, before crying out, 'Oh, Izy, I can't ask that!'

'Why not?'

'Because . . . because my mother didn't believe in marriage!'

The girls stare at each other, wide-eyed for a moment before collapsing into laughter. They have already declared themselves disciples of Mary Wollstonecraft – and Godwin, Mary's father. They have read Godwin's *Political Justice* and pored over

Wollstonecraft's *A Vindication of the Rights of Woman*. They have vowed to follow Wollstonecraft's principles, entering only into relationships with men who are brave enough to defy the world and offer them equality. They long to work hard and earn their own living, living lives full of intellectual endeavour.

'Oh, well then,' sighs Izy practically, 'let's ask who we might love to eternity instead!'

'I'm not going to ask that,' says Mary hesitantly. 'I'm going to ask for something different.'

'And what might that be?'

'I'm going to ask if I'll ever be a writer. I mean –' Mary stumbles a bit, shy now that the words are spoken – 'whether I will ever earn a living by it and be truly independent, like my mother,' she finishes.

'Aye,' says Izy, 'that makes sense.'

And with her friend's easy acceptance of the idea, Mary begins to feel that it might really happen.

'Did *you* ask who *you'll* love to eternity?' she asks Izy.

'I mustn't say, or it'll never happen!'

'Then I'll guess!' laughs Mary. Izy blushes. 'It's David, isn't it?'

'He's already married,' says Izy firmly. 'And to *my sister*. Or had you not noticed?'

'And yet you love him, Izy, don't you?' Mary says seriously. Izy looks away. They often speak of how wonderful her brother-in-law is, describing David's many virtues – especially his green eyes – but to admit that she loves him? Mary says nothing, waiting for her friend to acknowledge the truth.

'Aye,' says Izy eventually. 'I think I do.'

The very next day, Mary starts writing a story. It is set in Scotland. She does not read it to Izy – it's too close to what is really happening – but she gives it to her when she leaves.

'I'll be back soon!' she says.

'Promise you'll come next year?'

'Cross my heart!' says Mary. 'And keep everything exactly the same for me!'

JUNE 1813 TO MARCH 1814: BROUGHTY FERRY

But when Mary returns to Broughty Ferry a year later, everything has changed. Izy's sister Margaret is dead, and by the time spring comes, David has asked Izy to marry him.

'I thought he might ask *you*, Mary,' Izy says, as they sit beside the loch together.

'Why?'

'Oh, you know, you being the child of two such famous parents and all!'

'But that's silly!' snaps Mary, irritated. 'A man would have to love me for myself,' she declares, 'not for my parents!' Izy says nothing. 'Anyway, it's you he loves! And I will never marry! I don't believe in it, remember!' The truth is that she is just a little bit miffed that David has shown no interest in her at all.

'I think I might get married in tartan!' replies Izy.

'Oh!' cries Mary, for she can imagine Izy in her kirtle and shawl, and David in a kilt.

'Would you like to be my maid of honour?'

'Oh, Izy!'

'And Christy – the two of you, I mean.'

'As long as I can wear tartan too! I don't think my mother would mind *you* getting married,' Mary says generously.

'Let's ask Papa to take us to the factory. I ha'e to stick to the Baxter tartan, but you can choose any colour you like, perhaps a green to go with your hair?'

Mary has never been fussed over before, especially not in the way Mrs Baxter fusses over her, declaring she must go for a dress, not a kilt, and choosing a dark green with a deep blue stripe in it and the merest touch of red. 'Don't the pair of you look bonny!' She hugs Izy.

Mary stands back, longing to be hugged but anxious not to get it wrong. Do mothers hug other people's children? 'Come here!' Mrs Baxter cries – she is soft and yielding, her arms strong around Mary's shoulders. Mary would like to sink into her but she holds herself stiff and unyielding, unsure of what to do.

'There, get changed now and we'll take it all home!' Mrs Baxter says. Later when the girls are in bed, she says to her husband: 'Stiff as a board the girl is – it's as though she's never been embraced!'

'She probably hasn't,' Mr Baxter agrees. 'Godwin's a thinker, not a feeling man!'

'Have you noticed how quiet Mary beomes every time she hears from home?'

'Mmmm.' Mr Baxter becomes tight-lipped, as he always does when he's trying to keep a secret.

'William,' his wife says sternly, 'what is it?'

'Well, Godwin's not the best of men when it comes to finances, and he has an awful lot of mouths to feed with a wife and two extra children, as well as the bairn of their own.'

'Do you mean to say they're sending letters worrying Mary? Well, I shall keep them back in future.'

'You cannae do that!'

'I certainly can!'

But the next morning there are two letters waiting for Mary next to her plate.

*D*ear *Mary*, Fanny writes,

I write with good news. Papa has met with a new benefactor. His name is Sir Percy Bysshe Shelley – and he is a young baronet who comes originally from Sussex. Sir Percy admires Father enormously, and especially his defence of the Twelve Radicals. Fortunately, Sir Percy has decided that he will raise money upon the promise of his inheritance, spreading it amongst those who share his principles yet do not have his own good fortune – he has promised to support Papa. I do not know if Papa has told you how seriously in debt we are. If Sir Percy had not arrived in our lives at this very moment, then we feared Papa might have to endure prison. With Sir Percy's coming it feels as though we are all lifted from the 'shades of the prison house'.

Papa likes to have him here often now that you are gone, for without you he has no one to debate with over supper! Suppers are no longer so serious with Sir Percy here. He winks at Jane and I secretly and then laughs aloud when we (rather clumsily) try to return the compliment. He has brought his young (and very beautiful) wife to supper once or twice. They went to Ireland together to support the labourers there in their fight for fair wages. He has written a poem, called Queen Mab, *and he is teaching Jane Italian. I know Papa is looking forward to you meeting him on your return, which will be soon, I hope.*

Your sister,
Fanny

Mary stares at the letter; she has a vague memory of a poet named Shelley, but she cannot picture him.

'Is something wrong,' asks Izy. 'Not bad news, I hope?'

'No, just that Papa has met yet another young poet!' says Mary, carefully closing the letter and putting it away before she opens the next one, the clear writing of Papa upon the envelope.

Dear Mary,

I have booked your return passage on the Osnaburgh *for Thursday, and enclose some reading that you might enjoy as you take passage. The pamphlets are written by Sir Percy Bysshe Shelley, who dines with us often. You will be able to judge the measure of him from the literature enclosed – and will no doubt meet him soon after your return. He offers to support my work with a generous loan, but the arrangement will take quite some time and we miss your company alongside such an illustrious guest.*

Your papa,
William Godwin

'Oh!' says Mary aloud. 'Now I won't be here for the wedding!'

'But we must at least run up Law hill one last time,' cries Izy, 'before you leave?'

It's a tradition between the girls that they make the trip at least once each visit. They race to the top of the hill, Izy winning easily, but slowing to reach the top alongside Mary.

'Perhaps,' says Mary when she finally has her breath back, 'this hill really is a magical place. It has granted your wish to marry David, and perhaps it might one day grant my wish to be a writer?'

'I think maybe it's harder to write a book than to fall in love!' laughs Izy.

'The first story I ever wrote was about Margaret dying and you marrying David.'

'True,' says Izy, 'but you already knew I was half in love with him!'

'But what if there is a magic in the stories we write,' Mary asks, 'so that when we write a thing we might make it come true?'

'Well, if you can do that then perhaps you could write a story where the church sanctions my marriage!'

Mary laughs, staring out over the loch stretching away to the horizon, the straw hills she has come to love, glowing in the spring sunshine: 'The church will never do that,' she says flatly.

Izy rolls on her back, and flings her arms out wide, facing the sky. 'I dinnae really mind!' she says.

'Mary?'

'Mmmm.'

'When David asked me to marry him, he kissed me.' Mary says nothing, sensing a revelation coming. 'It's no' just a pressing of the lips.'

'No?'

'No.'

Mary wonders what else it could be. She and Izy used to imagine kissing David, even tried briefly pressing their lips to each other's before drawing away, shocked by the sudden intimacy and softness of each other's skin.

'It's more like touching tongues.'

'Ugh!' says Mary, throwing her chewed-up blade of grass away.

'I know,' sighs Izy. 'I knew you'd say that. I'd have said it myself before it happened.'

'And now?'

'Now I like it,' she laughs.

'If you like him that much you can probably survive excommunication,' says a stunned Mary.

Izy laughs aloud with joy at her comment. 'I'll tell him you said that!' she says – but Mary can't see the joke. She is being completely serious.

'Must you go?' asks Izy. 'Can't you stay, at least until the wedding?'

'I can't. Papa wants me back, to meet Sir Percy Bysshe Shelley.' She rolls the name across her mouth.

'Why does he need you when he already has Jane and Fanny?'

'Jane and Fanny do not have my mind.'

'Do you want to go back?'

'No! I hate leaving here,' cries Mary. 'Every time I go I fear it will be the last time I set eyes on these hills or gaze out over the loch. Until you have been in London you cannot imagine the stench of it or the misery. Or how alone one can feel, even when one is surrounded by buildings and people!'

'I hope you find someone for yourself, Mary,' cries Izy, holding her tight. 'Find a man as wonderful as David and come and live in Broughty Ferry with us.'

'I cannot,' says Mary calmly. 'Papa will never have the money to marry me off, and I would refuse anyway. I do not want a husband. I have decided on a life of solitude, a life of writing!'

MARCH 1814: 41 SKINNER STREET, LONDON

Jane clambers into bed with Fanny. 'I think tomorrow I shall ask Sir Percy to decline the verb "to love"?' she suggests, her eyes shining and her hair lying loose across the pillow. 'Do you dare me?'

'Go on!' whispers Fanny, her eyes alight. She would never admit it, but it is a relief, sometimes, to be free of Mary's presence. Jane is fun. And so is Sir Percy – especially when he pulls faces at them across the table. 'You'll tell me what he says, won't you?'

'Of course! Do you like him yourself, Fanny?'

'Perhaps,' whispers Fanny shyly. 'But he's married, and Harriet is so beautiful and clever!'

'He told me that she hid seditious pamphlets in her skirts,' laughs Jane, 'and carried them through the Irish customs!'

'I'd blush at once, and be discovered,' says Fanny hopelessly.

'Sir Percy doesn't behave as though he's married, does he?'

'But he is,' says Fanny, 'and we've met her, and so we shouldn't really be too forward with him.'

'Mmmm,' says Jane, getting back into her own bed.

Sir Percy waits for Jane in the dining room, flicking through the books he has brought with him to teach her. He does not look up when she arrives, or stand as most men would, but remains immersed in his reading.

Jane does not mind, for it gives her the opportunity to stare at his face, the perfect symmetry of it allowing her eyes to slip from one feature to the next, like being caught up in a never-ending circle. His eyes are shaped like delicate, slightly rounded almonds. His hair is a soft curly gold and his skin so smooth that she clasps her hands together, stopping the longing in her fingers to reach out and touch it. Her eyes skim over his face searching for flaws, but there are none, his skin knitted into an ivory silk far fairer than any woman's she knows. Perhaps only Mary's pale skin might come close to matching it. When she's not scratching. Jane is not looking forward to Mary's return. It is lovely to have Sir Percy to herself.

Quietly she slips up to stand behind him. '*Amo, amas . . .*' she begins.

'Oh!' he starts, and stands immediately; his jacket, she notes, is slightly too short, his frail wrists protruding from its sleeves. 'Forgive me,' he says, bowing slightly. 'I didn't see you!' When Sir Percy remembers them, his manners are exquisite.

'Or hear me!' laughs Jane. 'I was attempting to decline the verb "to love".'

'I am not sure the feeling is amenable to declension,' he returns, before rattling off the endings and asking her, very seriously, to repeat them.

Bored at once, Jane seeks to distract him. 'Tell me again why poets must also be agitators?' she asks, neatly deflecting him. 'I'm not sure I fully understood your meaning at dinner.'

'Wordsworth,' he replies, 'says "a poet is man speaking to men". He lived amongst the poor and destitute so that he might understand them better in his fight for their right to live on the land that is being stolen from them. Lord Byron may be rich beyond measure, yet he defends the right of weavers to break the looms that put them out of work and into poverty. Blake writes of the blood that runs down palace walls, unacknowledged by those who feast and become fat within them. What good is any poet who ignores such things?'

'Mmm,' agrees Jane, nodding seriously and wondering what Mary might say. 'Did he win?'

'Who?'

'Lord Byron. Did he win the weavers the right to – um – destroy things?'

'No,' says Sir Percy earnestly. 'The government believed it preferable to sentence to death the men whose livelihood they have stolen and so driven into poverty. They did not listen when Byron said that only utter desperation could have driven the men to such hazardous action – they preferred to believe those desperate men desired destruction – and yet Byron's words will last, and history will judge; and that is what poets should be doing . . .'

He is away and Jane can sit back and watch the words fall from his beautiful lips, the passion light up his dark blue eyes. She puts a serious expression upon her face.

'But Mr Godwin says we must encourage change slowly, through offering education, and so teaching reason to the poor.'

'That may be right in principle, but how, I wonder, does sitting by the fire spouting ideas ever really change anything?'

Jane glances at the door; she doesn't want Papa to hear him. She wouldn't have Sir Percy in trouble for the world, but his righteous indignation makes her want to laugh out loud, especially as she has heard him agreeing so wholeheartedly with Mr Godwin over dinner. She bites her lip and widens her eyes to keep them serious. 'So what should we do?' she asks, leaning forward. She'll do anything to keep him talking. He is easily the most wonderful being she has ever met.

'Yes, we should teach the poor,' he says, 'but we must also encourage them to fight against their bondage. In *every* way they can,' he cries. 'They must do it through learning, but also through poetry and action – and if it's required, even sedition!' He is almost shouting. Jane reaches out and grasps his elbow in an attempt to calm him; to stop him before anyone in the household hears. He looks down at her hand in confusion as though, for a moment, he really has no idea at all why it might be there. She raises her finger to her lips but he smiles confidently at her caution. 'We are in the home of William Godwin, author of *Political Justice*, a home where they understand revolution,' he says. 'Mrs Wollstonecraft herself reported on the French Revolution, and Mr Godwin tells me his daughter Mary is a true radical!'

'You can ask her yourself when she returns,' snaps Jane, for it seems as though Sir Percy is already as entranced by the idea of Mary as every other poet and philosopher who enters the house.

'Be your best self, Mary,' Mr Godwin says as he does up his cuffs, 'for without Sir Percy's investment the bookshop will sink. We are out of money.'

Mary nods. She raced back to London only to find that Sir Percy had disappeared. He went off to Wales with his wife Harriet, and is only now back in London and coming for dinner in Skinner Street tonight.

'Are you listening, Mary?' her father asks.

'Yes, Papa,' she dutifully replies, but she is not listening; she is thinking that she has been hearing about Sir Percy and waiting to actually meet him for weeks, when she could have been in Scotland. Mary wonders what Izy's doing right now, at this very moment. Perhaps she's walking down by the loch with David, waiting for the sun to set, or is at her father's factory choosing a fabric for Christy's dress. London is boring and it stinks after the clean Scottish air. The noise in the narrow streets is overwhelming; the butchers calling out their wares amongst the metallic, rank smell of meat and blood that follows her along the road she lives in; the looming brick walls of Newgate prison at the end of the street a constant reminder that men are meat too, whose lives can be ended with a sharp drop.

She hates it. She's already written to Izy and asked if she can come and live with her when she's married. Back in Broughty Ferry she feels she can write, but here? Here, everything presses in on her. She looks out of the window; even the sky is smaller, a tiny patch of blue stuck between the high roofs of the endless buildings.

Staring out over Skinner Street, Mary feels a familiar sense of irritation. Her skin started to itch as soon as she stepped over the threshold, the dark panelled rooms closing in on her, the long narrow staircase stretching up five flights sapping her strength. She herself has changed so much and yet everything – everything – in London remains the same; her hated stepmother still angry that she will not call her Mamma, her sister Fanny creeping around trying to please everyone but merely succeeding in irritating them. Charles her stepbrother is barely ever around, and little William, ten now, spends almost as much time locked away with Papa in the study as Mary once did herself. In her absence it feels as though Jane has taken up all available space. She is everywhere; even now the sound of her practising her singing echoes endlessly up and down the staircase as she runs from room to room, taking particular care over her Italian phrasing.

'Sir Shelley's teaching Jane Italian,' Mrs Godwin says proudly. 'She'll be quite the catch!'

'It's Sir *Percy*,' laughs Mary contemptuously. 'Not Sir Shelley!'

Mr Godwin shakes his head and goes to his study. The tension between his wife and daughter is already rising.

Mary sighs. As soon as her father leaves the room she picks up Izy's letter for the hundredth time.

Dearest Mary,

The church has indeed threatened us both with excommunication. Thank goodness for my father. He stands so firmly by us, and our right to love one another. I do not know what we would do without him. Elope, I suppose! Please, do come back to Broughty Ferry as soon as you can, and by the time you arrive I will be able to tell you ALL about married life! It is wonderful to know that the church with all its power cannot overcome our love – or my father's support for us. I hope, dear Mary, that your mother is looking down upon us from whatever it is that we must call heaven – now that the church has rejected us – and is proud. Of course she would rather

we did not have to marry at all, but needs must. I miss you, Mary.
Marriage, I hope, will be wonderful, but it can never be the same
as having a dear friend.

Izy

Yes, thinks Mary as she gazes at the rooftops, London is
boring, and so is the idea of having to charm yet another poet.
But she is practised at charming poets. When she was a child
she wanted to marry Mr Coleridge.

'He's already married, Mary!' said Marguerite, her nurse.

'Well, he can marry me too, can't he? If he wants to.'

'No, he can't,' said Marguerite.

'Well then, marriage is silly!' claimed Mary, and was
surprised when her nurse wasn't angry at all but only laughed
out loud saying: 'That's exactly what your mother believed!' It
made Mary feel warm and happy inside whenever Marguerite
said she was like her mother. 'Anyway, you won't want to marry
Mr Coleridge once you're older.'

'I will!' Mary remembers crying out loud, furious at being
gainsaid, but Marguerite was right after all; she doesn't want
to marry Coleridge any more – she doesn't want to marry
anyone at all, but if she could choose a poet to love, then it
would probably be Blake, she thinks. In comparison with Blake
or Coleridge, Sir Percy Bysshe Shelley is barely a poet at all.
He has published only one poem and a short pamphlet denying
the existence of God. He is a mere boy at only twenty-one.

Mary decides to wear her tartan dress to supper; it will be like
a flag, marking her as different. No one in London wears tartan.
She walks into the dining room slightly late just to demonstrate
that she is not entirely bound by the rules of Skinner Street.

Sir Percy stands as soon as she enters. 'Miss Godwin.' He has a clear, high voice.

Mary smiles, bobbing a careless not-quite curtsey in response before remembering that she is meant to be on her best behaviour. 'Sorry, Papa,' she says as she sits, ignoring her stepmother, who is the person she should properly be apologising to. 'I forgot the time!' Papa nods. He is irritated but Mary cannot bring herself to care. 'I'm afraid I always lose my London manners after a time in Scotland,' she sighs, taking up her spoon. She looks across the dinner table, preparing to be bored.

It is a shock, that first proper sight of him: a visceral physical feeling. She cannot look away. The deep blueness of his eyes is startling as they gaze back at her. They remind her of the loch under a rare sunny sky, a deep and endless dark blue. She finds she cannot speak but manages to wrench her eyes away from him, mechanically lifting food to her mouth because she knows she must at least maintain appearances, but her appetite has gone. She barely tastes the soup. *So this is what it feels like*, her mind says over and over. *This is what it feels like. To be struck by love.* Already she cannot wait to be free of the table and write of it to Izy.

'You're wearing tartan; do you owe allegiance to any particular clan?' Sir Percy asks her, smiling.

'Oh, Isobel's father manufactures textiles so we chose it for the colour rather than the clan. It was illegal to wear tartan in the Highlands until recently – an act of defiance,' Mary manages, and to her surprise her voice does not give way but sounds quite calm and collected, her usual self.

'The tartan gives people a way of belonging to each other rather than to king and country, so of course the powers that be would wish to make it illegal,' Sir Percy says passionately.

It is so exactly what Mary herself thinks that she can only nod at him, dipping her head to her soup. Jane stares at her, quizzical – this is not like the Mary she knows, who is usually so full of her own opinion.

At the sight of Mary Godwin sitting opposite him, a blade comes down inside Sir Percy, cutting him away from his young wife. He is already aware that he has fallen out of love with Harriet, but now he feels a physical sensation of something parting inside him, as Harriet is cut away from his imaginings and fades into the distance. He can see only Mary sitting before him dressed in green tartan, her unruly cloud of gold-red hair defying the pins that try to hold it back.

Mary touches her hair, aware that he is staring at it, before remembering that she has a task to fulfil. She is meant to be flattering him. 'Papa gave me a copy of your pamphlet, *The Necessity of Atheism*,' she says admiringly. 'Is it true you were sent down from Oxford for writing it?'

'Yes,' he says easily, 'we both were. I wrote it with a friend, Jefferson Hogg.'

'In your argument,' Mary goes on, barely registering his friend's name, 'you accept that whatever it is that creates humans is both eternal and incomprehensible?'

Jane sighs, aware that the next half an hour will be taken up with an intellectual debate that she cannot take part in. She too has been given Sir Percy's pamphlet. It is short and that is its biggest blessing as far as she is concerned.

'Well, we acknowledge,' Sir Percy says seriously, 'that whatever force created man is incomprehensible to us at this moment in time. I suspect at some point we might come to understand how and why humans exist.'

'So when you say "the thing that creates us is unknown", what do you actually mean? If whatever makes man is not God, then surely you must offer some alternative?'

'Why,' asks Sir Percy gently, 'should we feel obliged to do that?'

'That is not an answer,' replies Mary.

'Isn't it?' he asks sharply.

Jane notices Mary blush – she is not used to this at all. Visitors to her father's house usually show deference to her greater intellect; if they argue with her at all they do so calmly and remorselessly. Not like this.

'Not knowing is a thing in itself,' Sir Percy is saying. 'We do not know who or what made us, and we cannot know for we have no evidence. Can we not at least accept that as a fact?'

'So,' says Mary slowly, 'we do not know if there is a God or not, and that is somehow preferable to a belief in the existence of God?'

'Yes, why must we always treat God's existence as an accepted fact? At least if we acknowledge that we are ignorant, then we leave open the possibility of discovering an alternative.'

'But you cannot claim that a belief in God makes everything worse when for so many of us it clearly does not.' Mary is calm now, notes Jane with envy, because she has practised such arguments with her father since she was a child, each of them taking up opposing positions as the rest of the family respectfully listened.

'I do exactly claim that practising a belief in God is worse than not knowing,' Sir Percy is saying, 'because any such belief goes against the evidence of both our senses and our reason – and so demeans us.'

'But faith is not a literal thing,' says Mary.

'Quite,' says Papa. 'It is a spiritual thing.'

'I do not claim a disbelief in the spiritual,' says Sir Percy, 'just in an all-seeing, all-knowing God. Surely you see what such a belief must make of us? It means we are always looking over our shoulders. Scared to think and scared to act, for ever terrified in case we are denied an entirely imaginary heaven.'

'But you are thinking only of the individual, aren't you?' says Mary. 'Which suggests that you have not learned from the lessons of the French Revolution, which are that without God and the church – or at least their morality – social order might collapse; and without social order, moral chaos will almost certainly ensue.'

'Is there not chaos already?' says Sir Percy, banging the table violently with his soup spoon, making everybody jump. 'And does not such chaos arise directly from this belief in the deity?'

His voice is rising. Jane and Fanny glance at each other, smiling in silent amusement. They are quite used to Sir Percy's passion as he discusses his ideas, to the way he drives his hands so fiercely through his hair that it stands on end as he bends forward, placing his elbows on the table and looming over his soup as he stares at Mary.

'Was it not chaos when women were burned as witches?' He throws his arms up into an imaginary pyre. 'Or when the Catholic church had a bonfire of Jews in Cordoba? Or was that not a matter of faith, Miss Godwin – but a matter of *belief*?'

Jane notices that he speaks as though the rest of them no longer exist; every remark directed solely at Mary. What might it be like to be the focus of all that furious, passionate attention? The thought makes her shiver. She watches as Mary takes a breath and leans away, driven deep into the back of her chair by the force of his feeling; yet her eyes refuse to leave his for a single moment. Her voice is cool as she speaks, as though she might damp down his vision with her own reason. Calm his fire.

'But we are not discussing the *effects* of a belief, are we?' she asks. 'We are only testing the potential reality of the belief itself.'

Mary's food is forgotten. Sir Percy's too. The two of them glare at each other across the table.

'It might be possible to divide the theoretical and the actual for the purposes of a pamphlet,' he declares, 'but to do so in everyday life would be a mistake. A belief in God and the afterlife is how the church has justified the torture of the human body by claiming it saves the soul. We cannot argue against a belief without recognising it has consequences. That would be truly inhuman.' He is almost shouting now.

Mrs Godwin sighs; the main course will be going cold and it costs a fortune to keep on feeding Sir Shelley, who does not seem to recognise that food costs money, despite the fact that he has offered to support them financially. This strange aristocratic young man believes in sharing his privilege and he certainly puts his money where his mouth is, but at this very moment she would quite like him to put his soup where his mouth is so that they can get on with supper.

'I have been taught,' Mary says, glancing at her father for approval, 'that it is the power of reason and education that best effects social change. If you set loose passion, rather than argument, then revolution is inevitable. And how does revolution end? My mother was a great supporter of revolution but even she was shocked by the destruction it unleashed in France. She stepped in a puddle and when she looked down saw that the puddle was not rainwater, but blood. The gutters of Paris ran with it! The revolutionaries claimed that afterwards all mankind would be equal, but it did not happen. Just like the aristocrats before them, they became drunk upon their own power; women were good enough when they needed us to fight alongside them, but once they'd won, we were subjugated once more. That is the nature of chaos and revolution – it feeds upon itself until it eats its own tail. Have you heard what they did to Marie Antoinette's friend?'

'Mary!' snaps her stepmother, for whilst Mrs Godwin is used to giving the poets and philosophers in her home considerable leeway it must stop somewhere; else the chaos Mary speaks of might descend upon her very own dinner table.

'I abhor all forms of violence!' declares Sir Percy passionately.

'It's true,' laughs Jane. 'He wouldn't even let me kill a lace-wing that interrupted our Italian lesson!'

Mr Godwin clears his throat. 'Quite fascinating,' he says, 'but can you tell me, Sir Percy, has your solicitor replied to your, um, request to formalise a loan?'

Sir Percy turns to him. 'I have done all I can to set everything in order. The money should be here within weeks.'

'We need it,' says Godwin baldly. 'You are our financial saviour, Sir Percy, and I'm sure you will be glad to be able to return to Harriet and your daughter Ianthe, as well as your own important work, when all of this is done.'

The three girls look towards Sir Percy. Life in the dark narrow house will feel so dull again without him.

Mary listens as Sir Percy and her father discuss the loan that will save them all from ruin; now that the poet's attention is elsewhere she feels cut off, adrift. Jane raises her eyebrows at her but Mary looks away.

Fanny has her head down, staring intently into her soup. Always Mary, she is thinking to herself as she spoons up the watery liquid. Always, always, always ... Mary. The words repeat themselves in her head. Mary is always the one who gets the attention, and now she is back and Sir Percy has not said a word to either Fanny or to Jane. He has not winked at her once, despite her keeping her attention firmly upon him. It is because Mary is back, and now she is all he can see. It is always, always, always the same.

'Fanny,' Jane whispers gently, touching her arm.

'Oh,' says Fanny. 'Sorry!' For when she looks down she finds she is spooning up nothing but air. Her soup bowl is empty. She shakes her head, embarrassed – but it does not matter, for no one has noticed.

*

'Well done!' Papa whispers to Mary as they rise. She stares at him blankly; she has completely forgotten Sir Percy was meant to be a task, an irritation.

'Perhaps the three of us might take tomorrow afternoon's walk together,' Sir Percy asks, nodding towards Mary and Jane as he speaks to their father.

'Of course,' Mr Godwin replies.

Mary arches her perfect brows. 'That is, of course, should we women agree to it, Sir Percy!' she says.

Papa sends her a sharp, irritated look. Fanny leans against the panelled walls, wondering why Sir Percy has not included her.

He seems to have completely forgotten her existence. He laughs aloud at Mary's comment, a free ringing joyous sound that seems to press back the walls, making the dark hallway brighter. 'Forgive me my assumption, Misses Godwin,' he smiles. 'With both of your agreements, of course. And please, my name is Bysshe.'

'Consider yourself forgiven,' says Mary.

Jane stares at them both, aware that her own agreement is neither here nor there, for Sir Percy is no longer able to see her.

15th June, London

*D*ear *Izy,*

Last night I met the poet Shelley. If these words sound portentous it is because I hope that one day they might be. I am in love. I do not know how to explain it; for once, my reason seems entirely at the mercy of my feelings. I cannot help it! Is this how you feel when you look at David; that you could look into his eyes for ever if only there were not the eyes of others also watching you?

I have already read both his pamphlet on The Necessity of Atheism, *and his poem* Queen Mab – *which is dedicated to his wife. Yes, he is married. A fact I am aware that I am, at least for the present, ignoring – as you once did. I will send you a copy of the pamphlet. He wrote it when he was young, and so perhaps makes assumptions instead of arguing from the basis of a truly sound proposition. Tomorrow we are going for a walk; he has asked Jane as well, but I hope that is only as a chaperone. I wish I was setting out with him from the door of your house, that we might stride together up into the hills and look down upon the loch. I wish we were anywhere but here, in London, where there is no fresh air and barely any freedom.*

Mary

It is but a few minutes before Sir Percy is due to arrive. Mary tries very hard not to look at herself too long in the mirror. 'I do not want a love based merely on physical attraction, but on a true connection of the mind,' she tells herself firmly, before leaning forward to the glass to check that her front curl is hanging in exactly the right place, turning neatly beneath her left cheekbone.

Jane knocks at her door. 'Are you ready? Can I borrow one of your tartan skirts,' she asks rapidly.

'They're kilts,' says Mary, 'and no, they wouldn't fit you.' It's true; Mary's walking across the moors has left her as thin as the stem of a thistle, whilst Jane has soft curves above and below her tiny waist. 'Your hips would stretch the pleats out,' Mary goes on. 'It would look awful.'

Jane looks down at her plain muslin walking dress, unaware of how lovely she looks, of how its high waist accentuates the contrast between her slender shoulders and rounded breasts, the flowing fabric hinting at her hips. 'At least my dress is not white!' she says. 'Mamma says the green in it brings out the green in my eyes.' Mary doesn't answer. 'I could wear the brown pelisse,' suggests Jane.

'It's June,' says Mary. 'You'd be far too hot!'

Still, Jane considers it. From far below, the girls hear a knock on the door. They glance at each other before racing to the stairs. On the small landing they both stop and compose themselves, before jostling each other. Jane gives Mary a sharp shove backwards and steps forward into view.

Sir Percy nods at her as she appears at the head of the stairs. Mary waits until Jane is at the bottom before beginning her own descent; she rests her hand on the bannister, lifts her head and walks down as though she were alone. Only when she gets to the bottom does she allow herself a glance up at Sir Percy.

'Sir Percy,' she says.

He stares at her. 'Miss Godwin.'

Standing next to him, Jane notices a small movement in his throat, a desperate swallow, as though he cannot take Mary in all at once. As though the sight of her is too much for him to digest. I could be wearing nothing but a tartan corset, she thinks, and he still wouldn't be able to see me.

'So,' says Mary, as the three of them turn the corner of Skinner Street, 'Fanny and Jane both tell me how very lovely your wife is.' I must mention her, she thinks as they walk to the end of the street. Whatever this connection we may have is, however it unfolds, it cannot begin on a lie. He nods at her words but says nothing.

'They went as a couple to Ireland to start a revolution!' adds Jane, pleased for once to know more than Mary. 'And they have a beautiful little girl called Ianthe.'

The thought of his daughter pierces Bysshe for a moment,

but it is only brief. He stops and bends to touch the petal of a plant growing out over a window box. The girls glance at each other, confused by his refusal to respond to Mary's comment.

'Are you pretending not to hear us?' asks Jane, giggling with nerves.

'No,' he says calmly, lifting his head. 'I'm just unsure as to how I might answer.' He stares at Mary, his gravity making Jane feel small and silly.

'Perhaps with the truth,' says Mary tartly, a question in her fearless eyes, for much as she wants to impress him she is not used to being ignored. The three of them stand in a small awkward group, unmoving.

'Well then,' Sir Percy answers, understanding her unspoken message that there can be nothing between them if he is not able to be honest with her. 'Yes, I am married. Yes, Harriet came to Ireland with me, and yes, we have a daughter named Ianthe, and also yes, my wife is with child.' He turns away, convinced that he has said too much, overcome by the truth of his own words. The fact of them. A story he can neither change nor re-imagine. He is married, to a woman he no longer loves, a woman who clings to an idea of marriage that he no longer believes in. And he cannot know if Mary, extraordinary as she seems, will ever be able to overcome such an obstacle.

The girls hurry after him, clutching each other's hands in excitement.

'I wanted to ask you . . .' Mary begins a little breathlessly as they enter the park.

He stops at the sound of her voice, turning so suddenly that she has to check herself and step back, almost tripping before coming to a standstill. Jane laughs nervously and they both glare at her. 'Anything,' he says eagerly. 'Ask anything at all!' suddenly aware that he might have been too abrupt or rude in walking away.

'I understand you doubt the existence of God, but I wonder if that also requires you to deny the meaning of the Bible?' Mary asks.

'Oh!' he says, startled, for he was expecting a more personal question.

'I could quite do without either,' declares Jane, sensing yet another of Mary's interminable philosophical debates. She is rewarded with a loud burst of Sir Percy's unfettered laughter. Several couples walking in the park turn to glance at him disapprovingly. Both girls step an inch or two closer to him, feeling debonair and dangerous.

'You are a free spirit, Miss Godwin!' He nods at Jane.

'Oh!' says Jane, wondering if his words might be true, that she might one day be something more than simply second best to Mary.

'But,' Mary continues determinedly, annoyed by the loss of his attention, 'you do not deny that there is meaning in the Bible?'

'Of course not. Bible stories remain as meaningful as any Greek fable or fairy tale!'

Mary smiles, for he does not appear to notice that he has said anything remotely radical. 'Seriously,' she asks, 'you see no difference between the three? Isn't that as good as claiming that the Bible is a mere story, holding no more meaning than a novel?'

Sir Percy frowns. 'I think you do the power of story a disservice. The story of St Peter denying Jesus tells us how painful it is to betray those we love.' He thinks of Harriet as he speaks. 'Whereas a myth such as Narcissus explains how easy it is to see only oneself, one's own beauty or desire, and to place that desire above those we love.' Yes, he thinks, that is what I have done. He sees now that his passionate desire to free Harriet from the oppression of her father, to liberate her, was all that mattered to him. He did not think of Harriet as a person at all beyond her obvious beauty and the wildness he sensed in her, the willingness to do whatever he asked.

'You are thinking of something personal to you, aren't you?' asks Mary gently. 'Something that makes those stories meaningful to you?'

He nods and she falls naturally into step beside him as together they follow the clearly defined paths of the park. Jane keeps a pace or two behind. Neither of them notices her careful kindness in dropping back. They are too deep in thought, too lost in each other. Mary feels as though she could watch him for ever, his thoughts haunt his features, feelings flit across his face.

'If God is but a story then it is a truly wonderful one, isn't it?' she asks after a while. 'I mean,' she qualifies rapidly, 'it isn't only about providing a justification for treating people badly . . . I mean . . . at least, for me it has more meaning than that.'

He turns to her at once, enquiring gently, 'In what way?'

'Well, I can understand the notion that God might not exist, but what it is harder to give up is the *feeling* that such a belief in God and heaven gives me.' Mary takes a breath, for what she is about to say is so personal, has been buried so deep within her, that she does not know if it is truly possible to say the words aloud. 'My mother was not an atheist and so religion,' she says slowly, 'allows me to feel that I am still in communion with my mother, and that I have not lost her entirely.' There, it is said.

'Mary!' he whispers, stepping so close that the drift of his jacket grazes her waist. 'Your mother is everywhere! She is in your bones, in your being. She is in the books she wrote. Perhaps even in the very air we breathe.' He forgets himself, clasping her hands in his passion, not noticing what he is doing.

A few paces away, Jane's eyes widen and her breath draws in. Have they forgotten they are in public?

Mary feels tears rise at his kindness; she blinks fiercely,

removing her hands from beneath his. She never cries, ever. It is something she prides herself on; she is not like Jane who cries at the slightest thing, is always at the mercy of her feelings.

'It is a challenge,' she says, unaware of her hands twisting together, transferring the remnants of his touch between her fingers, 'to connect feeling to reason when one is not used to it.'

'When you open the caged bird's door,' he replies quietly, 'the bird does not fly, but think, Mary! What if it is not heaven but the world itself that holds its breath, waiting for that one bird to fly, to lift up its beak, open its tiny wings and sing its own peculiar song! What if there is no other world but this one, with all we need in it, right beneath our very feet? Does that thought not hold its own peculiar wonder?'

Mary's heart flies towards him at the sound of such words, but her eyes close against him. He is too bright, too burning. Yet there is no escape, for behind her closed lids a vision of him remains, impressing itself upon her: asking, what if, what if, what if she should defy all reason and lift up her arms to the sky in that same abandoned, carefree way of his, allowing herself to fly; but she cannot, she must not, for that way lies chaos and despair; the triumph of feeling over reason. Her father's firm training and her mother's experience will not allow it.

'You have given me much to think about,' she says. 'Perhaps we should return now, they will be waiting.'

'Of course!' he agrees immediately, but he walks slowly now, reluctantly – aware that each step takes him closer to separation from her. They walk towards the exit of the park, Jane following along behind them.

A few days later, as soon as Mary and Jane leave on yet another walk with Sir Percy, Fanny begins to pack. She has made her decision. She cannot bear to watch Sir Percy fall in love with her sister. She does not know whatever possessed her to think that Sir Percy might truly notice her – why on earth should he when no one else does?

'Would you like to take the blue walking dress, and perhaps the brown pelisse, Fanny?' Mrs Godwin stands beside the open trunk, folding clothes for her.

'Oh, thank you, Mamma!' It is a generous offer. 'But it would be a waste to have it out in Wales,' says Fanny. 'Let Jane or Mary wear it here in London.'

Mrs Godwin sighs; her stepdaughter's voice has that dead quality to it that so often comes upon her when she is either hurt or troubled. 'Fanny?'

'Yes,'

'Are you sure you want to go to Wales? Sir Shelley . . . I mean Percy . . . will be leaving once the loan to Papa is secured, and Mary will almost certainly return to Scotland then.'

'Thank you, Mamma,' says Fanny, without looking at her stepmother. 'I like spending time with Mamma's sisters. They tell me about her.' Fanny takes over, carefully folding and packing as she speaks, and Mrs Godwin watches her with a confused affection, wondering, as she has so many times before, if her husband is really doing the right thing by Fanny.

She is tempted to tell her stepdaughter the truth, that she is not really Mr Godwin's daughter at all, that her mother had a wildly passionate affair that resulted in Fanny's birth, that Mary Wollstonecraft had loved Fanny's real father so much that she caught a boat to Sweden with Fanny in her arms and only Marguerite by her side, chasing her lover's lost treasure to the very ends of the continent in the hope that if she found his goods he might return to her. He didn't. He abandoned them both anyway.

When Mary Wollstonecraft married William Godwin he

insisted that Fanny be known as his own child. That decision worries Mrs Godwin, for it is obvious that her husband prefers Mary, and poor Fanny has no idea why, imagining it must be due to some failing of her own. Surely it would be better for the girl to know how loved she was, to have a romantic, passionate story of her own, something to help her match Mary?

But Mrs Godwin cannot go against her husband's wishes. He has saved her and her children from another stint in a debtor's prison, given them a home and Jane the education Mrs Godwin would have liked for herself, and so she will not betray him. He has had enough of powerful women, however much he writes about equality between the sexes. There are ideas, she thinks to herself, and then there's the reality – and the two don't always match.

'You don't have to go away, Fanny,' she hears herself say, when what she'd really like to say is; if you really like that young man as much as you seem to, plant your feet down firmly and fight for him; but she knows it would do no good. Fanny has spent a lifetime watching Mary carry off the honours. Mrs Godwin is not at all impressed with that young man: he could at least make an effort to remember the existence of Jane and Fanny; let alone his young wife! They were worthy enough of his attention before Madam Mary returned.

'It's all right,' says Fanny as she closes the trunk. 'I really do want to go.' And it is true, she does. She cannot bear to watch Sir Percy falling so inevitably in love with Mary.

Fanny climbs into the carriage, she does not look back. London passes by in a blur as she finally allows the tears to roll down her cheeks. She has been so stupid, allowing herself to believe that somebody might really love her. After all, didn't her mother die when she was only two? Didn't Marguerite, whom she had loved all her life, leave her too?

'Fanny, look at me,' Marguerite had said before she left.

'I have to leave you. I do not want to go, but have been told by Mrs Godwin that I must. Your mother loved you and I love you.' Fanny clung to her, trying not to weep because she knew it would annoy Papa and her new stepmother to see her tear-stained cheeks.

'Look at me, Fanny,' Marguerite continued, her soft French voice firm, as it could sometimes be. Fanny looked up at her. 'Now, say after me: *my mamma loved me.*'

'My mamma loved me,' Fanny said seriously.

'And I love you.'

'And you love me,' Fanny repeated.

'Now all at once.'

'My mamma loved me and you love me.'

'Promise me that you'll remember that whenever you are sad.' Fanny nodded, then Marguerite kissed her, holding her tight for a long, long while before letting her go.

Fanny remembers standing at the nursery window, watching Marguerite walk away through the small square. 'Turn around,' she'd whispered. 'Please turn around.'

At the corner she did turn, just as Fanny had wished, but then she had waved, blown her a kiss and walked on.

She did not come back, however hard Fanny had wished it.

'My mamma loved me and you love me,' Fanny whispers the words to herself. The words fall into a rhythm with the rocking of the carriage wheels. The tears stop and slowly the words merge one into another, becoming something meaningless, a chant that does nothing to touch the grey dead space inside her. Her lips move soundlessly as she stares out of the window, wheels turning.

19TH JUNE 1814: 41 SKINNER STREET

'Perhaps,' suggests Mary quietly to Bysshe, 'we could visit my mother's grave. I used to go all the time,' she says quickly, before he can answer. 'With Papa, I mean, until we moved to Skinner Street. And recently, as you know, I've been in Scotland.' Stop talking, she says to herself, let him answer. But she goes on in spite of herself, unable to leave any space for fear of rejection. What will she do if he says no, or fails to understand the significance of her offer? 'It's been so long since I was able to visit her!' she finishes.

Liar, thinks Jane, for Mary visited her mother's grave only yesterday, she is sure of it. Probably to ask her mother's blessing for this very visit, telling her that she will be bringing Bysshe.

'Are you sure?' asks Bysshe, rising up from the bench and pacing up and down, unable to keep still in his excitement, for surely this is a sign that Mary is interested in more than just debating with him, that she too might have been falling in love over the last few days.

'Yes,' she says, and then, 'yes, I am.' He holds out his arm and she rises. They set off together at a rapid pace, fuelled by their excitement. Jane scurries after them.

'It is an honour that I had not expected,' he says, picking up his pace in the hope that it might encourage Jane to fall back as she usually does; but Jane remains stubbornly in step with them – determined not to be left behind. As a child new to the Godwin household she often stood at the nursery window with Fanny, watching as Mary and her father walked together towards St Pancras churchyard, wishing she was with them.

'It's not FAIR!' she used to shout, beating the words out in a tattoo upon the nursery window as she screamed, but Mary and her father could not hear her; unaware of the two small girls staring longingly after them. 'She's your mamma too!' Jane would cry out, furious on Fanny's behalf, banging even harder upon the window. 'Stop! Stop it, Jane,' Fanny said gently, holding on to her wrists and pulling her away from the window. 'Mamma will hear you.'

Jane determinedly keeps pace with the pair of them. They walk together over the wooden bridge that leads into the graveyard, the River Fleet flowing dark beneath them, then on to the grass and up the slight incline towards the old church. As they approach her mother's resting place, Mary shoots Jane a look of such pleading that she finally relents, continuing on past the grave to a small bench in the corner of the graveyard, as far away from the neighbouring tavern as she can get.

She sits and opens up a book. She knows that Mary and her father used to read Mary Wollstonecraft's books beside her grave, and has decided she will do the same. She has deliberately left her favourite volume of Byron's poetry at home so that it will not tempt her. *A Vindication of the Rights of Woman*, Jane reads on the cover. She opens it up and is soon lost in the text, surprised by how easily the thoughts speak to her. '*For my arguments, sir,*' Mary Wollstonecraft writes, '*are dictated by a disinterested spirit: I plead for my sex, not for myself. Independence I have long considered as the grand blessing of life, the basis of every virtue; and independence I will ever secure by contracting my wants, as though I were to live on a barren heath.*'

As Jane reads, the ideas lodge in her mind and turn over. She feels as though Mary's mother is speaking directly to her, describing a world where she might neither need nor long to be married, where to be deserted by a man, as her mother was, might not be a crime – or to be dependent upon Godwin, as they are now, might never be necessary. She has heard such ideas before, many times, but she has never really considered them. She imagines feeling so fiercely about an idea that she would be prepared to live on a *barren heath*, *contracting her wants*, which she thinks might mean having nothing. In her imagination quite a lot of people visit her on the heath. They are impressed by her determination. And she is beautifully dressed.

Mary and Bysshe stand before the square gravestone, heads lowered. Mary remembers tracing the letters with her own small fingers, slowly coming to understand that they also formed her own name. Now that they are here she does not know what to say; the enormity of the occasion overwhelming her. She takes hold of one of the branches of the two willows that her father planted, the deep bell of them covering her mother's resting place. The thin fronds are in leaf, golden underneath and green on top. She holds them aside like a curtain and the two of them step inside. Cocooned.

'My father planted these,' she says.

'One at her foot and one at her head,' says Bysshe, 'eternally weeping for her.'

'Oh, I hadn't thought of that!' she exclaims.

'Why else would he plant them?' he asks.

'Well, because they're beautiful and—' Mary stops, startled by a sudden memory. Bysshe waits, the green light beneath the branches reminding him of home, of sitting beneath the willow in his own garden, telling stories to his sisters. This gentle waiting for her to speak is one of the things that Mary is beginning to love most about Bysshe, the way he allows her thoughts to form and deepen in the space of his watchful silence. Now, beneath his gaze, she remembers standing in the churchyard with her father. She is four years old and looking into a hole with broken, splintered boxes at the bottom. Her father is shouting at a man as he fills in the holes, digging a spade into the roughly piled turfs beside the wide-open grave, and throwing them on to the tops of the coffins where they thump and spatter.

'Papa?' Mary asks, for the sight is alarming. She remembers turning so confidently, expecting her papa to make sense of everything as he always did. But this time he did not.

'Not now, Mary,' he said and pulled her away, setting off immediately for home.

'Why are we going home?' she wailed. 'We haven't spoken to Mamma yet!'

Her father did not answer, pulling her along even harder, increasing his pace so that she had to run, her feet flying almost to the point of falling in an effort to keep up with him. She was breathless by the time they returned home. In the hallway Papa dropped her hand, walked into his study and closed the door behind him, leaving her alone in the hallway.

Mary stood there shaking. 'Papa?' she whispered, but the door stayed closed. She still does not know how long she stood there, unable to move.

Back in the churchyard she turns to Bysshe. 'I came here often when I was young, with Papa.' He nods. 'And once I saw an open grave with splintered boxes at the bottom of it. I didn't know what they were, and I never guessed until years later.'

'How? How did you guess?' he asks.

'We moved,' she says, enjoying his rapt attention, 'to where we are now, in Skinner Street. I hated it from the start. Soon after we moved there was a hanging,' she says, her hand tightening upon the willow branch.

Bysshe does not ask her what she means, for he can see she is lost deep in a memory and he does not want to disturb her. She swallows. 'We were all in the shop and my stepmother was wearing a dress of deep red, with fluted sleeves, the colour of blood. There was a noise like a humming and then the crowd came around the corner, the mob. "Shut the door, Jane. Now!" my stepmother shouted, and Jane's hand trembled as it reached out to bolt the door against the crowd rushing towards the prison to see the hanging of two men. It was so shocking that even my father came out from his study, and I remember that his appearance at the door between the house and the bookshop made everything even more frightening. "Ridiculous!" he said, when he saw the mob running and falling over themselves in their haste to see the men die, yelling and laughing as they ran. "This is what happens when we fail to educate the masses. They kill each other in their desire to witness death," he added, before turning away and closing the door. "More meat for the grave robbers!" said my stepmother, and as soon as I heard those words I saw the splintered boxes again, remembered my father's fury, and understood that he was not angry with me that day, but frightened that my mother's body might be stolen from her grave.

'Just then the bells of Newgate began to toll. Have you ever heard them?' she asks.

Bysshe nods again.

'They mark the final steps of the condemned men, the bell tolling for each step between the prison and the scaffold. The people in the street ran even faster. I remember one of them calling out: "Hurry up, or we'll miss it!" But all the time I was asking myself if my mother's body had been stolen. The thought that Mamma's body might be lost somewhere, her spirit alone and wandering haunted me. I wanted to ask Papa so badly if it was my own mamma's grave, which had been robbed, but somehow I couldn't. I did try, the very next morning, but he was too angry. "Twenty-eight people," he said. "Twenty-eight people trampled to death in that melee yesterday. If that doesn't prove the need to educate the masses then I don't know what does." And somehow, my question, well, it –' she looks up at him – 'it withered under his fury.'

'Mary?' Bysshe touches her shoulder; she looks up, her fingers still curled around the thin fronds of the willow.

'So I think he planted the trees because he was frightened of grave robbers,' she says. 'People do that, don't they? They say the roots are as good as bars.' She notices his hand upon her shoulder, finds it comforting. 'I never knew if she was really here or not after that,' she says slowly.

He reaches out for her other shoulder, steadying her between his two hands. 'She's always wherever you are,' he says gently, 'always. No one can take away your sense of her.'

'I didn't know that though,' she whispers, 'because I was a child.' Actually, she thinks, I didn't know it until this very moment, until the words came out of his mouth; and it is only now that he has said them that they make sense, taking away the fear that has lain inside of me so secretly for so many years.

'Yes,' he is saying, 'as children we cannot speak. When they took me away from home, and sent me to school, I was in despair and yet to say so felt impossible. As children we live with our sadness. Silently.'

She nods, lifting her hands and briefly clasping his elbows to steady herself before stepping back, so that his arms drop empty to his sides.

'I will always remember this moment,' he says.

Mary is silent.

'Have I offended you?' he asks anxiously.

He has not – but she cannot speak, afraid that if she does her words will emerge strangled and broken, overwhelmed by emotion. She shakes her head in response, grateful for the sight of Jane heading towards them.

'Shall we walk back through Somers town, past our old house?' Jane suggests.

'Yes, let's!' says Mary gratefully.

The three of them walk home together past the park and through the crescent that was once the girls' home. The memories rise thick and fast now, set free by the familiar streets. 'The square below our windows was often full of French refugees, and they would call out to us sometimes, "*Bonjour, ma petite!*" I think

Marguerite our nurse must have told them about Mother because they used to mention her sometimes. Marguerite was with her during the Revolution in Paris.' Mary talks on happily, wanting Bysshe to know everything, wishing she could take his hand and travel back in time with him so that together they might each watch their young selves. Beside her he asks question after question, never wanting the story of her life to end.

'Do you remember Marguerite teaching us "The Marseillaise"?' Jane says quietly as they stand in front of their old home. The sound of her voice makes them both jump, for they had forgotten her existence. Without waiting for an answer Jane begins to sing. Her voice is sweet and clear and she sings in a low whisper, aware that the war is still close, and the Revolution not a thing to be heard celebrating. The quiet singing gives her words an unearthly air in the empty, late afternoon street: '*Allons enfants de la patrie, le jour de gloire est arrivé*,' she sings. 'Children of the country, the day of glory has arrived.' When she finishes there is a silence, for her rendition is beautiful. Bysshe claps gently and Jane curtsies. 'Marguerite told us that the man who wrote that was in love with Mary's mother,' she explains.

'We are all a little in love with Mary Wollstonecraft!' declares Sir Percy.

'I remember,' Mary says dreamily, 'one of the watchsellers in the crescent frightening me. He said, "You see this little thing here." And he showed me a watch. "Listen!" And he held it to my ear. I heard it so close it felt like it was right inside my head. Tick. Tick. Tick. "You hear that?" he asked, and I nodded. "Those are the seconds of your life, *mademoiselle*, ticking away. You cannot stop them and you cannot slow them down, you can only listen as they pass, make sure you use them well!"' Mary shivers at the memory.

'He was right!' laughs Bysshe.

'Perhaps! But I was only six years old, and it frightened me.

I wondered how long I would have on earth, and whether I would soon lie under the ground with my mother! I hate watches – they speak only of time passing, of never knowing how much we have.'

'But if we had for ever, what then?' he asks.

'We'd have time to learn,' says Mary at once. 'We'd have a greater sense of what history has to teach us.'

'And would it make us any better at living?' he asks. 'Would it help us to live each moment as it comes, rather than believing in a perfect heaven?'

'You *can* do both, Bysshe!' laughs Mary. 'It is possible to believe in a better world *and* to believe in heaven!'

'But what if,' he goes on, determined now, 'what if we had to make our own heaven right here on earth. What would yours be?' he asks.

'Well, there would be equality between men and women,' Mary says at once. 'No marriage contract, and proper education for all – not only boys and girls, but rich and poor too! And the rich would support the poor, and in doing so they would not be driven so far apart.'

'And would people be able to believe freely in your world, whether they be Mohammedans or Christians, or maybe even non-believers!'

'Yes!' declares Mary. 'We would all learn from each other, and respect each other. But tell me about your heaven on earth,' she asks passionately.

In my perfect world, thinks Jane, exasperated, people might simply kiss when they adore one another, rather than talking on and on until they are exhausted.

Bysshe readies himself to answer Mary's question. Perhaps she will be appalled by his thoughts, perhaps after he has spoken she will no longer wish to walk with him; yet the thought of failure does not paralyse him, instead it drives him forward. As always when excited, the words fall flawlessly from his lips.

'In my world,' he begins, 'there would be no God, nor even thought of him. We would be governed by our own being, expected to follow our own instincts and learn from our own experience. There would be no discussion of equality between men and women, nor adults and children, only an assumption that we are already equal.

'In my world we would refuse to insist that the poor pay in taxes what would easily keep them from hunger and cold; we would not grind them into abject poverty, and then accuse them of being abject. How abject would *we* be if we had no food and no heat, if we worked fourteen hours a day, every day? If we could not walk amongst the trees when we felt like it, or pick up some bread because we were hungry? How much would we feel like reading a book or staring at a painting with our guts growling in hunger? How civilised would we be then? In my world it is the rich who would pay more taxes!' Carried away by his words, he has already forgotten his fear that Mary might not agree with him.

Jane and Mary nod in unison, entranced by his speech, unable to look away from him.

'And there would be no marriage because we would love each other as freely as we share ideas, as easily as we hand each other a book to read from. In my world there would be no shame in a man loving more than one woman, or a woman loving more than one man. Shame would only exist for those who subject others to their own will, or who act against the cause of freedom.' He stops, remembers where he is, sees the faces of Mary and Jane intent upon him.

'Yes!' whispers Mary, for she can see the world he creates as though it is rising up before her eyes, can imagine him willing it into being; her steady belief in the ideals of her beloved papa begin to crumble within her.

Bysshe looks into her eyes and sees not rejection, but acceptance and excitement as she gazes back at him.

Bysshe's words stay with Jane long after he has stopped speaking and the two of them have moved away; they mix with the recently read words of Mary's mother. She stands a while, staring up at windows of the houses on the Polygon, imagining her mother living next door to Godwin, alone with two children.

She knows the story of her mother and Godwin's meeting, how they each stood on their separate balconies one evening and her mother said: 'Can this be the famous William Godwin standing beside me!' The obvious flattery in her mother's words fills Jane with equal amounts of shame and sympathy. Her mother must have seen Mary's father on that balcony and blessed God for her good fortune; the sight of a man so obviously in search of a wife.

In a world such as Bysshe paints, her mother would be free of the shame of having no father for her children. She wonders what her mother might have done then. Have Mr Godwin and her mother ever truly loved each other, or has her mother simply done the best she could? The word *independence* rings within her, repeating itself, forming new and different pictures in her mind; perhaps, one day, the world might truly be different. Perhaps, one day, she might be free to love exactly as she chooses. Perhaps, one day, she and Mary might share Bysshe as easily as they each read the same book, or perhaps she might one day have a poet of her own.

Jane turns away from the Polygon with a head full of possibilities, born by the presence of Bysshe. The life her mother has imagined for her – and that Jane too has longed for – of a successful marriage and a home of her own, feels dull now. And boring.

Mary strides ahead by Bysshe's side, lost in a world of potential wonder; she has found a man who seems to be able to put into words the very thoughts and feelings that exist within her. Is this what love is? Will a life with Bysshe ever really be possible?

Perhaps, thinks Bysshe, I have finally met a woman who can live alongside me outside the bond of marriage, who might help me create a new world where equality in mind and body is not just an idea but a reality? He glances at Mary as she walks beside him, lost in thought as deep as his own. She is extraordinary. He loves her straightforward calm, her reason and capacity for steady thoughtful debate in the face of his wild passion. He loves her red-gold hair and the light in her eyes. He feels she was made for him.

Their steps slow as they approach the house, neither of them wanting their time together to come to an end, both already longing for tomorrow afternoon when they can be together again.

They loiter in the porch of the door.

'Perhaps—'

'I—'

They both speak at the same time, and then stop and smile at each other.

Jane runs up beside them. 'You should have waited for me so that we all arrived together,' she hisses in a whisper.

Yes, thinks Mary, we're getting careless, but does it really matter? If we are to be together eventually, then at some point we must be discovered.

Mrs Godwin opens the door. 'What on earth are you three doing standing on the doorstep chattering like tradesmen! Have you no sense of propriety?' She can do nothing about Mary, but she will be damned if her Jane is going to be dragged down alongside that little madam. She reaches out to pull Mary inside.

Before he knows it, Bysshe finds his arm between them, stopping Mary's stepmother from reaching her. Both women step back. Jane's eyes widen. Now Bysshe will see a different side of Mary Godwin, she thinks. Now he'll see the rage she exhibits whenever her stepmother tries to reprimand her.

'I'm sorry we are late,' says Sir Percy, his arm remaining firmly in place. 'I'm afraid it is entirely my doing, for we were discussing the relative merits of a heaven upon—'

'Yes! We're sorry we're so late!' Mary interjects rapidly before he can declare himself both a poly-amorist and an atheist upon their very doorstep.

Mrs Godwin is so taken aback by Mary's easy apology that she allows them to pass without comment; never in all her years as a Godwin has Mary ever deigned to utter a single word of apology to her stepmother. Jane's jaw drops. 'Careful,' says her mother, 'or the wind will change and you'll be stuck like that!' Jane lifts her jaw.

'Ah,' says Mr Godwin, emerging from his study, 'just the man, Sir Percy! Come in, come in.' He gestures to his door, wondering if the young man has any idea at all of how deeply in debt the bookshop is, indeed if anyone except his wife does. Godwin has sold debt after debt, made loan after loan, the interest increasing each time until now his debtors circle like sharks, sensing his desperation – and longing to attack. For they know him as a man who would happily distribute their wealth amongst the poor if he could.

So far Mrs Godwin has managed to keep their family of five children from poverty – and yet if this eccentric, revolutionary poet does not come up with the goods, the debtors' prison still hovers. At least with Mary and Jane entertaining him, Sir Percy will not be tempted to slip away with his wife and forget his fine promises. Nonetheless Godwin will be relieved when his household can return to normal; he does not like disruption. Routine is essential to good work; breakfast and study in the morning, exercise in the afternoon. Mary has perhaps lapsed a little since she has been in Scotland, but undoubtedly all will return to normal when Sir Percy leaves, and surely that time must be close now. It will be good to have Mary back helping in the shop. She can certainly hold her own in arguing with the young man, he thinks with pride.

Bysshe tips his head to the two young ladies and disappears into the study. Mary walks decorously upstairs to her room. Once inside she throws herself upon the bed, wrapping her arms around her body. She closes her eyes and relives the moment again – her hated stepmother reaching for her as she so often has, and Bysshe's arm appearing between them as if by magic, keeping Mrs Godwin from her. Papa has always steadfastly refused to take Mary's side against her stepmother, but Bysshe did not hesitate. She sees his arm again, striking out so rapidly, holding on to the doorframe and remaining in place even as he apologised, making sure that Mary and her stepmother were separated. The feeling it gives her is extraordinary. It is the very thing she has dreamed of Papa doing. But he never has. 'He must feel something for me,' she whispers to herself, 'wife or no wife!'

She wishes, yet again, that her mother was alive to meet him, to advise her in whether her feelings should be acted upon, or whether falling in love with Bysshe is something she should resist. 'Mamma,' she whispers into the air. 'Did you like him?'

There is only silence. Mary sits up, aware of a familiar feeling that her mother is close, that she may have been sitting over by the window whilst Mary's back was turned, and yet, as ever, she melts away the moment Mary turns towards her.

'Where are you, Mamma?' she asks. Sometimes the longing for a mother of her own is overwhelming: such as when she catches sight of Jane and her mother laughing at some secret thing together in the kitchen, or when she watched as Mrs Baxter ruffled Izy's hair.

She stands and walks to her desk, picks up a book of her mother's and holds it in her palm. When she was younger she used to do this often, ask Mamma a question and then open one of her books at random, pointing with her eyes closed to a place on the page. She did it secretly and shamefully – for it was a superstitious thing to do, not based on reason and thought, but feeling and intuition: things she has been taught to be suspicious of. And yet the urge is overwhelming, the longing for her mother's blessing acute. And so she picks up her mother's book and opens it, closes her eyes and points. She looks. The words stare up at her from the page.

'*Women,*' her mother writes, '*have ever been duped by their lovers as princes are by their ministers, whilst dreaming they reigned over them.*'

She reads the words over and over, shocked by the precise power of them, the relevance to her own life. Is this really what her mamma would say if she were here; is it what she is trying to tell Mary from beyond the grave? 'Mamma?' she asks again, but there is no reply, just the pages fluttering open on her lap; and the sense of safety she held so powerfully within her a moment ago now gone.

25TH JUNE 1814: THE JUVENILE BOOKSHOP – 41 SKINNER STREET

'He is so beautiful!' sighs Jane. 'I think I could look at him for ever!' They are unpacking books and cutting the pages prior to stacking them on shelves. It is a job neither of them likes, but Mrs Godwin insits they do it for it sets the bookshop apart, and means the children can read the books immediately. At least the room they are in is private, a small room off the bookshop, where they can talk.

'You do look at him, very obviously, every time he speaks to you,' laughs Mary.

'He doesn't even notice me now you're back.'

'He's tortured,' says Mary, 'by no longer loving his wife, and he cannot find his way forward, cannot see that he is a poet, not a philosopher or essayist. Do you really think he ... that he might be ... fond of me?'

'I know so!' Jane admits, swallowing her hurt at Mary's easy acceptance of her own rejection by Bysshe. 'When you walked into the dining room in that tartan he looked like he'd been struck by lightning! And he's dined here nearly every evening since he met you.'

'But he's married, Jane!' Mary is appalled to hear a note of petulance in her voice, but she cannot help but feel aggrieved, for surely he is meant for her.

'But he doesn't *believe* in marriage,' says Jane stoutly. 'He believes ...' She sits back on her heels, trying to recapture Bysshe's words, but she cannot. Only a feeling remains, a sense of possibility, of difference, of a world where she might be something other than Jane Godwin, born Clairmont – always second best, ashamed of her beginnings, and of her mother – of her very name. Which is not Wollstonecraft-Godwin. Mary's parents are famous the world over. The vice-president of America, Aaron Burr, came to offer Mary and her father his condolences upon the death of her mother; whereas Jane's father is unknown. Jane does not believe the tales her mother tells her, of a respectable man, now conveniently dead. She and her brother Charles have long since understood that her father was most probably a mere shadow in the night, a momentary attraction.

'But you are loved just the same,' explains her brother Charles, holding her close whenever she feels upset and ashamed. In Bysshe's new world, all that could change.

'He makes me feel,' whispers Jane, 'as though ... as though ...' Again the words elude her, for his way of thinking is so new to her that she cannot quite keep hold of it.

'That the world might be different,' finishes Mary.

'Yes.'

They smile at each other. Mary sits back and tucks her hair behind her ears. 'When I came back from Scotland I thought I'd die of boredom,' she says, 'and yet now, now I feel as though I could live anywhere as long as he were near me. I try to remind myself he's married, and that I shouldn't feel such things, but I can't help it. Can he really feel the same?'

'Has he said anything?'

'Oh, everything and nothing! He looks at me sometimes as though he would like to say something ... and he ... he touches me sometimes, I mean just a hold of my shoulder, or a helping hand, nothing untoward! But he declares nothing!' She lets go of Jane's hand and brushes her skirts. 'Perhaps we're both just silly girls imagining what we long to be true.'

'No!' says Jane. 'I've seen the way he looks at you, Mary. It's not whether he loves you or not, it's what he chooses to do about it.'

'Really, you really think so?'

Jane nods. She is sure of it.

'Then why does he not say something!'

'He's married, Mary,' she says, 'so perhaps that stops him. I've met Harriet, his wife. He persuaded her to leave her father, to risk everything and run away with him. Perhaps he fears his power to persuade you, and longs to know that you come to him of your own volition.'

Mary knows immediately that Jane is right, and is more than a little irritated by the knowledge. Am I so bound by convention that I have been waiting for Bysshe to declare himself when I am perfectly capable of doing the same myself? she wonders.

'Of course,' she mutters, 'that is so like him! So thoughtful!'

Jane sighs – for whilst she too adores Bysshe she is not quite so blinded by him. She has inherited the clear practical mind and instincts of her own mother.

Broughty Ferry

D*ear Mary,*

I read your letter with such excitement, but you do not tell me what Sir Percy looks like! Or whether you have spoken alone with him yet? What does your father think? I have read Shelley's pamphlet, it is true that we cannot ever, at least through our own senses or experience, prove the existence of God, and yet, even as one who has been excommunicated I can see that it is not about proof, but belief, and perhaps we simply sometimes need to believe? As to the power of the church (as opposed to the love of Christ), then of course I am in agreement: it exists to keep us all subjugated, and when we desire to break free of it, it exacts the terrible punishment of ostracism – or in past times even torture and death. Are you ready for that, Mary? The reaction will be stronger if you 'take' a married man, and especially one with children.

Up here we can manage whether or not we are approved of, but in London where you described so much coming and going and gossip it must be harder to be vilified. I have such need of my family now. We are so blessed, Mary, in our fathers. I remember you saying that excommunication would be as nothing compared to touching tongues! And now what do you say?

I am looking out over the loch with a rug on my knees, because it is cold now in the evening, even in June. I am hoping that your love is returned, that you can share love with a man who treats you as his equal, who loves you as a woman and never tries to belittle or demean your intelligence – who longs for your success as a writer as much as you do yourself, and is not envious or afraid of your fearsome mind. Who can love your body with his own and for you both to find equal pleasure there. Mary, if all that is true then what does society matter? And yet it is a high price to pay, to be cut off from all normal social intercourse. I want you to know that, so that your decision is made with your eyes wide open. Oh, Mary! I cannot help but be happy for you. Write soon.

Izy

26TH JUNE 1814: ST PANCRAS CHURCHYARD

Mary decides that she must declare her love. She makes the decision as they walk towards the cemetery, which has become their regular trysting place. Even the day itself seems to encourage her; it has been a cold summer but today the fields beyond the bridge to the churchyard are full of tall buttercups, the sunlight lifting them into a hazy field of gold. She looks up at Bysshe walking along beside her, unaware of what is to come. At this precise moment in time she is the only person in the world who knows what is about to happen. The sense of power is delicious; in fact the enjoyment of clasping the momentousness of her decision to herself is so wonderful that perhaps she will not tell him today after all. She will wait until tomorrow, hugging the knowledge to herself for one more day – oh, but no – she cannot, because somewhere inside her, as ever, she can hear the tick, tick, tick of those tiny watches and feel time passing. What if he decides to leave suddenly on the morrow and she is left with her declaration unsaid. No! She must tell him today, with the sun beating down upon them and the fields full of buttercups.

Jane follows a few paces behind them both. She has a powerful sense that Mary has come to a decision; there is something freer in the way she walks, a secret pleasure in her frequent glances up at Bysshe – who seems not to notice. He looks tired, thinks Jane, his beautiful eyes shadowed, the fragile skin beneath them bruised and blue. The not knowing if Mary returns his love is beginning to tell upon him. 'Soon,' Jane imagines whispering to him soothingly, 'soon everything between the two of you will be different, nothing will remain unspoken and everything will be said.'

The truth of it strikes her then, causing an almost physical pain in her heart. He will never be hers. She veers away from the two of them, entering the small church itself. The cool dark of it a relief in the heat of the day, the smell of clean wax and candles strangely reassuring. This place, she thinks, represents everything that Bysshe detests, and yet there is a peace here. She sits on the wooden pew, rocking. Help me, help me, she thinks silently, and in her mind she sees not God but Mary's mother, smiling down upon her. '*Independence*,' Jane hears Mary Wollstonecraft say gently, '*does not mean belonging to a man, not even one as wonderful as Bysshe, but belonging to yourself.*'

The thought is so startling that her pain is eased for a moment by the need to think about it.

Mary kneels down, tracing the letters of her mother's name with her forefinger. 'Whenever I did this as a child I imagined my mother's finger on the other side of the stone, following my own.'

Bysshe holds his own hand to the name. 'May I?' he asks. She nods. He takes a deep breath and slides his own finger across her mother's name, gently, reverently. 'I feel,' he whispers, 'as though I ought to introduce myself, even though we've been here many times.'

'Mrs Wollstonecraft,' he begins, 'I am Percy Bysshe Shelley, and I . . . I hope you will bless my friendship with your daughter.'

They wait for a moment in silence, hoping perhaps there might be some response, but all that happens is Jane appears on the other side of the church, sits on a bench and opens her book.

Bysshe lays down his jacket for Mary beneath the secret branches of the willows. 'As a child did you ever just lie back and feel the sun upon your face?' he asks, lying down himself and turning his face to the sun filtered through the leaves.

Mary lies beside him, feeling the grass tickle her ankles and rise up around them, hiding them further from the world.

He leans up on one elbow beside her. 'Close your eyes,' he says.

She does so and immediately the dappled sun feels stronger upon her face, the shape of him dancing in red shadows behind her lids. 'Proper young ladies are not meant to expose their skin to the sun!' she smiles.

'And neither are they meant to lie in the grass with young men!' he replies.

She does not answer, enjoying the feeling of her closed eyes clarifying the sense of everything around her. She feels like she is floating. She feels that together they can do anything. She allows her hand to drift through the grass closer to where she imagines his own might lie. The edges of their hands touch and she stops. The world seems to hold its breath, solidify behind her closed lids. He moves neither towards her nor away but she hears his own breath stop and then start again. Slowly, deliberately, she places her hand upon his and feels it turn beneath her own, his palm flattening and shaping itself to hers: 'And palm to palm is holy pilgrims' kiss,' she whispers.

He says nothing. He cannot, his hope is too wide and the fear of its failure too great. They lie together joined in effigy, facing the sky. Mary wishes this moment could last for ever, that they could step outside of the tick, tick, tick of time that confines them, making them subject to an endless forward momentum. There is a beauty, she thinks, in the perfection of a moment, and a sadness in the knowledge that once she speaks, and the declaration is made, they must inevitably set the world in motion again, take a step forward and allow consequence to unravel.

Speak, thinks Bysshe, please speak.

'When I was young,' she says softly, without opening her eyes, 'I used to say that my mother was beneath the earth and up in the sky!' She laughs at her younger self, and yet the truth is that she feels closer to the child she was then than she has ever felt before.

His fingers move to clasp hers and their hands hold. She turns her head towards him, opening her eyes. The intensity of his gaze, the question and naked longing there, makes her sink the fingers of her other hand deep into the damp grass, needing the feel of the earth between her fingers, grounding herself and her resolve to test him.

'I wish she was still alive,' she says simply.

'So do I,' he whispers, their gaze unbroken. 'May I?' he asks, reaching out even as he speaks to pluck a blade of grass from her hair. He has wanted to sink his hands deep into that hair from the first moment that he saw it. It glows a red-gold halo.

'*Women,*' whispers Mary, '*have ever been duped by their lovers, as princes are by their ministers, whilst dreaming they reigned over them!*'

The remark stays his hand even as it moves towards that second blade of grass stuck so enticingly behind her ear.

'That is something my mother once wrote,' Mary says, continuing to gaze at him, her eyes holding a clear challenge in them. 'Perhaps that's what she would say if she saw us now. That I am a fool who is being duped by a man already married.' The shock in his eyes almost stops her, but if she is to give herself to him she must know, must be sure, all doubts expressed – a clean beginning.

'I cannot change what is already done,' he whispers slowly, 'but my marriage to Harriet was dead to me from the moment I saw you. From before I saw you.'

Mary lets go of his hand, kneeling up and peering through the leaves of the tree. She sees Jane, her head deep in a book. The world beyond them feels a strange and separate thing; powerless to touch her. She sinks back down. 'Married or not, my mother believed in commitment between a couple,' says Mary.

'I am not . . . I am not . . .' Mary has never heard him stutter before; it startles her into a recognition of his desperation. 'I *am* committed to Harriet,' he says. 'I will always be committed to her and to our children, but I can no longer *love* her. When love is dead must we go on being chained to each other for ever, dragging each other's unfeeling bodies into an unloving future?' The image exerts a horrid fascination over Mary. 'I will always support Harriet. I hope she can find a love such as . . . such as I hope to find myself, that is equal in both mind and body, but if she does not then must I sacrifice myself to something that is dead? In my world,' he goes on gently, 'in my heaven, Harriet and I could each find another love and yet live close enough to share our children.'

'But what does that life offer a woman?' Mary asks.

'Freedom,' he answers, 'to love wherever she chooses. It is an extension of your mother's thinking. She did not believe in marriage, because she did not think women should be chattels, hiding their intelligence lest it threaten a man – yet has anything changed? We cannot just change the law, Mary; we have to change the way we think. We have to free ourselves from the very idea of possession. And yet we do nothing. My sisters remain at home, waiting to be passed from our father to some other man, any man that will have them, as though they were pots or pans rather than living breathing people with brains that might think, or bodies that might feel. They are trapped. That is why I married Harriet, to save her from her father! I did not understand that marriage was yet another trap. You see the measure of my problem, don't you? I have a wife who believes in holy matrimony when my whole soul rebels against such a state. For either man or woman!'

Mary says nothing, and so he goes on, fighting with each word. 'What if my sisters felt free to choose, and what if they made a mistake and so were free to learn? What if they loved more than one person, and were loved in return? If they lived in a world where they were free to share not only ideas, but also to love with their whole beings. Where women live as freely as men – not only in the mind but also in the body!' He stops, he is finished and he dare not look at her.

'Look at me,' she says. He looks up. 'So in your world you and I are free to love?'

'Yes, but are we free to love in your world, Mary?' he asks, lifting his hands to hold her face.

In answer she lifts her finger, tracing the perfect shape of his lips. 'In my world . . .'

They lean towards each other. He hesitates. 'Mary?'

'In my world, yes.'

His lips are soft and pressing. 'Then let the earth be our bed,' he whispers between kisses. 'And the sky our church.'

As her lips part, she thinks briefly of Izy, remembers her own repulsion at the idea of such intimacy – and then she forgets. She forgets that they lie upon the earth of her mother's grave, she forgets everything except the feel of him, and their moving together. Above them the sun travels across the sky, the light changing from its bright, bleaching rays into a golden evening glow. In time the ground begins to throw back the heat of the day, alerting Mary to the fact that somewhere outside of them time goes on ticking and she should speak. 'I love you,' she says.

He rests his head against her shoulder. 'And I you,' he whispers. 'And I you.'

Jane hums a sonata beneath her breath. Afternoon turns into early evening and still they do not come. She wonders what will happen now that Mary has declared her love. As the sun lowers she stands, making her way over to where they lie. They do not notice her slip through the grass and stand watching. Bysshe's golden curls bend forward as Mary's hair falls from her tipped-up face; the pale skin of her thigh gleams between the bars of light that fall through the leaves that surround and cover them. Jane sighs and, despite the pain it causes her, notes how beautiful they look together, how perfect.

She recreates the sight of them now as she hums: his hand running the length of Mary's body, tracing the curve of her hip, stopping to shadow the shape of her shoulder with his palm before sweeping on to hold her face so gently towards his own. They were so lost in each other she was invisible to them as she stood there, entranced, caught up in the intensity of their love for a brief moment. The vision of them together will not fade, the knowing that they were entwined as in a painting, their eyes open and gazing into each other's as they kissed. Nothing in her short life of sixteen years has prepared her for such a sight – it is burned upon her brain and she cannot free herself from it. It makes her ache with longing and loneliness. Perhaps, Jane thinks, only poets can inspire such a love, or hold within them such passion. She feels blessed to be near something that feels so sacred, and wonders if this is what becomes possible when one discards God and religion, that the holiness is imbued into everyday objects, becomes held within oneself. She cannot find the words to explain such a feeling, only knows that she longs to be near it and vows to herself that she will do all she can, whatever she can, to preserve the love between Mary and Bysshe and allow it the freedom to exist.

'Jane?' She looks up. It is Bysshe speaking. Mary stands beside him. The three of them look from one to the other and Jane smiles with a generosity that is almost as intense as the couple's feelings for one another.

'You've told him?' she says, and it is not a question but an understanding.

Joyous in their declared love, Bysshe holds out his arms, and without hesitation Mary joins with the movement. Jane rises up and they hold her between them, the three of them standing together.

They head homewards in a daze.

'When shall we tell Papa?' asks Mary, happily reaching out for his hand and then withdrawing it as she remembers they are in a street.

'Why not savour it for a while?' says Jane, for she does not share their confidence that Mr Godwin will be quite as happy as they imagine he might be.

'But why keep it to ourselves?' asks Bysshe. 'I want the whole world to know! I want to shout it: "Mary Godwin loves me!"'

Jane says nothing; for they are contrary creatures and insisting

71

might only make them more determined to do the opposite. Mary imagines lying in bed and holding the knowledge of his love to herself, replaying every moment of this glorious afternoon in her imagination. 'Yes,' she says, 'let's wait, at least one night.'

'Really?' he asks. 'You're sure?'

'Yes.'

'Whatever pleases you.' He leans towards her, brushes her cheek, his love so palpable Jane has to turn away from it.

'You're late!' snaps Mrs Godwin angrily. Jane is sure that the change in all three of them must be obvious, written in wide letters, high across their foreheads. Mary and Bysshe are glowing, and Jane shines in their reflected glory. But Mrs Godwin simply says that they must eat the food cold for it will not be heated.

'Of course!' cries Mary. 'We wouldn't want to inconvenience Martha.'

Jane almost gasps, for this is so obviously not the Mary they know that her mother must surely notice, but Mrs Godwin has already turned away and is saying, 'Mr Godwin would like to talk to you as soon as you've eaten.'

'Yes,' replies Bysshe. 'I can go now if necessary, I am not hungry.'

'You don't eat enough anyway,' snaps Mrs Godwin. 'You could hide behind a candle.' There's a short silence. The girls' nostrils flare with suppressed laughter as they watch her recall that she is still meant to be treating Sir Percy as their saviour, for his money is not delivered to them yet. 'Of course you must eat, Sir Percy,' she adds hurriedly. 'Take him through, girls, and I'll speak to you both later!'

Jane and Mary risk a glance at each other, eyes shining with conspiratorial joy.

*

72

The three of them sit alone in the kitchen. Martha, the servant, has run off, terrified by Bysshe's suggestion that she might break bread with them. 'Until we can do something as simple as break bread together as equals the world will remain an unhappy place!' he declares.

Mary caresses his arm. 'I can't eat,' she sighs. 'I'm not hungry, could not put a morsel past my lips!' At the mention of her lips both Jane and Bysshe gaze at them. They are slightly swollen, still red from long kisses.

'Well, I can,' says Jane, helping herself to the food on Mary's plate, 'and asking Martha to eat with you scares her, Bysshe,' she tells him, 'and that's not a kindness.'

'Forgive me, Miss Godwin.' He bows a little.

'But the sentiment is laudable, is it not?' declares Mary, for she cannot bear to have his gaze stolen from her for even a moment. He turns to her to answer.

Jane says nothing. Perhaps one day someone will look at her like that – but it will not be him. The truth of it drives her up from her seat, the pain too raw to allow her to be near them. He reaches out, casually clasping her hand as she passes. She closes her eyes and is about to return his brief pressure when he releases her. 'I think I'll . . .' she turns to say, but they are already lost in each other, unaware of her existence, and so her sentence remains unfinished.

26th June, London

Dear Izy,

I do not know what to say about the feelings the act of kissing engenders. I remember so well throwing away my blade of grass in disgust at the mere thought of touching tongues! I understand now

*what I did not then. What a child you must have thought me,
but you are kind, Izy; it is your strength and perhaps also your
weakness.*

*I was in despair at having returned to London the day I met
Bysshe, and feeling that my life of solitude, dedicating myself to
writing, was impossible for me in London. How quickly life
changes. I declared my love to him freely as we sat upon my mother's
grave, and with no art from him to persuade me. In truth he did
not have to, for his whole being is made to fit mine; and he has
convinced me that my love is not responsible for his abandoning
of Harriet, for he had stopped loving her long before he met me.
Others may not believe it, yet I know it to be true.*

*What does he look like? Perfect. He has wild hair that moves
with every thought, mostly because he runs his hands through it.
At times he does not seem to know where he is, he becomes so lost
in his own thinking! He is passionate to the point of madness, and
so I need calm him at times, to help him apply reason to the
wildness of his mind, and he in turn encourages me to feel
passionately as well as to reason calmly. In that sense we are truly
made for each other. We speak of so much together. We talk endlessly
of our past, as though we might somehow be able to comfort each
other for our losses I, for the death of my mother, he for the pain
of his schooling, which was brutal for a boy of such imagination.
We restore each other.*

*All we need to perfect our union is Papa's blessing. Soon the
loan Bysshe is making to Father will be settled, and he does not
want the two confused, so would rather ask sooner than later. We
are, as you say, so blessed in our fathers, who see beyond the
strictures of convention, allowing us to find love wherever it falls
to bless us. I cannot imagine, now, a life without him. Or believe
that a few short weeks ago I had never met him. I will bring him
to you as soon as we can, and you will both see immediately why
I feel as I do.*

Do not worry for me, Izy. I was a woman who had settled upon a life of solitude and so if I am forced to share my life with him alone, without the sanction of society, then I will do so. Happily. More than happily; with my whole heart, with all of me.

Mary

27TH JUNE 1814: 41 SKINNER STREET

The following afternoon, Mary leans over the bannisters as Bysshe comes out of the study to take a walk with her father. As they open the door she imagines their return. Perhaps Papa will call out to her, the way he used to when they lived alone with Fanny? He will congratulate her, making the comparison, as he so often has, between her and her mother. She feels a profound relief that in choosing Bysshe, an atheist and a believer in equality and justice – a poet, as so many of those who loved her mother were – that she is finally about to live up to her heritage. Now her own story will be no less exciting than her mother's. The fear that it might not be has often plagued her.

'Ah, Sir Percy,' she hears her papa say, patting the younger man's shoulder as they leave. 'Well, I suppose you will be moving on soon! Free to pursue your own path again. Where will you and Harriet be settling? London? Or will you return to Wales? You will no doubt be relieved to get back to Harriet, and Ianthe.'

Mary feels a cold trickle of premonition. Can Papa truly be so completely unaware of their love? Have they really hidden it so well? Over the last few days she has unquestioningly imagined that her father knows exactly what is happening and is offering them his silent approval. After all, he instructed her to entertain and charm Bysshe, didn't he? What did he believe might happen? It is only now, as Mary hears the front door close behind them both and it is too late to stop their declaration, that the doubt begins to take hold of her.

It is not long before they return. The front door is thrown open before being slammed shut. They disappear into Papa's study, she hears raised voices and then: 'No!' She has never heard her papa shout out like that before. The sound drives her to her feet and down the stairs out of concern for him. She throws open the door to find Bysshe standing in the middle of the room with a look of such devastation upon his face that she immediately forgets her father and goes to stand by him.

'Mary!' her father snaps. 'Come here.'

She takes a step, stops and stands between the two men, her head turning from one to the other.

'Is it true that you have allowed yourself to be seduced by this . . . this . . . vagabond!' he hisses at her.

Mary cannot take it in, does not know which way to turn and so stands rooted to the spot, unable to take a step in either direction.

'I did not seduce her, Godwin,' says Bysshe. 'She declared her love freely, and of her own volition.'

'How dare you!' Mr Godwin splutters, made even more furious by the man's use of his surname. 'How dare you speak of her in such terms. How dare you even imagine my precious child in such a way?'

Mary is stunned. Her father has never spoken of her as his precious child. He is rarely affectionate, despite their obvious love for each other.

As though he realises he has exposed himself, he turns to her. 'Leave!' he demands.

She is halfway to the door before realising that she is obeying without thought; that she is behaving like the child her father is assuming her to be. She stops, turns back and stands beside Bysshe, reaching for his hand.

'I am not a child, Father,' she says, although her voice is shaking like a child's, 'and I would rather not be treated as one.'

'You are most certainly behaving like one!' Papa retorts. 'He is a married man with a wife and child!' The facts crash down upon Mary then. They sound so freshly damning coming from her papa's mouth, but she summons up her arguments, as she has been taught, and manages to respond.

'You have always asked me to apply reason and yet you have not waited to hear what I have to say.'

'You were always bold, Mary, but I did not expect this, and I have heard quite enough from the blackguard himself!'

Mary is stung by the description of Bysshe. 'I am not your possession, Father, and he is not a blackguard. We have fallen in love. If marriage is a contract in which the woman is treated as a chattel why should anyone be deterred by its existence?'

'Do NOT –' her father crashes his hand upon a table, overturning it. Mary jumps and Bysshe tightens his hand over hers. She notices the colour has leached from his face; his perfect skin has the pale green cast of shock upon it. They hold each other's eyes before turning to her father.

'I repeat, do NOT quote my own wife at me in my study.'

Mary is dazed into submission, for a moment, the shock of her papa's loss of control throwing her back on herself. She stares at the two men standing at loggerheads.

'Perhaps you should leave?' she suggests to Bysshe, her voice calm and unmoved.

'Without you?' he asks. She nods. He does not move and she is grateful in spite of herself. She takes a breath and looks at her father. 'I will quote my mother whenever it feels right for me to do so!' she declares coldly. 'A man may have another wife,' she continues pointedly, 'but a daughter can never have another mother!' She notices him wince but feels no pity, only an intense determination not to falter.

Father and daughter glare at each other. Godwin is reminded of the first time he met Mary's mother. He had not liked her at all. He believed she was far too full of herself, talking equally with the great American philosopher Mr Paine, and interrupting his own attempts at conversation with the esteemed man with an assumed freedom that he found shocking. He had not thought that his own Mary, whom he has raised to always think first and act later, could ever make him feel the same way. He watches as she turns away from him, walking with that blackguard to the door. Together they disappear into the hallway. He hears their voices, conspiratorial and close, and then the front door closes. Her feet rush up the stairs and he calls her name – 'Mary!' – but there is only the sound of her chamber door shutting loudly.

Mary sits in her room. She cannot take it in. She cannot understand how in one quick tick of the watch, the perfection of her world has collapsed so completely into despair. She picks up the volume of *Queen Mab* that Bysshe has given her. He has crossed out the inscription to Harriet and addressed it to her. She stares at the small change, wondering if it is really possible to simply cross someone out of your life; to draw an ink line through their existence and believe that it is done.

'Mary?' Jane is at the door.

Mary shakes her head at her, she cannot speak to anyone. She must think, must try to understand what has happened, and yet her mind keeps on returning to that look of devastation on Bysshe's face, the raw shock of abandonment in his eyes that creates a longing in her to comfort him. What will happen now that he has gone? Will her father ban him from the house?

Her heart lurches inside of her at the thought. No! he cannot, he'll come to his senses. It's been a shock to him, that's all.

'Mary?' insists Jane.

'I told you, not now!' snaps Mary.

'But Mary, Bysshe left you this.' She is holding a scrap of paper, hasty words scribbled across it.

Mary snatches at it. 'It's really from him?'

Jane nods. 'I slipped outside and waited whilst he wrote!'

Mary does not say thank you. She reads the note and closes her eyes, holding it close to her chest.

'What does it say?' asks Jane.

Mary does not answer. She sits with her eyes closed and her head raised as though she might somehow be able to sense where Bysshe is and send her thoughts flying through the air straight to him. Jane waits a while before turning to leave, closing the door behind her. Mary straightens out the note and reads it again.

In the solitude of your chamber, he has written, *I shall be with you. You are ever with me my sacred vision.*

She turns the pages of *Queen Mab*, adding her own inscription: *This book is sacred to me and as no other creature shall look into it I may write what I please. Yet what shall I write? That I love the author beyond all power of expression and that I am parted from him. Dearest and only love, by that love we have promised to each other although I may not be yours, I can never be another's.*

THE KITCHEN: 41 SKINNER STREET

'Right!' says Mrs Godwin. 'You tell me everything, and you tell me now! How long since the pair of them decided they were in love?'

'What?' asks Jane, her eyes open wide. 'I've no idea. Are they in love?'

Her mother's slap is sharp and unexpected. She has not done that for years. They stare at each other, shocked by how easily the years in the Godwin household are stripped away. Jane is once more a grubby, starving child and her mother desperate not to hear her wailing. But I have changed since then, thinks Jane, I will not lift my hand to my cheek or return my mother's strike with my own, much as I want to. I will live on a *barren heath* before I allow my mother to know that I am hurt. Jane is neither a Godwin nor a Clairmont now; she is a disciple of Mary Wollstonecraft and an admirer of Shelley.

'You've been out walking with them every day,' says her mother. 'You must have noticed something!'

'I noticed that he preferred her to me,' continues Jane stoutly, 'but not much else.'

'So when did they find the time to fall in love if you were watching them as closely as you were meant to be?'

Jane throws her head back, staring her mother defiantly in the face. 'They bored me!' she declares. 'They were always talking about Mary's mother and how wonderful she was, and what she wrote and how Sir Percy thought it meant this, but how Coleridge thought it meant that. I . . .' She risks a glance at her mother who seems to be falling for it. 'I stopped listening,' Jane lies, 'because it was so dull.'

Her mother sighs and nods. 'It's true it can be more than a little tedious,' she agrees. Jane looks away, surprised and a little disappointed to have so easily fooled her mother. 'But I've seen the way you watch him, Jane, and I doubt whether you could take your eyes off him for very long, whatever nonsense happens to be falling from his pretty lips. Never mind. If that's the line you need to take with Godwin, then take it. He might fall for it but *I* want the truth, and so after he's spoken to you, you will tell me *everything*. All of it. And then we'll see if we can clear up this mess.'

Jane says nothing.

'Look at me,' says her mother. Reluctantly Jane looks up, and is at once made tremulous by the love in her mother's face. 'If Mary or her father can blame you for this,' she says softly, 'they will. You know that, don't you?' Jane shakes her head. She might believe it of the old Mary, but not this new vision, softened and made generous by love. 'Well, more fool you then, because all those two care about is each other.'

'She loves Bysshe, Mamma. And you don't know him!'

'She may well love him, but she loves her father and her comforts more, and when she remembers that, you will be the scapegoat, and my job is to make sure that you are not! So don't you lie to me.'

Jane nods her head in agreement, which means she is not really lying. Not quite.

GODWIN'S STUDY: 41 SKINNER STREET

'You understand the gravity of the situation?' asks Mr Godwin.

Jane nods again; it seems it's all that she's required to do recently.

'It appears that Sir Percy has brought out a side of Mary that is not . . . not entirely within her control, and we must protect her, not only from Sir Percy, but also from herself. Do you agree?'

Jane nods yet again. She wonders if it is possible that this man ever lay in the long grass kissing Mary's mother. She looks up at the portrait on the wall. Mrs Wollstonecraft looks away into the distance. '*Independence*,' she hears herself think, '*means belonging to yourself.*' She thanks Mary's mother silently, for it is a thought that Jane holds close constantly now, taking it out and turning it over whenever she is alone. Does it mean she has the right to form her own beliefs, to think, as Bysshe has declared, her own thoughts, and whenever it feels right, to act upon them; as she is doing now? Mrs Wollstonecraft has a sweet face, thinks Jane; there is a kindness and compassion beneath her wild hair, and a sense of steel in her bearing. Unconsciously she straightens her own shoulders.

Mr Godwin looks at the bookcase behind her as he speaks, avoiding her eyes. 'For various reasons we cannot, um, banish the man from our lives entirely.' He stops as though expecting to be challenged. Jane supposes, quite rightly, that the reason might be that the loan hasn't arrived yet, and to banish Bysshe immediately might mean risking the money.

'So your mother and I are relying on you, Jane, to ensure that there is no communication between the two of them beyond that which we can see, hear and manage. If there is any sign, any sign at all that they are communicating, I expect to hear about it.'

Again Jane nods, whilst making a silent vow to Mrs Wollstonecraft that she will do all she can to support her daughter's love. Godwin, assuming that she is too frightened to answer is satisfied, and dismisses her. He might have understood if the man had dallied with Jane. There's something about her dark eyes and temper that belies a passionate nature, that suggests a lack of control that might be compelling to a man like Sir Percy; but Mary – his perfect Mary – that he cannot understand. He readies himself to call in Mary.

She is standing waiting at the foot of the stairs, her small face pale, and for once she is not wearing her tartan.

'Mary.'

'Papa.'

'Come in, come in.'

Mary steps over the threshold and into the room. Here they read together, here she was given her mother's books to study, or a case to argue, or asked to demonstrate how to apply principles to a particular argument. She does not have the same affection for this room as she did for his study in the Polygon, but it was here that she thought her papa would bless her union with Bysshe. Well, he has taught her to argue and she will argue now, for she must make him understand. For a moment they stand staring at each other, so alike and yet so different, neither knowing how or where to start, both sensing the precipice of separation a mere step away.

'You must be wondering why I am so against this match?' he starts.

'Yes, Papa.'

'I've been considering . . .'

Mary's heart leaps, for he is calm and that is a good sign. Perhaps he is at least contemplating their union.

'And I have come to a decision that there is something I must tell you. Not in any desire to despoil your mother's memory . . .' Instinctively Mary looks up to the portrait of her mother and back at her father.

'Please!' she says, and they stare at each other, for it is an unspoken rule that you do not ever disturb the person speaking and disrupt their thinking. Her father stops. 'I'm sorry,' says Mary, 'but please don't!' She doesn't know why she feels so sure that whatever it is he is about to say should remain hidden, but the feeling that it is so is overwhelming.

'Mary,' he continues, irritated now, 'as I have already said, I do not progress without careful and profound consideration. And I am sure your mother would be in agreement with me.'

Mary drops both her eyes and her head. How would you know? she hears herself think. Are you a woman?

'Long ago before she met me, your mother fell in love with

an American. It was during the Revolution, and whilst he wasn't already married like—' He stops, finding he cannot bring himself to say the name.

'Sir Percy,' says Mary.

'Whilst he was not married, like . . . Sir Percy,' replies her father, 'he was, like him, a blackguard. She – ahem – I hope you understand this is not easy . . .'

Mary looks up and sees that it is true; her father is struggling, his face haggard with the memory. She wishes she could wrap her arms around him, the way she has learned to do so easily with Bysshe, and yet the act feels impossible for they have never really touched and she wonders why. Why, when it is so effortless with one man, should it feel so impossible with another?

'Yes, Papa,' she says.

'Well, your mamma, my wife, fell passionately in love, in much the way you seem to have done. She allowed such passion to overrule all reason. She believed this man would remain with her, that they might start a new life in America.'

Mary is silent. So her mother has felt this feeling, this longing. This love. The thought fills her with a joy that she manages to hide by keeping her head bent.

'Of course the inevitable happened. She was deserted. She was—' He stops again.

Mary dare not look now, for she is too full of confusion. What if Bysshe should desert her, what would she do, how would she manage?

'And this man not only deserted your mother,' her father continues in measured tones, 'but also their child, for she had a child by him, and that child was Fanny.'

It is only in the silence that follows this statement that Mary truly hears what has been said. The shock of it is as powerful as the sense of rightness it brings with it. For with

84

his simple surprising statement so many things fall rapidly into place. Her father has always loved her best and now, for the first time, she considers that it might not be because of her natural talents, but because she is the only daughter who is truly his. Her father has not hesitated to allow his news to sink in, but continues talking.

'Your mother did many things to try and save her relationship and bring this man to a recognition of his duty, but in utter, and I repeat, Mary, utter despair and abandonment by this man – if he can be called a man – she decided that she would take her own life.'

Yes, thinks Mary. Yes, I can imagine no longer wanting to live if Bysshe ever deserted me, but I cannot stop loving him for fear that he might leave me. She lifts her eyes to the portrait beyond her father. Her mother stares, as always, into the half distance, at something either real or imagined. The portrait remains unchanged, and yet, thinks Mary, everything is changed. I see you differently now, Mamma.

'She must have felt very desperate,' Mary says softly. She longs to protect her mother from being revealed to her.

'She did, and I only tell you, Mary, because I am sure your mother would want you to learn from her experience, because she would not want you to make the same mistake. You cannot trust a man who is prepared to abandon his wife and child. You can never be sure that he will not do the same to you.'

Mary can easily believe that her mother might choose to reveal herself to protect and cherish her child – and yet she senses something quite different within her father, something she cannot quite put her finger on, as though in the telling of the story he is somehow finally triumphing over her mother. She cannot understand it and yet she is quite sure that it is there.

'Have you anything at all to say?' asks her father, surprised by her silence.

'I need to think,' she whispers.

'That is exactly what I had hoped you would say.' He comes towards her and gives her one of his rare, tentative pats on the shoulder. For years this was her only understanding of physical affection; but now she knows the feeling of a hand that does not fly away as soon as it has made contact, of palms that remain and hold. She knows what it is to melt into the side of another until she is unsure where she begins and he ends. In the light of this new knowledge, her father's slight, fearful touch fills her with sorrow.

23RD JULY 1814: MARY'S BEDCHAMBER, 41 SKINNER STREET

Nearly a month has passed. Mary holds two letters before her. In her left hand a letter from Harriet, Bysshe's wife, begging for the return of her husband: *If you desist, these feelings will fade . . .* she writes: *you are not the first woman he has had such feelings for. The first was when I was pregnant with Ianthe, the second is now, when I am pregnant again. It does not take a woman of your intellect to recognise that there may be a pattern here. I believe it might calm him if you wrote suggesting he subdue his passion.*

In her right hand she holds Bysshe's poem to her:

> *Upon my heart thy accents sweet*
> *Of peace and pity fell like dew*
> *On flowers half dead; – thy lips did meet*
> *Mine tremblingly; thy dark eyes threw*
> *Their soft persuasion on my brain,*
> *Charming away its dream of pain.*

I would rather not live than not have you, he writes. *Your father cannot keep you like a possession to be adored for his pleasure alone. Come away with me, Mary. I await your word.*

Every bit of Mary aches. Her body longs for Bysshe, and her mind for the approval of her father. She must convince her papa. There is no other way. If her own mother believed that it was possible for a woman to share a man and love freely, as Bysshe also believes, then surely it is a path she can follow? Perhaps Harriet and Ianthe can live with them?

She closes her eyes, hears his voice whispering to her as they lay in the grass. She can hear the breeze in the willow above them. Feel the tickle of a sharp stem across her thigh. '*The earth will be our bed*,' he whispers, '*the sky our church.*'

She repeats the words aloud, alone in her bedchamber. She has no words to describe the deliciousness of allowing her lips to part beneath his. *Your mother was right*, he writes, *and the question is no longer of whether women must marry or not, it is whether both men and women can love freely. Must our bodies remain chained where our minds run free? Your father is of the old guard, frightened by the Revolution and any change that is not sanctioned by him alone. He believes in possession not freedom!*

'But my own papa,' she whispers to herself. 'Can I really abandon him?'

24TH JULY 1814: GODWIN'S STUDY, 41 SKINNER STREET

'I will write to Harriet and reassure her, Papa,' she says the next day.

'Even so,' he replies, 'you will never be allowed to see that man again.' Mary says nothing. Her father smiles, touching her shoulder. She represses a shudder; his touch has become something questionable. And yet she cannot stop loving him.

*

'I must try and give Bysshe up,' she whispers to Jane later that night, hoping that somehow the sound of the words spoken aloud might convince her that she is right.

'But Mary,' says Jane dramatically, 'he's DYING of love for you! He's threatened to kill himself rather than live without you. His friend Hogg says he cannot rise in the morning nor sleep at night for fear you might abandon him!'

'I *can't* betray my father,' Mary replies, her small face paler than ever and her mouth tight with despair. 'I'm all he has!'

'He has Fanny and William, myself, Charles *and* my mother,' Jane persists, 'whereas Bysshe has no one except his friend Hogg!'

'He has a wife, Jane. And a child! Please,' whispers Mary, 'don't tempt me. My resolve is weak enough, but Papa is right. If I look at this with reason, it is something he has done before. Papa wants to protect me from myself. In time Bysshe and I can share a friendship perhaps . . .' She tails off.

'What is it?' asks Jane.

'It is just that it can't . . . that it can't be . . . would never be . . . anything more.' Even as she speaks she remembers the feel of his lips upon hers, remembers the rapid strike of his arm across her body, protecting her from her stepmother's fury. She scratches at her arm. 'Don't scratch,' says Jane. Mary looks down; her skin is beginning to break out again, the tension inside of her erupting across the surface of her body.

'Even your skin is weeping for him,' whispers Jane.

'And so what was it weeping for all those years before I met him?' asks Mary wryly.

'For your mother.' The reply startles both of them into understanding how closely they are bound together now, how the world apart from themselves and Bysshe feels distant and unreal, unworthy of their attention.

'He's changed both of us, hasn't he?' Mary whispers.

Jane nods. She sits on the bed gently pulling Mary's sleeve across the scaly skin and buttoning the cuff for her. 'Bysshe wants to come into the shop, Mary,' she says. Mary closes her eyes; beneath Jane's palm her arm shakes with the effort of maintaining her refusal to see him. 'He says they cannot stop him being a customer!'

Mary closes her eyes; her hands twitch in her lap. 'I don't know.' She speaks without opening her eyes. 'If I see him, Jane, my resolve will crack.'

'Yes,' she replies simply, 'and he knows that, why else would he want to see you?'

'But perhaps it won't.' Mary opens her eyes. 'Perhaps,' she says, allowing herself to imagine it, 'I'll see him differently. Perhaps the scales will fall from my eyes and I will see him as Papa does!'

Jane wrinkles her brow; Mary has always been good at finding arguments that allow her to do exactly as she pleases. She says nothing, hoping Mary agrees to see him, for if she doesn't Jane is frightened of what Bysshe might do.

'How is she?' Bysshe asks Jane in the secret moments they steal together. He is thin now to the point of emaciation.

'She longs for you,' says Jane quietly, 'and yet she loves her father. He is all she has ever had.'

'Tell her I am waiting, that I will die without her.'

'It's true,' says his friend Hogg, standing quietly beside him. He pulls Jane aside. 'He has threatened to take poison if she refuses him,' he whispers, 'and please tell her that whatever her decision, he will not return to Harriet. Mary cannot save what is already broken.'

Jane has barely noticed Hogg before but she sees now that he is like a shadow to Bysshe's light. Dark where Bysshe is fair, and his features firm, with a powerful, jutting nose, where

Bysshe's are soft. He has thick dark hair and eyes that flit from her own face to Bysshe's – and on to the bookshop. He is like a powerful bird taking everything in.

'I will tell her,' Jane answers, before turning back to Bysshe, who leans listlessly against the wall, so thin from lack of food that it is possible to imagine him dissolving into air for loss of sustenance.

'Eat something,' she says. 'You'll be no good to her dead, Bysshe.'

'Will she stand by me,' he asks, 'now that the loan has finally arrived, and her father no longer has need of me?'

'She loves you still,' says Jane. 'She keeps your book by her bed where she used to keep her mother's.'

'So there is hope,' he says. 'And yet if her father refuses to see reason, what then? Will she still come with me?'

'I don't know,' Jane has to answer. 'I don't know.'

'Please!' he says. 'Give her this.' He hands Jane a pamphlet. She looks down and sees it is a copy of *The Corsair*, Byron's poem.

'She's already read it,' says Jane. 'Everyone has!'

'It does not matter – she will know why it is meaningful.'

Jane takes it, but she does not give it to Mary immediately. Alone in bed that night she opens it herself and begins to read:

> *Ours the wild life in tumult still to range*
> *From toil to rest, and joy in every change.*
> *Oh, who can tell? not thou, luxurious slave!*
> *Whose soul would sicken o'er the heaving wave;*

She understands at once what it means. Come with me, leave everything and walk into a future unknown, except for my presence. Jane sighs aloud, imagining her life after they have gone; no secret meetings with Bysshe, and no negotiations with Mary. She squeezes her closed lids tight. It is unbearable. Impossible. She reads the the next few lines:

> *Oh, who can tell, save he whose heart hath tried,*
> *And danced in triumph o'er the waters wide,*
> *The exulting sense – the pulse's maddening play,*
> *That thrills the wanderer of that trackless way?*

The next morning she hands it to Mary. 'He'll come tomorrow, at lunchtime, when Mamma and Papa are eating and I am in the shop,' she says. 'He says he'll come with his friend Hogg, who will enter first to make sure my mother is not there.' Mary nods. Jane does not ask if that is an agreement; she has delivered both the poem and the message. She stands up to leave, but Mary clutches at her sleeve.

'Am I deluded?' she asks. 'Will he desert me?'

Jane stares down at her. For a brief moment Mary is no longer her superior but her supplicant. 'No, he loves you.'

'But he must also have loved Harriet.'

'He wanted to free Harriet from the oppression of her father,' she replies gently, 'and he mistook a physical attraction for love.'

'He has told you that?' Mary is startled and dismayed by the idea that he has shared so much with her stepsister.

'He loves you, Mary. He cannot see anyone else, he cannot think about anything else. You have only to glance at him tomorrow to know immediately what I cannot describe.'

Mary sighs in relief, letting go of Jane's sleeve. She must convince Papa of the rightness of their love, and to do so she must do as she has always done. She sits at her desk, opens her notebook and lifts the pen to begin her fight for a life with Bysshe.

25TH JULY 1814: GODWIN'S STUDY, 41 SKINNER STREET
'Papa?'

'Yes?' He does not look up as she enters the study, and the absence of this small, everyday action, so redolent of her father's love and respect for her, sends a shiver of fear through Mary. Is this what she will face if she refuses to accept his judgement? Is this small ignoring of her done deliberately or without thought? Is Bysshe right? Has the love and respect her father offers her only ever been based upon her existence as his possession?

'Can we discuss this, Papa?'

'We have discussed it, Mary, and you have understood that this separation is for your own good. It's hard for you to believe, but there will be other men who are more worthy of you. You are only sixteen and so you must – at least in this – defer to me.'

'But Father, I have been thinking about it and I do not understand.' He looks up then, as she knew he would, for she has put herself in the position of supplicant, and that has always proved irresistible to him. 'I understand that my mother was driven to despair by her love, but the man she loved conducted commerce; he was not a poet or philosopher. He—'

'Is this all you have to say, because if so it is not an argument, Mary, is it? It is a mere statement of fact.'

'That is not my argument, Father; my argument is not only that Bysshe is of a different mettle, but also that in the fight for women to be equal my mother says quite clearly that "Freedom strengthens reason!" And I need to be free to be with the person I feel born to love. Free of marriage or expectation of marriage, free to know that what we offer each other we do so freely and with the hope that our love will remain simply because we fulfil one another. I do not want to be the "abject dependent" – of you, nor of Bysshe or any man who would partner with me. And I tremble to think that I have met a man who is my own equal, and yet am stopped from living with him merely by convention.' There, she has laid her case.

Her father sighs. 'I have asked you before, Mary, not to quote my own wife at me. She believed that education would lend comprehension to a woman's duty, not that it would encourage desertion of duty. That it would raise the female mind above "simple affection". This love you speak of for that man smacks of the very idolatry your mother abhorred. You elevate him above where he belongs. How can you fail to see that?'

'I do not fail to see it. I reject it and am offended by it. You yourself taught me better than that. I am beginning to understand my mother as a woman, not a set of ideas. A woman who could both think *and* feel, as I am only now learning to do.'

Godwin listens to her with a sense of dread – this has gone far further than he thought, and she has indeed surrendered to the power of passion, forgotten her own mind.

'You attempt to do justice by retaliation! By ignoring my teaching?' He is beginning to shout now. 'The very thing your mother accused ill-educated women of doing! I have brought you up to fare better than that!'

'You cannot hear me, Papa,' pleads Mary. 'I am begging you to allow that, alongside reason, feeling must also be given its place. My mother says that the tyranny of those in power will ever undermine morality, and she does not mean only the morality of churches and paternalistic institutions, but the morality of knowing oneself, of understanding that love is not possession. Is that what is happening here, that you must demonstrate your power over me?'

'It is not tyranny to exercise experience over youthful ardour! Both you and Jane have been beguiled by him – at sixteen, that is perhaps understandable, but . . . to act upon it? Mary, this man has already eloped once, and with a woman your age. You will be wronging her, another woman and her child.

Your mother would never have encouraged such a thing. He is already married, and that is a fact you cannot overcome!'

'How can it even matter,' Mary says passionately, struggling to contain her fury, 'when their love is a dead thing?'

'No, Mary. This is the counsel of an unwise child. Again, I speak as your mother to you and command you listen.' He waits.

The effort of controlling her fury and remaining still, whilst waiting for him to continue, is immense. He is playing a game with me, thinks Mary, exercising his power. If I lose my temper he will win, so I must remain calm. I must remain calm.

'*The father of a family,*' he finally begins, '*will not then weaken his constitution and debase his sentiments by visiting the harlot, nor forget, in obeying the call of appetite, the purpose for which it was implanted.* Those are the words of your mamma, Mary, and a man's purpose is family. The very thing you are destroying.'

Mary closes her eyes; they have so often duelled this way before, with the words and thoughts of others, but never with the words of her mother, stabbing each other with them, twisting them to reach deeper, both claiming ownership of her as she smiles from her portrait, looking away from them unmoved. Mary feels sick with the horror of it but she will not give up, cannot countenance the consequence of losing.

'And is the notion of family not yet another shackle? A shackle my mother could not yet see as even she was blinded by the strictures of her time. Did she not birth me so that I might see further and be not so blinkered myself?'

'We seem to be at an impasse.' The calmness of her father bemuses Mary; was she truly like this so short a time ago, arguing always from the head as though she had no heart?

'Are you sure you have questioned yourself,' he goes on relentlessly, 'as to whether you are more anxious to inspire love in this man, than to exact respect?'

'If you have brought me up to apply reason then surely you

know that I am capable of judging that he both loves and respects me, as he loves and respects you, Papa!'

'Firstly, Mary, you must command the respect not only of the man you choose but also of the society you inhabit. Secondly, how can you be so sure he respects you and will go on doing so when he shows so little respect to his current wife and child? The education of the rich – and he is one of them, Mary – renders them "vain and helpless".'

'You know him too well to believe that he is either vain or helpless. He has done more to encourage change than any other man of his age in the whole of England. He has spent his inheritance on maintaining you, because he believes in your philosophy. And what is the alternative for me, Papa? Do you want me to remain in a state of perpetual childishness, as Mother says all women are, moving from father to husband, belonging never to herself?'

'Mary, you could never be other than yourself, whoever you live with – and you are wrong. You are dressing up a childish feminine passion in the clothes of a great love.'

'No! I am asking for the right to make my own choices, to be free to make my own mistakes. Did my mother become wise because she was told so? Or did she become wise because she loved first and learned later? I do not want to be so subordinate that I am never free to learn, to feel love or pain and regret. I cannot come second to you, for how then can I be myself? Am I to follow only you, only my mother? Where then am I, Papa – and who am I?' She feels the flourish that is always there in the conclusion of her thinking, only this time it is greater, for she is fighting not only with logic but also with her whole self, *for* her whole self, and she is sure that her father will respond. She searches his eyes expectantly.

'What *do* you want then, Mary? What magical piece of thinking will bring this perfect state about?'

'I want to be equal! That is what Bysshe offers me and that is what I am prepared to brave all for, just as Mr Baxter braved the rejection of his church for the love of his daughter!'

Mary knows at once that she has crossed an invisible line. Her father feels an inexpressible fury at being compared to another man and found wanting.

'Equal?' he scoffs. 'Then you will have to grow some facial hair and put on muscle!'

Her father has never spoken to her with such contempt before. Her own reply is cold and furious: 'You mock me in my despair!'

'My view remains the same,' he replies, calm and dismissive now. 'Sir Percy will not come to the house, your union is not possible and he must be brought to understand that he has a duty to his wife and child.'

'He does understand that duty; he wants Harriet and her child to live with us. He has no intention of either rejecting or abandoning them!'

'Mary!' Her father's palm strikes his desk so hard they both jump. 'It is not possible. It is an inhuman expectation for a woman to live with her husband's lover! Only a besotted child could EVER believe it possible!'

'Was my mother a child then, when she suggested it? Was she unworthy of your love and your respect? Or does reason only become applicable when it agrees with you?'

'Enough! There is no point in us continuing!'

'So I must simply accept your judgment without understanding?'

'Yes.'

'And what does that make me, Father, other than your chattel?'

'It makes you my child whom I have a duty to protect.'

'Thus men have argued through the ages, have they not?'

'I doubt many of them have encountered women such as you!'

Mary cannot help feeling a burst of pride at his words, but her mother's face staring down at her returns her to herself. 'I am torn, Father,' she almost whispers, 'because I cannot accept your approval at the price of my very self. Please, do not ask it of me!'

'I do not see that there is any compromise necessary once you accept that I want only what is best for you. If you do not believe me then you must look to your own mother's experience.'

'And what of love?' she asks hopelessly, sensing that this is what lies at the heart of all her attempts at reason, defying her parent's careful logic, insisting only upon the truth of its own existence. 'Is there no place within reason for the madness that is love?'

'It need not be a madness,' he replies. 'It can be a balm to the soul, a steadying of the ship!'

Then you leave me no choice, thinks Mary as she turns away from him. I must go with Bysshe. At that very moment her father calls out her name – 'Mary!' – even though she has barely moved away from him. He frowns, puzzled by his instinct to call her name, and raises a cursory hand, ready to wave her away.

At the door Mary turns back. In that final glance everything feels both intensely familiar and for ever changed.

Her father's hand falls, dismissing her. Mary drops her eyes and turns away. She wonders how it is possible to feel such anger and pain all at the same time. How they can be so close in spirit that her father senses her imminent abandonment of him and yet so far away that he ignores it, dismissing her so easily?

Mary writes to Bysshe at once, before she can change her mind. '*I am ready. Make arrangements.*' Her heart beats wildly beneath the bars of her ribs as the ink flows across the page. '*I am taking up my life,*' she adds. '*And my heart can barely believe that I have offered it its freedom.*'

She folds the paper in half and kisses it, staring down at the small white square between her slim fingers. 'I hold my future in my own hands now,' she whispers to herself, and feels sick with both the pleasure and the fear of it. She cannot quite bring herself to call in Jane to take the message away from her. Although her decision is firm, something within her remains unwilling and unable to let this moment go, to allow time to move forward and the inevitable consequences of her action to unfold.

Behind her closed lids the French watchseller bends close to her ear: *'These are the seconds of your life, mademoiselle, ticking away. You cannot stop them and you cannot slow them down, you can only listen as they pass, make sure you use them well!'* And yet, in this one glorious moment, time feels suspended as she is caught between leaving her father whilst Bysshe waits somewhere in her future. She senses that it is only in such moments that she can ever truly be free.

She does not know how long she sits, before she finally rises, and with a sharp twist of her wrist opens the bedroom door. 'Jane!' Immediately there is the sound of feet running along the corridor.

'Yes?' asks Jane, her eyes eager. Mary hands her the letter. Jane looks at her, but Mary's demeanour demonstrates only that she has come to a decision.

'Remember, he and his friend Hogg are coming to the shop when Mamma and Papa are at lunch,' Jane whispers rapidly, 'but I can deliver it before if it's important.'

'It is,' says Mary.

Jane's face gleams with fascination but Mary says nothing. Already she is wondering which things to take and how she can transport them to her room without arousing suspicion. She does not know how the elopement will be done, or when, but she does not doubt it will happen.

Bysshe will come for her and their future will begin.

26TH JULY 1814: THE JUVENILE BOOKSHOP – 41 SKINNER STREET

The shopfront is cool, despite the heat in the streets. Mary waits silently behind the door between the house and the shop for the sound of the bell and his beloved voice.

'Do you have a copy of – um – *Trelawny*?' she hears Bysshe ask the boy serving.

'We're a juvenile bookshop, sir, we only stock children's books.'

'Well, a copy of *Mounseer Nonpaw's Trip to Paris* then!' declares Bysshe, managing to remember the name of the book Mary herself wrote for the shop, when she was ten.

Behind the door Mary smiles.

'Very good, sir.' The boy disappears to find the book.

Mary slips through the door. Bysshe is standing in his shirt, his hair wild around his head and his eyes so deeply shadowed that even the lids are bruised blue by lack of sleep. His shirt lies open at the neck and the sight of his frail collarbone jutting from beneath the soft white cotton makes her swallow with both pity and desire.

'Mary,' he whispers, his voice low and desperate.

'Bysshe!' She does not notice his friend Hogg staring at her in fascination. She has her tartan on again; it reminds her of the freedom of the Scottish hills and the hope that she, like Izy, will fight successfully for her love.

'You mean it?' His voice is shaking, his hands as unsteady in her own. She nods.

'At four o'clock, on Thursday morning. You will be there?' he asks.

She nods again, unable to speak, overcome by the sight of him. He slips a piece of paper across the counter and she meets it with her palm, sliding it off the counter and into her pocket.

'You promise?' he asks again. She understands that he needs

to hear her speak, that he has misconstrued her wordlessness for doubt.

'I promise.' He bows his head in relief.

'He has been threatening to take laudanum!' his friend Hogg whispers.

Mary grasps Bysshe's hand. 'We will be together!' she says. 'I promise.' He raises his eyes to hers, sees that she is determined. 'I must go now,' she says.

He nods, unmoving. 'I will wait for you,' he says, his eyes watching her until the very last moment, 'at four, at the end of the street. On the corner.'

She nods again, slips through the door and is gone. He gazes after her.

'Ah! Here's the very book,' says the shopboy, appearing from the stockroom.

'I shall treasure it,' shouts Bysshe, both too suddenly and too loud, making both Hogg and the bookseller jump. Jane, who has been standing listening – a silent witness – begins to giggle. 'For ever!' Bysshe shouts, holding the book aloft! Hogg gently holds his elbow and lowers his arm. 'Do not make us quite so noticeable, Shelley,' he whispers.

'Quite so, sir,' says the boy imperturbably, wrapping it up.

In the safety of her room Mary unfolds the piece of paper. Bysshe's handwriting is as flowing as his mind – it sweeps and loops and returns to invisible lines, anchoring itself for but a brief moment before setting itself loose again across the page. *And we shall walk as free as light amongst the clouds,* he writes.

It is quarter to four on a Thursday morning and London sleeps. Mary puts on her black silk travelling cloak and lifts her case. She has a change of clothes, the tartan dress she wore when she first met him, and a light dress of her mother's that she has always loved. She imagines she may have worn it in France and feels guilty for taking it; it is one of the few things Papa has kept. She has packed a small box with her most treasured possessions: her early writing, letters from Izy and her mother's letters to her father. She looks around her chamber and realises that she will not miss it. She turns to the door ready to go . . . and lifts her hand to stifle a scream.

There in the door stands a premonition, a black figure dressed exactly as Mary herself in a dark cloak and bonnet. The figure carries a similar case and stands in exactly the same way, staring back at her. For a wild moment Mary thinks that, finally, she is about to meet her mother. It is only that thought which stops her from screaming and waking the whole household.

'Shhh!' the figure says, lifting a finger to her lips. And Mary sees that it is Jane.

'What are you doing?' she asks.

'He said four o'clock?' Jane replies. 'And it will take some time to walk there.' Her eyes alight with excitement.

'What do you mean?' asks Mary.

'He didn't tell you I was coming?'

Mary shakes her head.

'I can't stay here,' Jane whispers urgently. 'They'll know that I've helped you, Mary, and what is here for me, now that I know another life is possible? Please, Mary!'

Mary says nothing. If she were Jane she would want to come too. Did Bysshe really ask her? Is this what he means by a community of souls – is it to include her stepsister? She does not want her there, but without Jane's help where would they be? She cannot just abandon her.

'Let me go and ask him,' she says, 'he will be waiting for me.'

'I can't wait here!' Jane begs. 'What if they wake?'

'They won't, and I must ask him,' Mary snaps. This last-minute confusion is not what she expected. She takes her belongings, walking as lightly as possible down the stairs. Outside, somewhere behind the tall narrow houses, the light threatens. Mary hurries silently down the street, a small black anonymous figure. Before she reaches the corner she sees him rushing towards her.

'Mary!' Before she can speak he takes her cases from her hands and sets them on the cobbles, lifting her face up to his. 'You came!'

'Yes!'

'Mary!'

'Bysshe.' They begin to laugh with anxiety and excitement. Mary knows that if she says nothing, if she allows him to pick up her case and lift it into the carriage then he will not mention Jane. If he ever suggested she might come he has forgotten her now, and yet she finds that however much she wants to leave her sister behind, she cannot do it. Without Jane's help she would not be here in his arms. Without her she would never have received his notes, nor had any way of making these arrangements.

'Did you say Jane could join us?'

'Yes, if she wants to,' he says casually. 'Does she?'

'Yes. She was at my bedroom door dressed and ready to go – I thought she was a ghost! Some terrible premonition!'

'Quick, we must hurry, tell her to come now!'

Mary has no time to express her doubt, to stop and think. Instinctively she turns to do as she is bid, and ten minutes later two dark figures appear at the corner, step up into the carriage and sit down as the driver cracks his whip and the wheels of the carriage begin to turn.

Jane tactfully turns to look out of her window, aware that the two lovers have collapsed into each other's arms, embracing passionately. Well, she thinks to herself pragmatically, at the very least this will be a chance to practise my French; for they are headed to the Continent.

'Will I really see Paris?' asks Mary.

'You shall!' exclaims Bysshe. 'Mary!'

'Bysshe.'

They whisper. Almost immediately, Jane begins to wonder if she has done the right thing. The sound of their adoration up close tests her resolve to put her own feelings aside in support of the lovers. She rests her head against the window, feeling the vibration of the carriage run through her. She closes her eyes. Gradually, the sound of their mutual excitement fades as she becomes lost in the growing light.

When she next looks up, Mary is asleep in his lap. Even as his own lids drift closed and his head begins to drop, Bysshe holds her in such a way as to minimise the rocking of the carriage, taking the strain in his own body. Jane turns away again.

Outside, colour begins to break up the sky, clouds hang above them and from somewhere below the dip in the horizon, light has broken, suffusing the clouds with a haze of pink. She turns to share the beauty of it but Mary and Bysshe remain asleep together, exhausted and relieved by the success of their plan. Again she is struck by the careless graceful beauty of them both; flung together as they are in the corner of the carriage.

She is tempted to reach out and touch one of Bysshe's curls. She could do it so easily, and no one would ever know. She lifts her hand and steadies herself against the rocking of the carriage; allows her fingers to rest lightly against the wiry, fiery gold mass of his hair. It is barely a touch at all and yet he immediately lifts his eyes to hers, answering the shocked and rapid retraction of her hand with an open untroubled smile of acceptance.

Jane gestures to the sky, as though the touch were simply a way of awakening him so they could share this moment. Together they stare out at the passing beauty of the breaking dawn as Mary sleeps. Perhaps, thinks Jane, it will be bearable after all.

Mary wakes with a start. She knows at once where she is and what she has done; there is no gap or lack of knowledge as she gains consciousness. Bysshe softly whispers her name and she grips his hand in response, but cannot answer or speak of her thoughts. It would feel like a betrayal to admit that her mind is full of her father. Has he found her note yet, left carefully folded on the mantelpiece beneath the portrait of her mother?

If my mother came to you now, when you are married, and asked for you to leave with her, would the shackles of either duty or convention keep you bound?

Will he understand? Perhaps he has already hired a trap and is chasing after them, not to forbid their union, but to embrace it now that he knows how far she will go to be with Bysshe? She sits up and looks behind her through the window.

'Do not worry, they can't catch us,' says Bysshe. 'We've gone too fast.' She sits up straight and pins back the loose strands of her hair. 'You should leave them,' he whispers, 'for they want their freedom, just as you do.' She smiles, and he lifts a hand to pull a strand free. 'See?' he laughs. 'How much happier is this strand when released from its pins!' She shakes her head at him in mock despair and wonders why he's whispering before remembering Jane. She's sleeping, her head rocking against the window. 'We watched the sun rise together,' he whispers.

Mary's heart dips into her stomach, becoming acid at the thought that she slept, unaware, whilst they shared the rising of the dawn on the first day of their freedom. 'You should have woken me!' she wails.

'Why?' he asks, gently pulling on the tip of the strand of her hair, edging her closer to him. 'You were exhausted, and we have so much further to go.'

She has no answer, only this gut-wrenching feeling that he has done the wrong thing. 'Was it beautiful?' she asks. 'The dawn?'

'I've seen better, but none which dawned as sweet.' They are nose to nose now, eye to eye. 'Soon,' he whispers, his breath mingling with her own, 'we'll be in Dover, then Calais.'

She closes her eyes, feels his palm clasp the back of her neck, supporting the burdensome weight of her thoughts. 'And then Paris,' she answers, feeling the breath of her words meet his cheek. She is torn in two between excitement and despair.

'Yes, Paris,' he agrees, 'in the footsteps of your mother.'

She lets her head drop back. There is something so abandoned about the deliberate exposing of her neck. How, she asks herself, as his lips connect with the hollow there, can something so public feel so intimate?

From beneath Jane's long dark lashes the couple blur and shiver as they meld into one another. She lets her eyes close and imagines her own neck falling back over his palm whilst his arms wrap themselves around her waist, holding her close. Mary's low groan sends a shaft of longing so deep into Jane's being that she turns away, closing her eyes properly now.

Mary knows at once that Jane is not asleep. She sits up on Bysshe's lap and moves to sit beside him. He smiles in bemusement but helps her pin her hair back up. 'Jane,' she says. 'Jane, I know you're not sleeping so don't try to pretend.'

Jane opens an eye. 'I'm not sleeping,' she says with as much dignity as she can muster. 'I am resting with my eyes closed.' Bysshe laughs out loud at her joyful mix of truth and fiction. Mary scowls. 'You missed a beautiful dawn,' says Jane.

They remind Bysshe of his sisters, arguing over who might sit in his lap and be told a story. He turns towards the basket resting on the floor and begins to unpack it. 'You must be hungry,' he says, hoping food might soothe them both. 'Mary, I tried to find the Scottish oatcakes you mentioned for your cheese – will these do?'

Mary is mollified; he has not brought anything special for Jane. 'I'm so hungry,' she says. 'I could eat a horse!'

'Well, soon you can,' says Bysshe, 'because soon we'll be in France!' And the three of them laugh, relieved to let go of the tension, to be returned to the excitement of their journey and the fear of being followed.

By the time the carriage rolls into Dover they are exhausted. 'We have to find someone to take us over the water,' says Bysshe. 'If we wait for the packet they could easily catch us up.'

'And then what?' says Mary. 'Papa would never take us by force. Perhaps when he realises how serious we are he might come to his senses.'

Jane and Bysshe glance at each other. 'What is it?' she asks them both, irritated by the dawning realisation that in the last weeks they have been together far more often than she and Bysshe, who reaches out now to pull her hood over her head, shading her from the sun. 'Your father might well be too angry to follow us,' he says gently. 'When men lose their most loved possessions they often pretend that they were meaningless to them.'

'I am not his possession but his daughter!' snaps Mary.

'And yet he has treated you as such.' Bysshe grasps her hand. 'We're free to follow your mother now, Mary, not your father.'

Mary smiles at him from beneath her hood, but within her chest she can feel her heart breaking; it's such a small strange feeling, like a step suddenly missed, a thing always assumed no longer there. As she stands staring at the sea she understands that all along she has been hoping that her father might pick up her note, left deliberately beneath the portrait of her mother, and that he might understand. That he might look up at his first wife and feel bound never to abandon their daughter. She has imagined him rushing to her, finding her just as she is about to step off the very edge of England and calling out to her. She looks back because her father's voice is so powerful in her mind, so present that she thinks she really hears it. But the quay remains empty.

She turns to Jane and sees that she has no such doubts. 'Hurry,' she is saying to Bysshe. 'We need a boat as soon as possible, because whatever Papa may do, my mother will definitely be after me the minute she finds out!'

The words bite into Mary, for Jane has no doubt at all that her mother will come and yet, she thinks, I have neither a mother nor a father to follow me. Can Papa really abandon her, the father who has loved her more than any other of his children, who has brought her up with such pride to impress poets and philosophers and vice-presidents of America?

Beside them a boat is already pulling in to the quay, turning in their direction. Bysshe runs towards them, his face aflame with excitement. 'I've found a passage,' he says, 'and they'll take us now, straight to Calais.' He lifts both cases and strides towards the boat, Jane keeping step.

Mary watches them go but cannot follow. She is paralysed by the enormity of that one step.

'Mary!' calls Bysshe, his hair whipped by the breeze. 'Come on!' He is already on the boat, Jane waving wildly beside him.

'Come on!' Jane repeats, her voice high and excited, her dark hair streaming in the breeze.

For a wild second Mary almost shouts, 'You go!' and turns away, for they look so exactly right together, so full of freedom and excitement and all the things she knows she should feel, but that are gone.

'Mary!' Bysshe calls her name again.

She takes a step, closes her eyes. '*And we shall walk as free as light amongst the clouds,*' she whispers as she runs towards him. He opens his arms out wide and she flies into them.

'To France!' he calls, and the sailors stare at them, shaking their heads.

'To Paris!' says Mary.

'*Vite! Vite!*' calls Jane, as the sailors cast off.

Mary sits in the prow of the boat between Bysshe's knees, her back held firmly against his chest, his arms trying to shield her from the seasickness that almost immediately engulfs her. She watches as the white cliffs and dots of gulls recede, the houses spreading up the hill become an indistinguishable line of buildings and the bobbing boats lose their masts against the blue sky. Everything, she thinks, that I have ever known is disappearing.

As though he can read her mind, Bysshe asks Jane to pass him Mary's mother's book and begins to read. Mary closes her eyes and rests against his chest. She hopes he cannot sense the tears slipping silently from beneath her lids, because she is happy, she is so very, very happy. She feels that she is meant to be here in this man's arms, on this boat, heading with barely anything towards a future unknown; it is just that she is also sad. And the sadness runs so deep that she is stunned by it.

Bysshe holds her as the little boat speeds away from the shore and out into the open sea. Once they are across the Channel it will be harder for anyone to find them, or to beg her to return. Barely conscious in his arms, Mary moans with sickness and loss. He holds her closer. One of the sailors at the mast shouts out, the waves begin to rise; the little boat kicks beneath them, lifting itself up over the waves and bouncing back flat on its prow before lifting again.

Mary takes a deep breath and holds on tighter. 'Uh!' She cannot speak, her whole being consumed by sickness, by an overwhelming need to lose either consciousness or the oatcakes Bysshe chose so carefully.

'It'll pass,' he whispers, taking the worst of the rocking boat in his own body, holding her steady, but it doesn't pass as again and again the open boat is pushed back from the shore, and the sailors fight the storm and waves through the afternoon and evening whilst Mary's guts writhe and she passes in and out of consciousness, half dreaming. At one point she thinks it is her father holding her and she is a child again. When she wakes to Bysshe's concerned glance she cannot take in what is happening and closes her eyes again. The boat goes on, dipping and rising, dipping and rising. The sailors shout to each other, working hard to stay afloat, ignoring the three of them crouched low in the prow.

'They cannot dock,' whispers Bysshe, 'for the sea is too rough.'

Mary cannot respond; the journey feels endless. When she next opens her eyes the sky is dark and stars are out. 'Is it night?' she asks, and Bysshe nods.

'Yes,' he whispers. They should be in France by now but still the storm keeps them at sea.

Soon there is nothing but the endless rhythm of the boat, the call of harsh concentrated voices, the feel of Bysshe's arms and the wet spray and splash of water; either in the air or coming at them in a rush over the sides of the boat. She holds on to his coat, her fingers curled in desperation. Occasionally she hears the cry of another voice, and opens her eyes to see Jane holding tight to her seat but with her hood flying free and her hair curling wild about her face. From the depths of her sickness

Mary feels a stab of hate so pure that she is surprised Jane doesn't immediately disappear over the side under the force of it.

'If we die,' she hears Bysshe shout out loud to the wind, 'we die in bliss. For we are together.'

Oh, please lord, no, she thinks. Don't let me die here, like this. Not like this. She'd like to say it out loud but doesn't want to disagree with her lover when he sounds so joyous, so passionate. She loses consciousness again. The night finally ends and they enter the harbour. Beneath her the boat stills and she sleeps on, soothed by the gentle motion of the boat.

'The sun wakes up the colour of her hair,' sighs Jane, and it's true – the growing light picks out the strands of red and gold in Mary's disordered curls as she sleeps. Jane and Bysshe smile together, united in their recognition of her beauty. 'When I was a child,' she whispers softly, 'I wanted to be her.'

Bysshe does not take his eyes off Mary as Jane speaks and she wonders whether he has even heard her. 'What was she like?' he asks.

Jane looks away, out over the sea. 'Whenever she entered a room the rest of us disappeared,' she says, her eyes crinkling up against the horizon. The pain of it is still there, she can feel it even as she speaks, that peculiar feeling of adoration and envy. She swallows as though she could somehow make it palatable, but it remains hard and unforgiving in her throat. She stares at the light dancing off the sea. Bysshe's hand lands so softly upon her shoulder that she barely notices it, feels only its spreading warmth. She looks up at him, grateful and surprised.

'Each person has their own beauty, even the envious angel!' he whispers.

Shocked, she shakes his hand away, but the words stay with her as she watches him bend over Mary, running his thumbs gently over her forehead. What can he or Mary know of her envy, how can they understand what it might mean to never be as beautiful, as desired, as feted or as talented as they are? An envious angel? Is that all she is? Would an envious angel do all she has done for them? Even as she asks herself the question it strikes her that her motives are far from pure, for like Lucifer she is entranced by the power of Bysshe's beauty and the passion of his ideas. She is here, in part, simply because she cannot stay away from him.

'Mary,' Bysshe whispers. 'Mary, look!' Mary opens her eyes. Sees his face bent over her own. He lifts her up and turns her towards land. 'Look!' he says. 'The sun rises over France.'

She tries to stand but immediately collapses, her knees giving way beneath her. He laughs, swooping her up in a single movement, one arm catching her failing knees and the other cradling her back as he carries her like a child, stepping off the swaying boat with ease and placing her gently on land before returning for their luggage.

Jane stares after them, wondering if he might return and do the same for her before shaking the thought away and turning to gather her belongings. She speaks some rapid French to the sailors; speaking the language is at least something Mary cannot do. They laugh and reply, something complimentary by the sound of it, thinks Mary from her position in a sodden heap on the sand. Bysshe picks up the remaining cases and manages a brief, '*Merci.*'

'What did you say?' asks Mary as the two of them stride towards her, their glowing cheeks an affront to her misery.

'Just thank you!' Jane tells her. Mary doesn't believe her.

'*Bonne journée!*' shouts one of the men.

'He's wishing us a good journey.'

'I can understand that much!' snaps Mary.

'Glad to see you're feeling better,' smiles Jane, managing not to raise her eyes.

Mary turns away. 'I need to get dry!' she says to Bysshe. 'Can you feel the ground still shifting beneath you?'

'It does for a while.'

'*Bonjour! Bonjour!*' the children cry up at them from the beach. '*Voulez vous un hôtel?*'

'Do we need them to help us look for a place to stay?' Jane asks Bysshe.

'Even the children speak French!' laughs Mary in delight. 'And look at their strange little hats!'

'Do we what?' asks Shelley.

'Do we need a hotel?' Jane repeats.

'We can go to the Hotel Dessin,' he says quietly.

'*Non, merci, mes petites,*' laughs Jane, but the children ignore her, gathering closer and clutching at her skirts.

Mary looks on, her delight in the newness of everything overshadowed by the thought that Bysshe clearly knows where to stay, most probably because he eloped here with Harriet. She pushes the thought away.

'Perhaps one day,' she smiles, grasping his arm and smiling up at him, 'we'll speak French just like the French children!'

'Or as well as Jane,' he says admiringly, who grins at him and curtseys. '*Merci*, Monsieur Shelley! *En marche!*'

'*En marche,*' repeats Mary, not to be outdone.

'*En marche!*' agrees Bysshe, holding out his elbows. The three of them link arms, the relief of dry land and the growing sun upon their skin overcoming the terrible crossing; the renewed excitement of their escape together stronger, for now, than the girls' differences as they march towards the hotel.

Mary sits in the lobby of the small hotel. The man at reception is clearly curious at the sight of the three *Anglais*, intrigued by the youth of the women and the fact that they travel with only one man. Mary cannot understand what he is saying, but easily translates the admiring glances he is trying to exchange with Bysshe, whom she loves all over again for he does not seem to notice the man's salacious glances as he asks Jane if she can find two rooms, and to explain that they are exhausted, but need to eat before they sleep.

'Nothing for me,' says Mary quickly. 'I can't eat yet; even the thought makes me feel ill!'

'One thing at a time,' begs Jane. 'I can't listen to you both and speak the language!'

Mary watches as she speaks to the man. He nods at her.

'*Oui, deux chambres,*' she says. '*Un doble pour mes amis et une pour moi.*'

'*Ils sont mariés?* Are they married?' he asks her.

Jane draws herself up, replies a little more coldly. '*Certainement!*'

Bysshe touches her elbow, asking what has been said.

'Nothing,' she says, 'it's nothing.' She dreads him insisting that they are not married to this man who might throw them back out into the street when they so desperately need rest.

The concierge lifts some keys and walks Bysshe and Jane up a stairwell. Alone in the lobby Mary closes her eyes and rests her head back. 'We're here,' she whispers to herself, 'and what some odious little man may think of us does not matter.'

'Come,' says Bysshe, returning. He guides her up the stairs into a small room. He has drawn the curtains back so the light floods in, and opened the windows wide to the sound of the gulls. He sits her on the bed and unties her black bonnet, undoes the silk strings that hold her cloak together. 'Rest,' he says, throwing the damp garments on to a chair and lifting her knees, removing her shoes. She shuffles back up to the pillows. The mattress is lumpy, but blissful compared to the hard benches of the boat.

'We're here,' she hears him say. 'We have done it.'

She opens her eyes. 'We're alone!' she whispers. 'Finally!'

He kisses her lips, stands up and removes his jacket, kicks off his shoes and pulls out his shirt. Mary traces his chest with her eyes, feels her mouth fill with desire. He lies down beside her and they stare into each other's eyes.

A loud knock on the door startles them both. 'Your soup, *monsieur!*'

They begin to laugh, Mary curling herself up and stifling her giggles into the pillow. Bysshe throws her travelling cloak over her, standing as he is in his stockinged feet, his shirt awry and his hair wild.

'*Merci!*' he says and takes the tray, standing guard in the gap of the door as the man moves his head, trying to glimpse inside.

'Madame is well?' he asks.

'She is fine! *Merci!*' he replies, kicking the door closed with a flourish. Mary laughs aloud. Bysshe caries the soup to her. It smells thick and rich with fish. It makes her stomach turn.

'I can't, really I—'

'Shhh,' he says. 'Sit up.' He rearranges the pillows and props her on the bed. 'You must eat – it's the very best thing for seasickness.'

Mary has never been fed, has never sat and watched as the spoon comes towards her mouth, never seen another mouth blow upon the spoon to cool her food, to choose just the right amount and to carefully watch as she sips. She is moved almost to tears by the way his own mouth opens slightly as the soup approaches her lips, encouraging her to eat. At first it is hard. She has to fight to keep the broth down, to stop herself from gagging. She notices he gives her nothing solid, carefully slipping the spoon into the broth only and wonders how he knows so exactly what is right.

'I used to feed Helen, my little sister,' he says. 'When she was ill I was the only one who could make her eat.' Mary nods, takes another mouthful. 'Better?' he asks after a while.

'Yes, thank you.'

He eats the solid fish himself, delicately picking around the bones, and eating the bread. 'I was hungry!' he declares as he puts the bowl down and wipes his fingers, dipping them in the basin of water. There is a strange silence between them now, a mutual question of whether and when. 'Shall we sleep?' he asks.

They lie side by side looking into each other's eyes, falling into an easy reverie that requires nothing except the fact of each other. Mary is sure that she will watch until his eyes flicker and close, but it is she who succumbs first.

Her last thought is that if Papa could see them now then surely he would forgive them.

29TH JULY 1814: HOTEL DESSIN, CALAIS, FRANCE

Jane is looking out of the window when she spots her mother walking along the quayside. She slips behind a curtain, even though she knows she cannot be seen. It's strange seeing her mother against a foreign background. She looks old, thinks Jane, and tired. She has never really noticed that her mother's walk is so ungainly, or how her body wobbles as she struts along. She looks ridiculous amongst the sailors and fisherwomen; and yet Jane cannot help but feel a stab of admiration for her mother; for the way she is walking so determinedly towards the hotel, her head up and the light of battle in her eyes. She disappears into the hotel lobby beneath the window. Soon Jane hears a knocking at Shelley's door.

'M'sieur Shellee! M'sieur Shellee!' The man's voice is vivid with anticipation.

'*Oui?*' says Bysshe, and Jane smiles, he has the accent completely, the curt word cut off in the throat as it finishes, but that is the extent of it, for he does not know what else to say. He is standing in the doorway looking completely flummoxed by the wave of words coming from the innkeeper.

'One moment,' says Jane, opening her own door, 'and slowly please, we are English!' It comes naturally to her to translate as she speaks.

'Thank you!' sighs Bysshe in relief. 'He came up earlier. I didn't understand him then either!'

'A woman is here,' the man shouts, jabbing his finger at Bysshe. 'She says you have stolen her daughter!'

'*Non. Ce n'est pas vrai.* No, it isn't true!' Jane says to him. She turns to Bysshe. 'My mother's here! She says you stole me!'

Bysshe pulls her into the room, shutting the door in the man's face.

'She waits downstairs!' the man shouts through the door, but hears only laughter. He draws himself up and repeats through the door: 'You must come and see her, or I will ask you to leave!'

'Of course I will come,' Jane shouts back through the door. 'But the woman is mistaken. No one here—' She stops because she cannot remember the words for free will, or captive, or anything else that might make sense. She begins again. 'We are all here because we want to see *la belle France* in the company of friends!' she says dramatically.

Bysshe leads her to the window and together they peer out.

'Can you see her?' asks Mary,

'I saw her arrive,' says Jane. 'I told you she'd come.' She does not notice how white-faced Mary looks, or how sad.

'You must go and see her!' Mary says. 'You can't leave her waiting; she must have travelled through the night.'

She might have a message for me, is what Mary does not say. She cannot expose her longing for her father, or her envy that it is Jane's hated mother waiting below them, whilst her own adored father has not walked a single step to call her back.

'Of course I'm going to see her,' Jane says casually, 'but she'll just make a drama out of it all! Imagine telling that horrid little man that you stole me!'

'It's already a drama,' says Mary shortly. 'Bysshe has just eloped with two girls not yet seventeen.'

'I'll just explain to her that I am here of my own volition!' says Jane, standing tall, imagining herself a free and independent woman, like Mrs Wollstonecraft on her way to write of revolution. Bysshe nods his approval. She takes a deep breath, straightens her shoulders and marches to the door. '*Allons, enfants de la patrie, le jour de gloire est arrivé!*' she hums, smiling as she leaves.

'I wonder if her mother will persuade her to go home,' says Mary as soon as Jane has gone, hoping he might feel it a relief for the two of them to be alone, but Bysshe says nothing. He looks out of the window at Jane and her mother, two women walking away from the hotel: one slender, who walks with an easy swinging gait, the other stuffed into an uncomfortable corset and shoes, her body carried along in rapid, stiff steps, struggling to keep upright as she trips along in inappropriate shoes. He does not like Mrs Godwin, has been infected by Mary's hatred of her stepmother, and yet he wonders what she might look like walking away from him in her bare feet, her body loosened and her shoes kicked off, unencumbered.

'What are you thinking?' asks Mary, for he looks so intent as he gazes out of the window.

'I was wishing all women could be free.' He sighs.

Mary jumps up from the bed, and wraps her arms around

him. 'If my mother were here she would bless our union!' she cries out. 'She would come after us to congratulate us, not to beg us to return!'

'Perhaps she *is* with us,' he says gently. 'Perhaps she looks down upon us even as we speak.'

Mary nods. 'I used to imagine that she was watching over me. I would go into a room sometimes and feel that she had just left, that she was always somewhere just beyond me, out of reach.' She gazes out at Jane and her mother. 'But Papa is not a bad man,' she insists. 'Without his guidance I would not have had the courage to be here now – you do understand that, don't you, Bysshe?'

He is touched by her need but cannot forgive her father's rejection of them both and so says nothing.

'You think he is to blame?' she says flatly.

'I think he is someone who does not understand the difference between love and possession. When your mother died he was more interested in making his knowledge of her public than he was in protecting her privacy. As a result of what he wrote about her, the world now calls her a whore. Now you have defied him he will cut you out of his life completely unless you conform to his way of thinking.'

'No!' she cries. His grip on her tightens as though he might protect her from the truth of his words.

'He is not here, Mary.' His voice is cold with anger at her rejection. 'He has sent his wife to reclaim Jane, but has no thought for you. How could he bear to lose something so precious? He can bear it because you have dared to lay claim to your own existence, to exercise your right to live as you choose. At heart he is no different to any other man.'

The words hit Mary like blows, for the truth of them is undeniable, and yet the love she feels for her father does not diminish but only retreats, for she is not sure if it is acceptable to go on loving someone who has so clearly abandoned her.

'You are all I have left,' she says simply. 'If you choose to desert me I will have nobody and nothing.'

'I will never leave you,' he says. 'You are my soul, Mary, my rock, my anchor. With you I might fly yet still know where the land lies.'

She hides her head in his chest, aware of the feeling flooding her face in a deep blush of pleasure – visible and naked.

Jane and her mother walk away from the innkeeper, aware of his fascination and needing to be free of it. Jane feels exhaustion like grit beneath her lids; she feels tired and dirty, knows that a part of her would like her mother to feed her and put her to bed, yet she must resist, she must remember the reality of each grindingly boring day without Bysshe's Italian lessons, or his presence at the table. She cannot go back. They find a small café. Men stare as they enter; clearly it is not meant for women. Jane shrinks a little, but her mother orders coffee in a louder voice than usual, her French immaculate and commanding, winning a rapid response from the man behind the counter. Jane feels a wave of unusual pride in her mother.

'If you do this, Jane,' Mrs Godwin begins as soon as they sit down, 'you will never be wanted by any worthwhile man ever again!' She sniffs the coffee and sighs. 'It is a long time since I've had truly proper coffee,' she says with pleasure.

'I don't want some boring, worthy man, Mamma,' says Jane. 'Not now, not any more.'

Her mother does not shout at her as she expects, but leans across the table and lifts her hand. 'Jane, we're not like them, the Godwins and the Shelleys, and as much as you might like to imagine that we are, we aren't. They'll get away with it because they always do. Some people, in that small world of poets and philosophers, are forgiven for their eccentricity – but never forget that our kind are not. When we try to play their games we are crucified for it! You're a child. Don't ruin your life simply because that little madam can't make her way through France without you speaking the language for her!'

'Mamma! That's not the only reason why they want me here!' Even as she speaks the words Jane wonders if they are true: is that why Bysshe asked her to come? Is her dream of being free and equal really as silly as her mother makes it seem?

'Isn't it?' asks her mother now. 'They've made good use of you, haven't they? Who was it that lied and covered up for Mary when she was seeing him? You did. Who arranged the rooms at this hotel, Jane? Was it Sir Percy and Mary – or was it you?'

Jane stops, because it is true; without her they wouldn't be here, but instead of feeling used and despairing she feels glad. She is more important to them than she thought.

'Tell me something,' her mother asks.

'Yes?'

'Has Mary thanked you? Has he? Have they once turned and recognised all you've done for them?'

Jane shakes her head. 'But Mamma, I don't need thanks. I've done it willingly because they are so in love – and what am I meant to do? End up like you? Married to a man who can't even look me in the face when he talks? A man who spouts nonsense about reason because he cannot understand feelings? He doesn't seem to care at all for Mary now that she disagrees with him. He's not here, is he, and yet she was always the one he took everywhere, the one he showed off to everyone. Why would I want a man whose love changes like that, the first moment you disagree with him?'

Her mother recoils from her as though slapped.

'Sorry, sorry, sorry!' says Jane at once.

Her mother doesn't speak and Jane wraps her arms around her in an agony of regret.

'What was I meant to do, Jane, can you answer me that?' her mother asks. 'I've lived the way those two think they can – and loved wherever there was passion – how else do you think you and Charles came about? And maybe with a famous mother and a father like hers, Mary will be celebrated for running off with a married man with children – but times have changed since the war. We're all more careful now, and so I very much doubt it.' There is a long silence. 'I know,' her mother says finally, 'that you and Charles have always believed your father was a man named Gaulis—'

'No! No, Mamma,' says Jane quickly. 'We worked out long ago that your story was probably untrue. Charles remembers a time when he was separated from you. When you were imprisoned. And when you returned you had a baby. We both knew it should never be mentioned.'

Mrs Godwin blushes. 'I was a fool, Jane. I believed your father loved me, and was honourable – but he deserted us! His name –' her mother takes a breath as though even to speak it might curse her – 'is John Letheridge.'

Jane stares at her. 'He is English!' she exclaims. 'When I have always believed he must be French, or Spanish, or maybe—'

'He is nothing, and nobody!' declares her mother. 'He paid me five shillings a week on the condition he never heard from us, and he left us in a debtor's prison to rot rather than claim you as his own. So now you know what happens to the likes of us when we go down that path. You have no excuse, Jane, because you *know* very well what I'm trying to save you from. And Sir Percy, with all his fine ideals and his borrowed money, will never know what it is to be thrown into a debtor's prison, but you do, and so why are you putting yourself in such danger?'

Jane gasps. In all her years growing up in the Godwin

household the debtor's prison has never been mentioned. Even when Jane and her mother are alone together they do not speak of it. Over time Jane had almost forgotten it existed, believed it might be a story that her brother Charles told simply to frighten her: that as a baby she had once lived with her mother in a prison. And now here is her mother speaking of it.

'And whilst we're discussing such things,' her mother continues, as though she has said nothing of any importance at all, 'Godwin may be a cold fish, and you may find that amusing, but he married me as a Clairmont, even though that was my chosen name, not our real name, and then he married me again, secretly, under my birth name, Vial, to ensure that it was legal – and in my eyes that makes him a good man.'

'I didn't know, I'm sorry. I'm sorry!' Jane holds her mother's hands tighter across the table.

'I did it all for you,' her mother says, 'and Charles! How can you abandon us, Jane, when you're on the very cusp of everything we planned together, everything I have worked for – a good marriage! You can sing and speak French. We're from a family that has some standing – and you're as charming as a little goldfinch. *She* can do whatever she likes but you come home. Please, Jane!'

Jane wonders how she could ever have abandoned her mother when she has fought so hard for her. How has she allowed herself to become the disciple of a dead woman when her own mother still lives and breathes? And yet. And yet. Bysshe's vision of a different world still flickers inside her.

'Mamma?' she asks. 'What if we lived in a world where women were not ashamed of loving more than one man? Or were not expected to be bound by marriage? Did you – and Mary's mother – each marry Godwin out of desperation, or love?'

'Jane,' her mother says sadly, 'what you cannot see is that your question does not matter. When and if a time of such freedom comes then you can behave in such ways. Until then your life will be made unbearable if you go against the world and its beliefs. Mary's mother was driven nearly to death by her wildness. Will you let that happen to you? Would I be a mother at all if I did? Come home with me and let others bear the burden of change.'

Jane bows her head as she clutches her mother's hands. 'I will! I will, Mamma. I'm sorry!' She feels her mother's body relax at the words, and is relieved.

'Go!' she whispers. 'Go and tell them now.'

Jane knows that she must go at once; she must go with her mother's words still ringing in her ears so that she is able to explain why she must leave.

Bysshe opens the door of their room before she can knock. As she steps inside, he returns to pacing up and down as Mary lies on the bed, her legs tucked up under her and her red-gold hair loose around the pillow, reading her mother's novel. Mamma's right, I can't do this, thinks Jane with relief. I can't watch them be in love when I love him so much myself.

'I . . .' she begins. They both stop and look up at her.

'Have you calmed her down then?' asks Mary dismissively. 'She looked ridiculous in those clothes.'

Jane feels a flush of anger. 'Well, at least she's here!' she snaps. 'Where's your beloved papa, or perhaps he was just relieved to be rid of you?'

As soon as the words come out of her mouth Jane regrets them, but it's too late. Mary is already displaying that icy distance that means she's hurt and will not respond, no matter how much Jane apologises. So Jane decides she will not even try. 'She was worried about me,' she says, 'and I've decided that if I go back then they'll probably leave you both alone, and so I'm going back with her,' she declares.

Mary blinks and lifts her book higher, covering her face. So Papa has not sent any message for her, but at least they will be rid of Jane. It was a mistake to bring her here.

'No!' cries Bysshe. 'You can't leave! You've only just found your freedom! You cannot give it up now!'

'I shall though!' Jane laughs, pleased by his response, wanting to provoke further the look of surprise on Mary's face as she lowers her book.

'Come with me,' he says, extending his arm. 'Let's go for a walk and talk about it.' Jane takes his hand.

Mary closes her book and unfolds her legs, ready to join them, but he shakes his head at her and she sinks back against the pillows, a look of irritation flitting across her face. She snaps her book open again, refusing to acknowledge them as they leave.

Bysshe says nothing as they walk together towards the sea. The seagulls screech and men shout and whisk past them. There is the smell of brine, the shout of boats loading and people disembarking. They walk until it is quieter and sit upon the sea wall.

'Are you serious?' he asks.

She nods. 'My mother . . .' she begins, but then realises that she cannot speak about what has happened between them in that little café. 'Everyone laughs at her, or despises her,' she blurts out. 'Don't think we don't know, or that we do not notice. We do. My mamma's never as good as the great Mary Wollstonecraft, is she? But she knows that. She's not trying to be. All she wants is for me and Charles to grow up safely, to have a family and a chance to be educated!'

Bysshe says nothing. The sea breeze makes the tears cold on her face. He wipes one away.

'She loves me!' Jane cries out.

'Obviously,' he agrees calmly, 'otherwise she would not have come!'

'And they don't know how we lived!' she whispers. She can feel the longing to tell someone the truth of her mother's existence building inside of her. 'How can they know, Bysshe, what it feels like to fear discovery, to feel so ashamed? We have different fathers, Charles and I. For a while we lived in a debtor's prison!' She stares up at him, her dark eyes wide with fear at finally speaking the words.

Bysshe notices only how the sea seems to dance in her eyes as he reaches for her hand. 'We make the abject, abject, and then we blame them for it, do you remember me saying that?' She nods. 'There's no shame in fighting poverty, Jane.' She stares up at him and he meets her eyes easily; there is no change there – the things she has said, that her mother has so feared revealing, make no difference to him at all. He sees her as he has always seen her. The relief she feels is immeasurable and she leans against him, not with longing, but from the simple desire to rest, a burden lifted.

'She translated a book once!' she whispers into his chest.

He puts an arm around her. 'Did she?' he says. 'She's a clever woman, Jane, and she has done what she had to, to survive. She found a man and married him. Is that all that should have been available to her, is it ever right when there is only one choice?'

She shakes her head against his shirt.

'You have that same spark in you that she once had; don't dim it, don't put it out. Celebrate it, Jane, don't go back and be married into servitude. If you stay with us I will protect you. I promise.'

'But it's not me you love,' she says hopelessly. 'It's Mary, and there's nothing you can do about that! I should go back with Mamma. I can't leave her.'

'What will you have then?' he asks.

'And what will I have with you two?' she returns.

'Freedom!' He pushes her away, holding her at arm's length and looking into her eyes. 'With us you may love whoever comes your way, without ever being abandoned like your mother, or made ashamed, and you will never, ever be left in debt because I promise that if you stay with us I will support you. We'll create a new way of living, Jane, with you, Mary and I at the heart of it. We'll live together, equally, we'll share love in the way we share ideas. Why should it be any different?'

'And Mary?'

'Mary agrees with me! We have always planned to invite Harriet to join us. She shouldn't be alone with our children. She should be here with us, as soon as we find a place we can stay!'

'You believe that?' Jane laughs out loud, but he looks so crestfallen that she stops laughing immediately. 'Harriet will not come,' she says. 'She is your wife and the mother of your children – not Mary's handmaid!'

'But you, Jane, will you stay? Will you be part of this new world, something people might talk about long after we're gone? Of how we broke open the chains of the church, of how you and Mary defied convention and proved that we may live and love together faithfully outside of marriage. My marriage was a terrible mistake. No church can keep people together; only love can do that. With us you'll be allowed to have the freedom of your thoughts. The right to act upon your feelings! Come with us, Jane!'

All memory of her mother's words begins to fade. He wants me, she thinks, he really and truly wants me. Maybe not like Mary, but as me nonetheless, and I love him. I can't help it, and in time who knows. 'Yes!' she cries. 'Yes!'

He wraps his arms around her, lifting her up in his enthusiasm, spinning her round and around until the sky and sea and air and everything – including the two of them – meld into one glorious rush of pleasure.

'Stop! Bysshe, stop!' she shouts eventually and he puts her down. They hold on to each other, gasping for breath and clinging to each other as the world carries on spinning around them.

From her hotel window, Mary watches as he steadies Jane, holding her shoulders as they catch their breath, before they turn and walk towards her.

She's staying then, she thinks.

PART

TWO

2ND AUGUST 1814: PARIS

It is only when they reach Paris that Bysshe reveals he has no money. He and Mary are walking along the Seine, oil lamps glowing against the warm night, stopping occasionally to gaze into the dark river. Distant footsteps echo on the cobbles and the sound of low French voices ebb and flow as Parisians walk past them.

Mary is alight with joy. 'I can feel my mamma here!' she whispers to Bysshe. 'It is as though her spirit flew home to Paris!' Bysshe squeezes her arm closer to his. They have escaped Jane; pretending to retire to bed, making love and creeping out to take the night air.

'We are almost out of money,' Bysshe says, as he looks up at the night sky, Mary's arm tucked up tight against his side and the memory of her nakedness singing all through him. 'Do you know the stars remain there in the light of the day,' he carries on, 'and it is only darkness that reveals them to us?'

It takes Mary a while to make sense of what he has just said. Surely it cannot be true. 'How?' she asks.

'How what?'

'How have we run out of money? The loan you arranged for Papa arrived before we left – surely you still have some of it?'

'It did,' he agrees, smiling at the way the moonlight sinks into her pale skin. 'But we left so fast!' he explains. 'I did not think to bring it with me! I have written to Hookham, our banker, but he is refusing to send the money to me. He has always favoured Harriet.'

'So how much do we have?' she asks. Passers-by turn at the

131

sound of their English accents, loud in the night, But Mary and Bysshe do not notice.

'Enough to eat, for a few days.' Mary stares at him, aghast. 'We will get more,' he says casually, brushing her hair back and smoothing her creased brow. 'I can sell my watch and we will find a French banker to loan us something.'

She shakes her head, her hair a halo in the soft light. 'So we are alone, in Paris, with no money?' she asks.

'Yes!' He smiles at her, 'But we will get some!' He lifts her face up to his and she tips on to her toes to meet him. The kiss is delicious.

'Shall we return?' she whispers, longing once more for the freedom of their tiny room where they have the time and space to explore each other, unafraid of the clock ticking or Jane waiting beyond the branches of the willow. This morning she awoke to find the bed empty, and Bysshe gone for a walk, a poem left on their pillow: *I felt the blood that burned in your frame mingle with mine and fall around my heart like fire.*

'So we are penniless,' she says.

'For now,' he agrees.

Mary feels even more of an adventurer. What more do they need than the bare minimum and each other? In the dark, beside the Seine, she begins to laugh at the sheer ridiculous joy of it all.

3rd August, Paris!

*D*earest Izy,

I write in haste. We are in Paris. I wish you were here, and that we might walk along the streets together, or sit in one of the many cafés and talk as the Parisians do. So much has happened. Shelley and I are married in all but name. I cannot know if the union of two people is as blissful for everyone as it is for us — but if it is then it is no wonder they do not tell us of it for we would all elope sooner! It is as though for years I have been but half a person and am only now become whole; I wonder if this feeling might be close to what it feels to have a mother.

I have witnessed the ease with which your mother might tousle your hair, or straighten a dress — a physical ease that I have only now experienced — and in a lover, not a mother. Such a love changes everything. The sun, when it shines is brighter; I think I must be the luckiest woman in the world. But see how my idiotic thoughts race, and despite so many words I find it inexplicable. Perhaps it's a good thing for once, not to be able to explain.

I must stop now, Bysshe and Jane have gone to try and raise some money — tomorrow they will buy an ass (can you imagine even writing that and it being TRUE!). It feels just like it used to when your mother called us in for supper and we wanted to go on talking for ever. Oh, Izy, I wish I could be with you for just half an hour up on Law hill. I know you'll be faithful and destroy this as I ask. You know how we are judged by the traces we leave. I cannot write yet of my father, the pain is too deep; you know how much I love him. If you or your father have the chance to speak in my defence, please, please be sure to beg my case, let him know that I am well, yet torn asunder by having chosen between the two men I love.

Reply to the post in Pontarlier — for we will pass through there on our way to Switzerland.

Your friend,
Mary (herself)

'Hurry, Jane. *Vite! Vite!*' Bysshe calls. He loves to try out his French. Whenever words fail him he releases a flood of Italian mixed with Latin, produced with such an enthusiastic and yet earnest look upon his face that Jane is made helpless with laughter. The sun is already bright as they step out of the hotel and head across the wide river towards the Boulevard St Germain.

'Shall we walk through the Isle de Saint Louis?' asks Jane.

It is not the quickest route, but Bysshe nods; he does not mind how far they walk. Mary is sleeping, made languorous by their love-making, and wishes only to write to Izy when she wakes. As they come off the Pont du Louis, Jane folds up the cheap parasol they share, grateful for the shade of the narrow streets. 'Do you think the ghosts of the Revolution watch us as we pass?' suggests Bysshe as they enter a dark cobbled street, set between high walls.

'Perhaps,' says Jane, 'but I wonder if it is wise to call up the spirits in such dark places?' She shivers.

'It feels as though the sun has never penetrated here,' he muses, running a light finger down the track in the back of her neck. 'What devilish deeds might be imagined!' She screams and he laughs.

'Bysshe!' she reprimands, but he can tell by the smile on her face that she is not really angry.

They enter the jeweller's and for a brief moment Jane wonders what it might be like to be here as his lover. Perhaps he might lift a strand of pearls over her head before clasping them upon her neck. But it is a foolish dream – Bysshe and Mary prize ideas far above jewels. The man behind the counter stares at them, an enquiring look in his eye.

'We have a watch you may be interested in, m'sieur,' says Jane, holding it out. He takes it from her hand and turns it over, naming a price. Jane feigns horror, holding her hand to her bosom. 'But it has been in the family for years!' she exclaims, as she wipes an imaginary tear from her eye. 'We could not possibly give it to you for such a price!' The jeweller smiles and makes another offer. Jane whisks the watch from his hand. 'We will return if we must,' she says, businesslike now. Taking Bysshe's hand she heads for the door.

They are almost in the street before he names a price nearly double what he has already offered. Jane glances at Bysshe, who nods, impressed by her performance and by her insistence that they are good customers, for – as she tells the shopkeeper, quite untruthfully – they will almost certainly be back as they have much to sell, so perhaps just a few more sous?

'Shall we have coffee?' suggests Bysshe, his pockets full of money.

'No!' laughs Jane. 'We must meet with the banker by lunchtime and Mary is waiting!'

They meet with the French banker on the wide, grand street of St Germain. He is a tall thin suspicious man. 'Tavernier,' he says as Jane introduces Bysshe, impervious to her charm and the value of Bysshe's proclaimed inheritance. He stares in horror at the flood of mixed languages emerging from Bysshe's mouth as he tries to make him understand his situation.

Jane watches in amusement as Bysshe's gestures become wilder and wilder, his indignation more and more apparent. 'But m'sieur,' she interrupts, smiling, 'Monsieur Shelley is a baronet!'

'I have never met an English gentleman who would wear such clothes!' Tavernier declares, before issuing an imperious: '*Non*, I will not lend you the money.'

Bysshe is angry. 'What is wrong with my clothes?' he asks.

'Nothing!' says Jane. 'Except perhaps they're a little too short in the sleeves.'

'Really?' he asks, staring at his cuffs as though that might elongate them.

'But we have sold the watch!' Jane reassures him as they walk back towards the hotel. The shops put up their shutters in the midday heat, tradesmen call to each other and women bustle past with long baguettes fresh for their lunch.

'True,' he says, 'and Mary will be waiting for me.' Jane can almost feel the longing in him to be near Mary now that they are heading home; it is in the rush of his feet along the cobbles and the swing of his arms, in the silence of him as he thinks of her.

Mary is looking out for him from the hotel window and the sound of her feet flying over the cobbles greets them as they walk towards the building.

'We have money for lunch!' says Bysshe happily, his arm clasped around her shoulder.

Jane closes her eyes for a moment, suddenly noticing how hot it is, how tired she feels. 'Did you rest all morning?' she asks.

'I wrote to Izy,' Mary replies, staring up at Bysshe.

'The bankers would not lend us a sou!' Jane declares, but neither of them hear, too intent upon settling themselves in a comfortable window seat, where Mary curls up against Bysshe, her head resting upon his shoulder, her legs folded on a cushion.

After lunch, a dim hush falls over the inn as guests retire to their rooms.

'We should rest,' says Mary, yawning as she stands, pulling Bysshe close.

'We should!' he agrees quickly. Jane notices his hand trail the length of her back as they take the stairs. The city seems to pulse with heat.

'Shall I read you some Byron?' Jane hears Mary ask as they

close the door, and Bysshe's laughing reply, 'There'll be time for Byron's poetry afterwards, perhaps when we wake up!'

Jane continues to her room. She closes the shutters and lies on her back, wide awake in the darkness. She recalls the feel of his finger, light upon her neck, and tries to erase the burning picture of the two of them lying together beneath the leaves of the willow, entwined.

The next morning, as Jane and Bysshe are about to leave the hotel, the concierge calls Jane aside.

'*Mademoiselle,*' she whispers.

Jane gestures to Bysshe to go ahead as she steps into the woman's small cubbyhole. '*Oui, madame?*'

The woman crooks her finger, beckoning Jane closer. Her teeth are bad and Jane does not want to get too close, the rot from them wafting over her. 'The gentleman,' she asks. 'He is your relative?'

'No, a friend,' explains Jane.

'You must not go with him and his wife, *mademoiselle.* It is dangerous in the countryside. The war is only recently finished, there are no inns open, and the people here are not fond of the English. Especially the soldiers. It is madness for you three to travel alone!'

'We are walking to Switzerland,' Jane says airily, 'where we plan to make a new world! A world where there will be no more war, for everybody will be equal—'

'Pah!' The woman laughs, cutting her off. 'If you are that much of an idiot then I cannot save you.'

Shocked, Jane retreats, rushing into the street where Bysshe waits.

'What did she want?'

'To warn us from walking to Switzerland! She says it is not safe.'

'It was not safe for Mary's mother to be in Paris but she came anyway,' he says.

Jane nods. 'She says the people do not like the English. But they do not seem to hate us . . .' she says tentatively.

'They are glad the war is over. They have had enough of conflict, it has brought them only poverty.' They both stare up at Montmartre, the abbey that gazes down upon the city. 'Imagine,' says Bysshe, 'four hundred thousand men surrounding that hill, and seventy thousand Parisians defending it! And still Bonaparte held them off!'

'I thought we would find freedom here,' shivers Jane, 'and the merry sound of people who have discovered what it means to live free of the aristocracy. I was a fool.'

'No! You were hopeful.'

The words of the old woman hang over Jane, turning the city from a place of romance to one of fear and darkness. She wonders which of the innocent-looking men standing on the street corners might have held a bayonet, or run someone through with a sword. 'I'll be glad when we leave here,' she says suddenly.

'If we can but find a banker who isn't a suspicious fool!' declares Bysshe.

'Let me negotiate with this one,' suggests Jane.

Bysshe stands in a doorway scowling as Jane whisks the man away from him, suggesting that they walk along the boulevard together whilst she explains their predicament. 'My friend is shy, and eccentric,' she begins, 'as so many of the English aristocracy are!' She makes a neat Gallic gesture of despair as she glances back at Bysshe. 'But he is in love!' she goes on. 'His fiancée's mother was French to her soul, but his father does not want them to marry and so they must elope, and raise money on his inheritance.' She shrugs again. 'It is the only way for them to be together.'

'Ah!' says the man, looking back at Bysshe who waits in a doorway, staring out at the street.

'His name is Sir Percy Bysshe Shelley,' continues Jane, 'and his family home is in Sussex. His father is a baronet. He is a poet and the eldest son!' Jane is amazed at how easily the words come to her, how insistent and yet charming she can be, her French already flowing more easily. She imagines Mrs Wollstonecraft making her way amongst the Parisians, exactly as she is doing now, buying and selling and arranging rents. But that was a different time. A time of hope, despite the killing. Determined that she no longer wants to be in Paris, Jane persists with the man, turning back his objections, placing a hand upon his arm and leaving it to linger in supplication.

Finally he agrees. 'Perhaps it was my charm,' laughs Jane as she gives Bysshe the good news, 'but I suspect he simply wanted to be rid of us! You can sign the promise now and pick up the money tomorrow.'

'You are wonderful!' shouts Bysshe, kissing her briefly upon the lips in his relief. She turns away, allowing her fingers to rest there.

'Will you be sad to leave Paris?' Jane asks as they pack their bags the next day, waiting for Bysshe to arrive with the money.

'Yes!' sighs Mary. 'Will you?'

It is different for you, thinks Jane, for this is the place you were truly joined together. She imagines the afternoon light falling across them through the bars of the shutters. 'No, I'll be glad to go,' she says. She does not like having to walk past the old crone in the lobby who shakes her head at them each time they pass, occasionally hissing that they should go home to England and leave Paris to the French.

'Look!' laughs Mary, pointing out of the window. Beneath them Bysshe is walking up the street with a huge sack slung over his shoulder. He sees them watching and pretends to stumble under its weight, sinking lower and lower until he is almost bent double as he disappears beneath into the hotel entrance.

'It weighs at least a ton!' he declares, throwing the sack to the ground.

'Is it really all money?' asks Mary, opening the sack and sinking her hands into it.

'We must be rich!' gasps Jane.

'No!' he says, grinning. 'It is just that French money is not worth so much, because of the war, and inflation!'

'Must we carry all this about?' asks Mary.

'We can tie it to the ass,' says Bysshe.

'But how?' laughs Mary.

Later, a small crowd gathers outside the hotel, shouting out advice as the three of them try to load their ass.

'We should have hired a driver!' says Jane.

'But we have no money apart from what we carry!' says Mary, 'and we wanted to walk, didn't we? To see France?'

Finally they are ready. 'It will be a relief when we are away from the streets!' says Mary, as they pull the animal along, embarrassed by its occasional refusal to move.

'We look ridiculous!' says Jane, and the three of them begin to laugh.

They are only a few miles outside of Paris, near the Bois de Vincennes, when Bysshe begins to tell them stories: 'In March,' he begins, as they walk past the thick woods, the air between the trees dark and impenetrable, 'there were soldiers hiding behind those trees. Soldiers from Austria and Russia and England. They were from so many different countries and yet at night each one of them lay down their heads and felt the same fear; the fear that they might never again see the women they loved, or their brothers or sisters. That this might be the last night they ever looked up into the stars or witnessed the sun rise.'

'And what were they fighting for?' says Mary contemptuously. 'They were fighting for a king to subjugate them!'

'They fought knowing that should they die, they would never return home!' says Bysshe, gesturing towards the woods. 'That their bodies would remain discarded and unknown, feeding the birds of prey and the earth.' As he raises his arms he trips on the road, tumbling into the verge. Mary leaps off the ass and stands over him as he lies pale and still on the roadside. For a moment both girls wonder what they might do if he never wakes and they are left alone; aware that it is only Bysshe who ties them together on this journey.

'Bysshe?' Mary shakes his shoulder, covering his face in frightened kisses as he sits up and shakes his head, grimacing at the pain in his ankle.

'You must ride the rest of the way!' the girls insist, and so he sits upon the ass, his feet grazing the road, as he tells them stories.

The French countryside lies flat, unrolling itself before them. The days are long and hard. The three of them start early, often walking thirty miles a day in the humid rain before finding some inn or housekeeper that might agree to offer them uncomfortable beds that Jane has had to negotiate hard for, her French becoming more confident as they walk through the scarred landscape.

*D*ear Mary,

I wonder where you are as I write this and what is happening? The news of your flight reached here before your letter – via a friend of Father's who arrived from London on the Osnaburgh. *It seems the whole of London is in uproar at your departure. You leave behind you a trail of outrage – most especially directed at Shelley. It is a relief to hear that you too seem to have had some choice in the matter. The way we hear it – especially from your stepmother – the blasphemer and wife-deserter has whisked you both away, enchanting you beyond your meagre powers of resistance, and overcoming any objections by threatening to take his own life. They talk as if you were both but fainting gothic heroines heading through the mountain passes towards his dastardly castle. Are you? Is he? You are certainly enchanted, but it seems to me that it is of your own volition.*

You seem so very far away, Mary. It's hard to believe that we ever ran up Law hill dreaming such innocent dreams. I am worried that in this world, where we are all so exhausted by war and fighting, so frightened of anything that speaks of revolution, that now is not the time for challenging and change. Your mother had thoughts before her time and your lover is the same. If Shelley had gone with only you, you might have managed to return and the rumours fade eventually; but already the talk is that you live not as a couple but as a three, loving each other freely.

Even I do not know what to make of that. I would not want to share David. I cannot believe that you are any different. I understand atheism but I am no convert to free love. Is it so? Even David is shocked; he does not know I am writing to you, so perhaps you might send letters care of Mrs Jenner at the post office. She'll know, of course, but she's a darling and won't say anything. I promise to burn everything you send, although it will break my heart to do so.

142

I think of you – MARY – perched upon an ass plodding through France and finding no room at various inns; the analogy cannot have escaped you!

Yours truly
Izy

MID-AUGUST 1814; ON THE ROAD THROUGH FRANCE

There are times when Jane can hardly bear to look at the two of them. Each time they accidentally touch, they glance up at each other, smiling. The heat seems to roll off them in a constant shimmer. Mary is luminous, and moves as though each muscle in her body has lost its formal stiffness. As the world around them grows ever more ugly, Mary appears ever more beautiful and startling within it.

It is unbearable, and so Jane begins to avoid walking with them at all if she can, pressing on ahead or hanging back until eventually they notice her absence and wave happily at her, believing she is being tactful when the truth is that she cannot stand to be too near them in their happiness. Has never felt so alone.

Perhaps, thinks Jane, love makes one blind and selfish, unable to see anything outside of oneself. In the long hours, walking behind them, or occasionally riding the donkey, she imagines having a poet of her own. She sees herself sitting down to supper with Lord Byron, just as Mary did one evening with Bysshe. She would be as wild as he is and so would tame him as no other woman has been able to – and he would write poems for her, and they too would journey together. On a boat perhaps, finding their own 'trackless way' . . .

'We should be at *Troy-ez* tomorrow,' Bysshe shouts back at

143

her, startling her out of her imaginings. She walks ahead to join them. He is on the mule they traded for the ass, his ankle still sore and swollen.

'It's not *troy-ez*,' she says grumpily. 'It's Troy*es*!'

'*Troyay*,' he laughs, knowing he has got it wrong.

'*Non*, you say it like this: *Twarrh*.' Jane comes up alongside him. 'There is a slight growl in the throat.' She touches her throat where the sound moves just below the bone. 'You can feel it here!' she says.

Bysshe leans down and places his fingers at her throat. 'Say it now?' he asks.

She swallows and he presses his finger closer, noticing her movement, the slight shiver at his touch. '*Twarrrh*,' she says. He places his fingers over his own throat and repeats the word perfectly.

'Such a small movement,' he cries, delighted. Mary tugs at the mule and it decides to stop.

The three of them sigh. 'I'll stay with it,' says Jane. 'You go on, I can catch up.'

Bysshe limps ahead on his bad ankle as Mary supports him. 'We'll stop if we come across any soldiers!' he calls back. For occasionally they do walk past a lone soldier, or more frighteningly a group of them. At least they assume that's what the ragged homeless men they come across once were. They are suspicious of them and make sure they are huddled close around the mule, hiding what remains of their money.

Jane leans against the animal, staring out over the devastated fields, thinking of the tales Bysshe has told them, of the spirits of dead soldiers stumbling after travellers delayed upon the road, desperate for the taste of warm, living blood. She shivers despite the heat, looking up to see how far ahead they are. The light fades quickly at night, dropping over the flat horizon in minutes.

'Come on!' calls Bysshe, his voice high and distant in the silent air. 'We need to stop at the next village, it's getting dark.'

Jane picks up the tether and begins to pull. If Mary and Joseph had had a mule like this, she thinks, they would never have made it to Bethlehem.

19th August 1814, Pontarlier

Dear Izy,

I read your letter over and over again, especially the last line, because you must have had a presentiment. I do not know how to say this – but – I am with child. I am sure of it. I write it to you before I say anything more to Bysshe. I felt it happen within me moments after we joined – in Paris – but he told me, very sweetly (but still as though he knew more about my body than myself!) that it was not always so, thinking it was the mere fancy of an innocent. So I am punishing him by keeping it to myself until I am completely sure. I insisted that we get rid of the ass after the first day; it was an unruly creature, and so we traded it for a mule that I'm afraid is not very much better!

The French are not at all as we imagined. They are rude and uncouth. We entered an inn one night, exhausted after forty miles of walking in a flat landscape, a bowl full of heat with no shade at all. The men sat by the fireplace and stared at us. They offered us neither greeting nor space to sit. Jane spoke to them in French. She claims they are exhausted by war and famine – and of course Bysshe then agrees with her. Personally I think they lack manners.

Three days out of Paris we began to see the signs of war, fields churned up and the houses reduced to rubble. We walked past two villages where we could find no shelter, for they had been all but destroyed. Finally, as late as nine at night, we came to a god-forsaken place called Ossey-les-Trois-Maisons. Desperate for rest and with the light failing we called at a cottage that had a poor light flickering from its windows.

Jane spoke to the couple who came to the door but her words were met with an uncomprehending laughter. It sounded strangely in the night and drove us away. As we paced the street a man called to us from his doorway; he offered us rooms, but made obscene suggestions towards Jane, who laughed of course, whilst Bysshe lost his temper. Nonetheless he gave us a room. It was up in the roof, a long low room with nothing but two awful beds. I do not feel sick or inclined to faint now that I am with child, but I do feel tired. At night I lie down and know nothing until morning.

Except for last night.

Perhaps we were unsettled by the sight of the fields lying so bare, and the destruction of the small villages, or by the surliness and suspicion of the people. The man who owned the place managed to find us some stale bread, and I was too tired to spend the time dipping it in the watery broth to soften it, and too tired to chew. I slept in my cloak because the room was filthy. I was in a deep sleep when we heard a screech loud enough to wake the dead soldiers that they tell us still lie in shallow graves beneath the fields.

The screech was not, however, supernatural at all – but landed on our bed, right next to Bysshe, and of course it was Jane, claiming that a rat set upon her. There are rats, but they are easily beaten off – at least that's what Bysshe tells me for I am far too tired to notice them. Jane clung to him for a while in apparent fear and despair; and then had a fit of giggles that required she cling to him even harder. 'I think the rat was probably the more scared,' he whispered to her. 'Don't worry, Jane, it won't come back!'

I have told him he must talk to her about her behaviour. She flirted with the innkeeper outrageously.

We are certainly not living in a three. Jane is our companion, and an impossible one at times – although it is also true that I do not know how we would manage without her. Tired of trying to persuade yet another animal to bear us, she has managed to hire us a driver, and so we progress faster now. Yesterday, Bysshe set sight upon an alpine waterfall and decided he wanted to bathe there. I did not want to do anything that might endanger our child – the water is very cold and I worried it might give my body too much of a shock – but of course I could not say so in front of Jane. It is hard enough having to share our elopement without having to share the fruits of our most intimate life.

'We have nothing to swim in or dry ourselves with,' I said, with a meaningful glance.

'Oh, but we can swim in our skin, and use leaves and moss!' he returned, for when a vision overcomes him, he becomes quite lost in it and determined to make it happen. 'We would be as Adam and Eve,' he said, 'in a Garden of Eden.' I laughed then, for he seems to have a miraculous way of knowing exactly what is happening, even though I have not told him! We are indeed like Adam and Eve, cast out of London and me with child.

Jane, of course, made it clear that she would be more than happy to swim naked in a mountain stream.

We speak often of the world we hope to create in Lucerne. Bysshe has written to Harriet in the hope that she will join us in our 'sweet retreat in the mountains', and perhaps there she too might find a love such as ours. I am not sure whether Jane has a serious enough cast of mind to be a part of our community. Dearest Izy, perhaps you and David will join us once we are established? It will be a world such as no other!

Do not worry about me.

Mary

24TH AUGUST 1814: LUCERNE, SWITZERLAND

'Let's live here!' shouts Jane.

'Oh,' sighs Mary, 'it is worth the effort of climbing these hills just to be away from those endless fields and destroyed villages.' Her exhaustion seems to lift up here, away from the squalid damp and heat of the plains.

'We could live in that little house right on the top of that crag,' Jane goes on.

'You say that nearly everywhere we stop!' snaps Mary. 'You wanted to stay in Neuchâtel and Pontarlier!' She is irritated by Jane's eternal enthusiasm, by her capacity to ignore the fact that they have so little money when it is beginning to play so heavily upon Mary's mind. If she really is with child and is to have her baby in a foreign country, then how is she meant to pay for it to be born? She does not know any midwives, nor will she be able to tell who is good and who is a charlatan – and yet it is unfair to blame Jane for her excitement when she knows nothing of Mary's predicament. The fact that Mary knows this only irritates her more.

'But this is truly the most wonderful place!' shouts Jane, undaunted. And when, a few days later, they finally arrive on the banks of Lake Lucerne and she sees the small house they *are* to live in resting on its banks, she throws her arms around Bysshe in delight. 'Let's live here!' she cries again, and this time even Mary smiles.

'Yes, let's!' she agrees.

'Oh!' cries Jane at the sight of her tiny room, up in the eaves, with a view back out over the mountains. 'It's perfect!'

'We have arrived!' says Bysshe, staring out over the lake. He turns to Mary. 'Can you imagine a life here?' he asks earnestly.

Mary reaches for his hand, looking up at the small wooden chalets clinging to the hillside. Their own tiny chalet has a deep roof and sits almost upon the lake itself, which shines a bright turquoise-blue in the sunshine.

'I have never seen such a colour,' says Mary. 'Yes,' she says, clutching his hands. 'Yes, I think we could live here.'

'They look like doll's houses!' exclaims Jane.

That first night they sit outside together, exclaiming over the beauty of the mountains reflected in the blue water, talking until the light begins to fade, their eyes becoming so used to the dark that it is deep into the night by the time they finally rise and go inside to light the candles.

Mary shivers, suddenly cold from sitting so long. 'There's a stove, Mary,' says Bysshe, delighted by everything about the place. 'Shall I light it for you?' He tries to set a fire but all it does is smoke, refusing to throw out any heat.

'We walked through France!' says Mary, coughing. 'Probably the first *Anglais* to do so since the war.' Perhaps one day the child within her might say: *my mother braved brigands to walk through France*. 'Shall we walk along the lake before we sleep?' she asks Bysshe.

'Yes, in the moonlight!' he cries.

Jane rises to go with them. 'Can you douse the fire, Jane,' says Mary quickly. 'I'm worried it might catch in the roof. Imagine how rapidly such a place might burn!'

'Would you, Jane?' adds Bysshe.

Feeling as though she has no choice but to agree Jane begins to spread the embers of the fire. She pours the water they have collected over the hot ashes, filling the small room with a thick acrid smoke. Coughing, she opens the door and runs upstairs to her small room in the eaves, shutting the door and opening the window, leaning out to breathe the fresh lake air.

She sees the two of them standing by the edge of the lake, the drift of their voices carrying up to her in the clear air. She leans out further but cannot hear what they say.

Drawing back into her room Jane lights her candle and in its small circle of light begins to write. She holds the pen between her teeth, thinking. One day, long after she is gone, people might read what she has to say. She thinks carefully before beginning:

We have rented a small house near the lake. Here we can settle and at last begin to write. I have a room with a window that looks out over the Alps. I am sitting at it now, writing this, and thinking that here is where we might change the world. Already I imagine how people might visit and be impressed by the simplicity and cleanliness of our abode. It is not a 'barren heath', but it is a place where one feels free. I could not have imagined it in London, and I can barely imagine London now that I am here.

'Shall we sit in the moonlight,' asks Bysshe, guiding Mary towards the water. The moon sets a shining path towards them across the lake. He takes off his jacket, placing it on the grass for her. 'Mary, finally we are here!'

She senses his deep happiness and fears that her news might disturb it. 'Bysshe?'

'Yes?' He slips her dress from her shoulders. 'Your skin in the moonlight!' he whispers. 'It is like alabaster.'

She stays his hand. 'There is something I must say,' she whispers gently. 'Do you know what it might be?'

'No,' he answers.

'I am with child.' She finds the words emerge easily as they sit beside the lake, perfect in the moonlight.

'Mary,' he lays a hand upon her stomach. 'Are you sure?'

'It has been over a month,' she jokes, 'and so I am more than sure.' She takes his hand, placing it over her belly. 'It happened in Paris.'

'Mary.' Again he whispers her name. She closes her eyes as he kisses her face, her neck; as he lays her down in the moonlight under the cry of an owl, delighting in the cold marble feel of her skin beneath the sky.

Afterwards they lie wrapped up tight beneath his jacket. '*Let the earth be our bed, and the sky our church,*' she murmurs, wondering if the child inside her might sense the perfection of this moment: the moment her father came to know of her existence. 'I am with child,' she breathes into his ear, over and over; the truth of it becoming solid and real now that she has told him.

'You are! You are,' he whispers back. They laugh aloud with joy, the sound carrying up to Jane who pauses in her writing – listening. One day, she thinks, she will tell others of how she heard their laughter on this first night. She will not mention the fact that it filled her not only with joy, but also with a stinging loneliness . . .

26th August, Brunnen, Lake Lucerne

D*ear Izy,*

I have told Bysshe that I am with child. He stared at me in wonder. 'You're sure?' he asked. Are all men bound to ask this question? At times I wonder, Izy: is this how my mother felt when she bore me? Joyous and scared, aware always of what might go wrong. I will write the child a letter in case anything should happen to me. I have asked Bysshe to heal the breach with Papa, should I die.

I am torn. Bysshe wants our child to be born here in the sunshine and believes we can grow not only a family but also a whole community here; but I think that surely now, with a grandchild of his own blood, my father can forgive us and we should return. What do you think? Please let me know – I need wise counsel! – for I have a hope that should Papa hear that I am with child then he might understand our love for one another.

We will struggle to continue here whatever we decide, for we expected to find letters and money awaiting us at Neuchâtel, but there was nothing. We barely had enough to get us into Switzerland, where we thought we might send for more. We have agreed to pay six months on our cottage but I do not know how we might manage it.

I hope, one day, that our children will run, as we did, Izy, down to the loch together. Perhaps they will run out and away all day as we did, speaking of how you defied the church and how I walked through a France barely recovered from the war. And we will stand together by the door, calling their names as your own dear mother once did. Such are my dreams, that we will have a life like yours, a family like yours, and all the broken bits of us will be knitted up together again and whole. Those are my daytime dreams. It is in the night that the fear comes and I see my mother, desperate to hold on to life, and yet slipping further and further away, until I am no more and she is gone.

Write to me, Izy. I can face the loss of society's sanction, but I cannot face the loss of a friend.

Your,
Mary

29TH AUGUST 1814: BRUNNEN, LAKE LUCERNE

'Jane?' Mary is standing in the door, holding her candle.

'Yes?'

'We are leaving tomorrow,' she whispers, 'as soon as our clothes are dry.'

'But why?' Jane asks. 'When we have only just arrived! We have barely had a chance to begin!'

'The stove doesn't work properly, and it's cold at night.'

'We can learn to riddle the stove properly. Mary, what is it?'

'We have no money!' Mary hisses.

'We can find a banker to loan us some in Geneva. We did so in Paris.'

'No, Jane, don't argue, Bysshe and I are already agreed; you need to pack and be ready by morning.'

'I am not walking all the way back the way we have come. Bysshe cannot agree to this! What of our dreams? Where else will we ever find somewhere so perfect that others might join us – and yet isolated enough to allow us our freedom?'

'We are not walking back,' says Mary, refusing to answer her questions. 'We are going by boat.'

'But why?' Jane wails. 'You hate boats! And Bysshe has already written to others to join us.'

'Do not shout!' Mary demands.

'Why should I not shout if I choose?' Jane raises her voice. 'There is no one here to hear us!'

'There is the landlady who often walks past after dark, as does her son,' Mary whispers.

'You mean we are sneaking away, like thieves in the night. Without paying! Is that what is happening?'

'We have no choice!' Mary whispers.

'No. It is *I* who have no choice. That is the truth of it, Mary. You two have already discussed the matter and agreed. It is only I who have not been consulted!'

For a moment Mary is tempted to tell Jane that she is free to stay here alone if she wishes; it is only the thought of Mrs Godwin's fury should they arrive home without Jane – and her influence upon Papa – that stops her.

'If you wish to come with us be ready by four.' Mary turns and is gone.

Furiously Jane picks up her pen:

We leave tomorrow; we are waiting only for our clothes to dry, before slipping away in the dark like fugitives. They must think I am an idiot myself if I do not realise that we are fleeing from having agreed to pay six months' rent. I agreed to travel with Bysshe, to be a part of a new world, but I have no say in the decisions we make, and am treated like a child. It seems to me that all our plans truly amount to are three people trying to survive without much money, Mary irritable, Bysshe concerned — and me with no power to decide upon anything. When we read our journals to each other we make our lives sound so brave and intrepid, but the truth lives in another place. The truth lives in the air between the leaves of the journal; and in all the things we do not write.

She puts down her pen and watches the ink dry on her words. Should she let them remain. Or rip the page out. It is not a very illustrious representation of their dreams.

30TH AUGUST 1814, MARY'S BIRTHDAY: LAKE LUCERNE

Dear Child,

I write to you on my own birth date. We are leaving for England, going the whole way by boat. I am frightened but I do not show my fear because if I am to die then I want your father's memory of me to be gay. I am writing to you, my unborn child, because I wish my own mother had written to me as I grew within her, that she had known that ten short days was all the time that we would ever have together. When I think of you within me my heart leaps up to the heavens, and yet almost before I can touch my joy in you it immediately descends to hell again, for fear that

I might die myself and so abandon you both. Or even worse – that I might live – and yet lose you. Please know, if you are in the world reading this – and I am not – that we have risked everything, forsaken the love of our families and the sanction of society to bear you; the evidence of our love.

Each moment of each day I am overcome by the fact of you. Again and again my knowledge of you overwhelms me, and I sense myself in the presence of something beyond knowing. I am become part of a chain that stretches interminably back and yet also forward – diminishing into the past and growing towards a future. I am a part of something bigger than myself, and you, so tiny and frail yet powerful enough to change everything, are both wonderful and terrifying. I fear sometimes that I am not ready to be a mother and yet you give me no choice.

Outside the window it is night, and I can hear your father sleeping. It is the time when fears arise. Beyond the light of the flickering candle they huddle and hover: the fear that my birth killed my mother, and that I am in turn destined to kill and lose to destruction each thing I love in payment for this evil deed. At other times – and I tremble to mention this feeling – for fear of inviting destruction, the very fact of you, growing away inside me makes me feel I might become whole again. A new bud on a stick I thought was broken.

And so I am seventeen today, and you are nought. But to your father and me, believe me – you are already everything.

Your loving mother,
Mary

30TH AUGUST 1814: ON THE RHINE

The small boat carrying all three of them swirls along the Rhine. Mary watches as Bysshe picks up a piece of paper, folding it rapidly into a boat. She cannot count the times that she has watched him write a line, decide that it is not at all what he wants and turn it swiftly into a boat.

'What will you do with it?' she asks, concerned for the writing, all twisted up and lost now within the folds of the paper.

'What else is one to do with the failure of words except offer them as a sacrifice?' he says, tossing the boat over the edge, where it bobs bravely for a moment before sinking beneath the froth of white water.

Their own boat makes a sudden turn and the spit rises up into her mouth, where Mary tries to hold it, desperate to hide her sickness for fear of Jane recognising her symptoms.

'Shall we walk for a while, when the boat docks?' Bysshe asks gently, noticing her distress. She nods, afraid to speak in case something other than words might emerge. It is a relief to be off the boat, to be away from the other passengers, a group of raucous, drinking Germans who laugh boldly at Mary's horror of them.

They find a guide who takes them to a small castle in the mountains. It is bliss to feel the ground solid and unmoving beneath her feet. The castle rests on a jutting crag, clinging to the cliff. 'That,' says the guide, 'is the Castle Frankenstein!' Mary gazes up at it, wishing fervently that she might live up there alone with Bysshe, free of Jane. And of the consequences awaiting her in London. 'The man who lived there was called Dippel,' the guide says, 'and he believed he could find a way to defeat death.' Mary is only half listening, leaning against Bysshe's side, enjoying the warmth of him. 'He dug up dead bodies, and ground their bones to dust, made an elixir with the substance and smeared it over the newly dead, hoping they might rise!'

'Oh!' says Mary. 'Perhaps he felt he was God himself, perched up so high above us all.'

Bysshe smiles at her. 'And did he succeed?' he asks. 'Do the dead indeed walk again?'

'Perhaps,' shrugs the guide. 'It is possible to lose yourself for ever in these mountains, so we cannot know what monsters might roam there!'

'And so perhaps we should not walk alone here,' laughs Bysshe, 'lest we chance upon such a monster.'

'Would they indeed be monsters,' asks Mary, 'just because they have been dead?'

'They might teach us of what lies beyond death,' says Bysshe.

'It is a terrible thing to imagine.' Mary shudders. 'Perhaps it is better that we do not know.' She has imagined her mother's body warm beneath the earth. She would not disturb it. 'I think it is wrong,' she says, 'to seek to join the spirit with the body once they have been parted.' She imagines the shock of it, the rising from the cold to live. Would one remember, or would one be born anew?

'I suspect,' says the guide, 'that we do not have to concern ourselves with such questions. If God had wanted us to rise from the dead as Christ did then surely he would have arranged for it to be possible.'

As the small boat carries them closer to England, the tiny being inside of Mary begins to call out to her. She feels its existence in the soreness of her breasts, and the unexpected rising of nausea in the mornings.

'I wonder,' says Jane one morning, as they begin to approach Holland and the end of their river journey, 'if Harriet will have a boy!'

'Why do you even think of her?' asks Mary as calmly as she can.

'Because if she does then he will be an heir, and it seems unfair when it is you Bysshe loves, and when he does not wish either himself or his children to inherit.'

Mary feels a bright fizz of fear. Has Jane guessed her state? As the boat draws closer to home the thought of Harriet begins to loom larger. Mary remembers the words of her letter: *It does not take a woman of your intelligence to see a pattern here.* And the pattern, Mary's remorseless intelligence reminds her, is that Bysshe found entertainment elsewhere when his wife was pregnant.

She takes comfort in the way he holds her tight as the boat twists and turns in the rapid current. Mary closes her eyes, determined not to show fear – especially not when Jane whoops so fearlessly, effortlessly bending her body to the swirling rhythm of the untethered boat.

Even after their arrival in Holland their journey is not over, and she must embark yet again for London. The sea is rough and Mary is confined to her cabin, able only to raise her head to groan as Bysshe holds her hair back from her face as she empties her stomach. 'How can you so love the motion of sailing?' she gasps.

'It's not the motion of the boat,' he explains, 'but the concentrating upon keeping it afloat; it takes me away from myself and stills the mind. When I return to land things are clearer.'

But Mary is not listening. Later, when he has gone up on deck, she remembers her journey on the *Osnaburgh* with its sweet ending at the Baxters', hoping that her violent sickness might pave the way for another such resolution with her father.

Jane is the only passenger up on deck. Occasionally a sailor walks past and salutes her as she holds on to the ship's rails staring directly into the waves. She barely notices. There is something going on. She can sense it but has no idea what it might be, or why it has driven Bysshe to return to England, relinquishing his dream of a new world. No doubt he is below deck with Mary. Jane wonders if she will ever hold sway over a man enough to persuade him to give up his dreams for her.

At last she sees Bysshe walking towards her, holding tight to the rail as he comes alongside, taking deep, shuddering breaths, trying to control the rise of his stomach.

'You're only ill because it's so disgusting down there!' she tells him. And it is true; the smell of vomit and the green-faced groans of the other passengers made even her own strong stomach turn until she fled to the deck.

Bysshe cannot answer; still fighting to find a place where he might breathe and the sickness subside. They stand together as the horizon shifts, up and down, up and down, and the wind blows so fierce that they cling tight to the rails, unable to let go for a second for fear of being swept overboard. 'I'm sorry we had to leave,' he says eventually.

'I would not mind if you had told me why,' she replies, refusing to look at him.

'We had no money!' he repeats.

Jane remains with her face to the spray. 'We had no money in Paris,' she says, 'and yet we found a way to continue.'

'Trust me, Jane, we had no alternative.'

'I do trust you,' she says, 'only I no longer know why! If we are to build something new, how can we do so in England, where Godwin will turn everyone against you?'

'Perhaps he will have reason not to,' says Bysshe.

'If lending him your money has not worked then what could possibly persuade him? You do not know him,' she says. 'He will never change his mind until you return Mary to him, or marry her – and that you cannot do.'

'No,' he agrees, 'that I cannot.'

13TH SEPTEMBER 1814: GRAVESEND, ENGLAND

As the coast of England looms towards them, Bysshe feels a dread enter his soul. They cannot pay the captain, and he must negotiate with a boatman for their passage to the shore. The lack of money that so amused him on the Continent fills him with fear as he approaches home.

He stares at the flat grey coast, listening idly to an English couple talking in loud voices behind him: 'If you truly wish to find a safe haven for your money,' the man is saying, 'then you should invest in a plantation, or the mills. They may have abolished the trading of slaves, but they have not yet abolished the owning of them!'

Bysshe slips closer towards them. Mary, noticing he has gone from beside her, hears his voice, furious and loud: 'Do you believe,' he is saying, 'that the colour of a man's skin bars him from the right to be treated as a human being or to be paid properly for his labour?' The man's companion, a well-dressed woman steps back, but Bysshe leans forward, stepping closer to her. 'And you,' he says, jabbing a finger at her, 'as a woman, should at least feel some sympathy for their plight!' People turn and stare, muttering.

'Do you truly compare my companion to a black slave?' asks the gentleman, appalled. The murmur of the crowd around them deepens.

Jane moves to defend Bysshe but Mary pulls her back. 'Stay with our cases.' She steps up beside Bysshe, placing her arm firmly upon his. 'Some women, sir,' she says calmly, 'are indeed treated as slaves, and in this very country, but my *husband* did not intend to cause offence to either you or your . . . companion.'

'I'll wager you enjoy eating the sugar the slave trade produces!' the man declares. The crowd laughs.

'Indeed we do!' agrees Mary. 'And thank you for drawing it to our attention. We would never wish to take pleasure from another's pain. We shall stop at once!' Her calm words affect the man far more than Bysshe's fury.

As they collect their luggage a boatman offers to take them to shore. 'It's good to hear it said, sir!' he says.

Mary nods, still stunned by how wonderful it felt to defend him – and to call Bysshe her husband.

'Bravo!' says Jane.

'Welcome home!' says Bysshe.

The three of them turn to look at Gravesend coming closer; it is only Mary who smiles as they approach, who lifts her face up and thinks of it as home.

14th September, 56 Margaret Street, London

Dear Izy,

We spent our first night in the Stratford Hotel, Oxford Street, and have now taken lodgings at 56 Margaret Street, where you might reach me. We are near to Harriet in the hope that we might manage to persuade her to be a part of our experiment in living together. Bysshe has written to her over and over, offering her a home with us, and also to suggest she on no account involves solicitors in their financial negotiations. The sad truth is that if she fails to trust us and asks for a separation and legal settlement from him then we will find it hard to procure a loan against his inheritance.

I do not know why I have not heard from you. I am sure you would write if only you knew how desperate I am to read your words. We arrived in London expecting to find money at Bysshe's bank – but it was gone, removed by Harriet. We then went to my

161

friends the Voiseys but they said they had nothing to give us, and seemed embarrassed by me. They did not invite us in. Bysshe's friend Hogg, who was so kind when we were parted, is away at his legal work in the north and so could not help us. I tell you this only to explain how, in desperation, we came to Harriet's house in Chapel Street, where Bysshe went in to ask her for money. We waited outside, with the boatman who we had not yet paid and so would not leave us in case we deserted him! Thankfully we were in a closed hackney so could not be seen. We waited outside for nearly two hours!

When Bysshe returned, Jane asked why he had taken so long and whether Harriet would come to live with us. He looked pained and could not speak, but only showed us the money. He paid the boatman and so we were left alone. Jane claims Harriet can only have given us money in the belief that he might return to her, but I do not believe he would ever promise that.

Mary stops writing to put a coal on the fire. They all feel the chill of London after the clean Swiss mountain air. Their rooms are damp, the mattresses and chairs cold to the touch; and yet, thinks Mary, it is still home. It is a joy to walk in the same parks with Bysshe, to exclaim over how much they have changed.

'I much prefer Whitehall to the Champs-Élysée,' says Mary, feeling a small thrill at how cosmopolitan the words make her feel. She is writing a journal from her diaries. 'Perhaps I might publish it?' she suggests to Bysshe as they walk together. Before he can reply, Mary spots an old family friend walking rapidly through the park, 'Oh!' she cries. 'Look, Bysshe, it's Mrs Boinville!' She rushes towards her old family friend, longing to tell her of Paris and the war-torn fields. Oh, but she is walking away from them, almost running in her haste to be gone.

'Mrs Boinville!'

The woman draws up and stops. 'Mary!' she says, her face flushing.

'Mrs Boinville, my companion Sir Percy . . .'

'I know very well who he is, Mary, and I am afraid that I am not at liberty to speak to either of you—'

'Liberty!' cries Bysshe angrily, before she can finish. 'You are at liberty to behave exactly as you desire towards us, madam; it is only that you do not choose to!'

'Exactly right!' she declares. 'Mary, you are perfectly capable of understanding the law of consequences. If you choose to behave outside of the moral law then you must be prepared to live upon the edges of society!'

Mary stands before her friend, white with horror. 'But what,' she manages to say, 'if the moral law finds itself immoral, and yet no one acts against it, as my mother did, to question it?'

'You are most certainly not your mother, Mary!' The words cut Mary to the quick, but before she can reply, the woman speaks: 'Your father has made it very clear that if I associate with you then I may not associate with him. My choice is clear.'

Mary remains wordless as Mrs Boinville walks rapidly away from them.

'It is we who are not at liberty!' shouts Bysshe at her back. 'To live as we choose!'

'No!' Mary pulls at his arm, for people are staring at them. Bysshe's lack of care no longer makes her feel debonair and dangerous. 'Let's go home!' she whispers, longing to be where no one might see her.

'No,' says Bysshe gently, 'we cannot hide, for it will not be the last time, Mary, and we must hold fast to the knowledge that we are not wrong, even when such shame is heaped upon us!'

She takes his arm and they continue walking. But the words of the woman will not leave her. '*You are most certainly not your mother, Mary!'* And that her own father has encouraged their friend to reject her!

'I think,' says Bysshe, in an attempt to divert her, 'that you should definitely write about your travels, just as your mother wrote about hers. What shall you call it?'

'I don't know,' she whispers.

'Something straightforward,' he suggests.

'Perhaps, "A history of a six-week tour"?' she says, her voice shaking, grateful for the opportunity to turn her mind to something else.

'Yes,' he says, walking and talking as though nothing at all has happened. 'Shall we walk to St Pancras, and sit under the willow?'

'Yes please,' for that is exactly what she would like to do. As they sit beneath the leaves, autumnal now and falling, Bysshe holds her gently. Their kisses are different now.

'Your mother is reviled, Mary, but does that change the value of her thinking?' Bysshe says.

Mary shakes her head. 'No.'

'Take strength from her,' he whispers, and Mary does as he says, sinking her fingers deep into the earth where her mother lies, drawing it up through her fingers.

'Perhaps I am not as brave as you, Mamma – or as talented – but I know now that I love as passionately as you once did. Protect our child, Mamma.' For Mary can bear rejection for herself, but the thought that it might extend to her child fills her with despair.

16TH SEPTEMBER 1814: 56 MARGARET STREET

Jane cannot get used to the cramped meanness of the city, the grey of it. She looks out of the window, half hoping that instead of bricks and mud she might see the Alps rising magically into the distance. 'Wouldn't it be wonderful,' she says to Mary and Bysshe as they sit together at a small table writing, 'if we could suddenly be transported to anywhere we imagined!' As she speaks she notices a familiar figure walking towards the house. It is her mother, who cuts a far less comical figure in London than in France, In fact, thinks Jane, she looks quite forbidding with Fanny trotting along beside her.

Jane stands in the window, watching as the two women come up close enough to be seen and her mother begins to gesture frantically, waving one hand towards herself to suggest that Jane should come outside, whilst holding the finger of her other hand to her lips to indicate that she should do so secretly. Fanny stands beside Mrs Godwin, glancing towards the window. Trying to get a glimpse of Bysshe, no doubt. How strange that her mother and Fanny have spent all this time in London, waking each morning and breakfasting around the same table whilst she has walked the length of France, slept in draughty rooms shared with rats. Negotiated with bankers. Does she look as different to them as they do to her?

'My mother's outside,' she says aloud, 'with Fanny.' Before she can move to the door, Bysshe rises from the table and runs into the street. Mary comes to the window. Jane watches her mother glare at her, angry that she has betrayed her presence.

It is easy to see what her mother is saying. She has drawn herself up to her full height and is holding her palms out as though physically restraining Bysshe. Fanny blushes red with embarrassment, and Bysshe touches her lightly upon the shoulder – forgiving. Mrs Godwin is about to turn away when Bysshe clutches at her arm, whispering something urgent into her ear. Jane leans closer, as though she might hear through the window. A sudden stillness falls over the three of them. Fanny reaches out to Bysshe, holding his cuff and asking something. He nods. Jane cannot decipher what is happening.

'What is he saying?' she asks Mary. Mary knows exactly what it must be. That she carries his child. Bysshe is talking urgently, his hands flying through the air, posture intense.

'I don't know,' she replies casually, but Jane notices her knuckles stretched tight as she grips the windowsill, her lips pressed thin with hate.

'It is always my mother who comes after us!' says Jane.

'It is not us she chases after,' says Mary, 'but you. Why don't you go out and talk to her?'

'She will only ask me to return home, and I cannot,' says Jane. She hears the bell of the bookshop door, remembers the boredom of the routine days unfolding with such monotony. No. She cannot go back. Not to any house that fails to have Bysshe in it.

They watch as Mrs Godwin turns away, leaving Bysshe standing in the street. 'I'm sorry!' Fanny mouths as she races to keep up with her stepmother. Bysshe stands alone for a while, staring after them, before turning back towards the house.

'What did she say?' asks Mary. 'Is there any word from Papa?'

'No,' he answers, unable to look at her.

'Nothing?' she asks.

'I learned only that they were too frightened to speak with me. Your old friend was right, Mary. Your father has forbidden anyone to communicate with us. Mrs Godwin came only in the hope of seeing you, Jane.'

Mary does not move from the window. 'Papa has not yet heard from us himself,' she says hopefully.

'He has heard that we are back,' cries Bysshe furiously, 'and he has denied your own family access to us, on pain of excommunication – from the church of Godwin,' he says bitterly, 'whose philosophy we still fund!'

'You cannot believe everything my stepmother says!'

'She is not a liar!' says Jane.

'She is!'

'Mary!' Bysshe tries to hold her but she is stiff and unyielding.

'But he doesn't know yet,' she whispers hopefully into his shoulder, not wanting Jane to hear, 'that I am with child.' Bysshe says nothing.

'I will write to him myself,' Mary adds.

'But why?' asks Jane. 'When he behaves so appallingly. He is a monster to treat you so.' Neither Bysshe nor Mary reply. Again Jane senses that there is something. Something she is not being told.

'I think I might rest on my bed and read,' says Mary.

Once upstairs, Mary begins to compose a letter to her father. It is no good for Bysshe to write to him; only she truly understands him, only she might convince him of the rightness of her actions.

Dear Papa,

We have come home in the hope that we might be reconciled with you. You have spoken to me often of your meeting with Thomas Paine, and how impressed with my dear mamma he was. Paine believed that neither government nor church should guide us, and that 'when a man seriously reflects upon the precarious effects of human affairs he will become convinced that it is infinitely wiser and safer to form a constitution of his own in a cool deliberation rather than trust any interesting event to time and chance.' Bysshe was such an interesting event in my life, Papa, and I trusted not to government nor church, but relied upon my 'own constitution' and I remain convinced of its rightness.

I respect that we have need of society, but alongside Bysshe I hope to build a society that mirrors your own thinking. If this is so, then I do not understand why you persuade our friends to choose between us, when we do nothing but live according to your own, and my mother's precepts . . .

Mary stops writing. There is a bold knock upon the door and she rushes down the stairs, for it sounds just like her papa's knock. Perhaps her stepmother has given him the news and he is here now, knocking on the door and waiting for her answer.

But it is only Charles, Jane's older brother, who stands upon the doorstep.

'Charles!' says Bysshe delightedly, for they have had no visitors at all since they returned and are beginning to feel as though they are merely ghosts of their former selves, no longer visible to the people who once hailed them in the streets. 'Hello!' he says as he pumps Charles's hand. 'Come in and tell us what is happening, for we find ourselves in exile and hear nothing!'

'Yes, Charles,' says Mary quietly, 'please tell us what is happening in Skinner Street!'

Jane stands beside them both. '*Bonjour, mon frère!*' she says, curtseying to him deeply.

'*Bonjour, mademoiselle,*' he replies with an equally deep bow. They talk together in rapid French, her accent and speech far better than his own now, as she asks him to be careful what he says, for Mary is in despair at her father's continued rejection. 'We are glad you are safe home!' he says to Mary, lifting her hand to his lips.

And then, 'Jane!' he says at last, holding out his arms to his little sister.

'Charles!' They hold each other close – and all at once she is not changed at all, but only his sister, tearful at the familiar feel of him, the comforting warmth.

'I swear you've grown!' he says.

'You haven't!' she replies. They hold one another lightly by the hand. Mary turns away, unable to bear the sight of their easy, familial love.

'Well, here you are,' he says as he sits down, looking around at the small room, the furniture spartan and squashed close, the fire drawing badly.

'We took the rooms because they are close to Harriet,' explains Mary quickly, 'and we are hoping that she might begin to feel that she might join us.'

Charles says nothing.

'It is practical as well as philosophical,' says Jane in French, 'for if she decides to ask for a formal separation from Bysshe he will no longer be able to negotiate a loan with his bankers, and we will be forced to find money with the lenders.'

Charles shudders, both at the idea of Bysshe living with yet another woman – even though it be his wife – as well as at the extortionate rates the moneylenders charge.

'It is rude to speak in French,' says Mary.

'Sorry, I am showing off!' says Jane. 'His French was always so much better than mine!'

'Are you glad to be back?' asks Charles, changing the subject. They each fall silent at his question, unable to answer easily. They have not been feted for their travels but disowned. Only Bysshe's friends, Peacock and Hogg, have promised they might visit. 'Well,' says Charles, anxious to fill the awkward silence. 'I imagine it is, at least, preferable to living in a convent?' An ironic smile upon his face.

'But we never visited a convent?' says Jane, confused.

'No! But I hear that Mamma plans to put you into one if she can get you away from here.'

'Really?' Jane asks.

'Yes! I come to warn you that she plans to suggest an outing

169

with you, but once she has you in her clutches you are to be carried away to a convent!'

Mary makes herself smile along with the rest of them, but the thought of Jane's mother's desperate love causes a deep and inexplicable pain inside her chest.

'Typical!' laughs Jane. 'She should write books rather than sell them!' But there is fondness in her voice at the ridiculousness of her mother.

'And does Godwin agree with this plan?' asks Bysshe. 'Does he now believe that it is better for a woman to be locked up against her will than to make a choice he disagrees with?'

'I am sure he has no idea of it,' says Mary quietly. 'But I am not surprised my stepmother has conceived of such a plan. She would far rather Jane were locked up than consort with us. I think that perhaps some people would prefer women were dead rather than be allowed to exercise the right to think for themselves.'

'They fear that if they set you free you will flee from them and so they lock you up, forcing you –' Shelley touches Jane lightly upon the shoulder – 'to revert to belongings that one can keep in a cupboard.'

'Not a cupboard, Bysshe – a convent,' she quips, and the three of them begin to laugh.

'But Papa would never agree to such a thing,' insists Mary.

'And yet he refuses so see either you or Bysshe,' Charles says, 'and he has ordered not only his family but all of his friends to have nothing to do with you. He has made it plain that any who do will be cut off completely.'

Mary nods, silently scratching at the smooth skin on her inner elbow. She will not cry. *She will not cry.*

'Charles!' snaps Jane.

'I'm sorry,' says Charles. 'I should not have mentioned it so suddenly.'

'It's not right!' says Jane. 'It makes no sense! He always loved you best of all, Mary. You know that, don't you?'

Their easy kindness makes it even harder to bear, and she must not cry. She fears that once she starts, she might never stop. 'I'm tired,' she says. Recently she finds she can barely stay awake beyond eight o'clock, her eyes closing even as she tries to listen to Bysshe and Jane's excited plans for a future she can no longer imagine. There seems no place in their planning for a baby. Mary stands and Bysshe at once goes with her.

Alone in their room she turns to him. 'How can Papa consider himself reasonable and yet do this to us?' she asks.

'He is not reasonable, Mary,' he replies, furious with Godwin for causing his beloved daughter such pain. 'Nor has he ever been when it fails to suit him.'

'It is not Papa! It is her, my stepmother,' Mary declares. 'He changed when she came to live with us, and it has never been the same since.'

Bysshe holds his tongue. 'Perhaps,' he says.

'So, sister?' asks Charles, once he and Jane are alone. 'I take it you are aware of the rumours?' He throws several coals on the fire and watches in satisfaction as they catch and blaze, filling the room with warmth. Jane grimaces, for they are running low and cannot afford more, have already learned to eke out each piece, coaxing it for as long as it will burn.

'Which rumours?' she asks. 'There are so many?' Aiming for an airy response to his question.

'That Sir Percy shares you, Jane, and that he does so because he is a blasphemer and does not fear the wrath of God! Even a poet as famous for his dalliances as Lord Byron does not share his women!'

'No, Lord Byron prefers to discard his women. Is that truly preferable to loving more than one woman?'

'How can you ask your brother such a question?' Charles is serious now. 'Can you not see the pain you cause our mamma?'

'She would have done the same when she was young – if only she'd had the chance!' flounces Jane, hiding her guilt behind bluster.

'You did not see her after she returned from Calais,' he says quietly. 'If you are not sharing him with Mary, then why do you not consider coming home?'

'Is that why you are here?' Jane asks angrily. 'Because Mamma sent you?'

'She did not send me! I came because I *wanted* to see you and warn you, you little idiot! But Mamma is frightened for you. She knows that you will no longer be accepted in polite society if you remain here.'

'And it is precisely that fear that keeps us women in our place, isn't it, Charles? That makes us do exactly as we are told lest the church and its moral guardians abandon us. And Mamma is right to be fearful for me. We are already no longer received anywhere, and none more so than Mary, who was once the most feted! But she can live with the world's disapproval – it is her father's behaviour that she cannot bear. Why does no one chastise *him* for the way he behaves?'

Charles nods slowly in agreement, surprised to see his little sister's anger turned to righteous fury.

'It's true they have abandoned Mary, and it is cruel, Jane, but you still have the chance of a home with us, and I do not understand what stops you. Is it his ideas that draw you, or the man himself that you follow?'

'I'm no longer sure I know the difference,' Jane hears herself say. Her brother stares at her intently. 'Why do you not speak?' she asks.

'Perhaps because I do not know what to say!' he declares.

'We are concerned for you. Mamma wants you either home or away from here; she pleads your case with Godwin, and for now he'll have you back, but he says that if you persist in this connection with them then he is determined to protect his remaining daughter from the infamy of you both.'

'You mean Fanny,' says Jane scornfully. 'If we had asked her to come with us she'd have packed her cases faster than either of us!' As soon as the words are out of her mouth Jane regrets them; they are cruel and unnecessary, even if they are true. At times, she can see why Mary believes she should try to manage her temper better. She can be too quick and unkind, and once the words have left her mouth it is too late to be sorry.

'You'll always have a place with me,' says Charles. 'You do not have to feel that Bysshe is your only hope.'

'But the truth is that he *is* my only hope,' Jane cries passionately. 'Even if I were to do as you ask, would everyone miraculously forget what we have done?' As she speaks the words she feels a fear rise up inside of her at the truth of them. She has burned her boats as surely as Bysshe burns the paper boats that he floats upon the heath at night, watching them flare up in flames before disappearing into the darkness. 'If I came home what choices would be open to me then? Eventually I will be expected to marry. But who would have me? Some man who pities me and wishes to reform me? Or even worse a man who joys in reprimanding me! I cannot do it, Charles. I cannot be what I was.'

Charles smiles at her; her passionate intensity remains entirely unchanged.

'The three of us believe in something different. I have tasted freedom, and believe that he will change the world. And when he does I want to be a part of it . . . I—'

'And what does your freedom taste like?' Charles cuts in.

'Bitter at times,' she says truthfully. 'Both Mary and Bysshe feel I am too much at the mercy of my feelings – and they remind me of it a little too often; but I have travelled through France and seen the consequences of war. I am reading Rousseau and James Lawrence. I live in hope of change, Charles, not in longing for the past. In France I negotiated with bankers,' she says proudly, before stopping, worried that her older brother might laugh at her newly acquired earnestness.

'But what you do not say is that you love him, Jane. It's true, isn't it?'

'Yes.' She cannot bear to look at him as she answers.

'It will not end well, Jane.'

'I do not feel like Jane any longer,' she says angrily. 'Jane was a different person in a different world. It is Mary who grieves for the love of her old life, not I!'

'And if you are no longer Jane then tell me, little sister, who are you?'

'A woman who believes in the freedom to choose her own partner, to refuse to marry merely for money or status, or simply because it suits the world around her.'

'And what is this new woman to be called?' Charles continues, knowing that he is riling her, enjoying the sensation. As children he would wind her tight until she snapped, and then they would tear through the house, the sound of his laughter and her fury bringing Godwin out of his study, causing her mother to shout and Mary to roll her eyes.

'I do not know,' says Jane, 'but I shall change my name to mark it. There! You did not expect to give me *that* idea, did you, brother?'

'There is nothing wrong with the name given to you by our own mother.' Charles is shocked, but the idea appeals to Jane. She is no longer the girl who left Skinner Street and so she will no longer be called by that name. Charles stands up, he picks up a copy of *La Nouvelle Héloïse*, a novel by Rousseau that Bysshe has given Jane to read.

At the sight of it her new name comes to Jane: 'I shall be called Claire!' she announces.

'It just so happens that I've read this too,' says Charles, holding the book up. 'Claire's the name of the heroine, isn't it?'

She nods.

'And doesn't she become the lover of her best friend's husband?' he asks, still smiling.

Jane nods again.

Charles raises an eyebrow. 'Well,' he says, seeing that his sister will not be drawn and impressed in spite of himself. The old Jane would have attacked him by now, fists flying. 'I can call you Claire if you insist, but you will always be Jane to me. It is not so easy to change who we are – Claire.' He lingers over the name, teasing her.

'And I will no longer be a Godwin either,' she returns angrily. 'He does not deserve for me to carry his name, now that he has deserted Mary! I will be called Claire Clairmont!' As soon as she hears the name it rings true and clear to her.

Charles smiles at her with that little twist to his lips that she knows so well; the one that means he feels his little sister might be getting above herself. 'Then you will be a double fraud, Jane, for Clairmont is not even our mother's name as you well know. What a made-up little person you will be!'

Driven to fury Jane kicks him.

'A very persuasive argument,' he says, still laughing, and so she punches him as well.

It is a relief to let go of her rage, to know that when she hits him he will not tell her that she must think before she acts but will simply punch her back; being careful of course not to hurt her. He rolls up his sleeves and soon they are tumbling together upon the floor, fighting as they have always fought.

Charles is the stronger but she is more vicious and flexible. Perhaps she fights harder than she means to for she has been trying so hard to manage her impulsive nature in an attempt to impress Bysshe that her energy erupts under the strain; and Charles has to pin her down afraid that he might hurt her.

'Surrender?' he asks.

'Surrender,' she agrees, her hair falling over the floor, eyes still filled with laughter.

'What,' asks Bysshe, appearing at the door, 'are you two doing?'

They stare at him from the floor. 'Did you never fight with your sister?' asks Charles, blushing slightly, embarrassed to be caught engaged in such childish things.

'No,' says Bysshe, brushing the hair from his eyes and helping Jane to her feet. 'I told them stories.'

Which makes all three of them laugh.

Above them Mary buries her face in her pillow. Bysshe has said that they must move at the end of the month, flitting in the evening for they cannot pay the rent. She cradles her still-flat stomach and thinks of her child, the knowledge of the little being easing the hollow loneliness brought on by their joined laughter.

27TH SEPTEMBER 1814: 5 CHURCH TERRACE, ST PANCRAS, LONDON

They move at dusk, carrying everything they own. Mary sits in the half dark as Bysshe struggles to light a fire, and Jane (who Mary continually forgets to call Claire) begins to try and make the place look brighter, spreading their few books upon a table and resting a blanket Mrs Godwin has given her over the back of a chair.

'At least we are nearer to Mamma's grave,' says Mary brightly, 'and I can visit often.' She is determined to appear brave even as she feels her spirits drop at the sight of the rooms they have rented. They are cold and unloved. There are no portraits or books adorning the walls, just blank empty spaces waiting to be filled with all of the possessions they no longer own. How, she wonders, can she have a baby here?

Again she goes to bed early, yet remains wakeful as the sound of Bysshe and Claire talking together comes up through the dust-ridden floor.

'Mary?' Bysshe whispers, waking her in the night.

'What o'clock is it?' she whispers back.

'Late,' he replies, not wanting her to know it is well past midnight; or how easily he and Claire forget the time once Mary has retired.

'Bysshe?' she says as he fits his arm beneath her head, wrapping his other around her.

'Mmmm?'

'I must finish writing to Papa. I am sure he will have us home once he understands that we are only acting according to his own beliefs. If he could see how we are forced to live then surely he would want us home. How am I meant to have a baby in a room like this?' Even as she speaks a voice within her warns: *Be quiet, Mary, you are becoming as Harriet did – a woman who can no longer engage in ideas but only think of the practicalities.* But she cannot stop herself. She isn't Harriet and she did not defy her father to become subordinate to Bysshe.

'We will find the money somehow,' he sighs.

'But how?' she insists. 'Now that Harriet has requested a legal separation no respectable banker will deal with you!'

'Which is why I must deal with moneylenders and speculators,' Bysshe says bitterly. 'With those men who give money to people who have barely anything, and then when they cannot pay them back rob them of what little they once had. They will lend to me, Mary, because they know that I have an estate to lose.'

'And when you have sold off your estate, where will we find the money then?'

He leans up on an elbow, traces her brows. 'Well then, we shall be like every other person who has to work for a living!'

'But we do not work!' Mary declares. 'And it is impossible to write when we have no home and cannot pay the rent. And if Papa could only understand, then we might live with him and that would be so much the—'

A gentle snore comes from above her head. Bysshe has fallen asleep.

After breakfast Mary takes up her pen ready to continue with the letter to her father.

'Put it down and come with us to the heath,' says Bysshe. 'Peacock and Hogg say they will meet us there. Peacock has given up his life as a clerk to write poetry. You'll like him, Mary. Say you'll come. You remember Hogg. He is back from his legal rounds in the north and longs to meet you. Do you remember him from the bookshop?'

Mary has a dim memory of a man who stood beside Bysshe on that day but it seems an age ago now. A time that she can barely believe existed.

'He kept Bysshe alive for you when he was pining!' laughs Claire. 'Come and say thank you!'

Bysshe disappears to find the coat that Hogg has lent him.

'I'm trying to finish this letter, Jane!' Mary snaps. She would like nothing more than to walk on the heath and play at sailing boats or talk poetry, but if she does not write to her father then nothing will ever change.

'Claire! My name is Claire now!' She twirls her hair and looks at her reflection in the glass, still searching to see how the name suits her. Mary's insistence upon doing the right thing and staying home to write to her papa suits her very well, for it means more time with Bysshe.

Mary grimaces as though in pain, touching her side low down on the left. Sometimes it feels as though the baby is pinching her there, its small fingers hanging on tight to the insides of her.

'Are you sure you're all right?' asks Claire. 'You are so tired these days.'

'Yes!' Mary says quickly. 'It is just a twinge from sitting too long!' She still cannot bear the idea of Claire knowing of her child – it has become the only thing she shares privately with Bysshe. 'I'm completely fine,' she adds. 'I just need some peace to be able to finish this letter!'

'We're leaving,' grins Claire. 'We're meeting Peacock and Hogg by the ponds upon the heath just in case you do decide to change your mind.'

As soon as they are gone, Mary sets down her pen. The empty rooms are blissful. Guiltily she gives up on her letter and lies down on the damp sagging sofa. This is not the life she imagined when she eloped, she thinks, as her eyes fight to stay open. Perhaps, one day, all women will be able to live with whomever they choose, whether married or not, and perhaps one day such women will walk through the streets without attracting the slightest interest; and if so then maybe she and Bysshe will have been a part of creating that freedom. And with that happy vision, she falls asleep.

'Dormouse!' The sound of Bysshe and Claire's voices startles Mary awake. Before she can properly rise they are in the room.

'Were you sleeping, dormouse!' Bysshe cries. 'Really, you can tell us! You can tell us anything!' he says, dropping a kiss upon her brow. 'We've walked the length of the heath whilst you slept! And sailed paper boats upon the pond. And Hogg has gone to buy more coal, and says he will take us all to supper!'

Mary heaves herself upright, stifling a sharp retort.

'Don't look so cross, dormouse!' he says, wrapping his long arms around her and threatening to pick her up from the sofa.

'Stop it!' she laughs – but at the sight of a few grains of sugar still clinging to the corners of his lips she is startled into complaint. 'You've been eating cake!' she wails. He wipes his mouth guiltily. 'Oh, Bysshe!'

She feels an impotent fury at the ease with which he forgets how desperate their situation really is. As soon as they find another place to live – or gain a little money – he spends it – as though it is of no consequence at all.

'We can't *afford* cake!' she snaps. She can almost taste it, imagines the delicious texture of sugar and melting sponge in her mouth. She is sick with longing and yet fears to complain. The sight of Claire hastily wiping her lips of any further evidence does not help. 'Do you know how much that cake cost,' she asks them as they stand guiltily, like children, before her.

'A penny?' suggests Claire, knowing that that is exactly what it cost, but suspecting that she will somehow have got the answer wrong.

'No,' cries Mary in righteous indignation. 'No, it did not cost us a penny. Because every penny we borrow costs us as much as five or six shillings when we are charged with paying it back!'

'Sorry, sorry, sorry, my elfin!' says Bysshe.

Claire bites her lip. 'I really am sorry, Mary,' she says. 'We should have brought you some back!'

'We shall bring you some!' declares Bysshe. 'Hogg is longing to meet you again, Mary. As soon as he arrives we will send him out for more cake!'

'Oh!' Mary cries in frustration. 'That – is – not – the – point! The point is that we cannot afford it! And we have agreed not to eat sugar, and you know it makes you feel better to avoid it, Bysshe, so why must you do it?'

'We forgot,' says Bysshe quietly. 'It is nice to forget sometimes, Mary. Can you not also forget sometimes?' he asks.

She shakes her head. 'No,' she says truthfully. 'No, I cannot!' But Claire, Mary thinks bitterly to herself, forgets easily – and that is why you so love to spend time with her.

'Shall I light a fire?' Bysshe asks, anxious to please her.

'No!' she says, rising. 'We have to save the coal for when it's colder, and I – I must finish the letter to Papa. I did not mean to sleep.'

He moves to help her.

'Hello!' Hogg's strong voice comes through the door. 'I come bearing coal!' he shouts. Claire goes to let him in.

'You see,' says Bysshe. 'Now I *can* make you a fire!'

'Did Hogg pay for your cake?'

'No,' admits Bysshe, remembering the deliciousness of the forbidden cake, of how he and Claire sat together, carefully choosing which cake it should be before sharing tiny mouthfuls.

'Was he with you?' Mary continues.

'No! We bought it before we met them.'

'So it was just the two of you together,' says Mary.

'Hello!' says Hogg, appearing at the drawing-room door. The two of them turn towards him. 'Have I interrupted something?' he asks gently, looking from face to face.

'Not at all,' says Mary, stepping forward and holding out her hand.

'Oh!' he says awkwardly, his hands full. 'Let me just . . .' He puts the basket down. 'We met before of course, but briefly.

I have heard so much about you!' he says, beginning to blush. 'When you two were parted, Bysshe could talk of nothing else!'

'And I could think of nothing but him.' She glances at Bysshe, remembering.

'We thought he might die for love of you, didn't we?' Hogg says to Claire, who nods, pleased that the memory seems to have lifted Mary's mood.

'Well, I am glad he did not!' laughs Mary.

Hogg realises he is still holding her hand and drops it rapidly. 'Peacock says he will meet us at the Cross Keys at five,' he announces. 'Apparently they do a good supper.'

'Then it is not worth making a fire, is it?' says Mary. 'By the time it catches properly we will be leaving.'

'I am sorry,' says Hogg, 'to hear that you are treated so badly by so many who should be supporting you.'

'Thank you,' says Mary. 'We are prepared to accept such behaviour if it means we can live according to our beliefs: "If one exercises all of one's intelligence to form a complete and just view of the circumstances in which we are placed before making a decision then one shall find that he could not, in any moment of his existence, have acted otherwise."'

'You quote your father,' says Hogg, recognising the words.

'I do, and I live in hope that he will be able to acknowledge that we have acted accordingly, just as we hope that one day perhaps –' she shrugs modestly – 'history might also be on our side.'

Claire sighs. Why must Mary challenge every man she meets with her intellect? 'We have a new plan, Mary,' she says, hoping to divert her. 'Bysshe thinks we should rescue his sisters from their boarding school and flee to Ireland. Perhaps there we might find a community willing to understand our philosophy?'

But Mary ignores her interjection, deep in discussion with the two men. Claire sighs again. Hopefully they will leave soon. It will be warmer at the inn.

7TH OCTOBER 1814: 5 CHURCH TERRACE

Mary tries to sleep but the sound of Claire's delighted screams rising up through the floorboards seem timed to wake her at the precise moment that she loses consciousness. She opens her eyes struggling to light the candle in the dark. Claire utters another piercing scream and then laughs again. 'Shhh!' she hears Bysshe say.

Mary closes her eyes but it brings her no peace. As her pregnancy progresses she finds it harder and harder to ignore the fact that across London there is another child awaiting its birth, and that it belongs to Harriet. Harriet's words continue to haunt her as she lies awake and sleepless: *it does not take a woman of your intelligence to see a pattern here.* And close behind follow her father's: *'you cannot trust a man who is prepared to abandon his wife and child. You can never be sure he will not do the same to you!'*

She wonders if Papa has read her letter and when he will respond. If only they could live at home then Claire and Bysshe could not stay up each night, keeping the household awake. Her papa must answer soon; now that he knows she is with child, surely he will forgive her.

Just as she finally falls asleep, rapid footsteps rattle up the staircase, waking her.

'I cannot calm Claire!' Bysshe says, holding a candle, his hair askew and his anxiety apparent in the twist of his hands. 'She is beside herself!'

'And why might that be?' Mary manages to say sleepily. 'Perhaps it's because you've been terrifying her with stories of dead soldiers who appear to young women with the flayed skin of their backs held in their hands, begging them to return it to their bodies. Maybe that's why she's so scared?'

'Perhaps,' he admits, 'but she says it is something she sees in my face. Do you see anything in me, Mary?'

'I see that you have scared yourself as much as her!'

'She says I have a strange power within me, and that I might make her do anything!'

Mary feels a cold chill of fear. Their games have gone even further than she feared. Claire appears at their door, her face white with overexcitement.

'I can't sleep in my room,' she gasps. 'Some spirit stares at me from the mirror. I can sense it but when I turn to see it there is nothing there. When I turned back to my bed my pillow had been moved. I left it at the head of my bed but it was on the floor!'

Mary is taken aback by how truly terrified she appears. Bysshe should know better. Claire has always been susceptible to such silly fancies. 'Do you not think it likely that your pillow simply fell off your bed?' she asks.

'No!' Claire's eyes search the room as she speaks, staring at thin air. 'Souls wander at midnight, and they inhabit the living!' she whispers, as though some invisible spirit might be listening.

'And you thought Bysshe possessed by such a spirit?' asks Mary.

Claire nods, staring at Bysshe suspiciously.

'He is possessed by silliness,' snaps Mary. 'You both are!'

'But he looked so strange!' Claire gasps.

'As people do when they are tired and overexcited.'

'Truly?' asks Claire doubtfully. 'You don't believe he is possesed?'

'No, he is merely convinced by his own tales.'

'And the spirits do not rise at midnight?'

'Not if you don't encourage them. And Claire, you must stop waking me. I need to sleep.' Mary makes a decision; she will tell Claire that she carries a child. She cannot be kept up each night by their silly games, and perhaps it will bring Claire to her senses, curb her flirting. 'I need rest, Claire,' she says. 'I do not retire each evening because I am boring, nor because

I wish to leave you both to your own devices. I do so because I am with child.'

'Oh! Mary!' Claire cries, followed by a subdued glance at Bysshe who, despite their long hours alone together, has never mentioned Mary's state. 'That is wonderful! I am so sorry – we did not mean to disturb you.'

'Go to bed now, Claire.'

'I will, and I will—' She stops at the door. 'I was going to say that I will pray for you,' she says, 'but of course I cannot pray to a non-existent God can I, I can only wish you well.'

Mary nods at her, too exhausted to speak. 'And you should come to bed too, Bysshe,' she manages.

'What would we do without you, Mary?' he whispers as he climbs in beside her. 'You alone make the world regain its balance.'

Mary feels a sharp twinge in her lower belly and suppresses a groan. 'Claire is not capable of controlling herself, Bysshe,' she says quietly. 'You must stop frightening her.'

'I suppose my sisters were used to it,' he says, happy now that she has contained their fear. Mary listens to his voice, close and comforting. 'Once,' he says as she sinks into his shoulder, able to rest more easily now that he is safe by her side, 'I linked them all together around the kitchen table, each holding a copper wire, just to see what electricity did when it flowed through us all. We felt the power of it simultaneously flowing through our limbs. Poor Helen was thrown back by it, and Elizabeth's hair stood up. What a force it is, Mary; perhaps it is that which sets us all ticking like watches . . . perhaps if we could only harness its power then we might truly ignite the bodies of the dead. It is not blood and bones that that man, Dippel, should have smeared upon the dead to bring them back . . .' His words become a soft, meaningless rhythm that permeates her dreams as she sleeps.

185

23RD OCTOBER 1814: 5 CHURCH TERRACE

Mary hears a gentle knock at the door and leaps up, hoping that it might be a message from her father. A letter lies on the doormat and she bends to pick it up. 'Someone's delivered a letter,' she calls, 'addressed to you, Bysshe!'

Claire and Bysshe rush to the window and spot a small figure disappearing down the street.

'Did you see who it was?' asks Mary.

Bysshe stands at the window. 'It was a woman,' he says. 'But I don't know who. A young woman.'

Mary turns the envelope over in her hands. 'It looks like Fanny's writing!'

'Yes, it could have been her,' says Claire.

Mary hands the letter to Bysshe and the three of them draw close as he opens it: *You are discovered*, it says. *The bailiffs know of your whereabouts!*

'You should go – now!' says Claire, looking around as though the bailiffs might burst through the door at any moment to cart him off to prison.

'But it is late and it is a Sunday,' says Bysshe calmly. 'The bailiffs cannot work from midnight yesterday until midnight today. We are safe until tomorrow morning.'

They stand together in the centre of the small room, unable to sit, ready to flee.

'Who,' ask Mary, dreading the response in case it is her father, 'who do you think has told them of our whereabouts?'

'It does not say, but I suspect Harriet,' says Bysshe.

'I shall go and see her,' says Claire at once. 'Perhaps we can persuade her to drop her claim and stop the bailiffs.'

Bysshe bites his lip as he stares at the letter.

'It is not only Harriet who is on the side of the bailiffs, is it, Bysshe?' sighs Mary. 'Who else is willing to inform upon you?'

'It could be anyone!' he declares angrily. 'You would have to visit Mrs Stewart our last landlady, or perhaps the coachmakers who made the coach that Harriet still likes to drive around the country – and yet has no desire to pay for with the money she has stolen. We are surrounded by creditors! How would I know which one it is that has set the bailiffs upon us?'

'And no hope of a loan?' Mary asks. She has not asked for weeks, holding her fear to herself, refusing to nag as Harriet once did, trusting that he will find them money.

'None yet,' he says, 'but Peacock has hopes of a man named Ballechy. An Irishman.' Mary sits down.

'I am going to Harriet.' Claire gathers her coat before they can object – and is gone.

'It will make no difference,' says Bysshe. 'Harriet is too full of a desire for revenge.'

'Then we have no choice, you must leave us, mustn't you?' Mary says dully. 'Or be found here and face the debtor's prison.'

He nods, mute with fury that not only are they ostracised but that there are those who would rather see him in a debtor's prison and Mary destitute, than allow them to live as they choose.

'But where will you go?' she asks. 'We have no money for an hotel?'

'I will ask Peacock if he can find me somewhere; perhaps I shall stay with him and his mother.'

'But how will we be together?' she asks, as he begins to write Peacock a note 'We cannot be parted for ever, can we?'

'Peacock or Hogg will tell you where we might meet.' He clasps her hand. 'They will look after you, Mary.' She turns her face away from him, hiding her fear that he might be caught and imprisoned. 'Mary,' he whispers, stroking her hair, 'let's not think of the morrow.'

She takes a deep breath. 'Then what should we think of?' she asks.

'Of Lucerne,' he suggests. 'And how bright the stars were there, of how you lay as pale and luminous as the moon beneath them.'

She closes her eyes, concentrating only upon his words, on the feel of his hands upon her and of her longing for time, once more, to stop ticking.

The sound of Claire opening the door rouses them and they rush downstairs. She shakes her head, ignoring their disordered clothes. 'She will not help,' she says.

'Then we must find a cab to take this to Peacock.' Bysshe hands her the note.

Peacock arrives and together they pack Bysshe's small case and a large bag of books.

'We can leave just before midnight. By then my mother will be asleep and you can meet her in the morning,' Peacock suggests, understanding that Bysshe and Mary will want as long as possible together. The last few hours of the evening drag as they sit and wait for the clock to strike eleven thirty. Mary fights to keep her eyes open.

'We should leave London,' says Bysshe. 'We are right to think of a return to Ireland.'

Mary listens, saying nothing, dozing and waking and asking the time. She does not say what she is thinking, which is: what difference would it make in Ireland, we would still have no money – and no time to write – we would remain for ever too busy dodging bailiffs or searching for someone to lend us money. She is almost relieved when the time comes to say goodbye. The two girls stand in the doorway watching Bysshe walk to the end of the street. It is only when he turns the corner and is gone that they look at each other.

'He's gone!' says Mary, the street empty and dark.

'Come in,' says Claire, pulling her arm and closing the door behind them.

Mary wakes with her hand clasping the note that Bysshe has sent to her from his room in Peacock's house:

Oh, my dearest love, why are our pleasures so short and interrupted? How long is this to last? Oh, that those redeeming eyes of Mary might beam upon me before I sleep. Praise my forbearance, beloved one, that I do not rashly fly to you and at least secure a moment's bliss.

They promise to lie in their separate beds each night, imagining that they are in each other's arms before they sleep.

Mary returns to her routines, reading and writing each morning, working hard as a way of holding back her longing for the days to pass and for it to be a Sunday, the one day each week when they can see each other freely, without fear of the bailiffs.

She hopes each day that tonight will be one of those evenings when Hogg knocks upon their door and takes them secretly to an inn where Bysshe sits hidden in the darkest corner. 'He has taken to carrying his pistols with him,' smiles Hogg, 'although whether it is preferable to face prison as a criminal rather than to land up in debtor's prison is debatable.'

'It is not funny!' snaps Mary.

'What isn't funny?' asks Bysshe, kissing her lips as Hogg watches, wondering yet again how his friend has found himself a woman even more enchanting than Harriet.

'The fact that you carry pistols,' says Claire.

'But he would never use them!' laughs Hogg.

'And yet the sight of them might frighten someone else into using theirs!' declares Mary. 'You must give them to me, Bysshe.'

'I would only ever use them as a means to escape,' he explains earnestly. Mary decides she will simply slip them into her bag when he is asleep and hope that he does not notice.

On Sundays they retire to whichever inn has the cheapest rooms.

'We seem destined to find love in the rooms of inns,' he sighs.

'We are outlaws, and I suppose we must make do,' she smiles.

Afterwards they lie face to face across the pillow, alternately sleeping and waking. It is a delight to know that he will definitely be there when she wakes. Often he sits beside the bed reading and watching her sleep. As her eyes open he reads aloud from wherever he is in his own text. At times she asks that he read her Byron's *Thyrsas*; at others he reads the words that he has written just for her: '*My mind without you is as dead and cold as the dark midnight river when the moon is down,*' he quotes softly.

As the hours pass and the time for parting comes closer Mary becomes anxious. Bysshe seems able to forget the passing of time right up to the very moment of parting; each leaving coming upon him anew and greeted with the same sense of unexpected sorrow, but for Mary the clock begins to tick as soon as the sun passes over the horizon and the dark begins to arrive.

'Has Hogg been looking after you properly?' he asks as they lie together.

'Yes,' she says. 'He brings food almost every other day and without him and Peacock we might truly starve. Your friends have been kinder to us than my own family!'

'And he is especially fond of you, Mary, isn't he?'

'Yes, he is kind,' she agrees.

'And that is all you feel for him in return, kindness?'

'What else should I feel?' she asks.

Bysshe places his hand over hers.

'That is not for me to say!' he exclaims. 'But you know that if either of you were to feel more than friendship – if my absence left space for an affection to grow, then you know that I would never stand in your way.'

Mary lifts her hand from under his, wrapping the sheet further up around her body. It is as though Hogg is suddenly in the room with them and she must cover up her nakedness. 'I feel nothing but friendship for him!' she declares.

'Then that is all you feel,' says Bysshe easily, 'but I wanted you to know that you are not bound only to me; that we might begin our new world anywhere, even here in London where we are so reviled.'

'We should get dressed,' says Mary.

Bysshe smiles at her as she rises. 'My moon,' he says, and she wonders how he can so love her and yet not fear sharing her with another.

Back at Church Terrace the conversation plagues her. Does he long for her to love another so that he can be free to be with Claire? Do they still meet, even as Bysshe writes so desperately of his separation from her?

'Do you ever see him when I am not there?' Mary asks.

'At times,' Claire admits.

'You throw yourself at him,' Mary says contemptuously, the fear spilling out of her.

'It is not reasonable of you to speak to me like that!' replies Claire. 'Those are the words of the old world, not the new.'

'Do you care nothing for me?' Mary asks. 'I brought you with us, when I could have left you in Skinner Street.'

'But Mary,' Claire answers calmly, 'you spoke of free love even as you fell in love with him. You claim to share his philosophy. How then can you accuse me of failing you? Even if we should choose to love each other – which we have not.'

'Our philosophy is that we share love as easily as ideas, not lust! And you cannot possibly love him as I do!'

'Mary,' sighs Claire, 'if your love for each other is truly without artifice then why do you not tell him that you want no part of free love – or that you are not sure that you are made for it? Instead you simply complain that I am not good enough – and then ask me to support you, as I always have.'

'Have you?' asks Mary. 'Then why do you take every chance that is offered to be with him, and why did you stay up alone with him each night when I was exhausted with my child and must sleep?'

'Because we are friends,' says Claire, 'and because he teaches me the meaning of his philosophy. I have done nothing wrong, but should we happen to love one another what blame could you reasonably attach to us?'

Mary turns away; she has never felt such rage, except with Claire's mother, who stole her father. And Bysshe, like her papa before him, might so easily fall under the spell of Claire's affections.

Mary wakes each day full of a double dread, fearing both Bysshe's intentions towards Claire and the bailiffs' knock at the door. They can call at any time, and when they do spring themselves upon them she is grateful for Claire's presence.

It is always Claire who opens the door, gaily asking them why they are here, even though she knows quite well why. And it is Claire who follows them around the house as they search it, suggesting that Bysshe might be hiding behind the coving or perhaps between the covers of a book. Would they like to take whatever they have in lieu of the money they owe?' she asks, sweeping her arms over their meagre possessions, unashamed of their circumstances.

If the bailiffs come when Mary is alone then she simply opens the door and continues to stand by it, waiting for them to finish and leave. 'Good day, ma'am,' they say on their way out, almost bowing. When they take their leave of Claire they tip their hats and whistle at her.

Most mornings Hogg brings Mary bread or oatcakes on his way to work. Sometimes they are all she and Claire have to eat, unless they are all able to meet with Peacock and Bysshe in an inn that evening. At times she cannot work, or sleep for hunger. Mary does not eat the food that Hogg brings immediately, hoping to save it until the hunger pangs become unbearable. 'Drinking a lot helps,' she says to Claire.

'Sometimes I dream of biting into meat,' Claire admits.

Bysshe often takes Claire to help him with moneylenders, whilst Mary writes letters to anyone she thinks might offer them aid. But there is nothing.

'You must do something, Mary is with child, Bysshe!' Claire says as they shiver together on the heath. It is hard to walk fast enough to stay warm, yet slowly enough not to bring on faintness from hunger. Mary is too tired to walk with them.

'But I cannot do any more, Claire!' cries Bysshe bitterly. 'Except hope that someone will loan us money. My father refuses to help, and Harriet will not retract her claim. I will find the money, Claire, I have told both Peacock and Hookham that I will accept any rate of interest if they will only find us a loan.'

'*You* should write to Harriet, Bysshe. She does not care what might happen to me or Mary, it is you she still longs for! And only you can explain what a terrible thing she has done!'

'It is not only her. Hookham *chose* to act on her instructions without warning us,' hisses Bysshe. 'He did not have to tell the bailiffs where we were.' He hands Claire one of the cakes he has stolen from Peacock's house. He waits until Mrs Peacock leaves the dining room each morning before putting them in his pockets. He has no idea that she cooks extra, leaving them lying there as she deliberately vacates the room.

'Have you saved some for Mary?' Claire asks.

'Of course! And Mary would not want me to beg Harriet.'

'Mary need not know,' replies Claire. The bulge of the remaining cake in his pocket draws her eyes. She imagines if she could only eat it then she might remember what it feels like to be full. She notices Bysshe pat his pocket every so often as if to reassure himself that it is still there, and that he has not inadvertently given in to his hunger and eaten it.

'Have *you* had one?' Mary asks as soon he offers it to her. He nods and she immediately raises it to her lips. She has never known such hunger before; it is a live thing, feeding on her attention so that as hard as she tries she can think of nothing else.

It is the sight of Mary, humbly eating cake, no longer able to refuse sugar for hunger, that finally drives Bysshe to write to Harriet:

4th November

*D*ear Harriet,

I am perfectly free from danger but so exhausted as to scarcely be able to walk. This however does not matter. I have not a friend in the world who can assist me. Once in prison confined in a damp cell, I must inevitably starve to death. We have sold all that we have to buy bread. I am with a friend who gives me food and lodging, but I think you will shudder to hear that before I could sell the last valuables, Mary and her sister very nearly perished with hunger. My dear Harriet, take pity and send supplies.

Bysshe waits a few days for a reply. There is nothing. 'I will tear out the hearts of those Hookham brothers,' he rages, 'not with my hands, but with sarcasm and irony.'

Claire bites her lip. She'd far rather he killed them with his bare hands and cooked their hearts so they might have something to eat. He disappears upstairs, returning with his microscope in his hands.

'We must sell it. We have nothing else,' he says.

'No, you have had it since your schooldays, Bysshe,' says Mary, trying to pull it fom his hands. 'You cannot!' she cries, for the things he sees through the slides fill him with such wonder and delight.

'We must, Mary.' He holds it from her and though she tries to take it from him she has no strength. Just the slightest pull causes a twinge deep and low in her side, causing her to sit down suddenly.

Bysshe and Claire take the microscope to Skinner Street, in the hope that the local pawnshop might favour Claire as a former neighbour.

'Come on hard times, have you?' Mr Davison the shopkeeper sneers. 'Aren't you the gentleman who bought the two young ladies?' he says with a suggestive sneer to Bysshe.

'Do you want it or not?' snaps Claire, pushing the microscope towards him across the counter as she pinches Bysshe's arm hard.

'Come back in half an hour,' the shopkeeper says, determined to make them suffer in their shame. They walk along the road away from number forty-one, towards Chatham Place, pacing the square, not wanting to be seen.

'I do not think I can stay on my feet for much longer,' whispers Claire, holding tight to his arm. 'I have had nothing since breakfast. Has that man no pity?'

'What pity should he have for us?' asks Bysshe. 'Do we even think of him at all unless we are in need?'

When they return Davison holds out five pounds.

'Thank you,' says Bysshe, reaching for it. Davison lifts it away from him, making him stretch.

Furious, Claire snatches the money from his fingers. 'Perhaps one day you will be in want yourself,' she says. 'Indeed I very much hope that it is so!'

They buy coal and candles on the way home, and take Mary to the Cross Keys. Mary eats slowly, the food landing heavy in her shrunken gut.

'Mary?' Bysshe asks.

She leans against him. 'I am not hungry any more,' she whispers. 'I think I have forgotten how to be!' She laughs, but her eyes are dim. The pain in her side deepens. 'You eat it,' she says pushing her plate away. She cannot bear the idea of being full again, only to face the hollow hunger once more, when the money runs out.

As if he can read her mind Bysshe says, 'No, Mary, you eat. When this money runs out I shall sell the pistols.'

'But they are the very last thing,' says Mary, 'and when they are gone?'

6TH NOVEMBER 1814: 5 CHURCH TERRACE, ST PANCRAS
The twinge in Mary's side is worse this morning. She lies unmoving, waiting patiently for it to pass before she can rise and dress. She has become used to the pain, the dull ache of it always by her side. She should get up and see if Papa has

responded to her letter. He is their only hope. She would like to point out to her father that when he was in financial despair it was Bysshe who saved him. Will he not do the same for them? She has not heard from Izy either. She does not understand why Izy fails to reply to her letters. The girl she once knew would surely find a way to disobey her husband if she did not agree with him. Mary falls asleep again as she so often does these days, avoiding the hunger. When she wakes the house has that peculiar quiet that means it is empty. Perhaps Hogg will have left some bread downstairs.

On the table Claire has left two letters. With a leap of hope she notices that the first has a Dundee postmark, and rips it open.

Dear Mary,

We have heard from your father and Mrs Godwin, and I am sorry to have to inform you that you can no longer expect any further communication from my wife.

Yours,
David Booth Esq

She blinks, and reads again before allowing the letter to fall through her fingers, unable to believe that Izy has not had the decency to write to her herself. It is only then that she notices the handwriting of her father upon the other letter. She reaches for it. It feels light. She cannot bear to open it straightaway but carries it upstairs, nursing her hope as she climbs back into bed. It is cold in the house. Hogg has promised he will bring more coal. She holds the letter briefly to her chest before opening it.

There is only one page with but a brief two sentences written upon it.

Mary – you mistake sophistry for argument. All that is required is for you to both acknowledge and rectify your mistake.

Your
Papa

The shock of the words runs through her whole body. Now they have nothing. No hope of money and nothing to sell. She must find Bysshe. And tell him it has not worked. They must knock on the door of Skinner Street and show Papa how destitute they are. Surely the sight of her will evoke his pity.

She lifts herself out of bed. At first she thinks she must have wet herself. A flood of hot childish shame runs through her as she looks down and realises it is not urine but a trickle of deep red blood dripping down her thigh. She knows at once that her baby is in danger and yet cannot immediately take it in, nor feel it to be real.

'Jane!' She does not sit for fear of soiling the bed. 'Claire!' she calls out, before remembering that she is alone.

She falls to her knees and crawls to the chamber pot where she cleans herself up and sees that the bleeding has stopped. She sits with her head in her hands. 'Mamma,' she whispers, 'if you are there, if you can hear me, please, please help me. I do not know what to do.'

The answer comes to her immediately. She must call for Mrs Knapp, the midwife who attended Mary's own birth and who still lives in the Polygon. Mary rises and dresses, a part of her mind alert and unable to rest, waiting for that telltale trickle. She does not know whether she should go and find Mrs Knapp or whether she should sit still and wait until Claire returns.

By lunchtime she is pale with fear. There is no more blood but whenever she goes to the privy it appears again. She decides that she can wait no longer; she must find a carriage and go to Mrs Knapp herself. She must know what is wrong; perhaps her anxiety as she sits and waits is as dangerous to her baby as the act of walking. She finds her coat and stands on the doorstep; carriages roll up the street, people walk by as though nothing at all has happened and the knowledge that the world still turns, unaware of the terrible change in her body steadies her a little. Almost immediately she sees Hogg walking towards the house – a bag in his hands.

'Hogg!' she calls.

'Mary!' He rushes towards her.

'Oh, Jefferson!' He is touched by her use of his forename.

'What is it?' he asks, wondering why she is standing so stiffly.

'I think the baby is in danger.'

He comes to her at once, holding her arms and opening the door, guiding her to the sofa and offering her tea.

'I haven't eaten,' she remembers.

He brings bread and cheese out of his bag, making tea so rapidly and efficiently that she smiles at the comparison with Bysshe; who might begin to make tea and then wander away to look up something in a book. The relief of no longer being alone is immense.

'Thank you,' she says as she begins to eat. He has put sugar in the tea and she is about to refuse it but finds she cannot, for the feel of it in her body is too reviving.

'Don't move,' says Hogg. 'I'll find Shelley.'

'Yes please.' She makes a decision. 'But first, will you go to the Polygon and find a Mrs Knapp, tell her I need her. Mary Godwin, make sure she knows it is me!' He nods and is gone. As soon as she hears the door close Mary lies down and closes her eyes. The bliss of having him take over is overwhelming.

'Bed rest,' says Mrs Knapp, once she has fed Mary from her own pocket. 'As soon as you feel or see a spot of blood you come up here and lie down; it's either that or risk losing your baby.'

Mary nods. 'Did my mother die from . . .?'

'No,' Mrs Knapp snaps before Mary can finish. 'Your mamma was as healthy as a horse with you. She didn't miss a day's work; although writing isn't really work as such, is it? I mean, in the sense that it doesn't challenge the body. All in the mind, isn't it?' Mary nods from her position high up on the pillows, which Mrs Knapp has been around the rooms gathering up into one place so that Mary is comfortable. 'Just sit, and read or embroider and let your mind drift, that's the thing,' she is saying. 'Babies like their mothers to let their minds drift and their bodies rest.' She is not at all impressed with Mary's diet. 'Your first principle should be your baby, not some black slaves in a godforsaken country you've never even visited!' she says. 'Your mamma was the same, always had her mind upon others, but it didn't seem to make any difference to her until—'

'Will you tell me how she died?' asks Mary quietly. 'No one has told me.'

'Well, it was Dr Lawrence who attended her mostly, although she personally didn't believe men knew a thing about babies and their delivery. It was your father brought him in.'

Mary listens. Mrs Knapp can see her mother in her, but to the ageing midwife Mary is a child having a child. Looking at her lying in bed she doesn't look a day over thirteen.

Mrs Knapp would like to spank Godwin for treating his child so badly. The house is a mess, full of books and papers and no proper food. It's too cold and the beds not cleaned recently enough.

'Do you have a maid?' she asks.

Mary shakes her head.

'Well, you'll need help when it's born.'

'I have my sister.'

'Yes, I heard she was with you. A flighty thing, is she any good?'

'She is quite practical,' allows Mary. 'My mother?' she asks gently.

Mrs Knapp sits down and takes her hand. 'So,' she asks, 'are you one of those women who frets if you aren't told the truth, or are you a woman who gnaws at the truth once she has it, worrying away at it so it would have been better not to know?'

Mary considers a while. 'The first, I think.'

'I think so too, but no harm in confirming.' She rubs Mary's hand as she speaks and the thought that the same hand once held her mother, touched her and spoke to her, fills Mary with comfort. It has always been men, Mary realises, who have spoken about her mother: Coleridge, or Southey, or her own father. Even Shelley. The women who knew her mamma best have long since been banished.

'Your mother bled too, but not when she was carrying,' says Mrs Knapp. 'It was after she gave birth. There's not much we can do with that. I always try henbane, and we did try, because your mother insisted. She was a strong woman, Mary. She never doubted, until the very end, that she would survive. She was so proud to have another girl. "I was made to be a woman, to have girls and to support women!" she said. And she'd already saved your sister's life, so of course she believed

201

that she could save herself too. She was not sorrowful if that's what you wonder, not at all.'

Mary nods.

'And she knew you were healthy!' The old woman smiles at the memory. 'You arrived all wrapped up in your caul, and when we broke you out you looked up so curious we both laughed aloud and so the first sound you ever heard was me and your mother laughing!'

Mary does not move, frightened the woman might stop, longing for the story to go on and on; for as long as the woman is talking her mother is there, beside them both. Sensing her need Mrs Knapp continues.

'Did you know that Fanny had typhus in France. Everyone told your mother to wrap her up and keep the house warm, but she said it didn't feel right when Fanny was so hot, and so she kept all the windows open and took her out twice a day. She barely slept for feeding her every time she wailed, and believe me typhus babies cry a lot, but she did what felt right to her and she saved her, and she was determined she could do the same for herself. But she couldn't; sometimes we can't, however much we might want to.'

There's a silence in the room as the old woman remembers, gathers herself for the final telling.

'She knew at the end that she had no choice. She held you and looked into your eyes and said goodbye. Not one part of her wanted to leave you but we could not stop the bleeding or the fever. She asked your father to raise you as she would have, but he . . . he doesn't have her warmth,' she manages, aware that criticising her father will not help Mary. 'She did not want to leave you, Mary, and her bleeding is not your bleeding. Bleeding after is a different thing, so don't you worry yourself about that.'

Still Mary says nothing.

'It's a gentle death,' Mrs Knapp almost whispers, 'a slipping away that allows for goodbyes.' Mary's hand does not relinquish its grip and the two women sit for a while in silence. 'Neither of you wanted to let each other go,' the woman says, and at those words Mary's hand finally releases. She sits on the bed, tearless.

And that's the way it takes some children, thinks the woman; losing a mother so young can freeze over the soul, and it can only be released by another love; be it a man or a child – or sometimes never at all.

There's a loud banging and clattering up the stairs.

'Mary!' Bysshe flies to her side and Mary's eyes lift to his. The old midwife sees it then, that glance; that look from eye to eye, an invisible string connecting them both, the look that mirrors so clearly the love between mother and child. She stands up.

'Well, I'll leave you two to it.' She turns to Bysshe. 'She needs meat, and perhaps some stout. Babies live off their mother's blood so it needs to be rich.'

He nods. 'Anything!' he cries. 'I'll cook it myself.'

Mary smiles. I hope not, she thinks, suddenly overcome by a violent longing for one of Mrs Baxter's meat pies, rich with lamb and served with gravy.

That night Bysshe visits Hookham. 'Tell the Irishman again that he can charge me any amount he likes, only he must give me a loan,' he cries.

Hookham stands behind his door, holding it close so that Bysshe cannot enter, terrified by the wild desperation of him. He is so thin he seems barely able to stand and yet the fury in him blazes. Hookham has no doubt that if Bysshe had not already sold his pistols he would be threatening him with them.

'I have a child's life resting upon it,' he cries. 'Are you so heartless that you would be responsible for the death of Mary and our child? We have sold everything, and must lose life itself if you fail to aid us now.' He pushes his way into the house. Hookham walks as calmly as he can to his study, where he stands behind his desk, Bysshe following. 'And it is you who have placed us here. That we should die penniless –' he laughs aloud and Hookham holds hard to the desk – 'when you know without a doubt that at some point I shall inherit!'

'Yes, yes, you must go to Mary,' Hookham soothes, 'and we will definitely find something.'

'Now!' yells Bysshe. 'Or I shall buy back my pistols!'

The next day Peacock tells him that Hookham has arranged a loan of five hundred pounds.

9TH NOVEMBER 1814: FROM 5 CHURCH TERRACE TO 2 NELSON SQUARE, BLACKFRIARS, LONDON

'Five hundred?' asks Mary. 'Five hundred pounds?'

Bysshe nods.

She cannot believe it, cannot help the tears of relief slipping out from under her eyes. 'Oh, Bysshe! It means we might move?' she whispers.

'It means we might eat!' he laughs.

Mary orders a beef and oyster pie at the Cross Keys every night for a week. She cannot eat enough of them.

'Harriet could never eat enough cake when she was carrying Ianthe,' says Bysshe. There is a short silence around the table.

'I shall begin to search for a house tomorrow,' Mary announces. She sits back, her belly full. 'Somewhere the bailiffs cannot find us!'

The house they move to is only eight years old. It has a bright stone fire surround and tall windows that look out across the square. Mary can imagine bringing a child into this home. She feels her body relax in the gracious rooms. They have chosen curtains, and books. They have an embroidered cover for the foot of their bed, and they heap the fire up whenever they choose, keeping the house as warm as they desire. They burn a fire in their bedroom and have candles everywhere.

'You must pay off the creditors, Bysshe,' says Mary. 'As soon as you can.'

'But why waste it on them,' he asks, 'when we do not know when we will next find more money? Once I inherit, the estate will settle our debts.'

'But Bysshe, your grandfather might live for years! And until then we will ever have the bailiffs after us!'

'And we will inevitably be able to move!' he replies. 'For I shall borrow against my inheritance at whatever rate it takes. I shall borrow until my father's estate is worth nothing,' laughs Bysshe. 'It will take us a lifetime to work our way through it, will it not? And with this five hundred we have the resources to build our new world,' he says, throwing his arm around Mary's shoulder. 'And Hogg can stay with us as often as he chooses now, for we have room for him and we must welcome him for we could not have survived without his help.'

'Yes!' agrees Mary. 'He must come often.' But her heart sinks at the thought of it, of the knowledge that Bysshe might still hope that she finds love with his friend.

*D*ear *Izy,*

I am alone in the house. I am often alone as my baby cannot seem to hold tight to my insides and so I must often rest. Claire and Bysshe walk long in the evenings, talking of how we shall one day be seen as pioneers. Claire imagines a world where women live free of all restraint. She is reading James Lawrence, whose thinking, to my mind, is not at all about female freedom, but only of how he might persuade women to be used by men for their own pleasure.

Dear Izy, by my side there lies a letter; it is addressed to Bysshe in Harriet's hand, and I feel I must open it yet cannot bear to open it alone, and so even though I know you cannot reply I write to you, so that I feel I have someone near me.

I shall open it now.

It is as I expected. The letter tells Bysshe that Harriet has been delivered of a boy . . .

As she writes, Mary hears the key in the door and the sound of Hogg's voice calling.

'Hello!'

'Hogg!'

'Oh, Mary, are the others out? I've brought you some pheasant; a friend shot it!' He stands in the hallway, holding the dead bird and looking so pleased with himself that Mary cannot help but smile.

'We have no one to cook it!'

'They'll cook it at the Keys if we ask nicely.'

'Hogg?'

'Yes.'

'We have had a letter from Harriet.'

Hogg's eyes widen. 'She is delivered safely?' he says anxiously, and Mary is reminded that he once knew her well, and of the rumour that he loved her.

'Yes. She has had a boy. They have named him Charles.'

'Oh!' He looks so ridiculous standing there, caught between his relief for Harriet and his desire not to offend Mary, that she takes pity upon him.

'Put that thing in the yard,' she says. He does as he is told. When he returns he comes to her at once.

'It is hard news for you, Mary,' he says.

'I suppose we must ring the bells loud and celebrate, for unto Harriet an heir is born. An heir to his *legitimate* wife!'

'Shall we walk?' asks Hogg, reaching for her elbow. 'Are you feeling well enough?'

They turn about the small square.

'You know that Bysshe does not care for legality, nor for his inheritance – you know that, do you not?'

Mary nods. 'But Harriet's child will have everything and yet mine—' She does not finish; it feels wrong to care so deeply that her own child will have no rights at all. What rights do the children of the poor have, and what right does she have to claim more? That is what Bysshe might say.

'You have not chosen an easy path, Mary,' Hogg says gently.

Mary looks at him; he is little more than a shadow in the dark. 'No,' she replies, 'we have not.'

'You must know that he will never abandon you,' he says.

Mary says nothing. He abandoned Harriet.

'And perhaps,' continues Hogg, 'one of the joys of our community lies not only in the sharing of ideas, or love, but in the sharing of children. Your child will have the love of all of us, not just of two parents, but of many.'

'Perhaps we could go in now,' suggests Mary. 'I am a little cold.'

Mary stands by the window. Beyond the glass people stroll through the square. She is amazed by how easily they flow along together; like a shoal of fish, she thinks, all moving in the same direction, all with the same beliefs and the same unspoken understanding.

But she is set apart; she is different. How, she wonders, could she ever have spoken so proudly of the ideas that now cause her such a terrible sense of despair. Bysshe leaves her alone with Hogg as often as he can, taking Claire on long walks. Mary thinks of the girl she once was, flying down the street, revelling in her difference. But the reality of a life set apart from others is not as she expected. When she ventures out into the square to walk, it feels as though the people she passes remain a race apart. She remembers walking in the park with Bysshe and Claire a mere six months earlier and feeling such pity for anyone who was not them, but now . . . although she would never admit it to anyone, she sometimes feels such an overwhelming envy at the joy of ordinary people that she longs to reach out and touch them, the way she might touch some precious ornament or artefact in a museum, with an intense longing to possess it whilst knowing it is not possible. She can never again be a member of their clan, never feel their sense of belonging. She has set herself beyond them. She wonders if this is how her mother felt.

'When you look at people,' she says to Hogg, 'do you ever wonder whether the freedoms they give up in exchange for belonging might be worth the choice?' In spite of herself she is coming to like him more and more; his close attention to her reminds her of how easily she once charmed everyone, of how there was a time in her life when she assumed that it would always be so. That feels foolish now. She can see that Claire had no such illusions, was wiser in that she knew exactly what she was giving up in leaving Skinner Street. Claire does not seem to regret their social isolation at all. Why would she? thinks Mary bitterly, letting the curtain drop; she has Bysshe to herself more often than I do these days.

And Bysshe seems determined that there will be free love amongst them – should they choose. 'Perhaps,' he suggests to Mary, 'being with Hogg might relieve you of your sorrow for the loss of your father. And Izy. He is such a good friend to you.'

Hogg watches as Mary looks out through the window. It is easy to forget that she is with child, for she wears the loose easy clothes her mother recommended for women with child. He remains entranced by her. She has a cool, contained reserve that seems to break only when she is with Bysshe. Hogg lives for those moments when something he says engages Mary or makes her laugh. He does not know if she might love him. But he hopes.

'I sometimes wonder,' he says, 'how lonely it must have felt for Mary, becoming pregnant with Jesus. We have not changed much, have we?'

Mary smiles; she has told him of Izy's comparison of Mary riding on a donkey and finding no room at the inn. 'He too was ostracised, and yet the whole world acknowledges him now!' she says. 'Perhaps, it will be like that for us – that we will die unrecognised only to find understanding once we are gone and can no longer enjoy it.' The thought makes her shudder.

'What troubles you?' asks Hogg, leaning towards her. Mary feels herself withdraw. She can sense his fascination with her, his constant search for the chinks in her love of Bysshe. She both longs for and enjoys his attention but wishes it only to go so far. She sighs inwardly; it is hard work maintaining his interest at exactly the right level. She feels a flash of anger at

Bysshe for leaving her alone with Hogg so often – before immediately berating herself; she is thinking like a woman who cannot manage without a man to protect her. Hogg offers her an oatcake. She shakes her head. She does not want an oatcake. She wants a proper cake, a cake full of sugar and currants and butter, but she has given up sugar once more. What is wrong with me? she wonders. Why do I find it so hard to live according to the principles we have chosen when Claire and Bysshe seem to so easily thrive upon them?

It's a relief to hear the sound of Bysshe's key in the door. 'Hello!' shouts Claire.

'Hogg!' Bysshe says delightedly as he enters the room. Hogg stands and they embrace.

'We've been talking of James Lawrence's book,' Claire says, coming into the room. She is glowing, the colour high in her cheeks. Mary cannot stop looking at her waist; it seems so impossibly tiny, she cannot believe that her own was ever so small. 'I started reading it in the carriage on the way home!' Claire sits on a chair opposite Hogg, turning her attention upon him.

'I haven't read it,' he says.

'I have,' snaps Mary, 'and it is nonsense! He believes that female freedom should be expressed in the right to behave like animals.'

'But we are animals, Mary,' says Bysshe mildly. 'Only animals that have the capacity to reflect upon our actions and to learn from them, should we ever be brave enough to choose to do so!'

'But the lack of marriage between two people,' she replies tartly, 'does not suggest that love is no longer for the purpose of procreation, or that it is not sacred?'

'Of course it is sacred.' He kneels by her side, reaching for her hand. 'It is just that it need not be exclusive.'

Mary's heart sinks, for she has nothing to answer him with, and yet feels with all her heart that it cannot be right. She does not want to share him with Claire, just as she did not want to share her father with Claire's mother.

'Lawrence,' suggests Claire, 'does not even believe that love must necessarily accompany desire.' All three of them turn to look at her. She raises an eyebrow and laughs. 'It is not me who declares it to be thus!' she laughs. 'I am only repeating what I have read!'

'Again I ask,' hisses Mary, 'if that is the case then what is left to place us above animals?'

But no one answers her. She must talk to Bysshe about Claire's behaviour. It is obvious that her stepsister does not understand the true meaning of free love, and it is well past the time when Bysshe should explain to her that it is not about lust, but love.

14TH DECEMBER 1814: HAMPSTEAD HEATH

Bysshe and Claire walk along the familiar paths of the heath towards the ponds, the cold ground crunching beneath them.

'Mary has asked me to talk to you out of concern for some of your beliefs!' Bysshe begins.

Claire pulls a face and he finds it hard to keep his own expression stern. She is an excellent mimic, reflecting his own expression back at him, the false furrow in his brow as he prepares himself to be firm with her. His lips quiver, as does his resolve. Sometimes he wishes he could drink her.

'Mary's angry with me,' she says, 'and the main reason she's angry with me is that we are spending so much time together!'

And yet she drives you into my arms by asking you to explain my failings to me. Do you not think I already know them?'

'Then what are they?'

'I am too impulsive. If I can laugh rather than cry I will, and when life hits me hard I slap it back, just like my mother. I am uncouth and unphilosophical, all these things are true. Yet Mary fails to acknowledge my biggest sin, doesn't she?'

'Which is?

'That I am far more your disciple than she can ever be,' she challenges.

'You're wrong,' he cries. 'She is my soul, Claire.'

'Am I wrong? Or are you only seeing what you long to see?'

Bysshe turns and begins to walk. He cannot bear to hear Mary criticised, but Claire cannot stop herself. Bysshe does not see the same Mary that she does and that no longer surprises her, for as she grows, Claire is beginning to realise that there are many different selves one might have. With Bysshe, Mary is her best self; with Claire her worst.

'Sometimes,' she snaps, at him, 'you are completely, wilfully blind!'

'What do you mean?' he asks, bemused by her irritation.

'She does not want to share you, Bysshe. She cannot – it's not in her nature. Her own mother did not really long to share herself with her lover but only offered to because she was afraid of losing him.'

'No, Claire, Mary is right, you presume too far and perhaps attribute your own base motives to a woman you adore yet fail to understand!'

Claire turns on her heel, storming away from him.

Sighing, he goes after her. 'Claire?'

She does not stop until she is ready. 'I do not attribute my own feeling to others,' she says calmly. 'In fact, it is you and Mary who choose to see only what fits with your own ideals, just as her father does. Mary Wollstonecraft was desperate and alone, so in love with a man who did not want her that she made a proposal that she share him – it was her only hope. It was not a choice. Oh, Bysshe –' she holds her hands out to him – 'can't you see that some women can only ever love one man, and they will share him if they must, whilst others can never love only one man, but search always for another, and another. That is what I think, and I am not ignorant, I have read Wollstonecraft and Lawrence. I have listened to you, and I know that I am a woman who can take love where she finds it – like my own mother. Only unlike her I am lucky enough not to have to marry.'

'No, you do not,' he agrees, enjoying her fury.

'And I am beginning to believe that there is more than one way to be a woman,' she goes on. 'Mary is one type and I am another. I am sick of feeling myself to be wrong, of always being told I should be more like her. She is *your* vision of perfection, Bysshe, not mine!'

'I have never claimed there's anything wrong with you being you,' Bysshe cries, forgetting the many times that he has done Mary's bidding in taking her to task over her behaviour, and trying to mould her differently. 'That's as stupid as saying a flower shouldn't be orange, or the grass green. You're made that way!'

Despite her anger Claire is stunned, expecting a denial at best or a further reprimand. 'Really?' she asks.

'Yes,' he laughs. 'You're like a storm. You're all dark clouds and fury and then a second later – sunshine. Mary's different. Her pain is like a dark river that runs all the way through her. You cannot help it and neither can she.'

'And in what ways does the perfect Mary have to change?' Claire asks.

'She has to manage the loss of her father,' Bysshe says, 'the rejection of her closest friend and the failure of so many she thought once loved her to intercede on her behalf. And she has to manage her fear of losing our baby, and Harriet having my heir. She has given up everything for me, Claire. Is that not enough?'

'I'm sorry.' Claire grasps his hand – immediately and impulsively full of sorrow for her sister. 'It is too much. She is extraordinary!' And she means every word, just as she means what she does not say, which is that Bysshe has failed yet again to mention the one thing that causes more sorrow to Mary than any of the many things he has mentioned, and that is that he will never be a man who can love only one woman – and that he expects her to feel the same way. To practise free love.

'Do you think that she will return Hogg's desire?' Claire asks, returning to their most oft-held conversation.

'Love,' says Bysshe rapidly. 'Return his love.'

'So you agree then with Mary, that desire is only legitimate if it is linked with love?' she asks, enjoying his look of surprise at the question. She is often taken aback by Bysshe's delicacy, his innate purity.

'Yes,' he says slowly, 'I do.'

'But what if it is not?' she asks. 'What if a woman were to feel desire without love – or is that a step too far for your philosophy? Why do we deny a woman's right to a desire without love? Is that not what men do?' she asks. She is thinking of her own mother now, who wrote no fine words and yet felt free enough to join with a man for the sheer joy of the act. Claire can imagine it because she can feel it in herself, the look that is held a fraction too long and the suggestion of something more. Bysshe might dress it up in fine ideals, tie it tight with ribbons of philosophy, but there are plenty of streets in London where

214

free love happens without any philosophy surrounding it at all, and the fact that neither he nor Mary ever acknowledge such poverty-stricken truths is beginning to irritate Claire.

'Is this what Mary fears in you?' he asks. 'You know, Claire, that we might read Lawrence and consider him, but I believe in free love, not free desire. Mary and Hogg might love each other, or you and I, and if it *includes* desire then that is what we practise—'

'I think,' interrupts Claire, 'that my own mother felt desire rather than love. I hope one day that women will not be censured for allowing such feelings to flourish. Why is it, Bysshe, that you – a man – should decide how I – a woman – might feel? Am I not allowed to experiment with the boundaries of my own freedom?' Claire has lain alone at night carefully crafting each word to appeal specifically to him and him alone.

'And what do you desire?'

'You!' she laughs. 'Who else? I have desired you from the very first day I saw you. Fanny and I used to sit in bed and scheme to be alone with you!'

'Did you?'

'Yes, you idiot.'

Bysshe stares at her. He has imagined that he was carefully building his community of like-minded souls – believers in free love – and that any pairing with Claire would come about quite naturally once Mary has decided that she might love Hogg. He did not expect a declaration now.

'You see,' Claire laughs, 'even you – who talk so well of freedom – seem undone by a woman who actually lives by it.'

'That's true!' he says, startled.

She takes his hand. 'Perhaps, 'she says, 'when the right moment arrives it will be me who is seducing you!'

Bysshe gazes at her with something approaching admiration.

CHRISTMAS DAY 1814: 2 NELSON SQUARE

'Thank goodness Christmas Day is a Sunday!' says Mary anxiously, looking out of the window. 'Or do you think that as it is Christmas it might not count and the bailiffs could still come?

'Sit down!' says Hogg, coming to the window to guide her away. 'And stop worrying. If they come for him today we will either pay them or fight them off together whilst he escapes out of the window. Have you never seen Bysshe slip down a drainpipe or climb a tree to enter a window? At Oxford he was known for it.' He has been quite free with the wine, as have Claire and Bysshe.

Mary's own glass remains barely touched; the taste does not agree with her. She has made each of them a small handkerchief, embroidered in her beautiful small stitches with their initials. Shyly she hands them around.

'Oh!' says Claire. 'Thank you!' She did not expect a gift, and is glad she has bought something for Mary. She rushes upstairs, returning with a small box. 'It is only small,' she warns.

Mary opens it. Inside sits a cake, a small currant cake. The smell rises out of the box. 'Oh!' she sighs. 'It is so exactly what I have longed for!' Claire blushes with delight. 'But I cannot eat it,' says Mary. 'I cannot.'

'Mary!' all three of them cry together. 'It's Christmas!'

'What Christmas do the slaves have?' she replies.

'Surely even slaves have a day off,' says Hogg.

'I imagine they are busy serving dinner!' says Mary tartly. 'Not eating cake.'

'And after they have served dinner,' says Hogg, lifting the cake from the box and holding it up to her, 'they will eat the remains with a pudding far greater than this little cake! Open up,' he demands, holding the cake steady at her lips.

'No!' She pushes it away. 'The thought of the gift is enough. Truly, Claire, thank you!'

'Elegantly said!' says Bysshe, but each of them feels belittled by her self-denial.

'I hope you will at least eat the food I have bought!' says Hogg.

Mary nods; she can smell the pie, and her stomach grumbles at the thought of the rich meat. She cannot wait – she would like to eat the whole thing. 'In fact,' she says, joining into the spirit, 'I think I shall have extra, as I will have no pudding!'

'You shall!' Hogg agrees. As they sit he cuts her a full half of the pie and she does not stop him. She eats every last morsel, slowly savouring the pastry, the rich gravy, but most of all the taste of meat. They eat in silence, enjoying the food.

'In Scotland they have the guisarts at Christmas,' says Mary, when they've finished. 'They come in dressed in white, like ghosts! And you must give them sup and ale before they leave, or your house will be unlucky for the whole year!'

'And what do they do, the guisarts?' asks Claire. 'Do they sing or dance?'

Mary blushes. 'Oh!' she says. 'They sing – a rhyme of nonsense.'

'What is it, Mary,' they all call at once, 'that makes you blush so, tell us?'

She shakes her head smiling. 'I can't remember!' she claims, pressing her lips together as she smiles.

'You have a flawless memory,' claims Bysshe, 'but are embarrassed, dormouse!'

'Would you rather not say?' asks Hogg gently. 'There is no need if you do not want to.'

Mary stands up at once and begins to recite:

> *'I saw roast upon rungs,*
> *tits upon tongues,*
> *ladies pissing, spanish needles, ten ells lang;*
> *auld wives flying in the air, like the peelings o' onions*
> *swine playing upo' bagpipes;*
> *cats gaun upon pattens,*
> *and hens drinking ale!'*

She lifts her glass and they follow her action, each supping deeply. 'And then they each take out a glove,' she says, lifting her own carefully embroidered handkerchief, 'and place it on the table with their partner's . . .'

The others each lift their kerchiefs, following her actions. Mary drops her handkerchief on to the middle of the table, remembering Izy describing how she had longed for David to place his glove on top of hers, ashamed of the feeling because he belonged to her sister. Hogg places his kerchief rapidly on top of Mary's and Bysshe follows with Claire's landing last. They sit in a pile together. Mary slips hers out from underneath before sitting down. Perhaps, she thinks, even one glass of wine was too much. She did not mean to give Hogg yet another chance to suggest that there might be more than a friendship between them.

On New Year's Day Hogg brings another dinner for them. Mary is tired. Christmas felt miserable without her father, without her usual whispered conversation with the portrait of her mother. She has had another bout of bleeding, and longs to go to bed. Bysshe rises almost as soon as they have eaten, suggesting that he and Claire might take a walk. Mary stands at once, sensing that this has been arranged between the three of them.

'No!' says Bysshe gently. 'There is no need to come with us. You must rest!'

Mary sits down opposite Hogg, who seems anxious. 'I hope you don't mind if I lie down and rest,' she says, rising again as soon as Bysshe and Claire are gone. She does not want to be alone with Hogg. She can feel his resolve building towards some kind of declaration. She stands and rushes to the stairs.

'Come and sit by the fire for a moment, Mary,' he calls to her. She stops for a moment with her back towards him, wondering if she might summon the courage enough to be rude and to pretend that she has not heard him. But what if, in his determination, he were to follow her upstairs. No, she must sit down and try to manage it as best she can. She turns and sits by the fire, carefully tucking in her skirts around her, as though they might protect her.

'Mary,' he begins.

She nods, staring into the fire.

'You cannot have failed to notice what regard I have for you?' She nods again. 'In the hours we have spent alone together, I have . . . I have –' she does not help him, but cannot resist a glance. He is staring at her deeply, wiping his face with his kerchief – 'developed such a deep regard for you, that I think it is not unreasonable to name it, and to call it love.'

A coal turns over in the grate. Mary takes a breath. She cannot pretend that it is not a pleasure to feel that she has entranced somebody, but *love*. That is something she feels only for Bysshe. Hogg is staring at her, waiting.

'Does Bysshe know?' she asks eventually. 'Have you discussed your feelings with him?' She hopes against hope that he has not, but Hogg nods and smiles. Mary feels her heart slip down through her body at his answer. So this *has* been planned between them.

'You are surprised?' he asks.

She nods again. 'You are so kind,' she manages, 'and of

course we have not known each other long. I'm afraid, in my present state, I did not expect a declaration.'

'I thought that Shelley might have let you know!' he says.

She shakes her head. He should have. He should have warned me, she thinks angrily, but only says: 'He is too scrupulous, and would feel that any declaration must be between us only.' But she no longer believes in the words she speaks, for what is such delicacy worth when he has clearly discussed the idea with the others – only not with her.

'Than I am sorry,' says Hogg, at once solicitous, 'for you do not need such surprises in your condition.'

She is touched, in spite of herself, by his kindness. 'Is there any more that I should know?' she asks, aiming to keep her voice light, for she is desperate to know if Bysshe has the same plans for himself and Claire.

'Is my love not enough?' He laughs, denying his hurt that she has said nothing about returning his feelings. He has risen and is holding out his hands to her. She gives her own hands up to him. He has a pleasant touch, but there is no part of her that longs to feel his hands move further; or his lips come closer.

'I mean,' she says slowly, raising her eyes to his, 'are we meant to be a four? Are the things people say of us to become truth, that Claire and I are shared!' She manages a smile.

Hogg looks at her, sensing her reluctance – not he hopes, towards him, but perhaps in sharing Shelley. 'He has not said,' he replies.

'And why should he?' she says lightly. 'For we are bound only in as much as we wish to be, and no further.' He nods, but says nothing, forcing her to speak further. She feels ridiculous holding his warm hands in front of the fire and can bear it no longer. 'I am flattered and moved,' she says truthfully, 'but also overwhelmed. I must rest.' She laughs a little shakily. 'In my condition even a pleasant surprise can be tiring.'

'Of course.' He lets go of her hands and she turns rapidly away, the tears already forming in her eyes. As she reaches the door he calls her name. 'Mary?' She turns. 'I need, I hope, I mean . . . I mean to say, you cannot imagine how much your consideration means to me!'

'Please,' she begs, 'do not imagine that I am ungrateful. It is only that I am a little surprised!' She manages not to flee, to run up the stairs and away from him as fast as she can. She forces herself to move slowly, knowing that the sound of her footsteps running away from him might hurt him.

As soon as she is under her covers she reaches for her pen and begins to write:

New Year's Day, Evening 1815, 2 Nelson Square

Dear Izy

I must write to you, even without hope of any reply. There is something I do not know how to express.

I do not even know how to think it – and for once even my parents' teaching fails me. Neither the classics nor all the modern novels can give me comfort or advice, for never in our world has anyone spoken of what we are trying to achieve. Why then if my mind believes that what is being suggested is right does my whole being revolt against it – and instead of rising to the challenge, or at least imagining it possible – am I in despair? I do not think I want to be shared.

Perhaps there are some people, like Bysshe and Claire and Hogg, who might manage such a thing effortlessly, and then others, like me, who cannot. I am unfortunate to be the only one of us four who feels such a way. I ask myself so often what is wrong with me. I do not know the answer. Do you ever long for another? Can you imagine taking a lover? I need not ask Claire the question, for it is only too obvious that she has no such scruples. In this way she is more naturally his disciple then I am myself, but how can I accept that? I have so many questions, Izy, and for once not a single answer. I am tired. So tired. And yet I must now manage this, must find a way not to fail Bysshe – or our philosophy – and yet somehow remain true to myself. Oh, if only this baby was not so troublesome and could hold harder to my insides – and yet I am so grateful for it, for it gives me the perfect excuse.

And now I must write to Hogg myself – and give him an answer.

Mary

Dear Hogg,

You love me you say – I wish I could return it with the passion you deserve – but you are very good to me and tell me that you are quite happy with the affection, which, from the bottom of my heart, you know I feel for you. You are so generous; so disinterested that one can't help loving you. But you know, Hogg, that we have known each other for such a short time that I did not think about love – so I think that will also come in time and then we shall be happier, I do think, than the angels who sing for ever.

Mary sighs with relief. It is done; she has bought herself time. She has stayed true to their ideals by maintaining the possibility of a physical relationship with Hogg, but she has also made sure it cannot happen for a while. Once she has the child she can use it as a further excuse. She lies down – she can sleep now that it is done – and yet as soon as her head touches the pillows and she closes her eyes she thinks of Claire – and of the time she spends with Bysshe.

8TH JANUARY 1815: 2 NELSON SQUARE

Almost as soon as Claire and Bysshe leave the house, Hogg arrives. Mary suppresses a wave of irritation at the sight of him; sure that Bysshe has let him know that she will be at home alone.

'I have brought the newspaper,' he says, holding it out to her, an offering. As ever Mary is torn between irritation and affection as she takes it. 'I was thinking that it might be helpful to me if we might also read some Shakespeare together,' he suggests. 'I have not been well versed in literature.'

Mary nods; she enjoys teaching, but really she would prefer having the house to herself whilst she reads the newspaper. 'Could you possibly pick up some tea for us, Jefferson?' she asks. 'I find I have a craving for it!' Hogg is immediately solicitous, and leaves the house vowing to be back as soon as he can. Mary picks up the newspaper and sinks into a chair. It is still a delight to have comfortable furniture.

She turns a page and is immediately drawn to the name of Shelley. At first she cannot quite believe what she is reading. Why have they not been told? She feels a growing sense of both anger and hope as she rereads the notice: *Sir Bysshe Shelley died 7th January.*

She reads it again. And again. She stands and walks up and down the room, staring out of the window, searching for Hogg, or Bysshe and Claire. Bysshe's grandfather is dead! If it is true,

223

if she has read it right, then their financial difficulty is over. The estate might pay off the bailiffs. Bysshe will inherit his half of the estate, his father the other. She holds the newspaper tight in her hands, looking at it as she strides up and down the room, holding it close and questioning whether it can really be true.

She is at the window, beckoning with it, as Hogg comes up the street, walking fast with the packet of tea in his hands. She waves at him and he begins to run.

'Hogg! Jefferson,' she says in her haste, 'read this. Tell me what it says. Tell me that there is no mistake!'

Hogg holds the newspaper and reads. 'Sir Bysshe is dead!' he cries. 'Shelley's grandfather is gone!'

'You knew him?' asks Mary.

'Yes! He was a man like Bysshe who never cared for convention!'

'And he has entailed the estate to Bysshe and his father,' Mary adds anxiously. Oh, to never be hungry again. To be able to move again. To have a servant. To be able to write freely because she can relax, with no fear of the bailiffs.

'Yes!' says Hogg, 'Sir Timothy and Bysshe might have to assert their right, for his grandfather has two families; but it was made clear by his brother, who originally left his money to Sir Bysshe that his intention was that—'

Oh, Jeff,' cries Mary. 'I don't need every single detail. Will we have the money?'

He throws the paper down. 'It is without question, Mary, Shelley will have inherited!'

'Oh, Hogg! His father cannot prevent him having the money?'

'No!'

She cannot help it. The relief is overwhelming. She throws

her arms around him in her joy. Hogg holds her close, stunned by the feel of her in his arms. 'Mary!' he cries.

'Oh!' She disentangles herself. 'We should go and find them.'

'No!' he says. 'Let me make tea and we can wait together.'

Mary falls into a chair, hugging her arms to herself.

'Bysshe,' cries Mary, as he comes through the door, 'you have inherited!'

He stands in the doorway. 'My grandfather is dead?' he asks. 'And no one has sent me news?' Hogg and Mary fall silent. 'My father has not sent for me? Nor my sisters let me know?'

'No,' says Mary.

'Oh, Bysshe,' cries Claire, clutching his arm, 'were you fond of him?'

'Not deeply, but still,' he says, 'no one sent news to me.' He sits down. 'Does it say how he died?' he asks.

12TH JANUARY 1815: FROM LONDON TO FIELD PLACE, BROADBRIDGE, WEST SUSSEX, SHELLEY'S CHILDHOOD HOME
THE READING OF SIR BYSSHE'S WILL

'You would prefer to stay with Hogg, wouldn't you?' Bysshe asks Mary. 'He will help you here. Claire can come with me, we are so used to negotiating together.'

Mary nods, unable to say what she really feels and not prepared to lie. She does not want to stay with Hogg. She does not want Bysshe to be alone with Claire. But she must acknowledge that is the reasonable thing to do. She remains unwell and occasionally bleeding. She cannot make the long journey in a carriage safely. She watches from the window as the carriage rolls away with the two of them in it.

'I preferred my grandfather to my father,' says Bysshe, as the carriage rolls towards Broadbridge and his childhood home, 'and am sorry he is dead!'

'And yet his death might free us?' asks Claire.

'We must wait and see. My father and I now share the estate. I do not know if I can revert my rights to him in exchange for the money. Hogg says the courts must decide. Or perhaps my grandfather has bypassed me in favour of my son. But I do not think so. My grandfather ran away with several women himself and I have always been his favourite. The lawyers must decide whether they will honour my debts, but once we have the money we can live as we choose. Mary and the child shall have a garden to run in, with a pond! As I did.'

He falls silent. Claire watches as his thoughts flit across his face as he smiles at some childhood memory.

'Will you come with me to the house?' he asks. 'I'll show you the tree we all sat beneath as children, where I told my sisters stories . . .' His eyes alight.

Claire laughs in delight. 'You were happy there!' she exclaims. It is a revelation to her, for he has always made his father sound such a villain.

'Yes!' he says. 'My childhood was a paradise and all my sadness stems from being expelled from it!'

'And yet if you had lived in such a paradise for ever you would perhaps never have had a single radical thought, nor any desire to change things?' asks Claire. 'I cannot imagine you as contented!' And it is true; she cannot. In her mind he is for ever worrying at the fabric of the world, longing to either change or understand it.

'I always wondered what it was that I had done to be removed from my family!' says Bysshe.

'I heard,' says Claire dryly, 'that you set fire to the butler.'

Bysshe stops for a moment, and considers. 'I did!' he says. 'But in my childish understanding there was nothing wrong with that.'

'But in *reality* there *is* something wrong with that, is there not?' she laughs.

'I was sure the butler would not be harmed!' he protests. 'And I did not deserve to be sent away for it, not from all I loved!'

'And in this new world, the world we will try to build with your money, alongside Hogg and Mary, you will feel loved by everyone again will you?' She reaches for his hand and he takes it up.

'I sometimes wonder,' she says hesitantly, 'what my own talents might be in this new world?'

'Because you are not a storyteller, are you?' he says easily, unaware of the pain his answer causes her, his easy acknowledgement that she cannot write as well as either he or Mary. Perhaps, she thinks bitterly, because she does not have Mary's heritage.

'And so what worth am I then?' she asks, stung by his comment, and removing her hand from his grasp. 'If I am not a storyteller.'

He looks at her, considering. 'You have the gift of living,' he says simply, 'and perhaps that is what Mary and I find so difficult to accept in you. That whilst we sit on the banks and consider life, you throw yourself in, allowing the current to carry you away.'

Claire turns away from him.

'Claire!' he cries. 'What have I said?'

'No! No! It is good, it is . . . it's that sometimes, when you speak of me, I feel that perhaps I am not second best to Mary, or to all those girls who have both mothers and fathers!' she finishes, laughing away the seriousness of her words even as she speaks.

He does not laugh with her. 'I am sorry if I have ever made you feel second best,' he says solemnly. 'I feel it myself, when I look at Mary and she is so lost in the coming child. I feel, and fear sometimes, that I can never be first in her eyes again.' A silence falls upon the carriage as they become aware that the moment they have so often skirted is upon them.

'I promised you freedom and love,' he whispers.

'And perhaps, if Mary returns Hogg's love, then you might love me?' Claire asks. 'But only when you are assured of Mary's happiness.'

He holds her hands tighter. The carriage stops: 'Field Place, sir!' the driver calls.

'Will you come with me, Claire?' he asks.

'No! Now is not the time to incite your father by turning up with yet another woman!'

Bysshe smiles. 'You have become wise,' he says. He gets down, shuts the carriage door.

'Bysshe . . .' she says, leaning towards him out of the window.

He looks up at her, but before he can speak the driver clicks his tongue and the carriage wheels turn, carrying her away.

He approaches the house through the fields, as he so often did as a child, running home before the sun dipped, forgetting he had not eaten lunch, hearing the echo of his sister Elizabeth's voice calling him from the door of the sturdy house in the distance. It is deep winter now, and the memories of his childhood do not match the landscape. The bare fields remind him only of arriving home from school after that first term away, the trees bone-stark against the sky, the wind whistling across the face of the house as his sisters tumble from the door, unable to wait, throwing themselves at him.

He wonders if his sisters are there now, inside the house, if he will see them again. He suspects not for his father has forbidden them to contact him. He approaches the wide door and knocks. There is no answer. He stands back. Upstairs a curtain parts and falls. Is it his sister Elizabeth? 'Hello!' he calls. No one answers. He lifts the letter box. Inside there is a shuffling and the noise of voices – from somewhere within a door bangs. They are in there. He walks around the house, tries all the doors – they are all locked.

Again he returns to the front of the house and stands upon the lawn, staring up at it. He is torn between pain and fury. In London his rejection by his father has become a story, a tale he tells of how he fights against the prejudice of the unthinking aristocracy; that story bears no relation at all to the fury he feels now: the pain of standing alone upon his own doorstep, the inhabited house closed against him. He would like to throw a stone through the window but does not want to damage the house he loves so well; and yet neither will he agree to silently disappear, colluding in his own rejection.

He takes a book out of his pocket and sits on the doorstep. They will have to come out sometime – everyone who is gathered to hear the reading of the will, and when they do he will be waiting for them, insisting upon his right to be alive and himself: his grandfather's grandchild, and directly in line to inherit the house he is barred from.

As he sits, the clouds pass and the sun shines briefly upon his hair. Lost in his book he does not notice how cold he is becoming, or how the curtains shift several times and eyes look down upon him, some fondly and some with anger or despair. After an hour the butler comes out. Bysshe does not notice and so does not see his fond smile at Master Bysshe's capacity to lose himself in a book.

'Your father does not wish to see you, Master Bysshe,' he says, eyes to the lawn.

Bysshe leaps to his feet, startled. 'Smith!' he exclaims, unable to stop himself, filled with a fond flood of feeling at the sight of the man whose trousers he once burned.

Smith's lips twitch. 'I am sorry, sir,' he whispers.

'So am I,' says Bysshe. 'I was reminded by someone today that it was not kind to burn your trousers, and I have not apologised!'

'Better late than never, sir.'

'Indeed!'

'Perhaps it's best if you go, sir. It's far too cold in January to sit out.'

'Will no one visit with me?' asks Bysshe.

As he speaks, the family doctor – Blocksome – appears. 'It's no use waiting, Sir Percy,' he says. 'Your father has arranged for the will to be read to you in Kingston, at Whitton's. It's best you go there. It is all most odd,' the man mutters as he turns and walks back into the house.

'Goodbye, sir,' says Smith, turning to close the door.

Bysshe begins to walk.

By the time he arrives at the inn, it is hours after dark and Claire is waiting. 'You're freezing!' she says, but it is not the numb hands he holds out to her that concern her; it is the look in his eyes, a distant staring that does not change even as he speaks to her.

'They would not let me in!' he whispers.

'Tell me later, we need to eat and have something warm.' She calls for food and ale; Bysshe sits and she wraps her coat around him.

'Smith came out, and I apologised to him,' he says.

'For burning his trousers?'

He nods. He eats slowly, mechanically, his eyes elsewhere.

'Where have you been all this time?' she asks after a while.

'I sat on the doorstep and waited. They locked every door against me, all of them. And then I walked here.'

She understands now why he is so cold. 'Come upstairs.'

He follows her as she guides him to his room, bids him lie down and wraps him fully clothed under the bedcovers, worried that he will never get warm. She lies on top of the bed next to him, then after a moment's hesitation she wraps her arms around him. He lies as still and cold as stone before beginning to shiver, his whole body shaking as it begins to warm. She clasps him closer.

'Don't let go,' he mutters, and she does not; she holds him until the shaking stops, alarmed by the sudden sweats that take him in their grip, consuming him for a minute or two before the shivering recommences and the sweat dries upon his skin, making him cold again.

In the deep of the night his body finally calms and he falls asleep.

Claire lies beside him, her eyes wide open. As he sleeps she rises and finds a cloth to wipe his brow. She runs it gently over his face, wraps it lightly around her finger to sweep across his lids. He does not stir, lying as still as the dead. She strokes his neck, lingers over the hollow at his throat, stopping short of his shirt, hesitating. When she looks up he is staring at her silently in the darkness. She startles, cloth suspended.

He reaches for her hand. 'Claire,' he whispers, holding her wrist. The cloth drops from her hand. He reaches up from the covers and touches her face as though to reassure himself that she is really there. She remains unmoving, unsure if he is

231

properly awake – or whether dreaming. But he is gazing at her, his eyes no longer lost but focused and intent. He lowers her arm, replacing it at the hollow in his throat.

Her fingers find the button of his shirt in the dark and release it. She runs her fingers over the bars of his ribs, flattening her palms and spreading them across his chest. She feels his breath move beneath her hands, the living being of him. He lifts his arms and takes her face between his palms, bringing it down to him. She touches his lips, feels their mouths open and blend.

Gently he pushes her away, sits up and removes his shirt. She does not know what to do; all of her imagined longings have ended here, with a kiss, a touch. She finds herself awkward. 'I . . .'

He stops her lips with his fingers, slips out of the bed and kneels before her, taking her hand in his. 'I, Bysshe, ask you Claire—' he begins.

'Yes!' she says. 'Yes!' before he can finish.

He stands, pulling her up with him. She leans against him. 'Turn around,' he sighs, and she does, shivering as he undoes the laces of her dress, turns her towards him and slowly pushes the fabric from her shoulders, kissing her skin where her neck joins her body.

Claire closes her eyes. Stops thinking.

She wakes, reaching across the covers for him, but he is not there. She sits up and touches her lips, stares down at her naked body, only the slight soreness inside of her confirming that they have made love. He must have left her in the night. She dresses and finds him asleep in her room. He has washed and is in clean clothes; there is no sign of what has happened between them. She does not know what to do, or whether she should wake him. Have they done something he regrets?

It would not surprise her, for now it has finally happened she can feel the guilt rising. In acting on their principles of free love she has no real doubt that she has betrayed Mary.

As she gazes at him, his eyes open. He smiles at her and she sits beside him. He rises, laughing, holds her in his arms. 'Are you well?' he asks.

'Are you?' she replies.

'Claire,' he says, between kisses, 'I cannot tell Mary, not now. Let us see what happens with Hogg, and with the baby. Do you agree?'

She nods at once, happily assuaging her own guilt. 'But until we arrive back, we can be as we are?' she asks.

At breakfast Claire leans her head against his shoulder, feeds him her bread. Moments of their love-making come alive in her mind, the sight of her loosened hair drifting across his chest, the weight of him, the deep concentration as they strove together. She is amazed and delighted by her body, her discovery at the hidden depths of it. As they sit in the carriage together on their way to London to see his solicitor she feels as though she has been freed – not to be his lover – which is what she expected, but to understand the nature of her own desire.

'Will we spend a night in Kingston?' she asks.

'Yes, I think we must!' he grins.

'Perhaps,' she says, 'when we return home, Hogg and Mary will also have found each other?'

'Perhaps,' he says. 'I wonder what Dr Blocksome meant by the will being odd?'

In Kingston, Bysshe leaps from the cab and leaves Claire waiting. She rests her head against the window, thinking of the night past and the one to come. Despite all she has said she believed love an act that might join them inextricably together; and yet it does not feel like that. She is lost in thought when she hears his voice call to the driver, 'To the best hotel in town!' He leaps into the cab taking her in his arms and kissing her lips.

'So?' she asks.

'It is confirmed,' Bysshe says. 'My grandfather has settled half the estate upon me. One hundred thousand pounds!'

Claire's jaw drops, no words emerge – it is an amount of money beyond her wildest dreams. A number she can barely imagine.

'A hundred thousand!'

'But only if I agree to entail the estate.'

'And will you?'

'No!' he exclaims. 'I have always said that I will never agree to keeping the estate whole; it should be broken up and sold, the money spent on supporting change.'

'Bysshe!' Claire is horrified, but he grins at her.

'My father will almost certainly agree to buying my half from me and giving me an annuity – he is terrified that I will borrow until there is no more to borrow against.'

'But a hundred thousand pounds!' gasps Claire.

'Whitton the solicitor is negotiating to see if the estate will pay off all our creditors! We shall drink champagne on the promise of it!' he laughs, holding her face in the palm of his hands.

When they return home with the news, Bysshe asks Mary what she would most like now that they have the promise of money.

'To pay off the creditors and no longer be hiding from bailiffs!'

'Oh, but I cannot, Mary,' he wails, contrite. 'The estate must decide if they will pay my debts. They must call in the bonds and decide the amount, so it could be months. But we have security now. Is that not worth celebrating?'

'Well then, we shall move again. To a house in Chelsea!' she declares. 'Where I can have our child.'

When she sees number twenty-one Hans Place, she knows that it is perfect. She does not care that the landlady stares at her still-shabby clothes as she is shown around. She will buy more clothes. She looks at Bysshe. 'Do you like it?' she asks.

'Do you?'

'I could have our baby here, Bysshe,' she whispers.

'And there is room for Hogg to stay overnight if he wishes,' agrees Bysshe.

Mary closes her eyes for a moment. 'We'll take it,' she says to the sharp-faced landlady.

'Very good, Sir Percy,' the woman replies, failing to look at Mary, with her bump visible and no ring on her finger.

22ND FEBRUARY 1815: 21 HANS PLACE, CHELSEA, LONDON

Mary is sleeping when the first pains come. They penetrate her consciousness only slowly. She is deep beneath the covers, huddling close to Bysshe's warm back in the cold. At first she simply curls up closer around her belly, instinctively protecting and warming it in the hope that the pain might pass, and for a while it does and she stretches out again. But it returns, deeper now, urging her towards consciousness, still she resists, curling over and pushing it down, clinging to the release of sleep. Refusing to be disturbed, she wraps her arms around the sleeping Bysshe's waist and he curls up closer to her. Again the pain releases her and she relaxes against him. He clasps his hands atop of hers and they lie together, peaceful, breathing in rhythm, her cheek warm against his back. Lovely, she thinks, before the pain returns yet again, insistent now, driving her hands tighter around his waist and waking him.

'Mary?'

'Mmm?'

He turns and lifts the covers to see her. With the arrival of the cold air the pain drives deeper, giving rise to a groan from deep in her gut. 'Mary?' She is awake now, and he sees that her face is sweating and strange. 'Mary, are you awake? Are you bleeding?'

She reaches down. 'Oh! I don't . . .' For it doesn't feel like blood. 'I don't know.' She groans again and then it dawns on her; she is having the baby – it is coming before its time.

'I think the baby's coming,' she says.

'It can't, it's not time,' he says, looking down at her. The pain arrives and she cannot speak for a moment. When it eases she says, 'We need to call Dr Lawrence, I don't think the baby knows it isn't time.'

Bysshe leaps up and lights a candle. 'I'll get Claire!' he says.

She shakes her head. 'No! Not yet! Send someone, and then come back, just you, please!' She senses that in his fear he does not wish to be alone with her, and yet she cannot bear the thought of Claire intruding upon this moment.

He lights a candle and does as she says, dressing and raising the landlady to send a cab for Dr Lawrence.

She is not happy. 'For *Mrs* Shelley, shall I say?' She stares hard at him.

'Say whatever you wish to,' he snaps. 'Just send for him.'

She turns to obey, for however much Bysshe wishes to believe himself a man of the people; his voice carries the authority of the aristocracy. He runs back up to Mary.

She is pale and trembling. She holds out her arms and he

lifts her on to his lap and rocks her. In between the pains they rest together, unspeaking. When they come again she grips tight around his neck, panting strangely, but he stays steady and unmoving. Even in her distress Mary is relieved, enjoying the silent closeness.

'What's happening? Is everything all right?' Claire's voice is soft and concerned. She carries a candle and fails to notice Bysshe warding her away.

'*Get out.*' Mary's vicious snarl surprises them both; Bysshe loses his hold upon her for a moment and she leaps to her feet, screeching at Claire. 'Go!' she demands. 'Must you force yourself upon us even now?'

Bysshe grabs hold of her arms. 'Come back, Mary,' he whispers as Claire scoots away, standing outside the door listening, trying to understand what is happening. Surely it can't be the baby. They aren't expecting it until the end of April. The candle trembles in her hand as she counts the months; it is not due for another two. She has a sudden thought: the dates would work if they had made love in the churchyard – but can that really be the case?

Mary's whimpering is soft and quiet, her groans subdued, but still the pain is evident in the sounds she makes. When a knock at the front door comes, Claire is quick to let the doctor in.

'It is only seven months,' Claire tells him as they rush up the stairs. 'Will it survive?'

'Probably not,' says the doctor, and Claire shivers at his casual tone.

'We cannot stop the labour,' he says to Mary matter-of-factly, 'so we must let things take their course and see what happens.'

'If there is any choice to be made, then save Mary!' cries Bysshe.

'There's no need for that,' the doctor says.

'But her mother!' he cries. 'She died birthing her!'

Hearing him, Claire risks coming in, grabs his arm and hauls him out of the room – manhandling him down the stairs.

'She doesn't need to hear how her mother died after giving birth,' she hisses at him. 'Not now. Not when she's in the middle of giving birth herself!'

'But the doctor needs to hear it! I can't lose her, Claire.' She lifts up the candle and sees that he is trembling with fear. He clutches his own side in pain.

'You can't help her like this. Either stay down here out of her way or go back and tell her everything will be fine; but do not frighten her.'

'You're right. Thank you!' He clasps her hands before disappearing back up the stairs.

Claire sits in a chair, her hands resting upon her stomach and her heart racing. What if she too is with child? What then? As usual she has not thought of the future but simply allowed her longings to overcome her, unheeding of Mary's warnings that she might do better to try and reason with her feelings. She sits alone, listening to the sounds drifting down the stairs. How can she have been so blind to the consequences of her actions? 'It's not as though I didn't know what might happen,' she whispers to herself, 'but simply that I didn't choose to think of it.'

There is another knock on the door and she rises to answer it, hoping it is Mrs Knapp. Mary would like her to be here, but it is the landlady. 'What's going on here?' she asks, her face sharp with curiosity.

'Mrs Shelley is having her baby,' says Claire with as much dignity as she can muster.

'That's right, is it?' asks the woman. 'Well, when she's done having her baby you can all leave,' she announces.

'Why?' asks Claire. 'Have you no feeling?'

'I certainly do, and my feeling is all for the Mrs Shelley

who I hear lives in Chapel Street and has a new son! Not the daughter of a prostitute!'

Claire feels the old anger rise up in her. 'Mrs Wollstonecraft was not a prostitute!' she says contemptuously. 'She dedicated her life to women like you, so that you could be free! Harriet is Mrs Shelley in name only; Shelley's true wife is upstairs giving birth!'

There is a cool dignity in Claire's reply that impresses the landlady, in spite of herself. 'You'd do well to distance yourself from them before your own reputation is as stained as theirs,' she says.

Claire closes the door before the woman has even turned away. She might have her own difficulties with Mary, but she will not allow anyone else to treat her badly. She will tell Bysshe and Mary in a few days, when everything has settled. Perhaps by then the woman will have calmed down and changed her mind.

Mary wants her mother, or Mrs Knapp. She does not want only men to herald the birth of her child. She closes her eyes, blocking out Bysshe's fearful face, feeling only her fingers clasping his wrist, clenching hard when the pains are in full flow. The doctor watches. Behind her closed lids, time passes beyond meaning. She enters the deep rhythm of her body as it carries her along on the swell of its own making. She sees her mother as she is in the portrait on her father's wall, she is no longer looking away into the distance but instead looking down upon Mary, smiling. She can hear her mother's longed-for voice muttering words that she cannot separate into meaning and yet that comfort her. The pain lifts and drops. Lifts and drops. The hand grasping hers becomes her mother's. She is gathered up, no longer merely held in the swell of the pain but becoming it herself, her whole body pushing the world along until something slithers, is breached, and the world comes rushing back. The rhythm breaks and her mother's hand lets go. Mary's eyes open.

'Mary!' Bysshe cries. She lifts her hands down between her legs and feels a head.

'Gently!' says Dr Lawrence as a body slips out of her. 'A girl,' he answers her unspoken question. 'A girl, Mary.' She closes her eyes. A girl; the knowledge spreads all through her and she feels her mother's hand brush across her forehead, the touch of her lips. '*Well done!*' she whispers, before slipping away from her.

She is so small her head fits neatly into Mary's palm, and yet she is perfect. Her dark eyes search out her mother's. They stare at each other, wordless. 'Hello,' Mary whispers, and again, 'Hello!' She cannot take in the perfection, the living being-ness of her daughter, the ancient sensibility so visible in her dark living eyes. Mary wonders how she can have both known she was having a baby and yet so clearly not have understood what it means. It is a surprise, this rush of love, this overwhelming flood of feeling that cuts through her defences as easily as her body has been breached and opened up by birth. So this is it, she hears herself think. This is love. The baby hiccoughs, and Mary instinctively turns her over, rubbing her tiny back, watching her skin become rosy and perfect.

'Don't become too attached, chances of survival are not good,' says Dr Lawrence. Both Bysshe and Mary look up at him. He is a dot, an insignificance. What can he know with his black bag and his lack of feeling?

Bysshe stands. 'Thank you for your help,' he says.

'We haven't delivered the afterbirth yet. I'll go when it's done,' the doctor says calmly. Bysshe sits, immediately becoming lost in his daughter.

*

'Well,' the doctor says, having efficiently delivered the placenta, tied the cord and cut it. 'You are not showing any signs of excessive bleeding. Keep her warm. Do your best. Try not to expect too much.'

Mary says nothing. She is lost in the eyes of her child.

'What will you call her?' asks Bysshe.

'Everina, after my mother's sister.' The name rises up in her; she does not question where it comes from, or why, simply knows that it is right. She will do exactly as her mother did for Fanny; she will save this baby despite the doctor's prognosis. She will have faith in her daughter's desire to live, her right to be born. She lifts the child to her breast and gazes into her eyes as she struggles to feed. Bysshe touches her arm but she does not turn towards him or stir. Her eyes remain lost in her child's.

Watching her he feels a strange mixture of both love and envy.

24th February 1815, Chelsea, London

Dear Izy,

I do not know if you might have a baby yourself, perhaps you have. If so then you will know the wonder of it. Even as I write I seem to stop every minute to turn and look at Everina as she sleeps, each time her perfection grows upon me. She is so small it terrifies me, and the doctor said she would not feed but she is suckling well. Izy, I did not know such love was possible. I look into her eyes and hours pass. It is as though the world has shrunk to the size of the two of us, and yet expanded so that I feel I hold the whole of it in her being. I cannot explain. It is beyond words.

As always when I write to you, the feelings that I try to bury rise up into my pen. Is it you I wonder, or is it the act of writing? I know now the depth of love my mother must have felt for me. I try not to think of it too much. Bysshe is busy with Claire finding new lodgings; our landlady does not appreciate housing an illegitimate child. I cannot believe that anyone could regret a new life, or believe it illegitimate. Everina is so herself, and yet she is both of us too. She has his mouth, a perfect, tiny replica of his lips that makes me smile each time I see it. And she has my forehead, poor child! And then there are her eyes, so dark with such intelligence in them, not the intelligence of acquired knowledge, but something deeper, something I have never seen and cannot understand except in those moments when I lose myself in them – and we are one. Beyond time. She has come out of me yet left the love of her deep in my bones.

I do not even care that Claire and Bysshe are still so often alone together. I try to but cannot. At times I sense that he feels the loss of me, but I can never hold on to the thought, for it feels ridiculous. How can either of us matter as much as she does? Her name is Everina; if you were with us you would be her non-godmother. I cannot believe you are not happy for me, in fact I know you are. She is whimpering and I must go now.

me

Claire is overcome by the sight of Everina; all at once so tiny and so powerful. She is reminded of how softened Mary was by Bysshe's love, and yet this love is different again. It is as though Mary has, for the first time, truly lost sight of herself – of her own importance and heritage – and so become

242

entirely herself. She is confident with the child, holding her easily to her breast.

Claire sits and watches, knowing that she herself might be with child. She will know for sure in the next few weeks and the knowledge only encourages her natural respect for Mary to deepen. She imagines their children playing together somewhere far from here, perhaps on the shores of Lake Lucerne, or in Italy. She has not yet told Bysshe of her concern that she might be pregnant.

Returning from Kingston they did not speak of their love, the return to their life with Mary making the act seem a thing apart from everyday existence. It is easy, thought Claire, to have a theory of free love – but the act itself failed to conform to any of their ideals. Upon their return they spent all of their time together buying whatever might be necessary for the coming child – as though that might make their transgression forgivable, as though they should feel themselves somehow sinful.

But now, with the birth of Everina, everything has changed once more. Now they cling to each other. Shut out from the bliss of Mary's motherhood they make love with a fierce-fuelled longing that takes them both by mutual surprise. They do not speak of what happens outside of the hotel rooms they frequent, and again, once it is over, find it hard to believe that it has really happened: their furious shedding of clothes and inhibition, so far removed from the act of everyday living that it fades almost as soon as it is over.

Only when she is alone at night can Claire begin to try and make sense of what is happening. She tells herself that it is unlikely that such a love will make children, but as she watches Mary with Everina she fears this might be wishful thinking.

And if she is with child, what then? She is terrified of what Mary might do, but calms herself with the knowledge that they are all agreed upon living together with free love as their guiding principle, and surely, thinks Claire, that must include the fruits of any union? If we are to share ideas and bodies, then how much more important is it that we make room for the children born into such a world?

She watches intently as Everina comes to the end of her feed, her dark eyes loosing their hold upon Mary's blue ones as they slowly drift closed; her lips falling off the breast. Mary leans forward, gently kissing her child's forehead.

'She is so beautiful,' whispers Claire, and Mary nods, her eyes still resting on Everina's face. 'Can I hold her?'

'Not now,' says Mary gently. 'Maybe later.'

Claire nods; there is no malice in Mary's voice, only a certainty that Everina is not yet ready for any arms other than her mother's own – and at times perhaps her father's.

'I need to get up!' says Mary. 'I feel fine, and now that she's feeding so well, I should be getting back to normal. There is nothing unusual in a woman having a baby.' The words sound hollow and unreal – a repetition of her mother's beliefs and not at all how she really feels.

'Stay in bed; it won't harm either of you.'

Mary leans back and closes her eyes, lifting Everina closer. 'We need to pack,' she sighs. 'We always seem to be moving about and never getting anywhere!'

Claire touches her arm. 'You've just had a child – isn't that getting somewhere?' she asks. Alarmed, she notices a tear slip from beneath Mary's lashes. 'What is it?' she asks, fearful that a revelation is about to be demanded. That Mary might ask her what she does in her time with Bysshe. Mary does not answer for a while and Claire stays silent, her heart beating fast and fearful. Is it coming, the question she so dreads, and should she tell the truth – how can she – when Mary is so newly a mother? She makes a decision then that she will do anything to avoid telling her the truth for as long as possible.

'Mrs Knapp spoke to my father; she told him I have a child, but still he does not want to see us. Your mother sent clean linen for us both but they do not want to see Everina.'

'But Fanny came to see you!' says Claire.

'She only came because my father was not home and would not know.' Mary's eyes remain closed; she cannot speak of it to Bysshe for it makes him too angry and upset, and since the baby he has suffered with terrible pains in his side. She lives in fear that Bysshe might refuse to go on supporting her father once he inherits, and whatever Papa has done she finds she cannot stop loving him, even though her logic tells her that she should.

'How,' she asks, the tears flowing freely now. 'How can he turn his anger upon an innocent child?' Everina stirs slightly as though she knows she has been wronged before settling again.

'I don't know,' whispers Claire. 'I only know it's wrong, Mary, and cruel, and that I can't say the things it makes me feel because I know it doesn't help you when we vilify your father.'

'Do you think your mother encourages him?'

'Maybe, but I think also that he is his own man.'

Mary nods. 'I have longed—' she breaks off, unable to carry on.' Claire waits but no words come, only sudden wracking sobs and a handing over of Everina as she wakes, startled by her mother's silently shaking body.

Claire lifts the baby away. 'Mary!' she cries out, surprised both by the sudden outpouring and the fact that it is happening in front of her. There has been so little love lost between them lately. Claire turns away, rocking Everina in her arms, giving

Mary time to recover. The baby rapidly returns to sleep, her tiny hand wavering over the edge of her blanket, clasping the edge of it as Claire watches. Her minute perfection is entrancing; the feel of her in her arms entirely natural and right. Everina half opens her dark eyes, giving Claire a suspicious glance before she closes them again. Claire cannot help but laugh in delight. 'Where's your mamma?' she asks. 'Mamma's fine, she's right behind us!'

'I'm fine now!' she hears from behind her. Mary is staring at her, her tear-stained eyes as suspicious as her daughter's, half rising from the bed to reclaim her child.

Claire hands her back immediately. 'She didn't want me,' she explains. 'That's what made me laugh. She took one look at me and she closed her eyes again because I was not you!'

Mary softens once Everina is back in her arms and Claire feels a profound longing rise up in her. The love she is witnessing is of a different order to the free love they discuss so easily, and yet practise with such difficulty – there is nothing free about the love between a mother and a child, she thinks, as the two of them gaze at each other, oblivious to Claire watching them.

'Your father could never love you as much as your baby already does,' she says.

Mary glances up at her. 'I know,' she says simply, 'but it is having such a love denied to me that hurts.'

Claire would like to hold her then, the part of her that has always adored Mary, that once longed to be her, to look out of her eyes and see the world as Mary saw it from the position of an adored and favoured child; longs to comfort her – and restore her to her rightful position. She takes a step forward, but Mary withdraws at once. She does not want Claire's sympathy.

'Bysshe says your father must love you very much to have to reject you so deeply.'

'I'd rather you didn't discuss me!' Mary says coldly, already regretting her outburst.

Claire nods. 'Let me know what you need packing, and we're going out today to buy you a baby carriage so you can bring Everina to the new lodgings safely.'

Mary does not answer and Claire considers herself dismissed. She is not surprised and nor is she particularly hurt. If she were Mary she would feel the same. Somewhere inside of her, Mary knows what is happening, despite choosing not to confront either of them. And she is angry. Bysshe has been unwell in the presence of Mary ever since the baby was born. He does not understand why his pains seem to disappear when he is with Claire, or how she can lift his spirits so easily.

'They are often together,' says Mary, alone with Hogg.

'It was the same in the days immediately after Ianthe was born,' admits Hogg. Omitting to say that it was with yet another woman.

It is Hogg who is always available, and Mary is both surprised and touched by the clear delight he takes in keeping her company whilst Claire and Bysshe disappear on their long walks together, searching for new lodgings, or negotiating with bankers in the light of his new prospects. Hogg's presence is calming; he seems content to simply watch her as she sleeps or nurses. She wakes and talks sometimes of her mother's ideas on raising children. She tells him of how her mother saved Fanny's life, of how she too lived apart from society, unmarried with her first baby. 'And in a foreign country!' Mary exclaims. 'So what we are doing is nothing by comparison!'

Hogg smiles gently. 'It is enough, Mary,' he says, 'isn't it, to face so much rejection? Perhaps in a country where one is not known it might actually be easier.'

She had never thought of it like that and is grateful for a

newer and gentler perspective than her own. 'Perhaps,' she admits.

'Don't worry,' he says, even though she has expressed no worry. 'Bysshe loves you more than ever, but he is not at ease with birth; he had to suffer it too often as a child.'

'That's true,' she says. 'All those sisters!'

'Yes, five babies in almost as many years, and so perhaps birth means something different to him.'

Mary finds that she is beginning to love being near Hogg now that she has had her baby. In his calm presence she finds a sense of peace, and as he talks about his boring cases, his days at court, the world outside of herself and Everina appears safe and unthreatening, rather than the frightening one that has rejected them all, offering no place to her tiny newborn child. When Hogg is not near she often falls into a deep despair, sure that not only has she lost her father but that Bysshe must inevitably desert her too.

2ND MARCH 1815: 21 HANS PLACE, CHELSEA TO ARABELLA ROAD, PIMLICO, LONDON

Mary sits and waits with Everina in her arms. They are moving today, she has spent the morning packing and is tired. Claire and Bysshe have traipsed backwards and forwards but the last load is done now and she is waiting for him, sure that he will return. Hogg is at his chambers and so she is alone.

The house is empty of their things and she sits, wondering how many more times they will have to move. The thought exhausts her; they have only been in the house for six weeks. She hopes this is the last move, and that the money will be settled soon. Whenever she looks at her daughter the tiredness lifts as she feels a burst of delight. They are doing well – she is a natural, as Mrs Knapp would say, just like her mother.

The day slips past. The clock chimes twelve, and one, then two. She feeds and dozes between the hours, roused by the bells and waking to feed Everina and stare out of the window at the day. A dull grey has set in over the city that has not lifted since morning, and occasionally spits the kind of rain that seems as nothing until one steps out in it, immediately becoming drenched. At three o'clock the landlady knocks upon the door and Mary shies away from the window. She does not want to see her or face her cruelty in forcing them to move, not with Everina in her arms.

'I know you're in there,' the woman shouts, 'and I told Sir Percy to be out by lunchtime.' Mary looks around her; Everina is wrapped in her shawl but there are no further blankets to cover her with. Her own travelling cloak, the light black silk she eloped in, hangs in the hall. She thought Bysshe would return and find a cab for them now that it is raining. It is not like him to forget, but perhaps something has happened.

He is with Claire; *that* is what has happened. The thought comes with such bitterness that she has to sit down. What should she do? She does not want the embarrassment of the landlady returning and forcing her to leave.

She shakes herself. It's but a short walk from Hans Place to Arabella Road; she has given birth, not become an invalid, so surely she can walk the distance. She takes up her cloak, wraps Everina tightly in her shawl, tucking her underneath her cloak. As she steps outside she calculates the distance, ignoring the wave of tiredness that almost immediately engulfs her. She has not eaten but it is only a mile and a half, she tells herself, which is barely any distance at all. When she was well, walking ten miles in an afternoon was easy.

249

She sees the landlady glaring up at her from the basement and turns and walks rapidly along Sloane Street, taking the most direct route. Almost immediately she leaves, the rain begins to fall in earnest. She does not want to stop in a coffee house with a tiny baby – people will stare, and perhaps even know who she is – and so she presses on, putting one foot in front of the other, glancing up only to note that she is on the right street, before continuing. She is surprised by how heavy Everina has become now that they are committed to walking some distance. She would like to stop and sit on a wall, to rest for just a moment, but she forces herself to keep on walking.

As she turns into Arabella Road, she sees Claire and Bysshe enter a house. They are laughing and Claire turns and tilts her face up to his, their intimacy immediately obvious. They neither touch nor kiss and yet she knows; knows now for certain what she has before only suspected. She watches as they disappear through the door. He was not getting her and their baby a cab, they have not bought the carriage they promised – he was not thinking of her and Everina alone in the house with an angry landlady. He was with Claire. Probably eating cake.

Mary would like to carry on walking straight past the house, but she has nowhere else to go. Her mother had friends to support her in France when she was deserted by her lover, but Mary has no one. Everina stirs in her arms; they are both soaked with the rain. Mary walks up the steps and raises her hand to knock. As she does, Everina cries out and Mary stares down at her. If you were not here, she thinks, this would not be happening. Shocked at herself, Mary holds her child closer, knocking furiously.

'Mary!' says Bysshe. 'You are sodden! I was just coming for you. Have you heard the news?' He takes her cloak and shakes it out.

'Get me some dry things for the baby,' Mary snaps at Claire. Once she is gone, Mary glares at him: 'You were *not* coming for me, Bysshe, you had forgotten us.'

'No! We were held up, Mary. Everyone is talking about the fact that Bonaparte has escaped and declared war.' Mary says nothing, for his answer is no kind of excuse, stating only that a piece of news is more meaningful to him than remembering her child's need. It is Claire's doing – she is just like her mother, stealing his attention away from them as her mother did with her papa. What chance has Mary alone against generations of such women?

'Claire must go,' she tells Bysshe as soon as they are alone together.

'But Mary,' he comes close, holding her arms. 'She is a part of us and she is learning so much. Why would we abandon her now? We cannot!'

Mary does not soften but stands rigid in his arms. 'She cannot change, her baseness is bred in her!'

He steps back, shocked by her venom. 'I promised her, Mary, when we were in France, that if she came with us we would protect her, that with us she would be free.'

'I do not want her here. She is too like her mother.'

'Bur her mother did not have Claire's choices; she had to find a man to marry and I am sorry it was your father. These are the evils of a society that condemns free love. You are tired and she irritates you. I'll ask her to keep away.'

'You cannot change her!' she cries, desperate and frightened for herself and her child. Appalled at her hysterical need to be rid of Claire, but unable to resist it. 'And that is what is necessary.'

'But I do not wish to change her,' he says, confused. 'Not at the very moment that she is finding herself.' He stares at

Mary and his eyes seem to accuse her. *It is you who is changing,* they whisper. Again she hears his accusation against Harriet: '*she changed after Ianthe, she no longer cared for revolution, only longed for comfort and money.*' Is he going to leave her?

'Try to rest,' he says gently. 'You're tired.' He leaves the room. Everina cries out and Mary picks her up, gazing into her eyes, longing for the reassurance that the rush of love for her child always gives her – but the feeling has gone, and there is nothing. She holds Everina to her breast but the hot flood of milk no longer feels like liquid love, but something merely painful and distant.

Hogg comes to the new house as soon as he can from chambers. His easy delight in herself and Everina lifts Mary's despair as easily as he lifts Everina to his chest. 'You should have taken a cab,' he softly reprimands Mary. 'Walking in the rain so soon after giving birth was not sensible!'

'We're here now and fine,' says Mary. She takes Everina back. With Hogg by her side she can once again stare into her daughter's eyes and feel the world recede, her love returned.

After supper Bysshe reads to them all. Whenever Mary looks up, Hogg's eyes are upon her and Everina, his gentle concentration connecting her to both herself and her child. When he leaves she bids him goodnight in a wave of relief and happiness, reaching up to kiss his lips. If she can feel this for another man, then perhaps she is more of a true believer in free love than she has realised. Perhaps she *can* love both men. Perhaps she will not lose Bysshe, after all. Hogg stops and holds his hand to her face, overcome by her attention and stroking Everina's brow to distract himself. 'Thank you,' she whispers. She turns back into the house. By the time she has reached her bedroom the love has gone again – the world once more devoid of feeling.

*

When Hogg returns the next day, Mary clings to him, picking Everina up and following him from room to room. Without him she seems to lose all sense of herself. 'Sit down,' he laughs, delighted with her affection, but concerned that she rest.

When Bysshe and Claire return with the new baby carriage they have promised, Mary hands Everina proudly to Hogg, asking him to place her in it. Bysshe smiles at her approvingly and Hogg sets Everina gently within, pushing the carriage with his foot as Bysshe reads to them again. He has chosen Godwin's book on Chaucer. Perhaps, thinks Mary, I must accept that I will only ever have Papa's books to know him by, which is all I have ever had of my mother.

Bysshe reads the Old English with an easy lilting rhythm that carries her away and she forgets for a moment that she is angry with him; feels again the adoration. When she turns to look at Hogg he is still smiling at her, but with a deep sadness in his eyes at the sight of her love for Bysshe.

'I must go,' Hogg says quickly. 'I am in chambers in the morning.'

'Must you?' Mary asks, frightened at the thought of him leaving, fearing the grey deadness waiting to engulf her. She would like to beg him to stay but she cannot. She stands and walks to the door with him, picking up Everina on the way, wanting to feel the last of that closeness with her before he leaves. 'Must you go?' she asks again.

'I really must,' he insists.

'Will you hold her for a while, before you leave?' she asks, hoping that might persuade him to stay.

He lifts Everina into his arms and it is as though a weight is lifted from her. 'She's hot,' he says, stroking her brow.

'But it is cold upstairs at night,' Mary says, 'and she needs to be wrapped up warm.'

He lifts the baby to his lips, kissing her gently on the forehead. 'Goodnight, sweet lady,' he whispers.

For a moment, Mary considers refusing to take Everina back, taking so long to lift her arms in response that Hogg drops her in Mary's arms himself, kissing Mary's brow as he turns to go. She stands in the doorway staring after him, watching until he turns at the corner, knowing that as soon as she turns back into the house the numbness will return. It arrives as soon as the door closes.

'Goodnight,' she says dully to the others.

'Goodnight,' Bysshe and Claire cry in unison.

Mary wakes suddenly in the night and stares at her daughter's sleeping face, at her limbs extended and relaxed. She does not feel the rush of love that once came so easily. She opens and closes her eyes, testing herself, like pushing at a rotten tooth, waiting for the feeling to return. Nothing. She turns over and hopes for sleep.

Her breasts wake her in early morning, heavy with unused milk; it is almost daylight, and Everina lies still in her cradle. Rigid and cold.

Mary reaches over, recoiling at first from the cold body before desperately picking her baby up, rubbing her limbs and searching for life. She holds the tiny lifeless body close, rocking back and forth, whispering sweet nothings. When the warmth does not return she goes on holding her child hopelessly to her breast, but the closed eyes fail to open, the lips – so like her father's – remain still and closed. She cannot let go of her, cannot return her to her cradle. Gazing at her she is filled with a terrifying sense of rightness. She was not a good mother – she stood at the door of this new house and blamed her child for Bysshe's lack of love. It is a long while before she calls for Bysshe.

'I am no longer a mother, Bysshe,' she says, the words flat and unfeeling. He tries to hold her, but she cries out and he retreats at once, leaving her with her baby.

As she sits in the bed holding her dead child, Mary returns again and again to the moment that she woke in the night and watched over her. Was she alive in that moment or was she dying? If she had reached out and picked her up, or perhaps if Hogg had stayed that night, if only she had begged him on bended knee, perhaps now her child would still be here, for when he was near her, her love for Everina was alive. She knew that. She *knew* that, and yet she let him walk away, too proud to beg. It is all her fault.

As the morning passes the child's body becomes stiff and unyielding, but still Mary cannot let go, believing that if she can only understand what she has done then her tiny daughter might begin to breathe again.

Claire comes in and tries to persuade her to give up her baby. 'You must let go,' she whispers.

Mary looks up at her through her tangled hair, her eyes gleaming with fury. 'Do you want to take her from me too?' she hisses.

'No! No,' Claire tries to soothe. 'I want to put her in her cradle, I want to—'

'*Get Hogg,*' Mary shouts. 'He does not faint with pain whenever I am ill, nor did he desert us when we were in need.'

'We.'

'You left us!' Mary says, her voice dead now. 'You and him, laughing together on the doorstep whilst I walked with Everina in the rain.'

'What can I do? How can I help?' Claire wails.

'Why are you the one crying,' Mary asks coldly, 'when it is me who is holding my dead baby?'

'Mary, I—'

'Get me a pen.' Claire runs for one, and Mary scribbles a note to Hogg, still holding on tight to the child:

My dearest Hogg, my baby is dead – will you come to me as soon as you can – I wish to see you. It was perfectly well when I went to bed – I awoke in the night to give it suck and it appeared to be sleeping so quietly that I would not awake it – it was dead then but we did not find that out until morning – from its appearance it evidently died of convulsions. Will you come – you are so calm a creature & Shelley is afraid of a fever from the milk – for I am no longer a mother now.

Mary

'He's coming. He's coming!' she whispers to Everina. It is only when Hogg arrives that she finally releases her child. He holds out his arms for her and she gives her up to him.

'Oh, Mary!' he says, sitting down beside her.

Mrs Knapp comes to bind her leaking breasts. Mary sits unmoving as she wraps the bandages. The world has stepped away from her.

She watches her child's coffin lowered into the earth. She would like Everina to be buried with her mother, not to be alone in the cold earth, but it is not possible. Sometimes she thinks she sees her lying on the bed or in the carriage that still sits in the hall, but when she looks again there is nothing.

'Will you stay,' she asks Hogg. 'Will you live with us?'

15TH MARCH 1815: LONDON ZOO

'Shall we go to the zoo?' suggests Bysshe when Mary's milk has dried up and he loses his fear of being near her. She does not expect help for she does not feel she deserves it. She has failed.

'Yes,' she says dully, 'let's go to the zoo.'

She concurs with almost anything anyone suggests. If there is nothing to do then she reads or works at her translations. Bysshe watches her as she dresses. There is an untouchable, impenetrable air about her. When Mary is like this, even taking her arm seems an imposition, and yet he does it as they walk to the park. She does not shake him off, yet neither does she sink closer as she used to. Claire follows slowly behind them.

'Look,' he says, 'a lion.'

Mary drops his arm. She stares through the barrier into the animal's eyes. The lion stares back. It is a relief to look into the lion's face, to feel the animal live in an endless present, where pain might pass quickly.

'Mary?' she hears Bysshe say. 'We should leave.'

'Why?' she asks, for they have not long been here. Claire takes her arm firmly, pulling her away. She stares at the hand on her sleeve, looks up at her sister and then submits. What does it matter now?

As they turn, a movement catches her eye and she looks up. Across the animal enclosure stands her father. She takes a step forward, but before she can call out to him he turns towards her stepmother Mrs Godwin. Together they walk rapidly away.

That night Mary dreams of her father. Again and again behind her sleepless lids she sees him turning away from her to say something to her hated stepmother. She hears his voice calling her as he used to – 'Mary!' – and imagines lifting her hand to find the comfort of his hand clasping hers, looking up into his face and knowing always that he will be there – but in her dreams he has no face, and her hand reaches up into empty air.

The next morning, as soon as Bysshe and Claire are gone, she leaves the house, heading determinedly towards Skinner Street. She runs to her father instinctively, beyond thought or logic; seeking the man who restored her from that first loss – the loss of her mother. She feels her heart begin to beat fast with love as she approaches the bookshop. How could she ever have found it boring, ever have felt that its doors held only a past and not a future? She knocks but nobody comes. She knocks again.

'Please!' she calls. 'Papa! Please!' Still nobody comes. Mary stands in the street refusing to move, unable to believe that her father can hear her and yet fail to come to her aid.

Eventually Martha appears from around the back of the house. 'No one's in, miss!' she whispers, wide-eyed at Mary's despair, at having to refuse her former mistress.

Mary straightens her shoulders. 'Thank you, Martha,' she manages.

As she walks away she feels her heart begin to close over within her; it is neither a clenching, nor a pain, but a slow inevitable drift of ice that buries all feeling. Deep beneath it lies a terrible fury at Mrs Godwin, who came and took her father from her, and at Claire, who is doing the same thing to her lover. Back at Arabella Road the house is empty. The two of them are out together again.

'They are always out and about together these days,' says Mary brightly, when Hogg arrives. Appalled by her haggard expression he puts her to bed and brings up tea. She lies, feeling the warmth of the blankets slowly seep into her frozen limbs.

He sits beside her bed and reads. With him beside her she feels no need to do the things she feels she should be doing. She has never, except when she bled and in those early days after birth, stayed in bed. Mornings are for working and reading, afternoons for exercise and evenings for food and discussion. Her guilt at doing none of these things fades as he sits beside her.

'I should be working on my Latin,' she says desultorily. 'Bysshe has given me some texts to translate.'

'Does it help?' he asks, looking up from his own book.

'Nothing helps,' she says, looking away, the truth of it making her feel inadequate. She should be able to manage her grief and yet she cannot. All feeling should be amenable to reason. 'I feel nothing,' she says, 'and then when I stop whatever I am doing I remember that I am not a mother, and yet I still feel like one.'

'Just because Everina is gone it does not mean you stop being a mother,' he says.

The sound of her child's name is like a bell tolling all through her. Mary dreams of her at night, alive and in her arms – each morning is a new death. She cannot tell Hogg that. 'But I am not a mother!' she cries at him. 'I have nothing in my arms and—' She stops. She was about to say that feeling her breasts shrink, the evidence of their uselessness, reminds her every day of what she has lost.

'I am not diminishing your loss.' He picks at his words carefully. 'I am trying to say that the experience is not lost. You understand now what it is to be a mother, whether or not Everina is here. I cannot imagine how terrible it must be, to have such feelings thwarted.'

'How do you understand such things?' she demands.

'By watching you,' he says.

259

She says nothing, knows only that when he is near, her fear that she is somehow responsible for the loss of her daughter is held at bay. She is sure now that she killed her mother with her fierce and fiery need to be born, and so she does not deserve a daughter of her own. Her own father has rejected her, and her lover decided to desert her for the love of her sister. She is unlovable. She cannot cry. She must not. She must not give in to feelings but try and think her way out of her despair. 'It is silly to sit and allow myself to be so overwhelmed,' she says at last.

'You are not kind to yourself,' Hogg says as the tears slide out from beneath her lashes.

'And you are too kind,' she manages to reply.

17TH MARCH 1815: ARABELLA ROAD

When Claire hears Fanny knocking on the door she is tempted not to answer. Godwin's refusal to see Mary has shocked them so deeply and they want nothing to do with Skinner Street. She makes Fanny wait a long while before she deigns to answer.

'Has Godwin sent you?' she asks brusquely. Fanny shakes her head. 'Do you remember, Fanny, how we used to watch Mary and your father walk to the cemetery together when we were children?' Fanny nods nervously. 'Then you know how it feels to be left out in the cold. How could you leave the door closed against her, when she has lost a child?' Claire asks in a whisper.

'I'm sorry!' Fanny can barely speak for guilt, but Claire goes on. 'She has nothing! And yet you still prefer to obey a father who has proved that he thinks only of himself – and his finances.'

Fanny bows her head, creeping into the sitting room to face her younger sister. 'I am so sorry, Mary! Please forgive me.'

'It's not your doing,' Mary says coldly. 'Did you order the doors closed against me?' Fanny shakes her head. 'I believed that if *he* saw me he would be unable to refuse me. I was wrong.' Mary's words fall flatly and without expression.

Fanny recognises that sound, hears the invisible pain behind it. She reaches for Mary's hand. 'He knew you were outside the house but he ordered us to stay inside. Mary, it is not you he hates but Bysshe. He said to Mamma it was strange that such beauty could be given to a person so wicked!'

Mary turns her head away.

'Mary! I am sorry!'

'What?' Mary asks. 'Must I feel sorry for you, Fanny? They reject me so that you are not stained by association with me but what use do you make of your precious purity?'

'I try to keep the peace,' Fanny says. 'I plead for you there and I plead for them here. I am all that he has left of our mother.'

'You should work; you should try and find a way to escape. That is what our mother would wish you to do.'

'I have tried to work,' she tells Mary. 'I work in the bookshop, and I might work for our aunts.' Mary says nothing; her brief burst of anger spent, she stares at Fanny wishing only that she would leave. 'I am the only piece of Mother that Father has left,' Fanny says again as she rises. 'I cannot desert him. I do not fit here and I am not right there. I do not seem to belong anywhere. I never have.'

'And yet Mamma saved your life. So you must be good for something!' snaps Mary.

'Did she?' Fanny flushes with delight and Mary wishes she had remained silent.

'Well, Mrs Knapp says so.'

Fanny would like to hear more, but Mary has returned to her book, and so she rises to leave. 'Thank you for telling me,' she says. 'I will ask her.'

Mary does not reply.

Bysshe enters as Fanny is leaving. 'Fanny!' he says, bending to kiss her cheek, failing to notice her blush. 'Come sit with us. Has your father sent you with yet more advice as to how I am to act upon my own inheritance?' He does not speak as though he feels it is her fault that she has to deliver Papa's messages; he makes her feel she is a person who might exist in her own right.

'I am so sorry,' she whispers, 'for your loss.'

He stands awkwardly for a moment. 'It is hard after our expectations were raised.'

She nods. 'I must go. I am sorry to have to say this, but Papa has asked me to let you know that he would like to read the codicil your own father has placed in the annuity agreement, for he fears you should not give up your inheritance for an annuity. I know you will help him when you can.'

'You have more faith in me than he does!' Bysshe laughs.

Fanny remembers how it felt to hear that laughter echoing up the stairwell, how it made her heart beat faster and the colour rise to her cheeks. She had hoped that her father would welcome the girls and Sir Percy home, even though her own hopes were dashed – still the presence of him would have been welcome, brought life to the house. Now there is only William left at home and he is a child.

'Sweet, sweet Fanny.' Bysshe stoops again to kiss her, sad he cannot rescue yet another of Wollstonecraft's daughters. 'Will you stay?'

'No, I think Mary would like to rest.'

'Well then, shall I walk you home?'

Fanny hesitates, she would love him to walk her home, but she cannot be seen with him. She does not know what to say. She is allowed to deliver requests but cannot be seen to be socialising with him.

He smiles, noticing her indecision. 'Or I could walk you halfway home perhaps?' he suggests, smiling.

'Yes! Thank you.' As they reach the street he takes her arm, her step lightens and her heart lifts. She closes her eyes the better to feel his hand beneath her elbow, the height of him and the warmth of his side.

'I am sorry we must be estranged,' he says.

'Yes,' she agrees.

'Hopefully it will not be for ever.'

'I do not think they will relent unless you were to marry her.'

'Then they will wait for ever!' he says. 'I cannot become a polygamist.' He notices Fanny blush. 'I'm sorry I have shocked you. Perhaps your father is correct and you should be protected from me.'

'You tease me,' she says with dignity.

'I am sorry, Fanny, it is done from affection not scorn.'

'There is not much chance for affectionate teasing in my life.'

He feels the desire to make an offer for her to join them; only the sure knowledge of Mary's fury, were he to do so, prevents him.

'I am sorry,' he says instead. 'It must be a cheerless existence.'

She nods and then, coming to a decision, looks up at him. 'There are moments that lighten it,' she says gently.

'Then I am glad,' he tells her.

They both stop; to go any further would risk discovery, they have already come far enough.

'Goodbye,' she says determinedly, letting go of his arm.

'Goodbye, sweet Fanny,' he says and stoops to kiss her brow. He turns quickly and walks away, running from his desire to scoop her up and so relieve Godwin of yet another daughter. Fanny stares after him, touching the imprint of his lips upon her forehead.

When she returns to Skinner Street, Papa will not speak to her, refusing to answer when she asks him a question, as though she has become Mary merely by having been in her presence. He does not ask after her and leaves the room if Fanny mentions her to Mrs Godwin, who only wants to know about Jane, as she still calls Claire.

'We could still save her,' Mrs Godwin says whenever her husband will listen, 'but only if we are clear that we reject Mary and that man. Jane would never have gone with them of her own volition. She was seduced by him.'

'I think she wanted to go,' Fanny almost whispers. 'She believes in the same principles as they do.'

'Principles!' Godwin explodes. 'How dare they grace their pallid thinking with such a word. They are not principles but merely an excuse for the basest behaviour! And in going there you expose yourself!'

'She is my sister,' Fanny mumbles. She knows she should be grateful to her father, but it is Mary she misses, Mary whom she links with the dim memories of her mother, Mary whom she knows is only scornful because she is so hurt by their father's rejection. With Mary gone there is no one left who imagines her mother, who talks about her as though she might be real. Fanny sometimes lifts up the book her mother wrote her as a child, and reads it to herself, the way Marguerite once did. It is a child's book and Fanny is ashamed that even now she sometimes chooses to fall asleep with it in her arms, clinging to a dim sense of a woman who once held her close, cradling her as she slept. When she wakes it is hard to find the desire to rise and get dressed. She wants to close her eyes and sleep again. Imagine that she is not alone.

PART

THREE

24TH APRIL 1815: TOWARDS THE WINDMILL INN, SALT HILL, SLOUGH

It is April and Mary has walked long distances doggedly every day, determined to regain her health since her loss – and slowly, in spite of the dragging sadness she carries in place of her baby, she begins to feel the pull of spring. At times, she looks down at her body and wonders how it can appear so exactly as it was before her Everina. There should be evidence, she feels – of the pain she has been through – and yet there is none.

The bailiffs have discovered they are in Arabella Road, and Mary has suggested that they escape for a weekend. She is sick and tired of sharing with Hogg and Claire, and if only she could be alone with Bysshe then he might remember how wonderful it can be when it is just the two of them.

Bysshe holds her hand as the coach carries them away from London. They have escaped the city – and Claire and Hogg.

'Do you remember this?' Bysshe whispers, removing the pins from her hair and stretching out a curl, before releasing it to spring back against her cheek. She nods. He longs to recall her to her past self, to remember the girl who leaped so freely into a carriage to France.

If only I had not turned back, thinks Mary. If only I had taken that moment when he held my case in his hand, and turned for us to step into the carriage without thought of Claire – then *she* would not be here. But no, she must not think of Claire now – nor of how intimately she might know Bysshe; she must look forward. And she must fight; with a smile on her face, and no sign of her sadness. The weeks of her physical recovery are past, and once they renew their love he will no longer need Claire. She will make sure of it. She will never, whatever Bysshe's hope, make love with Hogg. She is profoundly grateful to him, but he is entwined with the memory of her loss in a way that Bysshe is not. And she does not love him – except as a brother.

But soon, soon, she thinks as their lips meet in the small carriage and they meld with their past selves, healing her hurt, I will find a way for us to remain together without Claire and Hogg. I will not let Claire win – as her mother has.

They both long for the journey to be over and the carriage to reach their destination.

'Mary?' Bysshe says as they finally pull into the hostel's yard. 'I have missed you.' He lifts her down. She is almost weightless in his arms once more.

'Would you like to eat, sir, or would you rather retire immediately?' the innkeeper asks.

They glance at each other. 'Retire immediately,' they say in unison.

For weeks they have done nothing more than hold each other. Now, they lie on the wide bed together, far away from Hogg and Claire, with no need to hurry, and no fear of disturbance.

'Do you remember Frankenstein's castle up on the crags?' she asks him. He nods.

'Oh, how I longed to be alone with you there,' she whispers. There is no mark upon her, he thinks, and yet she is so wounded. He rests his palm on her cheek and she covers it with her own.

'I sometimes long for that castle,' she says wistfully. 'I imagine us living there, away from society, and friends. No Claire and no Hogg. Just us together.'

'We are there now,' he says, brushing her eyes closed with the palm of his hand. 'Just the two of us.' She feels the thrill of knowing he is about to tell her a story that will both bind and release her. 'Outside it is almost dusk. If we were to look out of the stone window we would see the stars beginning to break through the blanket of the sky. In the empty forests that surround us a wolf howls and far below us the river shines in the moonlight.' He watches her breath slow to the rhythm of his words, her body relaxing. 'We are high up in the solar, with a fire burning in the grate. It is not the sun you feel upon your skin,' he whispers, gently lifting her arm into a ray of light that falls across the bed, 'but the flames, casting their heat upon you. There are no servants for we bid them leave each evening so we can have all within the walls entirely to ourselves.' She sighs. 'Are you with me, Mary?'

She lifts her hands to his neck, pulling him towards her. They hold each other and remember how deeply they have loved each other. Afterwards they fall into a deep sleep. They do not wake till dusk, simultaneously blinking into each other's eyes and laughing with the joy of rediscovery.

They are ravenous and eat more than they need, barely noticing the other residents of the inn.

'I feel I have stolen you from Hogg!' he says.

'And I have stolen you from Claire.' Mary manages to keep her voice light, not wanting to destroy their intimacy with her jealousy.

'We are wrong to think of stealing and yet the feeling is there.'

'Perhaps it is because we belong to each other more truly than we do to them,' she suggests as she pops a morsel into his mouth.

'Hogg will miss you!'

'I shall write to him so he does not!' She smiles. 'And then we can stay here a few more days!'

'Yes! I will go to London from here by the next coach and come straight back. The lawyers need not stop us staying!'

Her heart lifts at how easily he rearranges everything, as though all thought of Claire has gone from him entirely. 'I'll be waiting,' she smiles. He offers her his hand and they walk up the stairs. 'I will never fail to love you,' she whispers. 'I could not.'

And he knows that it is true. Is once more overcome by the reality of her love for him. It is wonderful to remember, to be together as they were in the beginning, before her loss – and his betrayal.

They wake and join together again before he leaves. After he has gone Mary lies back and closes her eyes, glorying in the fact that she is entirely and completely alone. It is well after luncheon before she gets up and walks. Beneath the beech woodland lies a haze of bluebells; she bends to touch them, releasing their delicate fragrance; she pinches a ramson leaf between her fingers and feels the physical world come close and intimate again – alive and full of beauty. If only, if only, if only it could always be like this. The refrain will not leave her, the belief that if they were not always surrounded by others, then they might be able to found not a new world, but a family. Like the Baxters.

She gets back to the hotel late, and scribbles a note to Hogg as she has promised.

25th April, Salt Hill

Dear Jefferson,

I am not hard-hearted, but Claire will explain to you how we are obliged to go away – you will perceive that it was indispensable. The bailiffs have discovered where we are.

We shall return tomorrow night, or the next morning, so dear Jefferson, do not think very hard of me, who would not for all the world make you uncomfortable for a moment if she could help it. Claire says that she will not get us new lodgings, she is tired with it – but she will, of course, and this will be the last time, we hope – for the estate will surely pay our creditors soon. Until then can you please send us some more money, and – dear Jefferson, love me all the time as I do you . . .

'See,' she says, as soon as Bysshe returns. 'I have written to Jefferson and explained.'

'I'll write too.'

He picks up a pen and folds the note over.

*M*y *dear friend,*

I shall be very happy to see you again & to give you your share of our common treasure of which you have been cheated for several days.

He throws the pen down and turns to Mary who carefully picks up the note. The words *'common treasure'* cause her teeth to grit in irritation. It is not how she wishes to be known, and she is about to slip it into her pocket, ready to tear his note apart from her own letter before sending it, but Bysshe pulls it out of her hand and puts it in an envelope, ready to send.

'Let's have soup,' he cries, 'and I shall feed you just as I did that first night of our freedom in Calais!'

'I doubt we shall find a fish soup like that in Slough!' laughs Mary.

'Then I shall feed you with whatever soup they have,' he declares.

'Did it go well, with Whitton?' she asks.

'It did. If the courts agree to allow it, then my half of the estate will revert to my father. Meanwhile he will pay our creditors himself, on the promise that I will no longer borrow money against the estate. I think my father shall settle a thousand a year upon my head!'

'We can leave London!' Mary cries. 'We can live here, perhaps.'

'And I can settle a proper amount upon Harriet! And upon Peacock, and maybe Claire!'

'Is Jefferson the only person that we do not keep?' asks Mary sharply.

'What is my money for if it is not for making the world as we would have it?'

'But is it wise, Bysshe, to support a woman if it prevents her learning to support herself?'

Bysshe hesitates. 'Would you like to support yourself?' he asks.

'No! Not me, for now you support me whilst I learn my trade, but once I write I hope I will support myself, as my mother did. That has always been my dream.'

'And so who do you mean?'

'Claire. She is not writing, is she? She spends all her time walking and talking and doing nothing else at all!'

'She reads,' mentions Bysshe tentatively. 'And she would like singing lessons.'

'But perhaps she would rather be a governess, or teach the piano. That is how my own mother began her career, and Claire is such an earnest disciple. My mother was never supported by any man!'

'Let us ask when we return,' he says. 'Perhaps she would like the idea.'

Mary smiles.

26TH APRIL 1815: PIMLICO, LONDON

Claire walks aimlessly through the rooms of Arabella Road. As each week passes the likelihood of her pregnancy increases, the fact of it becoming unavoidable. She tells herself she is waiting until they are all more settled before she mentions it to Bysshe, but really she knows that she is hoping it might not be true. Tired of being trapped in the house she reaches for her coat, deciding that she must walk somewhere briskly. Very briskly. And then perhaps bathe – in hot water. She does not notice her brother walking towards her.

'You look tired, Janey-Claire,' he declares, taking her arm. 'I was just on my way to see you all!'

'Bysshe is away with Mary – avoiding the last of the bailiffs, but you can find him in London today at the lawyer's. If you need him.'

'You will do just as well,' he laughs. 'Shall we walk?' he asks, taking her arm.

It is a relief to see Charles; Claire wonders why she had not thought of telling him. 'Perhaps we could just sit in the park?' she suggests. When they get there she drops on to the bench. Although it is sunny, she is cold. Her coat is an old one that Fanny has lent her, barely covering her wrists, and her hands are freezing.

'I'm with child,' she says suddenly. 'From Bysshe.'

Charles says nothing for a while, only frowns at the floor, unable to look at her. 'You are sure?' he asks eventually.

She nods. 'I think it was February,' she says, remembering how cold Bysshe was, how much she longed to warm him.

He falls silent. 'I am shocked,' he says after a while. 'What will you do?'

'He will support me, I am sure of that.'

'And Mary?'

'She too believes in free love and so has no right to

disapprove of me!' she says stoutly. Even to her own ears the words fall flat.

Charles shakes his head. 'She will never love anyone as much as she loves Bysshe,' he says, 'and will not take kindly to sharing him! What can I do? How can I help you?'

'You already have,' Claire says. 'I did not want to be alone with the knowledge, and yet I cannot trust Bysshe not to tell Mary straightaway, and it is not the right time. She has lost her own baby – the thought of another so soon after . . .'

Charles stands up, holding out his hand. 'Come on, let's walk, it's too cold to sit and you must be careful now.' He takes her to a coffee house and buys her warm milk. She holds it gratefully, the cup warming her hands. 'Claire?'

'Yes?'

'You understand I do not share your philosophy of free love. Atheism interests me, but free love, you understand I do not believe there can be any such thing.'

'But—'

'No! Wait, I will support you in whatever you do but I need you to listen to what I have to say first, and then we need never mention it again.' Claire subsides, for he is rarely so serious. 'What you believe in cannot work. It requires a change in biology before it can ever be so. For men there are no consequences – they can sow their seed wherever and perhaps feel nothing but relief – but for women the consequences come in the form of another life. For Mary who has lost a baby and now for you; and I believe a child is not a simple thing. Our mother had three separate fathers for each of us, and finally found that the only way to survive was with a husband. Until a woman's body changes there can be no freedom.' He looks at her across the table. 'I will not mention it again. It is not a moral argument I make but a practical one. What freedom is there in the position you find yourself in now? It makes you more dependent upon him, not less.'

'He has said he will support me and I believe him.'

'What meaning can there be in that when he can barely support Mary? When you move from place to place, always avoiding bailiffs?'

'Yes,' Claire says excitedly. 'There has been no place for us to rest. They throw us out of lodging after lodging, because we dare to live as we please, and not as we are told we should!'

'Or more often because you cannot pay the rent,' Charles reminds her.

'That too!' Claire agrees. 'But that is because we need the money we have borrowed to live on, and can never be sure when there will be more until Bysshe has his annuity,' she explains.

He squeezes her hand. 'When our mother was abandoned, only the women of the parish helped her. I will always try and help you.'

Claire nods. 'I am lucky. Mary has no one.'

'She will not be happy for you.'

'I know.'

'It is rare that ideology works in practice,' he says sagely.

Claire finishes her drink. 'But it is not just theory, Charles,' she says tentatively. 'I do not feel made to be a wife, to sit and embroider quietly in a parlour. Do you remember when we first moved to the Polygon, to live with the Godwins?' She grins as she says it and he is glad to see her smile.

'I remember it better than you do, you were but a babe!'

'But I remember nonetheless,' she says with some dignity. 'I could not bear it. We had to sit in silence. Eat in silence.'

'You stole bread,' he remembers delightedly, 'and stuffed it up your sleeves, still expecting to be hungry.'

'And I was ashamed of that until I met Bysshe! Ashamed of our poverty, and of our mother – of our illegitimacy.'

He covers both of her hands. 'If he has freed you from that then I shall always be in his debt.' He smiles.

'Are you not ashamed?' she asks.

'Godwin saved us from that life. I do not understand how he can be both so kind and yet so cruel.' Charles shakes his head and Claire laughs.

'That is exactly what he says about Bysshe! That he is so beautiful and so wicked.'

'Well, perhaps he sees his own faults in him, and so cannot bear him!'

'Why don't you join us, Charles!' Claire asks.

'Because I disagree with your philosophy. When I find a woman, I want her for myself and I want her to love only me. I already have a mother I could not have to myself, so why would I want the same from my wife?'

'We are so different,' she muses.

'And yet we love each other, don't we? And Bysshe is not the only man who offers you his protection!'

'If only Mary had a brother!' cries Claire.

'She does,' Charles reminds her tartly. 'She has a half-brother in William. He is half her blood through her father, and yet she never acknowledges him and so she cannot know the joy of him.'

'You are like Bysshe, you have an answer for everything!'

'No!' says Charles gently. 'I am not like him at all. I aspire to nothing but normality, for I have understood that that in itself is hard enough to find.'

'Well,' sighs Claire, 'I must find us yet another place to live before they return tomorrow. Will you help me?'

27TH APRIL 1815: 26 MARCHMONT STREET, BLOOMSBURY, LONDON

'We should leave London as soon as your annuity is settled,' Mary says as the carriage rolls towards their new home in Marchmont Street. 'We could rent somewhere in the country, or we could tour the whole of England, just us!'

'Perhaps we could return to Switzerland,' suggests Bysshe, 'or Italy, somewhere warm where we can breathe again – and write.'

'Without Claire,' Mary says firmly. Bysshe does not reply. 'If she returned to Skinner Street then her mother might persuade Papa to forgive us,' Mary persists.

'Do we require his forgiveness,' Bysshe asks stiffly, 'when he forced you into disobedience by his own actions? When as soon as he heard I might inherit he asked for more!'

Mary grasps his arm. 'But if Claire returns then he will not have my stepmother plaguing him with her notions. You know my father, and the work that he has done, the things he believes. Can you not see that it is that woman's poison always pouring into his ears that stops him from seeing reason,' she goes on. 'You must know that!'

'I will always respect him,' says Bysshe, 'but we cannot desert Claire and Jefferson; we have made promises to them.'

Mary sits back, her lips pinched and angry. 'Have you not enjoyed our time together?'

'Mary, it has been a time beyond joy. To have you back.'

'We need to have order and solitude to be able to write. Claire's excitement does not help, and although Jefferson is helpful, he is in essence a lawyer – he does not know what it is to try and create something, whether it be an idea or a poem!'

'We have offered them a place with us. They are our friends.'

'Jefferson maybe, but Claire is joined to me only by circumstance, and her remaining with us merely incites her mother against us.'

Bysshe does not answer. They are turning into yet another street, with yet another set of rooms. Mary sighs as she spots Claire, already standing on the steps ready to greet them. Mary kisses Bysshe as he hands her down, lifting her hand to the back of his neck.

Once, thinks Claire, as she watches them arrive, I would have wondered what that felt like, and longed for it. Mary sweeps past her, ignoring her greeting; Bysshe stops, still holding their bags.

'I need to talk with you,' Claire whispers.

Bysshe nods. 'Yes we must.'

'Mary is not happy,' he tells Claire as soon as they enter the park. 'She feels your mother would be happier if you went home, and then her father might be freed of the persuasion that I am evil.'

'And you?' asks Claire. 'What do you feel?'

'I feel her father will remain as stubborn as he always is. He is not persuaded by your mother but by his loss of Mary. He would have all of her or none.'

Claire nods. 'And she would have all of you or none,' she suggests, 'whereas I, like my mother, will settle for whatever I might get.' She enjoys the flinch of pain in his face at her words. 'I might have agreed to leave, but I am with child,' she says sharply. It is not the way she would have liked to announce such news, but the circumstances force her to it.

He turns to her – shocked.

'What?' she asks. 'Were you unaware that what we did might result in such a thing?'

'I am surprised,' he says. 'I don't know why!'

Claire softens almost at once. 'I felt the same,' she says. 'That our love is not the kind that might make a child, and yet it has. We must tell Mary. I cannot pretend to be interested in returning to Skinner Street. If I am to have this child then I want to have it here, with both of you. I know very well how much it will suit you having Mary near whilst I am with child. I do not mind; I only need to know that any child of mine will have a father – as I never have.' Even as she hears the words she speaks she cannot believe the truth of them. *A child*, the refrain continues in her head. *A child*?

'Oh, Claire!'

'If I am to have a child,' she repeats shakily, 'then I would like my child to have *you* as its father.'

'You are right, we must tell her; and perhaps she will soften when she understands.'

'No, she will not.'

'But she has found strength in loving Jefferson; perhaps she can understand that I find a similar release in you.'

'You go,' Claire suggests gratefully. 'I need to sit for a while.'

He walks away from her. From behind he could be a boy, the light spring in his step, a tall slim figure with abundant hair. She sighs. It is not that Mary will not understand, thinks Claire, but that she will not agree.

Mary will not talk to her, withdrawing into an icy silence that refuses to acknowledge Claire's existence, as though, if she tries hard enough, Claire might disappear, no longer representing such an intractable problem. As soon as Claire enters a room, Mary rises to leave it.

'Mary,' Claire begs, 'we must talk.'

'About what?' Mary asks, her face piched with anger. 'There is nothing at all to talk about.'

'About how we are going to manage.'

'You should go home to your mother. Is that not where you

might naturally expect support?' Mary pauses in the doorway to wait for her answer; the knowledge that Claire carries his child when she has lost her own eats at her.

'You cannot change what has happened,' shouts Claire, 'and turning away from me will not make me disappear!'

Mary walks towards her. 'Do not remind me of how easily a child can be lost,' she says coldly, inches from Claire's face.

'Mary!' Claire is aghast. 'You know that was not my intention. I am only asking that you help me! I do not know what to do,' she begs.

Bysshe is upstairs writing and so Mary speaks quietly and up close. 'What exactly is it that you expect me to do?' she hisses. 'You have taken advantage of my loss to steal the only thing left to me! You already have a mother, Claire, and through her you have my father. Must you have everything of mine? I cannot bear to be near you. That is why I leave the room whenever you enter.'

Claire pulls away from her. 'But my child must have a father.'

'Must it?' Mary asks. 'Your mother took my father without any thought of what it might mean to me.'

'But Mary,' Claire tries again, 'we both know that Bysshe can never love me as he loves you. I do not need him to be entirely mine. I am not fighting you for Bysshe but for a father for my child.'

Mary turns to go. 'Go back to Skinner Street. Your mother found a father for you there.'

Claire stands very still after Mary has left. She sometimes feels as though if only she can keep still enough then everything might resolve itself around her. It is her impulsiveness that has brought her to this pass. She does not hear Bysshe enter.

'She will not hear of you staying with us,' he says. 'Perhaps if you spend a few days away at Skinner Street it might help.'

'I cannot tell them!' Claire cries in despair.

'No, you need not tell them,' he agrees, 'but perhaps it's best for now if you are out of her sight. Allow her to have some time.'

'Did she tell you to say that?' Claire asks, suspicious.

'No,' he declares, but it is always obvious when he is lying.

'I'll go,' agrees Claire. 'I need to be away from her myself, and at least I am still welcome there.'

41 SKINNER STREET

It is strange stepping through the door into the bookshop. 'Jane!' Her mother wraps her arms around her.

'Mamma . . .' she manages, almost immediately longing to tell her mother everything, whilst knowing that she mustn't, or at least not in her usual impulsive rush.

'Mamma?' she asks a few days later, when they are alone in the kitchen. She likes being in the warmth with her mother, who still sometimes gives Martha the afternoon off so that she can bake herself.

'Yes?'

'What do you know of Sir Percy's beliefs?'

'I know that he would make a whore of you!' Mrs Godwin declares stoutly.

Claire laughs out loud at that; she has missed her mother's protective fury. 'But only with my consent,' she responds.

'What child knows her own mind in the face of such seduction? You are but sixteen!'

'But Mamma, what if you had not had to marry Godwin? What if you had lived in a world where to be unmarried with children carried no shame, where you might work and be proud!'

'Pipe dreams, child, you blow them away with the gift of age. And you forget that I did work! That man has made you believe in dreams, but at heart he is no different. He longs to surround himself with adoring women!'

'But they are my dreams too!' says Claire. 'And I will not relinquish them. Wollstonecraft said marriage is servitude. I can live with you, Mother, but I cannot live here as I did before. I must be allowed my own beliefs,' she declares. 'I have changed.'

'Not in this house you have not!' says her mother, and suddenly they are angry at each other. 'You return only to shame me!' yells Mrs Godwin.

'You do not think that, you cannot!' Claire screams back. 'Have you forgotten the years before your marriage? I believe you were magnificent then!'

'I was not. I was rotten with misery. What servitude do I suffer now? A man who provides for and loves me?'

'He does not provide for you, Mamma, Bysshe does, even when he has nothing, even when Harriet has stolen all of his wealth, still he tries and tries and tries to soothe your husband's creditors and love his daughter. Even when she lost her child, Godwin did not visit. He is not a man but a monster.'

'How dare you!'

'I dare because I am free of the chains that keep you blind.'

'Well then, you can be free elsewhere!'

Claire returns to Marchmont Street.

'They would not accept me as I am,' she says proudly.

'And neither can we,' retorts Mary.

'I must go and see Jefferson,' says Bysshe.

Both women almost glance at each other, almost sigh with a shared grimace at the man they both love running from their fury, but they resist, harden their hearts and turn away from each other.

Alone at night Claire grinds her teeth at the fact that it is

Mary whose bed Bysshe retires to. She has those precious hours for persuasion, whilst Claire has only the walks they take together – no longer happily discussing some perfect, imaginary world, but each desperately hoping that the present might change. 'She is hurt,' says Bysshe. 'She has lost a child.'

'I know,' agrees Claire, 'but I do not know if she will ever forgive me. When I think of how determined her father has been in rejecting her, and I see that same stubborn hatred in her face, then I give up hope.'

'I know you carry my child, Claire. I will not pretend it is not so.'

She holds hard to his hand. At night she wonders how it can be that what once felt so free and wonderful now feels so desperate and fearful. Her brother was right; if she has this child she will be truly dependent upon Bysshe and Mary.

'She must go,' says Mary. Bysshe does not reply. 'Are you listening to me?' The truth is that he is not listening. He cannot bear to listen for he can see no resolution to the problem. It is always Mary who calms him, who has soothed Claire when he overexcites her, and this time she will not. Cannot. 'Bysshe!' He jumps at the sharp tone in Mary's voice.

'But where can she go?' he asks. 'She has already tried to return home.'

'I do not care where she goes. I cannot live with her. It is impossible!'

'But why, Mary?' Bysshe asks.

Mary remembers her father's rage when she suggested that Harriet might live with them. She understands now why his fist landed on the table so harshly. He was right. *He was right*, she thinks silently and in despair. It is not possible to share the man I love with another woman; to sit by whilst she has his child, and yet it is exactly what I expected from Harriet.

'Because,' Mary says, 'she will steal you from me, just as surely as her mother stole my father. She will not be content with part of you but will want all of you.' Even as she hears the words emerge, she recognises that she is speaking of herself, not Claire, and is horrified. But she cannot stop.

'She wants her child to have a father!' begs Bysshe. 'She has never had a father of her own.'

'Why?' Mary cries out. 'Why must she have a father for her child when I have lost my own father? And must she have my lover's child too, when I have none? Then what am I to be left with?'

'Mary, I will always love you. Without you I do not know myself.'

'Then why must you have her too?' The words wrench themselves out of her – she cannot help herself, feels exposed in all her weakness, her possessiveness – all the things he despises.

'I think,' he says slowly, 'that it must be the way I am made.'

'I'm sorry!' she cries. 'You did not lie to me, you never have, and for that I am grateful.'

'Can you not try?' he begs.

'No,' she says sadly. 'I cannot watch her have your child when I have lost my own.'

They next morning begins in yet another icy silence, for fear that speaking might invite a sudden burst of fury from Mary.

'Would you like some bread, Claire?' Bysshe eventually offers.

'Yes,' says Mary, before Claire can respond, 'and perhaps you'd like some butter with that, and cake as well, and whilst you're here why not take anything else that so happens to please you?'

Claire presses her lips and does not answer. Bysshe passes her the bread. Mary stands up and leaves the room only to return almost immediately, not wanting to leave them alone together. The three of them sit silently, Claire sick with fear and Mary raging, Bysshe eating rapidly so that he can leave.

The tension in the house erupts into his body, compressing his chest so that he cannot breathe. He escapes the house on long walks across the heath where he sails his paper boats obsessively, staring at them as they finally soak up water and sink. He has failed. The idea of a world where love is shared as freely as ideas lies crumbling around him.

Hogg no longer visits. 'Why don't you come?' Bysshe asks him.

'Because Mary does not want me,' Hogg replies. 'Surely you can see that?'

In despair Mary visits her mother's grave. She rests her head against the stone. 'I don't know what to do, Mamma.' she whispers. There is a deep silence beneath the leaves of the willow. Mary closes her eyes. It is so peaceful outside of the tension-filled house; the odd breeze carrying the dim sound of voices from the inn, reminding her of long afternoons with Bysshe, when free love was an idea rather than a painful reality. She lies down, as she did then.

She thinks of Claire. *She is your sister*, she hears her mother say. *And a woman.*

When Bysshe returns, Mary is sitting at the table with their journal in front of her and Claire's journal beside it.

'Hello,' he says tentatively

'Will you call Claire,' she asks stiffly. 'We cannot continue to live like this. You are ill and she is refusing to act. We must think together. We must find some resolution.'

He nods, relieved to have the Mary he has learned to depend upon back. 'Will you come down, Claire?' he asks.

'Not if it is only to be told that I am everything she is not!'

'Please,' he asks. 'If we are to find a way to live together then we must at least be able to talk together.'

'And that is still what you want?' Claire asks. 'For us to be together?'

'If we can. But we cannot continue like this.'

Claire walks down with him and sits at the table. Mary nods at her. 'We must come to a decision,' she says.

'Why have you got my journal?' asks Claire.

'One day people will read this,' Mary says, 'as they now read my mother's journals. They will read of how Bysshe and I fell in love and eloped to France. Perhaps, when we are long gone, they will think of Bysshe and his poetry, or me and my travel journals.' She holds the diary up in front of both of them. 'It is all in here,' she says, 'our history.' Claire nods, sensing Mary's subdued but furious rage – and her efforts to control it. 'And you wish to be in here too, don't you, Claire?'

'I don't *wish* it,' Claire says stoutly. 'I *am* it. Without me you would have had no one to chaperone you, without me you would have had no one to pass your notes to each other – and without me you would have stumbled through France never knowing how to hire a room or arrange a loan. You cannot change that.'

'And yet all the time you were desiring him, planning, waiting – until you could have him yourself?'

'No!' Claire manages. 'It is true I loved him – but I saw that he loved only you, and so I wanted to . . .' It is hard for her to remember the joy of those days. 'I wanted to protect your love.'

'I think that is true,' says Bysshe quietly. 'I remember it.'

'And now?' asks Mary.

'And now I believe in the principles of free love – that we are not bound by anything except the love we feel.' She dare not mention desire. 'And that we might share such love.'

No, that is not at all what is going to happen, thinks Mary. She calls up the Mary who sat across from her father and calmly argued each point, applying reason to emotion, curbing passion. 'So we find ourselves in a position where we must manage the consequences of a shared love,' she says. 'If you have this child, Claire, then you will be bound by it and you will be known as a woman who has had a child not only outside of marriage, but also with the man who eloped with her sister. You will be reviled in ways that we have not yet even begun to experience. Your mother will know – and so will my father. You will never be allowed back into Skinner Street.'

Claire swallows. It is true, only she has been too terrified to even think of it.

'And I cannot have a child in my house when I am still grieving,' Mary manages to say calmly. 'Can you not see that?'

Bysshe places his hand over hers. 'Do you have a suggestion?' he asks.

Mary nods. 'You need time, Claire. Perhaps if you were to go away somewhere . . .?'

'But where?' cries Claire. 'And why?'

'So that you can make a decision,' says Mary quickly. 'Do you truly want to bring a child into the world in such circumstances?'

'There are times,' Claire admits slowly, 'when I wish it had not happened, when I would like everything to return to the way it was between the three of us.' She hesitates. 'At times,' she admits, 'it does not feel real.'

'I know of a place in Lynmouth,' says Bysshe, 'where you might stay.' At the sound of his words Claire feels a flood of relief – perhaps the problem can be taken away from her, and be over. But to have to leave . . .

Mary closes her journal. 'Will you arrange it, Bysshe?' she says quickly. 'Because whatever you decide, Claire, you cannot stay in London and be exposed.'

'You promised me,' Claire says to Bysshe, 'that if I came with you, if I left my mother and was brave enough to come with you, then I would never find myself in her position, would never fear for my child or my future.'

'And you will not,' he promises. 'I will support you, Claire. You will never have to marry a man for his money!' His words do not reassure her; she does not want his money as much as his presence, his desire to be a father to her child.

'Why,' Claire asks Mary when Bysshe has gone to post his letter to Lynmouth, 'have you got my journal?'

'Because we must change them,' says Mary. She picks up the journal she shares with Shelley and flicks through the pages. 'Here is what I wrote on the day you revealed that you are pregnant with Bysshe's child!' Mary rips out the page. Claire watches, motionless. Mary drops her own journal and lifts up Claire's. Claire reaches for it but Mary lifts it easily and lightly away from her.

'That's mine.' Claire's voice shakes. 'Give it to me.'

'No,' says Mary. 'I do not want a record of this. It is for your good as much as mine.' She tears out the pages, precisely, calmly, one after the other. Claire swallows – she does not try to stop her for there is something about Mary's rage that is too terrifying. 'That,' says Mary, ripping out the final page, 'is how easy it is to wipe a mistake from history.'

13TH MAY 1815: CHEAPSIDE, LONDON

Mary does not say goodbye. Bysshe takes Claire to catch the post to Bristol. They wait in the same coffee house she sat in with Charles when she told him she was with child. Claire feels both relieved and terrified by the idea that she might soon be free of this burden.

'But if I do decide not to keep the child then how will it be born?' she asks. 'And where?'

'We will find somewhere. But Mary believes it is important that you are able to return to London with no stain upon your character. We are already ostracised and if it were known that you are with child and not yet married then your chances of a normal life are ruined! Oh, Claire.' He rests his hand on hers, suddenly deflated.

'You mean that I cannot return to live with you if I keep the child?' she asks. 'And that you are in agreement with Mary?' He says nothing. 'Are you ashamed?' she insists.

'No! I am not ashamed, Claire, for we have done nothing to deserve shame. It is not we who think that way but the rest of the world. And Mary is right – you must be protected from it.'

She does not answer, cannot. He is slipping away from her, his promises melting in the face of Mary's resolution. The minutes tick past.

'Shall we walk in the park?' he asks, and she agrees, for it seems there is nothing else she can do. It is happening. She is being sent away from him. Bysshe holds her arm, the pain in his chest a constant dull ache. He is torn between longing to get on the coach with her, at least to deliver her to the tiny cottage he has rented for her. 'I am sorry,' he says again. She nods and they carry on walking in circles, waiting for the time to turn towards the post to Bristol.

When the moment comes she steps up into the carriage and he loads her trunk. She holds her cheek up for a kiss, a simple trusting movement so like one of his young sisters that it undoes him. He holds the carriage up, standing in the doorway and refusing to get off, full of a terrible confusion.

'I don't know what to do,' he whispers in her ear. 'Should I come with you?'

The driver eventually gives up remonstrating with him and sits waiting; the passengers stare at them both, disapproving. For once Claire cannot help him, she sits there, silent. Just go, she thinks, for this is already far too difficult. As though he senses her silent message, he finally steps away and the driver clicks his tongue. The horses begin to move, slowly at first, heaving into their load and then faster, catching the rhythm of their movement.

Bysshe stands watching, hoping she might turn or her hand appear at the window, but it does not although he waits until the carriage is out of sight. When she is gone he stands unmoving, drivers swearing at him to get out of the way, until one touches him with a flick of the whip and he stumbles, stepping aside, continuing to see that small, dignified tilt of her cheek towards him, like a sacrifice. He promised her and he has failed her. He has tried to live according to the beliefs he holds and he has failed them.

He cannot return to Mary. He walks long hours through the city, unable to go home, for when he does he will have to confront himself. He walks in a wide circle, retracing their steps, passing the coach stop and at each turn wondering whether or not to follow her.

At home, Mary waits. At three in the afternoon a light rain begins to fall. It must be done now. She imagines the post carrying Claire away; hears its wheels grinding through the mud and feels a light sense of relief at the thought that when Bysshe returns there will be no one between them. He will be turning away from the carriage now and back towards her, the rain clinging to his hair. She will dry it for him when he arrives. It will have been a hard thing for him to do; she understands that. She goes to find a cloth; he never notices the cold or rain until it is too late and he is ill.

She sits and waits. The clock ticks and he does not come. She stands and checks outside the window. Perhaps the post left late?

She picks up some of his letters to her. She has destroyed any evidence of his love for Claire and now she collects together the evidence of his love for her, running her fingers over the phrases as she reads: *Remember love at vespers!* he wrote. *I did not forget to kiss the image of your body before I slept!* She holds the next one to her chest for it is her favourite: *My mind without yours is as dead and cold as the dark midnight river when the moon is down.* She whispers the words to herself. These are the words their love will be remembered by. She sorts out her letters, carefully ripping out any remaining pages in their journal where she has been too honest. Time passes. He does not return. She pushes the letters into a bundle.

He is half an hour late, and now an hour. And now two.

Slowly it begins to dawn on her that he might not return, that he too is in the post, rolling towards Lynmouth as happily as they once travelled to the Windmill Inn together. She gets up and runs into the street. There is no sign of him; he is neither in the coffee house nor the park. The post left on time and yet he is not here. He has gone.

Her eyes smart and she notices she has forgotten her coat. She walks home, sure now that he has abandoned her, that she has pressed too hard and pushed too far. How could he abandon Claire when she holds so closely to his principles? She has been stupid, blind, refusing to bow to the strength of her reason and allowing passion to rule her as her father always told her was wrong. She has been cruel beyond reason and now he has left her. As has her mother, her father – and her baby. She is finally alone as she deserves to be.

She returns to the house and lights the lamps, using the cloth meant for him upon her own hair, unpinning the long curls and remembering how gently he dries and brushes them, how he loves to wind the long strands around his fingers as they sit beside each other, almost as though they were his own. Will he never do that again? She must not think about that now, it will undo her. She walks to the window, some forlorn hope lingering – and sees him walking towards her.

Is it he?

It must be and yet she dare not believe her eyes, even though there is no other man in London who dresses with that strange careless elegance, who walks along to his own distant rhythm, speeding up and slowing down to some internal, invisible pattern of thought. He does not glance up and see her waiting. He opens the door with a loud bang.

'Bysshe?' she calls.

'I'm here,' he says. 'I'm back.'

She knows from his tone that his return was no easy thing. That she has nearly lost him.

14TH MAY 1815: LYNMOUTH, DEVON

At least the cottage is pretty, thinks Claire as she arrives at the door. The garden is in full bloom; roses and honeysuckle circle the arch above the gate, and long blooms of varying colour line the path to her door, which is painted a deep, peaceful blue.

'Shall I show you how to manage the fire?' the landlady asks, hesitant, not wanting to insult her, but knowing Claire has not employed any servants.

'I know already,' smiles Claire. 'I cannot afford a servant.' She hesitates and then adds, 'Not since I lost my husband.'

The words resonate with a truth for she may not have lost a husband but she has definitely lost the fight for her man. She twists the ring Bysshe has given her. 'Dishonest,' he said, 'but it will help, it's a small village.'

The woman pats Claire's shoulder. 'Plenty of us have to make do without a servant,' she says.

When she is gone Claire sits in the small garden. She has never smelled a country garden in May and is captivated in spite of her sorrow. The birds are full-throated in the evening. She closes her eyes and listens, drinks the cold water; it tastes cleaner, fresher than in London. In the tiny kitchen there is bread and cheese and a neat square of butter under a cloth. She is touched almost to tears – she had not expected to feel cared for, to feel, along with the sadness, a sense of release from the brooding, furious presence of Mary. Well, she thinks to herself, surely this is better than becoming a governess, which seems to be what Mary feels both her sisters might try, although, thinks Claire bitterly, Mary herself does not care to emulate her mother's work as a governess but only to take up her glory as a celebrated writer.

When she wakes on that first morning with the sun in her eyes, Claire wonders where she is. There are no noises below the window of horses' hooves or carriage doors shutting, no call or click of a driver's tongue. But there is also no furious silence as the three of them sit around the table. She imagines Mary and Bysshe waking up together whilst her own room stands empty, the two of them leaning close and talking, perhaps between kisses. To erase such thoughts she throws herself into activity, cutting bread, setting a fire, cleaning an already spotless house, and as the afternoon arrives taking a long walk along the riverbank, wondering how long it will be before Bysshe visits.

Because he has promised he will come. As the day progresses she is surprised to find that she misses even Mary, or at least the idea of her.

She gets back at dusk, glad of the tiredness in her limbs and the smell of the evening garden. She is determined not to be sad, or at least she will not be seen to be sad. She picks up her pen and writes to Fanny.

As the days pass Claire finds her own way of managing; practising her singing in the mornings, and walking in the afternoon. Reading and working on the garden in the hours in between. She finds she can sleep almost anywhere and at any time. She does not think of the child growing so slowly and turning within her, for there is no one here to remind her that she is with child – and so in those long, early weeks in Lynmouth, she allows herself to forget.

When she sits to write to Bysshe, as she does most evenings, she imagines him separate from Mary. Sees him suspended somehow – alone and lofty in her imagination. Belonging nowhere – like herself.

It is strange to think that there is war again in France, she writes, *that there are now British men in those fields we once walked through together, but it is also a blessing, for there are one or two women who have lost husbands and so the people of the village are kind to me. But I do not like deceiving them. It feels wrong. There is a girl in the village who is with child without a father. I watch as they shun her and feel a fraud. I offered her tea and the poor thing said: 'I would not if were you, they might think badly of you.' We had tea anyway. Perhaps one day the world will be as you imagine it, Bysshe – although it is hard to believe a woman will ever be able to bear the children of those she loves, freely and without shame, unless she is married.*

MAY 1815: FROM LONDON TO BRISTOL LODGINGS

Mary and Bysshe leave London almost immediately Claire has gone. The city has come to represent everything that they have lost: the love and respect of Godwin, the life of their baby and now the presence of Claire. London, with its filthy, stifling air holds no pleasure for them. The parks where they once walked and fell in love are become mausoleums. They flee from what they have done, deciding they will tour the south-west of England just as they once travelled across France, desperate to recapture that same spirit of freedom and adventure. And this time, thinks Mary as she steps up into the carriage that once belonged to Harriet and that Bysshe has now commandeered, there will be no third person standing between us.

'The sea!' Mary cries as they arrive at the coast, her heart lifting at the sight of the wide, empty sky and the freedom of being in a place that holds no memory of Claire. They get down from the carriage immediately to walk along the beach. It is evening; people drift away to their lodgings, children laughing, as tired, sun-drugged nurses chivvy them home. Mary sits and takes off her shoes and stockings, Bysshe watching as she slowly rolls the delicate fabric down her legs. Lifting her feet free and digging her naked toes deep into the sand, she throws her head back to the sky. 'Ahh!' she cries in a gasp of relief.

'What?' he laughs.

'*Absentia Clairae!*' she answers without opening her closed eyes, breathing out as though she is blowing all thoughts of her sister away. She does not notice him flinch or feel his sharp withdrawal at her obvious pleasure in her sister's absence. He is pained by Mary's lightness of spirit and yet he says nothing for he also loves her and is relieved to see her happy.

They travel slowly along the coast and into Bristol, Bysshe sometimes walking for long days along the cliffs, alone, or taking the carriage to return to London, still engaged in settling with his father. The courts have ruled it illegal for Bysshe to sell his right to his titles and all his inheritance – and so they fight the courts. Bysshe is tired of fighting.

'If you were to inherit, then after you your land and titles should go to Ianthe,' says Mary, 'and not her baby brother Charles. How can it be that women are still not thought fit to run an estate?'

'I cannot take on that issue as well!' he laughs. 'They have not yet agreed to allow me to renounce my own baronetcy.'

'But would you leave it to Ianthe if you could?' she insists.

'I would not have anyone, anywhere, own any rights to anything,' he says angrily, 'that they did not earn, or make or build with their own hands. It is not a question of male or female, Mary, but of privilege by birth! If there were no lords and ladies then there would be no fight over whether men or women inherit.'

'But privilege *does* exist,' she insists, 'and until it changes there remains the question of women being treated as lesser than men!'

Whenever he is away she wonders whether he is truly in London, or Windsor, where he claims to be staying with

Peacock, who has moved; or whether he is simply crossing North Devon to visit Claire.

It takes several hours in the post from Bristol to Lynmouth, but Bysshe makes the journey as often as he can. He arrives at noon and Claire meets him with a basket of food. They walk along the River Lyn together, finding secret shaded glens to sit and picnic in. Occasionally Bysshe takes out his pen and notes the way light strikes a branch or the sound of a river in the distance. Often he watches her as she sleeps.

'Are you sure,' he asks her, 'that you want me to arrange for the child to be given away?'

'I think,' she says slowly, 'that I must.' Although her body is beginning to change, yet it still does not feel real that she carries a living being within her: a real child. Her mind cannot take it in and so it baulks, allowing her to continue as though it is not real at all, whilst knowing that it must be. 'If I keep this baby,' she muses, 'then I must give up on the hope of us ever creating the world we dreamed of – that is the truth of it, isn't it?'

He says nothing.

'I mean,' she goes on, 'that if I decide to have this child, and live here with it as I do now, then everything will remain exactly as it is. You might see us occasionally but we will be hidden from the world – and alone. I cannot have you with me as well.'

'Yes,' he agrees.

'Well then,' she says, leaning against him in the hidden glen, 'I think we must find the child a home where it will have parents that will love and cherish it. If I must choose between this child or you, then I choose you. And once it is done, we will be together again?' she asks.

'Yes,' he whispers.

'And we will fight for a world where we might love each other freely, and have children who are born without shame?'

'Yes.'

'And you believe Mary will agree to us all being together again?'

'We will find a way,' he agrees, for as ever when he is with Claire, the world seems full of possibility. It is only when he is faced with the reality of Mary's determination to keep them all apart that he fears it might never happen.

BRISTOL LODGINGS

'Have you been with her?' asks Mary.

'I have seen her,' he replies. 'She is alone in Lynmouth and must soon give up her child, Mary. Have you no pity?'

'I cannot bear to think of her,' she says, 'with your child inside her.' It is the truth and yet her feelings fill her with shame.

She does not know how to tell Bysshe that she is with child again herself. Alone at night she crosses her arms over her belly and invokes her mother. Please, she thinks silently as Bysshe sleeps beside her, do not be angry with me. She closes her eyes and tries to recall the touch of her mother's hand upon her brow as she gave birth, the whisper of her presence in her room as a child. She tries each night but there is nothing – her mother has deserted her. Is ashamed of her treatment of her sister.

Often, when Bysshe is gone and she is alone she stands with her mother's book in her hands, daring herself to close her eyes and choose a page at random. But she cannot. She is too afraid. 'Of what?' she asks herself, and the answer comes easily. 'Of knowing that your mother is ashamed of you.' She is terrified that it will be Claire who has a healthy bouncing child upon her knee and she who will fail again.

'We must stop travelling at some point,' she says to Bysshe, 'and should find somewhere we can rent for a good while soon. Perhaps we might rent somewhere in Windsor, near the inn where we were so happy?'

'I'll visit Peacock and find somewhere. It will be good to settle in the country.'

Neither of them mention that it will be harder to visit Claire from Windsor.

SEPTEMBER 1815: LYNMOUTH

When Claire is alone she often retraces their steps up to where the waters meet. It is autumn now, and the child is active within her. Claire watches the leaves falling, wondering if she can really shed this child as easily as a leaf? She does not know and would rather not think of it. She finds that if she sits staring at the river for long enough then her mind drifts and merges with the rush of the water, allowing the hours to flow past without notice until Bysshe comes again, and once she is with him anything feels possible.

'How is Mary?' Claire asks.

'Almost happy, I think,' Bysshe says slowly. 'It is strange; it is as though she has forgotten what has happened.'

'And so you never talk of me,' Claire says. 'I do not exist in your life just as I no longer exist in your journals.'

'Things will change, Claire,' he says.

'Will they?' she asks. 'And if they do not, then what will

you do?' she asks suddenly. 'If I abandon this baby, can I trust that you too will not abandon me?'

'Mary cannot face the thought of you with my child,' he says sadly, 'just as Harriet could not face the thought of Mary having my love.'

'And yet I would willingly share you with either of them,' Claire says simply.

He kisses her goodbye, lifting her into the air and making her laugh. In the future he will often recall that moment, the radiance in her face, the hidden fullness of her as he lifted her up – the moment when Claire was last her young self.

From Lynmouth he goes immediately to Windsor. He has promised to look for a house they might rent near Peacock.

He finds a small red-brick cottage upon the edges of Windsor Great Park, and writes for Mary to join him. There, in the peace of their own home, Bysshe finally begins to write – not in the house but outside, building bowers as he did as a child – finding a place for his confusion and the failure of his grand dreams in the words of his poem. One day, as he arrives home, the sun shining and his hair smelling of the woods, Mary takes him by the hand and leads him up the steep stairs into their bedroom. After they have made love she holds his face in her hands. 'I have something to tell you,' she says. He stares at her, sensing what is coming and yet not knowing. 'We are having another child,' she whispers.

'Mary!' He begins to cry, filled with relief and pleasure at her joy, even as the thought of Claire's coming grief rings inside him.

'I know,' sighs Mary. 'It is wonderful news.'

'I am so happy for you!' he declares.

'For us,' she says gently.

They do not mention Claire and yet she haunts them, the knowledge of her hovering at the edges of Mary's mind.

She is become a dybbuk, a shadow-self, a thing never to be acknowledged. A woman who warns of what Mary might so easily become should Bysshe decide to leave her. She says nothing when he disappears, afraid to call the same fate down upon herself, yet knowing where he is going.

20th September 1815, Lynmouth

Dear Bysshe,

It is almost October and we know what that month brings. My brother Charles is asleep in the chair by the fire as I write. I will be so sad to leave here. I never thought I was made for solitude but this time has changed me. I shall miss the river and the trees and being amongst them with you more than I miss the people, kind though they are. I feel the woods have kept a kindly eye upon me and the river has always been beside me, and yet this will always be a place of sadness for I leave my memory of my child here and I do not think I shall return, for there would be so much to explain. Where my child is and what happened to it.

I will leave with Charles for Ireland, as you arranged, where no one will know us, and there will be no trace of the birth. Charles claims we are travelling to visit a brewery that he might invest in. I hope the family you have found for our child is kind. If I did not love you with all my being, if I did not think that we might change the world, then I would not leave here. I know that we are agreed that I will never be a poet or a storyteller; but I think I might have been a good mother, only not to this child.

Claire

Bysshe destroys the letter at once. By now she will be there, in Ireland – with Charles – giving birth to his child. He feels his gut begin to cramp in sympathy and stands up straighter, stretching and breathing deep, determined to keep the pain at bay. He walks into Windsor clinging to the solidity of the buildings, seeing her face as he lifted her into the air, or as they read the drafts of his new poem together on the banks of the Lyn. He stops at the post office and sends her ten pounds. Then he walks into the Great Park, hiding in the bower he has made to write in.

There he allows the pain to take him, shuddering under the shock of it, the brutal wave of his abdominal muscles overwhelming his body. He bends his head to his knees and groans. When it is over he walks until dark; filled with the loss of his dreams, his children and his Claire.

The next day he finishes his poem, its birth completed with the birth of this lost child. He lifts it from his pocket; it has the sound of the River Lyn running all through it, of their hours shared together. It speaks of Claire's solitude – and her determination to begin again; to found a world where she too can be with him. He does not want the solitary, internal life of a poet, but to live out his philosophy and to fight for it. He folds away the sheaf of papers and carries on walking.

Perhaps Mary was right and a part of the reason they could not make their new world work was that Hogg was not a poet. He must find a way to give new life to his philosophy and for Claire to be with them. He must recapture that spirit of freedom and hope, the desire for a new world that sent all three of them spinning towards France together.

He remembers the words of Byron's poem that he sent Mary, so full of hope, so sure they would succeed:

Oh, who can tell, save he whose heart hath tried
And danced in triumph o'er the waters wide
The exulting sense – the pulse's maddening play
That thrills the wanderer of that trackless way.

The words echo as he walks, repeating themselves until out of them comes an idea as to how they might move forward – together. He has made provision for Claire to return to London. She is free now to spend her time between Skinner Street and Arabella Road, which he has rented for her.

'Claire has been delivered of her baby and I am going to see her,' he tells Mary.

'She is back from Ireland?' Mary asks. 'And well?' Now that it is done she feels a dreadful sympathy for her sister.

'I have not seen her, but I shall go now.'

Mary crosses her arms over her belly. 'You will come back?' she asks suddenly.

'I will,' he says, 'but I cannot desert her entirely.'

'No,' says Mary, and for once the thought fills her with relief rather than fury, for it means he is unlikely to desert her either.

NOVEMBER 1815: ARABELLA ROAD

'I did not know,' cries Claire as soon as he walks in the door, her face white with grief. 'I did not know what it would mean to lose him.'

Bysshe tries to hold her, shocked by the sudden smallness

of her, the changed shape without any evidence of a child to make sense of it.

'I cannot believe what I have done,' she says, 'or remember how I thought it possible.' Again he says nothing; staring at her in a mute pity that ignites her. She has been waiting and longing for him, hoping that with his coming something might change, and her baby be restored to her.

'I do not know where the child is,' Bysshe says miserably.

'You promised he would be safe!'

'Charles was with you, Claire. He met the family but he does not know where they live. That was the agreement!'

She thumps him, her curled fist smashing into his chest so that he stumbles and recovers, only to step forward again, closing his eyes ready for the next blow.

'Yes, close your eyes,' she shouts, 'so you cannot see what you have done.'

He opens them and the pain for her that she sees there only drives her fists forward harder. She beats him over and over as he stands with his body bent forward accepting each blow, saying nothing and making no attempt to defend himself. She goes on until her fists are sore and her recriminations begin to dissolve into silent, furious tears. He wraps his arms around her and she beats him with her head, banging it into his chest, feeling the relief of her pain made real.

'Come back to us, Claire,' he whispers. 'It is not the same without you.'

'Why?' she asks hopelessly. 'What good can it do now?'

He does not answer.

'You cannot bring back what we have lost, and you will always love her best,' she says hopelessly. 'I thought it would not matter, that I could let my child go. Mary must have known how it would feel, she should have told me. How could she allow me to do this?'

'She thought she was helping you!'

'No,' says Claire, wiping her tears. 'She was helping herself. She sent me away when she knew I was with child. She persuaded me to give up my child and encouraged you to desert me in my hour of need. She has failed to live up to every principle you share and yet still you love her.'

'Yes,' he admits. 'I love you both.'

'But she has you,' says Claire.

'And so do you.'

'But only in part; it is what we agreed,' she says dully, 'but it is no longer something I can return to.'

Outside the small room, the sky begins to darken but they do not move. Claire imagines what it might be like to stay in Skinner Street for ever. To go on pretending that she has never given birth, that she is happy and carefree. It isn't possible. She can go neither forwards nor backwards, just as her body can never be innocent again and full of longing.

'Perhaps there is a way,' Bysshe suggests after a while, 'that we can try again. It is done now, Claire. Should we not try and make something of what remains of our lives?' He takes her hand, pressing it to him. 'Of our love?'

'Mary and I can never live together,' she says, her voice flat. 'I was a fool to think so. I see that now. I was a child playing make-believe. You have both lost a child – you should have warned me what pain it would bring!'

'A man cannot know what a woman feels,' he says. 'Tell me what I can do?'

'Stay with me for a while. Don't go back to her. Not yet.'

And so he remains in London tending to her every need.

They do not talk of the child, and he says nothing of the idea forming in his mind, until she asks him herself.

'I do not believe there is any way that the three of us might truly begin again,' she says one evening as they walk through the streets, her coat wrapped tight around her in the freezing air.

'But perhaps there is,' he answers, 'if we can only understand why we failed?'

'But we know why we failed,' she says sadly, as they reach home and open the door. 'We failed because Mary could not share you – and now we cannot be together for we have both lost the children born of our love for you.'

'That is our failure as humans,' he says, bending rapidly to rekindle the fire as she lights the candles. 'As a community perhaps we failed because we tried to make it happen with people who were not our equals, who did not share the creative mind! Mary could never love someone as pedestrian as Hogg, and neither could you. A community must be made up of equals before it can succeed.'

'I am not your equal and yet I love you.'

'You are still the girl who stood beside me in a park and told me that she had no time for God or the Bible . . . You are the woman who had the courage to see that passion does not always mean love. It is not only poets and writers, like me and Mary – but also women like you, Claire – who can see how the world might change. We should never have included Hogg. He's a kind man – but a lawyer, not a man of vision.'

'Then who?' she laughs, longing to be convinced.

'If you could think of anyone, a poet who defies convention, then who might you choose to help build a new world?' he asks. They sit close by the warmth of the growing fire.

Claire remembers walking through France, dreaming of Byron – a poet of her own. She remembers thinking that only poets could inspire a love such as Bysshe and Mary shared. There is only one poet who would place her so far beyond Mary that she need never fear her again.

'Lord Byron, if I could choose anyone in the world, then it would be Lord Byron – he is the kind of man it would take to make it happen.'

'Exactly!' laughs Bysshe.

'But that is ridiculous,' says Claire, smiling in spite of herself. 'He is the greatest poet in the land, and he has every woman who has ever read him clamouring for his attention.'

'And yet,' says Bysshe eagerly, 'they say he is in despair, that his wife has taken his only child and left him, and that the public are as ready to despise him now as they adored him once. Perhaps he too might like to build his own world, a community of like-minded radicals?'

'What interest would such a man have in me?' she says. 'He has women from all over the world requesting locks of his hair!'

'Any man would be interested in you. He would be interested because you are young and beautiful. Because you inspire poetry as you have inspired mine, and Byron, of all men, will admire your freedom of spirit.'

'Perhaps once,' she answers, unconvinced. The thought of her old self exhausts her. 'I am going to bed now.' She does not invite him to share her bed with her. She cannot. Not yet.

'Claire,' he whispers from the doorway of her room.

'Mmm?' She is sitting on the edge of the bed, caught up as she so often is in a sudden memory of her child.

'I am so sorry,' Bysshe says as he lies her down, removing her shoes. 'I do not know if you can forgive me.'

'It is myself I cannot forgive.' She holds her arm over her eyes, turning away from him.

*

'Claire!' he persists, over the course of their days together. 'We do not have to give up on our dreams. If we can make a poet as famous as Lord Byron believe in our ideas, then the whole world will be more interested in what we have to say. And maybe all our . . . difficulties . . . will not have been for nothing,' he finishes.

'No!' she says sharply. 'Nothing can make what has happened meaningful. How can my life have meaning when I have agreed to something so monstrous? When my life has been ripped from the pages of our journals – and I have been turned into an irritating child! No one will ever know I loved you or was loved in return.'

'But would any of that matter if you were known as Byron's lover, the most notorious poet in the land? No one then could deny your existence,' he declares. 'You would have a story of your own, with a far greater poet.'

'No,' she says again, but when she wakes up the next morning the idea is there, waiting for her. She finds heself imagining what it might feel like to finally eclipse Mary.

She imagines Lord Byron carelessly slitting open an envelope and beginning to read the letter that is already forming in her imagination. She could write something that Mary will be unable to destroy, a document that will be her own testament to history where she might be seen as the true disciple of free love. As a woman who, if she offers herself at all, does so with freedom. She will be no Mary Godwin longing for that one love.

Bysshe watches that evening as Claire sits in the pool of candlelight, her eyes glinting as they disappear into thought, searching for the words she will write to the magnificent Lord Byron. She dips her pen and begins.

When she has finished she stands, leaving the letter lying

on the desk. It does not really feel possible that Byron will ever read it, or reply. It feels like a game they are playing in an effort to avoid the pain of her loss. Deep down, she does not believe anything will come of it.

Dear Sir,

An utter stranger takes the liberty of addressing you. It may seem a strange assertion but it is nonetheless true that I place my happiness in your hands. If a woman without either guardian or husband to control her should throw herself upon your mercy, if with a beating heart she should confess the love she has borne you many years, if she should secure to you safety and secrecy, if she return any kindness you may choose to bestow with affection and devotion; would you betray her, or would you be as silent as the grave?

E. Trefusis

As Bysshe reads, Claire allows her mind to drift, the pictures behind her eyes fragmented and broken. Nothing whole remains – only moments or sharp images, for the midwife was rapid. She remembers a rosebud mouth clenching her breast and the tiny dark eyes that opened and stared so directly into her own; the electricity of it, the invisible string that for a brief moment tied them so tightly together.

Claire opens her eyes unnaturally wide and stares at the ceiling, forcing the straight lines of the wooden beams to claim her attention and block out her imaginings. She senses Bysshe reading but she cannot look at him, cannot turn her eyes from the grain of the beams for fear of breaking. When he is finished he comes to sit beside her.

'Claire, I must return for a few days,' he whispers. 'I am sorry,' he adds.

She says nothing for there is nothing to be said. He must return to Mary. After a while he lets go of her. A little after that the front door closes and he is gone, back to Mary.

It is a while before she spots the note he has left beside her own to Byron.

Mary is with child, it says. *I am sorry to tell you such news in the midst of your own loss.*

Claire feels a wave of hate so powerful that it drives her to her knees where she rests her forehead on the floor. Because of Mary, she has given away her child, and Mary's actions are repaid with a child who will be born acknowledged, a child who will exist and have a father.

Claire squashes the note into a tight ball within her fist, paralysed by her powerlessness. Words run through her mind: '*A poet of your own, a poet far greater than me.*'

Claire thinks of the words of her mother: '*We are not like them, they are allowed to be different.*'

And of the words of Mary Wollstonecraft that once so inspired her, now transformed by hate. I will live on a *barren heath* she promises herself, before I allow Mary Godwin to banish me from Bysshe's life, or destroy any hope of ever having his child.

Her fury brings her alive; it fizzes inside her, diminishing the pain of her loss as she plans what she will do. She will send her letter to Byron, and she will take her chances. She is no longer sure if any man can hold her heart, but that one glance into her lost child's eyes has captured her for ever. That is what she truly longs for – and if Byron and Shelley and Mary create a world where they all live together, then who is to know which man's baby she might be carrying?

Bysshe can never be openly acknowledged as father to any child of hers – for Mary would never allow it, but Byron . . . If Byron were to be seen as the father of Claire's child, then it

could never be stolen from her. Her child would, she imagines –
be untouchable. It would have wealth and status and all the
protection that Bysshe once promised. And she would like to
partner the most famous man in England, perhaps the
continent. And as a woman unmarried, free and equal.

Her child, if she were to be blessed with one, would be a
Byron. And a Clairmont. And people would love the child for
her parentage. And her brilliance. Just as they once loved Mary.
But first Claire must make amends with Mary – for if she
cannot then it cannot work.

DECEMBER 1815

Dear Mary,

*You do not wish to hear my sad news and I do not wish to speak
of it. Bysshe, and my mother, kindly keep me in London. I wonder,
at times, how we have moved so far from our lives in Skinner
Street. I think of how we once sat together and imagined a new
world. Must we remain apart rather than live together as sisters
who have both suffered loss? We have done each other harm but
in my own grief I cannot wish you and your growing child
anything but happiness. If you should find it in you to remember
the dreams we once held, of a place where we might all live as
equals, then perhaps one day we might resolve our differences.*

Your sister,
Claire

22nd December, Windsor

Dear Claire,

I am glad you are well. We are happy here in Windsor. You will no doubt be pleased to hear that Shelley has worked well throughout the summer upon on his most recent poem – Alastor. *At times he was so lost in his work he arrived home only to asks me: 'Mary, have I dined?' I fear to disturb him at the very moment he is finally able to put imagination to paper. In writing of solitude I believe one requires it also and his visits to London (and you) disturb him. We have had so much turmoil that I hesitate to change anything. Thank you, Claire, for your good wishes. I hope you understand. Perhaps we might meet at New Year?*

Yours sincerely,
Mary

DECEMBER 1815: 2 NORFOLK STREET – BYSSHE'S NEW LONDON LODGINGS

'Disturb you, did I!' laughs Claire. 'You might write well in Windsor, but your poem is an elegy to our love in Lynmouth; it has the river rushing right through it – and the cave and glens! Has she read it?'

'I do not share the work with her until it is done,' he says.

'But you did with me?' She is touched.

'A part of me must have always been with you,' he says simply, 'only I did not know it until the work was written. And it has Mary within it too.'

'Yes,' agrees Claire, kissing him. 'She is, as ever, your moon, but should the poem ever succeed – then my part in your work will never be known, whilst hers will be celebrated.'

'You will be known as the inspiration of a far greater poet,' he whispers between kisses.

'Will I?' Now that she is committed to capturing Byron, Claire is worried that their plan will not work. 'I have had no reply from Lord Byron, and I have had a clear one from Mary. She does not wish to see me.'

'It is hard that you are welcome in Skinner Street when she is not. But if you should succeed with Byron then I am sure that she will want to meet him. And she will not be able to except through you.'

'If,' laughs Claire. 'But he does not seem at all interested.'

'Send him another letter; let him know that we are friends, and that you too write.'

'But I don't!' laughs Claire. 'Or only letters that no one responds to!'

'Send him *The Idiot*, the story you wrote in France, it will set you apart from the other women.'

26TH JANUARY 1816: WINDSOR GREAT PARK

Mary and Bysshe are walking in the Great Park when the pains arrive. Mary hesitates, Bysshe carries on walking then stops to look back. 'Mary?'

'He's coming,' she says quietly, holding her hand to her stomach, not noticing that she has let slip that she hopes it will be a boy. In fact, hopes desperately that she will not have another girl, not yet. Not so soon.

'Can you walk back?' he asks.

'And if I couldn't,' she laughs, pointing at her huge belly, 'would you carry me?'

'Yes!' he says simply. They turn and walk towards the house, each silently concentrating on what is to come. Mary stops, occasionally overcome by light early contractions. Bysshe holds her as she leans into him, each of them praying silently that the child will be well. As soon as they arrive home she retires upstairs. All is ready.

'It will be different this time, different this time,' she whispers through each pain. Bysshe insists, much to the midwife's annoyance, upon staying in the room and is the first to look into his son's eyes as he emerges.

'A boy!' he cries, and Mary closes her eyes in relief, feels her son's wet flesh land upon her breast and holds him tight, feeling the warmth of him.

'Open your eyes, Mary,' whispers Bysshe, 'for he is perfect!' She opens and sees that it is true. Relief floods her being, followed almost immediately by horror. What if he were to be taken from her now, as Claire's child has been. What has she done?

'William,' she says, 'we shall call him William after my father.'

Bysshe purses his lips; her longing for reconciliation makes him bitter with anger at Godwin. 'William,' he repeats. 'Then William Shelley he shall be.'

From Lord Byron to Claire, AKA: E. Trefusis

Dear M Trefusis;

I do not read unsolicited manuscripts, however you may visit at Drury Lane Theatre if you wish. Arrive at the stage door and ask for the green room.

Byron

EARLY MARCH 1816: COVENT GARDEN

Claire walks down Southampton Row towards Covent Garden. A group of chidren in neat pairs pass her, returning to the foundling hospital in their navy-blue pinafores. She smiles at them and blinks. It might have been her own child abandoned at the door of the hospital, given a new name and some token to identify him should Claire ever decide to return. She is grateful as she turns into Drury Lane for the thought that her child will have a family.

Drury Lane is busy, cabs stopping and servants coming and going to buy tickets for this evening's performance. She searches out the foyer with its new gas lamps before she knocks at the entrance to the side door, introducing herself under the name Trefusis, and is allowed to pass. It feels special being given entrance.

The stairs up to the green room are narrow and she holds her skirts high, clenching her hands deep in the fabric, whilst assuming a bold air. She must appear neither too afraid nor too full of adoration. Byron has enough women who appear before him as supplicants, asking only for a glance from those dark eyes, or a lock of his hair; that is not what she wants. She wants to be as Mary is for Bysshe, his equal.

'Miss Trefusis,' he says as she enters. 'Unless you are yet another married woman in disguise.' He peers at her. 'Are you?'

'Lord Byron.' The sound of his name in her mouth makes her eyes gleam and a smile break out across her face. 'No, I am not married! My real name is Clairmont,' she says. 'I thought it best to use a *nom de plume*.'

'Is it so dangerous to associate with me?'

She looks him in the eye. He has a face that should be beautiful but falls short in her estimation, for she is used to the finer, less fleshy symmetry of Bysshe's face. Byron's eyes are wider and darker and his lips more sensual; a smile twists them up into an expression that she is not sure is a sneer or laughter.

'Women will persist in believing they can write novels,' he says, picking up her manuscript. 'But you have a nice hand, perhaps you could do some transcribing for me.'

Claire ignores his offer for her to become his handmaid. 'They do not merely *believe* they can write novels,' she says. 'They have already proven that they can, but perhaps not all of us have that capacity, just as not all men can write poetry!'

'What on earth did you send me a novel for if you don't believe you can write?'

'I thought I might have the gift once – you cannot blame a woman for trying!' she laughs. 'I wrote under the guidance of a poet named Shelley and his lover Mary Godwin.'

'The pretty boy who wrote *Queen Mab* – amongst other things.'

Claire nods. 'And *The Necessity of Atheism*,' she reminds him, 'when he was but nineteen. He was a boy then but he is a man now.' She looks up as she says it and smiles.

Byron laughs aloud. The girl surprises him. She is not quite eighteen but has the feel of a much older woman, of a life already lived. A sense of something wild comes off her. She intrigues him, lifting the depression at his failed marriage. And perhaps she might be useful in deflecting the rumours that are beginning to circle. Byron knows that he has led a charmed life since he became a lord and a published poet, but he fears it is about to end. There are rumours of a love affair with Augusta, his half-sister, and his estranged wife is threatening to expose his love of sodomy. Claire arrives like a gift – a girl with a public-enough history to perhaps deflect from his own.

'So which of my poems is it that so intrigues you?' he asks.

'I love all of them! Shelley and Mary and I used to read *The Corsair* to each other as we walked across France.' Claire can hardly believe that she is talking to the man she once dreamed of as she watched Mary and Bysshe falling in love. 'Shelley sent its verses to Mary, to persuade her to elope with him. It is a popular poem,' she says confidently, 'but it is most definitely not your best.'

Byron laughs aloud at that; her response surprises him for he thinks the same himself.

'You have read me carefully,' he says.

'With both Shelley and Mary Godwin. Mr Godwin is our father, but he spurns us for we chose to live freely with Shelley rather than become spinsters, or suffer marriage to men who might refuse us our freedom! Even at fifteen I believed that principles should not exist merely upon the page but be enacted in life!' she finishes, wondering if she has perhaps overdone it.

'And those principles are?' he asks, amused by her seriousness.

Claire does not answer immediately, caught up in the intensity of Lord Byron's attention in spite of herself. He has that same quality that Bysshe has, of concentrating upon what one has to say. She does not want to fall in love with Byron, cannot bear the thought of losing her heart to anyone except another child, and yet he could perhaps be a good companion. She considers his question carefully.

'They are derived from Mrs Wollstonecraft; she is my first principle,' she says. 'I lived in her home and her husband was my father. And then there is Shelley himself.'

'The poet who elopes with children!'

Claire stops. 'I did not think you would be so minded to believe in gossip,' she says with dignity, 'for you have suffered from so much of it yourself. Rumour has it that you consort not only with women but also with butterflies!' Byron laughs aloud at that; there cannot be many women who know the name of the theatre boys who sell themselves to men like Byron.

'And so what is the truth of your running away with Shelley?' he asks.

'We went willingly. He promised me freedom from a marriage that would merely bind me to a life of constraint.'

'You do not believe in marriage?'

'We do not,' she says proudly. 'We believe that until women are allowed to love as freely as men, might exchange their bodies as freely as their ideas, and until the world understands the same of us, then there can be no such thing as equality between men and women.'

'Do you know what they say of you, Miss Godwin? That your father sold you both to Shelley!'

'And they say of you that that you slept with your sister,' Claire snaps back. 'Does that make it true?' She is angry and he is not used to the women he invites to his green room challenging him in such a way. He enjoys the combination of her fiery temper and serious philosophy; and is attracted by her youth.

They stare at each other, Claire furious and Byron amused. In that moment they each have the same thought; that the other has a secret, and that neither of them are particularly minded to discover what it might be. Byron laughs aloud, it will be amusing to spend time with her; she is more than just a pretty face and he is in desperate need of distraction: his wife loathes him and is determined to ruin his reputation even further – and his half-sister, whom he loves deeply, is heavily pregnant and must stay away from him to scotch the vicious rumours that he might be the father. He sighs. If the public knew the truth – which is that he loves men as much as he does the women he is so famed for bedding – then they would find it far more compelling than the rumours of incest that so consume them. And so Byron breathes fire into the rumours that do exist, stoking them anew in the knowledge that they hide a far greater, more forbidden love, and Claire will undoubtedly provide a pleasurable way of helping that process along.

'Well,' he says brutally, testing Claire's mettle for he does not want to waste his time on some fainting lily-livered specimen of a woman who cannot bear to hear the truth about herself, 'you certainly cannot write, so what other talents do you have?'

Claire hides her irritation at his rudeness; it does not really matter for she senses that they are using each other. She stares back at him, a hint of amusement in her own dark eyes. She lacks fear, he thinks. I like that.

'Bysshe himself has told me I am no storyteller but I have an eye for description and even Mary says that my letters are more lively than her own, but my talents are mostly for music.' Without hesitation she begins to sing. Her voice is rich and deep, moving easily from a contralto up to a clear sweet soprano. She sings entirely for herself, so lost in the song that he is free to gaze at her. Her voice is beautiful but it is her lack of self-consciousness that really captures him. It is so long since he has been able to lose himself in the presence of another. To watch rather than be watched. He decides he will see her again, if only for the amusement provided by her strange mix of youth and maturity – but mostly simply for the pleasure of her voice.

That evening he writes her a sonnet – sending it with a request to meet him at his town house.

MARCH 1816: WINDSOR, BERKSHIRE

'Please, Bysshe, will you go to London yourself this time, and tell my father directly that we have a child who is named in his honour,' Mary asks as she holds William. 'I do not want it to come from my stepmother.'

Bysshe says nothing; he does not want to meet with Godwin, who has shown no sign of care for Mary – either in her pregnancy, or by repaying the loan he has had, instead of asking for more money, assuming Bysshe will continue to support him.

'Will you?' Mary begs.

'If you ask me then I must,' he says, bending over the child and kissing its tiny head.

Godwin refuses to allow Sir Percy entrance to his house. Bysshe can hardly bear to return with the news that Mary's hopes are once more dashed.

'Did you see him?' Mary is waiting in the garden with William in her arms.

'No!' he says shortly. 'He refused to see me.'

'But do you think he might agree to see William and me?' she insists.

'No, Mary! He does not wish to see either us or our child – and we are fools to stay here, in a country where we are not wanted.' He leaves her there, walking straight to his desk and taking up his pen. He knows what will frighten Godwin and he is angry enough to threaten it.

I think perhaps that we shall leave this country, he writes. *I shall hide Mary and myself from the contempt which we so unjustly endure here in England. Should it continue, and the evil from our desolate and solitary situation flow to my children then we shall once more go into exile, as the only resource left to us against such injustice. In my judgement neither I, nor your daughter, nor our offspring ought to receive the treatment we encounter upon every side. It appears to me that it should have been your especial duty to see that a young family, innocent, benevolent and united, were not, and by your own mouth, confounded with prostitutes and seducers. My blood boils in my veins when I think of the contempt we have endured from you – and all mankind.*

He sends it before he can stop himself. Let Godwin appeal to someone else for money whilst he and Mary live in comfort in a warm climate. The idea, born of anger, begins to take root.

EARLY APRIL 1816: 13 PICCADILLY TERRACE, HYDE PARK, LONDON

Claire arrives early at the Hyde Park town house Byron has specified for their meeting. She emerges from her carriage and walks to the door, nodding to the servant who immediately opens it. He is discreet but she wonders what he thinks of her. How many women have entered the house in this way and what does this man, with his eyes so politely lowered, truly think of them all?

'Madam?'

'Yes'

'Where would you prefer to wait?'

Despite herself she blushes. 'The drawing room,' she replies as haughtily as she can.

The fire is lit and the room is very grand. Far grander than any of the lodging houses she or Bysshe and Mary have rented. The walls are plastered, with gold gilt roses adorning the lamps and gilt coving around the edges. It is a wide, open room, with tall windows and heavy velvet curtains drawn back with sashes. She takes a breath, perches upon a seat near the fire and waits. When he fails to arrive, she plucks up her courage and rings a small bell she spies upon the mantelpiece. A servant arrives.

'A glass of . . . of . . . champagne, please,' she says, the effect of her attempt to be haughty undermined by a sudden, unstoppable smile at the ridiculousness of the situation she finds herself in.

The man nods and disappears, reappearing with a small glass.

'Would you be kind enough to show me to my room?' she asks, having decided she must behave as though she is merely a weekend guest.

Again the man simply gestures towards the door and takes her to a room, which is equally sumptuous. When he is gone she sits on the edge of the bed and drinks the champagne quickly, hoping it might alleviate her nerves. She both longs for Byron to come and yet hopes that he might not. As she sits on the edge of the grand bed she cannot help but remember the small inn at Slinfold, and the inevitability of her coupling with Shelley, as opposed to this arrangement. Her feelings veer between a glory in her power at bringing the great poet to her and a creeping concern that her attraction for him is merely a shadow of her love for Bysshe.

She sits and waits. He is very late and she flips between relief and disappointment. Should she leave? Or perhaps she might stay? Sleeping alone in the grand bed seems preferable to the defeat of leaving. She has almost given up by the time he arrives.

'You came?' she cries, aghast at the note of relief in her voice. It is not at all what she intends to convey.

'What would you have done if I hadn't?' he asks.

'Slept a little, had some more champagne, left in the morning,' she replies airily.

'It would mean nothing to you?' he questions.

'Not nothing,' she says. 'Shelley advocates free love but James Lawrence allows that a woman might simply desire without love.'

'And you, Claire Clairmont, are you merely a collection of the ideas of others?'

'I would not know,' she answers. 'I am not so experienced in love as to have formed many views of my own.'

'But you have known Shelley – as a man?'

'If I had it would not be your concern. You cannot give a woman the freedom of free love and yet continue to claim the right to question her!'

'You are well versed in the theory,' he laughs, stepping closer, 'but perhaps we should experiment with practice?'

Claire does not know what to do. She thought that he would come to her as Shelley had, to slip her dress from her shoulder or make some move to aid her, but Byron stands before her, waiting – that strange smile that is almost a sneer upon his face. She lifts her fingers to the buttons of his jacket, remembering the double bone below Shelley's throat, the fragile sweep of his collarbone. Byron is more muscular, his shoulders strengthened by swimming, his ribs invisible. Claire is intrigued by the difference, feels the tension and power alive beneath his stillness. She slips his shirt from his shoulders; copying Shelley's own gesture she stands upon her toes and reaches up with her lips. Byron bends and as her lips touch his shoulder, sweeps his hands beneath her legs, lifting her into the air and dropping her on to the bed.

'Does Claire still visit Skinner Street?' asks Mary.

The news from her father has depressed her; the sun is shining on the beech hedge that surrounds their garden and yet she cannot take her usual joy in it. The day, despite its sunshine, feels grey and overcast. When she picked up William this morning she felt that strange divide she once felt with Everina begin to open up between them, and looked away from him in horror.

'She does,' says Bysshe, 'but not often, and she has certainly paid a high-enough price for the privilege of their company.'

Mary looks down at William, who begins to grizzle. She is full of the fear that he might die, like Everina, that she will do something wrong again. 'Perhaps we should find a nurse for William?' she suggests.

If Claire were here, we wouldn't have to, they both think, but say nothing.

'How is she?' Mary dares ask.

'She is well,' he says. 'She has asked after you and William.'

'Has she? She doesn't wish us ill?'

'No!' he smiles, coming towards them. 'She has a different life and a poet of her own now.'

'Who?' asks Mary, curious; she holds William close, unable to tear herself away from his gaze for more than a few minutes at a time.

'Lord Byron,' Bysshe says as casually as possible, reaching up for a book from the shelves.

'Lord George BYRON!' she exclaims. 'And Claire!'

He smiles to himself before turning back to her. 'Yes! The very same!'

'How,' she asks, disbelieving, 'did she meet him?'

'She wrote to him,' he says, 'and declared her interest.' He comes and kneels by her, stroking William's cheek, entranced by his child, delighted to find that he is not driven away this time by Mary's absorption, but able to join with it.

'And he replied to her?'

Bysshe looks up at her. 'He did! And so you see Claire has her own poet now, and a far greater one than I.'

'Lord Byron!' says Mary again, shaking her head, before hearing what Bysshe has said. 'And he is not necessarily the greater poet, only the more successful.' Bysshe laughs so loud at that, that William starts at her breast and begins to wail. 'Oh, Bysshe!'

'Give him to me!' he says and takes him up easily, swinging him over his shoulder in a way that makes Mary's heart leap in fear before he begins to walk up and down with him. When he is settled again Bysshe says, 'In fact, Claire wonders if you would like to meet Lord Byron?'

'Oh!' Mary thinks for a moment; Lord Byron, the greatest poet of their generation – and Claire. She shakes her head, but the words that come out of her mouth are: 'Yes! Yes, of *course* I would like to meet him!'

'Well, we should hurry to arrange it, for he is leaving for the Continent soon; the rumours around him grow and public hatred is beginning to mount.'

'We are so far away from London,' sighs Mary. 'I hear nothing! What do they say of him?'

'His wife claims he is a sodomite,' says Bysshe casually, still pacing with William.

'A *sodomite* . . . so does he love men as well as women?' whispers Mary. The word has a terrible power. It is not a word that they have ever mentioned to one another. For Mary it means darkness and death. For a man to love a man and enact such a love is a crime worse than treason. It is an offence against God, mankind and the natural order of things.

Bysshe laughs at her fearful need to whisper, as he pats William's back and the child belches, the look of surprise upon his face making Mary laugh and Bysshe hold William up to see what has amused her. 'Very clever!' he laughs, and tickles William's nose with his own before resuming his walking.

'Really?' whispers Mary again, as though someone might hear her utter the word. 'A sodomite? Does Claire know? Does she not mind?'

'There is no one to hear us here,' Bysshe laughs. 'You do not have to whisper, and no, Claire does not believe it is of any consequence at all. It is not the worst they say of him. They also claim that he is the father of his half-sister's child!'

'It is not funny,' says Mary. 'If it is true that he indulges in such practices then he might hang – an English mob might truly tear him apart!'

'And yet they so loved him once,' answers Bysshe, 'didn't they? Is he not still the same man who wrote the words they so adore? Does loving a man instead of a woman change him?'

'In the eyes of the public it does.' She shivers, remembering the mob that rushed past the bookshop window, trampling over each other in their keen desire to witness death.

'In the eyes of the mob, you and your mother are whores, and I am nothing but a blasphemer and deserter of wives. Are we to see ourselves as nothing more than that – just because they tell us so?'

'Of course not!'

'Mary?' he asks. 'You do not eat sugar because there are people who believe that black men are no more human than animals, and yet when we saw them in Bristol, what did you see?'

'People, just like us.'

'Yet we treat them as slaves. Do they not bleed red? Do their hearts not beat in the same way? They do and yet we choose to believe what suits us, do we not?'

'Yes!' Mary is irritated now. 'But we are not talking of slaves, we are talking of choice!'

'Are we?'

'Of course!' she replies. 'Those men are born black, Byron was not born a ... a ... sodomite.' She whispers the word again as she says it.

'Did you choose to love me?' Bysshe asks.

'You know you need not ask.'

'Answer me! Did you choose to love me?'

'No.'

'As I did not *choose* to love you. Love comes upon us. We do not choose it, and so if Byron loves a man it cannot be a choice, can it?'

'It is a choice to enact such a love!' Mary says stoutly.

'I think,' says Bysshe slowly, 'that is exactly what your father claimed, when he begged you to refuse me.'

There is a stunned silence between them.

'That is different,' Mary claims.

'It is not different,' he insists. 'It is the same. The only difference is that people do not choose to see it.'

Mary feels a deep rush of love for Bysshe as he walks with their child, seeing so easily beyond prejudice. 'But would you risk death for the right to love a man?' she asks.

'I would have welcomed death,' he declares, 'if I could not have loved you.'

Mary remembers how thin he was when her father separated them, how he declared that he would die if he could not have her and of how she believed him. 'Sometimes I wonder,' she says, 'what we are really made of. If there is no God to guide us, or if he proves unkind, then how are we to know what is truly good and what is evil?'

'Perhaps,' says Bysshe, 'we should not think of right and wrong so much, but only of what is kind.'

'I should like to meet Lord Byron!' she says. 'And . . . also . . .' He turns, William asleep upon his shoulder, 'to see Claire.'

10TH APRIL 1816: DRURY LANE

The journey from Windsor to London is not a long one but Mary feels a frisson of excitement as the carriage enters the city. She is filled with a sense of the familiar: the smell, the traders calling to one another, the busy, rapid mess of it all. In spite of herself she cannot help but think of it as home.

The chaise turns into Drury Lane where Claire is waiting to meet her. She is dressed in a deep crimson velvet Angoulême pelisse, tied high at the waist and with a rising collar that frames her face and dressed hair; the white of her dress, beneath the deep-red velvet, peeking through. She searches up and down the street, walking towards the carriage as it stops, looking elegant and composed.

Oh! thinks Claire, as she catches sight of Mary stepping out of the carriage. She looks so strange and old-fashioned in that dress. And so small!

'Mary!'

'Claire.'

They do not linger together but walk rapidly towards the stage door. 'He is so looking forward to meeting you,' says Claire.

'And I him!'

'Hello, Paulie!' Claire says gaily to the boy at the stage door.

'Miss Clairmont!' He smiles, letting them pass. She is so at ease here, thinks Mary with a stab of envy, whilst I am buried in Windsor with a baby.

'Lord Byron,' says Claire as they enter the green room, 'may I introduce my sister Mary Godwin.'

Mary holds out her hand. 'Mary Wollstonecraft Godwin,' she corrects, as Claire stands back.

'My pleasure, Miss Godwin! I am familiar with both your mother's and father's work – as well as Shelley's.'

'And I with yours,' she says shyly.

'Would you like some tea?' asks Claire. 'I can call for some,' she says, enjoying her familiarity with life at the theatre. 'Albe?' she asks Byron – using her pet name for him.

'Would you like tea?' Byron asks Mary, who nods. 'Then yes, Claire, find tea!' He turns back to Mary. 'So you hide in Windsor, with Sir Percy Shelley?' he says.

'I do, and our son William.' Mary has a recollection of how easy this used to be; of how she once thought meeting poets boring.

'And is he writing poetry or polemic at present?' asks Byron.

'He has just finished a narrative poem.'

They talk easily of poetry, Mary losing her shyness and becoming more and more herself as Claire watches, feeling that familiar sensation of Mary taking centre stage. Lord Byron is on his best behaviour, impressed by Mary's intellectual pedigree.

'Oh!' Mary says afterwards. 'He is not at all as I expected!'

'And what did you expect?' asks Claire.

'That he might be improper!' she says. 'Or perhaps too fond of himself.'

'He can be!' says Claire, handing her into a carriage.

331

'Have you . . . have you been to Skinner Street recently?' Mary asks abruptly, as the carriage is about to set off.

'Yes,' says Claire, 'it is the same as ever.'

'I shall hope to meet Lord Byron again,' says Mary, blushing, disliking to ask Claire for a favour.

'I wish we could, but it won't be possible, Mary. He leaves as soon as possible, for the Continent. Life here is becoming dangerous for him.'

'Oh!' cries Mary. 'It is such a shame, and just when we have met. Do you think he might come to Windsor?'

'No! He cannot, he must leave in haste, for the public have turned against him, and his friend Hobhouse says they might do him harm.'

'Then we must lose him just as we have met,' she says sadly.

'But perhaps not!' suggests Claire. 'Maybe we might all meet together on the Continent?'

'How did you find him?' asks Bysshe when Mary arrives home.

'Oh, he is wonderful!' she says. 'He spoke quite normally and not as though he was so famed at all!'

'Have you heard that he is leaving England? Has been driven out, as we were?'

'Yes,' she says, 'it is a great shame to drive such a man into exile.'

'Claire suggests that we might meet with him in Switzerland. Wouldn't you like to return there, Mary? To be where we were neither ignored nor despised?'

Mary hesitates; the taste of London life has awakened something in her, but she is not sure if she would leave England, she still longs for her papa to relent and admit them to his house once more.

'Perhaps,' she says.

'Away from here,' Bysshe says wistfully, 'we might become again what we once hoped to be!'

'And what is that?'

'A community of like-minded souls,' he says, 'with the most famous poet in the land at its heart!'

'Perhaps,' says Mary, again, 'but what about our Wilmouse?'

Bysshe holds her hand. 'He's happy and healthy, Mary, and you have found him a wonderful nurse in Elise. We could go soon, just the two of us, and William and Elise can follow. You have so often said how much you long for us to be alone.'

'And Claire?' Mary asks. 'What of Claire?'

'She would be with us; after all, she is the one introducing us to him!'

'But once we are there, she will not spend every moment with us?'

'No, she has her own life now. It is different.'

Mary imagines the sun as she stares out of the window into the park, the rain dripping off the leaves. She remembers the heat of Paris and lying together in strips of sunlight shining through dark shutters.

'Perhaps,' she says.

PART

❴❵

FOUR

24TH MAY 1816: HOTEL D'ANGLETERRE, GENEVA, SWITZERLAND

The three of them have been at the hotel awaiting the arrival of Byron for almost two weeks now. It is late afternoon and Claire walks along the wide promenade keeping a lookout. He might arrive at any moment in his ridiculous carriage with its golden wheels and family crest painted so brightly on the door. She has a fondness for Byron and he for her, but they are not in love. Claire knows that, but she makes sure that every letter she writes sounds as though she is in the grip of a great passion – for it is not what actually happens in life, but only what is preserved of it that makes history. Mary taught her that lesson and she has learned it well.

To the left of her, Lake Geneva gleams a deep blue in the spring sunshine. She walks down to its edge, gazing through the clear water all the way down to the rocks beneath the surface. A fish glides out, the flip of its silver underside above the surface reminding her of the movement of a child within; so rapid that she can never be entirely sure she really feels it. And yet she is sure she is with child.

She has told Bysshe. 'Perhaps this time,' he whispers to her in one of their rare moments alone together, 'we might succeed in being able to live together. Mary with a child of her own and you with yours.'

'But only if she believes it is Byron's child,' Claire says anxiously. 'You must never think that she could accept that we remain lovers, and that the child might be yours!'

'We will keep this child safe,' Bysshe promises, 'whether mine or Byron's.'

Claire hopes her child belongs to Bysshe because she loves him; she sees that now. She enjoys Byron's company, he is strong and experienced and they often laugh together in his wide bed – but it will never be the grand love she hoped might arise. Claire knows this because no matter how often they make love he never removes his left boot. His left leg is withered and his foot clubbed. If he would only remove that boot then she would know that he stood naked and vulnerable before her, and she might love him in return. But he cannot. She looks up at the sound of wheels along the promenade, but it is not Byron. She longs for him to come, for she needs to persuade him that he is the father of this child. All their plans depend upon Byron's deigning to stop and spend time with them, and yet he is not here. She looks up again; surely he will come – as he has promised.

Bysshe has taken the cheapest rooms at the very top of the hotel. In the day the heat rises, staying trapped in the tiny suite, where they can open the windows and look out directly over the water. Across the lake the dark mountains rise up into the sunshine, Mont Blanc peaked and majestic in the distance. In this weather the mountains appear harmless, but Mary has heard tales of people walking into them and disappearing for ever. Beyond the fertile lower slopes lies a landscape of ice and snow, the coldness of it unimaginable as they lie naked on their bed together in the early summer heat, grateful for the odd breeze through the window.

'I'm so glad that Wilmouse does not have to suffer this heat!' says Mary. She longed for time away from her child but now both misses him and dreads his arrival with his nurse Elise, not knowing whether her love for him will reignite after their absence.

'One day,' says Bysshe, 'we'll ride up to *La Mer de Glace*. Can you imagine it? A sea stopped up and sculpted into ice!' Mary closes her eyes, imagines waves curling high up overhead, never to fall. 'Perhaps we'll all go together once Byron has arrived,' Bysshe says.

'Mmmm,' mutters Mary, for she does not want to think of Lord Byron and his arrival.

She longs for things to remain exactly as they are. In their small rooms tucked away in the roof of the hotel they have easily recaptured those first days of love. They write poetry to each other: '*Thou wert lovely from thy birth,*' Bysshe murmurs as his lips glide across her skin. She loves those words more than any other he has written for her.

She pulls him towards her, looking up into his face, hovering above her own: 'Do you ever fear,' she whispers, 'that you might not do anything of consequence?'

'I fear more that all I have done might be lost,' he answers, 'or that I might do no more.' He kisses her forehead.

'You have done so much more than I have,' she says. 'What if we were to die tomorrow? There would be nothing left of me except the knowledge that I was the child of one famous couple and the lover of another.'

'There would be the life you have lived,' he reminds her softly. 'And William. Does that not mean anything?'

'Perhaps not if it simply passes and is forgotten.'

'Mary,' he says, 'you are only eighteen; you have a lifetime still to live and we are here now, where we can rest and write.'

'But I am only writing scraps!' she cries. 'Nothing of consequence.'

'But that is how it starts. We cannot write things whole all at once, Mary!'

'I think I can,' she says stubbornly. 'When it comes I think it will arrive whole and complete in my mind and I will know it – and yet it is not happening.'

'Perhaps I am right,' he says gently, 'and it is not solitude you need to inspire you but company. Perhaps when Byron arrives,' he says, turning to lie on his back with his hands behind his head, 'then we might find inspiration in each other.'

'Mmm,' mutters Mary, unconvinced. She remembers standing in her room in Skinner Street, her letter agreeing to elope written, and a sense that she held destiny in her hands; knowing that once the letter was gone all would be set in motion, unstoppable. And so it was, and here she is, but what has come of it all, she wonders. She has not written a great novel and Bysshe has only managed one poem. They do not live as part of a world-changing community but have only once more been driven from London. As a child she had no doubt that she would rise to the challenge of matching her mother, but now she is not so sure. Now it does not seem as though it will be quite so easy. Now she wonders if she is quite as talented as everyone once believed.

25TH MAY 1816: HOTEL D'ANGLETERRE

Claire is still awake when Byron finally arrives. It is midnight and her candle flickers as she opens the window, leaning out to see his grand carriage tumble past the window. She is wondering whether or not to go down and greet him, when he appears beneath her window with a companion.

Their voices rise up to her: 'I did not say that I would give you a thrashing, Poli, merely that I could do so if I chose. There is a difference!'

The sound of his voice, the irritated fondness in it piques her interest and she leans out further, but she can only see the top of a dark head and wonders who the young man might be. There is something close and intimate about the way they speak, something that stops her from throwing the window open wider and calling out, or creeping up to his bedroom and surprising him.

They disappear into the hotel and she shivers. The evenings are becoming chilly. She closes the window and writes a note for him: *Direct any arrangement under cover to Shelley, for I do not wish to appear either too curious or in love.* She folds the note over and addresses it to him. It must work, she thinks, unconsciously holding an arm over her belly, whispering to her child, feeling a need to comfort the little being in its darkness.

'He arrived late last night,' Claire says happily as they eat breakfast the next morning, 'and with a companion, I am not sure who!' Mary nods. 'And he always rises very late especially when he is writing,' Claire goes on, 'and so will probably not appear until after lunch!'

But Byron does not appear at all – even after lunch. Claire and Bysshe glance at each other; the fear that he might choose not to stop but simply move on remaining silent.

'He has not rushed to greet us,' says Mary. Claire feels the humiliation of knowing that Bysshe would rush to Mary if he had not seen her for so many weeks.

Mary continues to embroider as they wait, the calm, dip-dip-dip of the needle making Claire want to snatch it up and stab her with it. She shudders. She has risked everything in the hope of Byron and this child. She stands and goes to check the hotel register full of a fear that he might have already left. But his name is there, and he has not signed out. The name of his companion, she notes, is John Polidori, aged twenty-eight, an Italian doctor; he has a neat italic hand. She smiles as she sees that Byron has recorded his own age as a hundred.

She writes him a note: *I am sorry you feel so ancient, but I have been in this weary hotel for over a fortnight and it seems so unkind, so cruel of you to treat me with such marked indifference. Will you go straight to the top of the house at ½ 7 and I will be there.*

That evening she hears the irregular beat of his footsteps as he climbs the stairs. 'Hello!' she says. 'You're here!'

'I am.' He makes no move towards her but stands a few feet away. Outside it is still light; she can see that he is browner, already healthier-looking than when they met in London.

'Mary and Bysshe are looking forward to seeing you.'

'Did you summon me all the way up here for that reason alone?' he asks.

She shakes her head. 'No!' Gesturing towards her small room. 'Perhaps we could talk in here.'

'You want to talk?' He laughs. She ignores him as she walks into the small room and carefully sits beside the bed, rather than upon it. 'I have tumbled every maid from Dover to Chamonix,' he says, 'and have no need of more.'

'You sound like a child, boasting,' she says impatiently. 'I am not interested in your conquests.'

'We must be more careful to hide our relationship here,' he replies. 'I have already had to flee England; I would not have my companion Poli made uneasy.'

'Who is he?' she asks.

'He is a young *dottore* from Italy, quite brilliant and recommended as a companion by my publisher.'

'I do not want to disturb either of you,' says Claire, 'and I do not care whether you are companions, or lovers!' she declares.

Byron smiles, this is the Claire he likes, fiery and with an easy acceptance of the unconventional. 'Then what *do* you want?' he asks. 'And what have you made me climb all those damn steps for?'

'Because I thought you would like to hear in private what I am about to say.'

'Which is?'

'That I am carrying your child.'

He laughs aloud at that. 'And am I to simply accept that the brat is mine,' he asks, 'when Poli tells me every soul in the hotel is already discussing the sharing of the misses Godwin with Shelley?'

'The child is yours,' she says simply. 'There has been no other since we—'

'Fucked,' he fills in for her. 'And what do you expect from revealing such news to me?'

'I expect you,' she says firmly, although she can feel her heart in her mouth, 'to acknowledge the child. That is all; to offer it a name.'

'Well,' he laughs, 'that is a strange expectation, when you do not believe in marriage, or do you not remember making that clear to me?'

'I do not wish you to marry me,' Claire snaps, her patience at an end. 'I simply wish to have a child who knows its own father!'

'Then you should make sure you are in a position to be certain of whom the father might be!'

Claire punches him; it is neither a slap, nor a lady-like tap but a well-aimed, perfectly executed punch to his jaw, made with all the strength of her fury – and it is so sudden, taking both of them by surprise, that he is overbalanced by it, falling to the bed. She rubs her fist. 'Women cannot run away from the consequences of your love-making,' she spits at him. 'Perhaps you have left a trail of your brats as you so proudly call them, from Dover to here, but that is no reason to brag about it, or to desert this child.' He rubs his jaw as she goes on. 'You boast of how you support the weavers, and the working men, and yet you spare no thought at all for the poor serving women you leave destitute and perhaps with child as you pass by on your travels.'

'You have a point,' he admits sombrely, 'but I will neither be trapped nor fooled by you, Claire. I have told you I am done with marriage.'

'And I have never been convinced enough by it to try it. I have said I do not want to marry you but you are too full of yourself to have heard me!'

Byron walks to the door. 'You have played an old, old game,' he says, 'and you have failed. Ask Sir Percy Shelley to father your child.'

'I would, if he were the father.'

'I look forward to meeting him,' he says on his way out. 'Polidori and I will be out sailing for the day tomorrow, but perhaps afterwards.'

In spite of her fury with him Claire is relieved she has not jeopardised a meeting between the two men.

The three of them spy Byron and Polidori the next morning, about to set off in a small sailing boat. 'Albe!' shouts Claire.

Byron turns and at the sight of them brings the boat in. All three of them walk down from the wide promenade on to the small beach. Almost immediately Claire realises that she has been thoughtless calling him in from the boat, for Byron must now limp his way along the beach towards them whilst they watch in an awkward, pitying silence, his club foot in its engineered boot dragging at his left side. It is only now, when it is too late, that she realises how rarely she has seen him walk and of how much effort it must have taken for him to arrange it to be so. Finally he arrives, straightening himself into an elegant pose. Polidori, sitting in the bow of the boat, remains where he is, staring at them. He is small – light and boyish – just Byron's type, thinks Claire.

'Lord Byron.' Claire sweeps into a half-ironic curtsey, hoping to lighten the mood. 'This is my dear friend Sir Percy Bysshe Shelley.' It feels good to be introducing the great lord and celebrated poet to Shelley. 'And of course, this . . .' She turns to Mary.

'We met in London,' Mary reminds Lord Byron rapidly, not wishing to be introduced to the great man for a second time by Claire.

'Of course!' he says. 'You are in no need of introduction, Miss Godwin! I enjoyed our meeting immensely.' Mary nods her head graciously.

'And you must be the poet and blasphemer Sir Percy!' Byron holds out a hand. Shelley lifts his own hand awkwardly in response. Byron grips it hard and Shelley tries not to grimace in pain, or massage it as soon as Byron lets go. 'A pleasure,' says Byron, the warmth of his words belying his vicious handshake. 'I wrote to you of course after *Queen Mab*, and Claire has given me a copy of *Alastor*.'

'Thank you,' says Bysshe rapidly, not wanting to hear what he might think of the poem, 'and we all await the third canto of your poem *Childe Harolde*!'

Byron waves in the direction of the man in the boat. 'That's Polidori,' he shouts, 'my doctor and travelling companion.' The man nods at them. 'Come to supper with us this evening, we can talk poetry then.'

'Thank you! I shall.'

'I dine late, so at seven?' suggests Byron, gazing at Bysshe as he nods. 'And Claire tells me you like sailing; well, we must go out together sometime!' Claire smiles, for she had guessed Byron might be as entranced by Bysshe's beauty as his poetry.

'This evening then,' Byron barks at Shelley. 'Just you alone.' Then, remembering his manners: 'After which we should all meet for breakfast tomorrow!'

They turn their backs as soon as he walks away from them, not wishing to witness that awkward gait through the shallow water, or the effort of his heaving himself into the boat.

'I do not think he would be so anxious to see you if he did not like the poem,' says Mary as they walk.

'He thought it fascinating,' says Claire, 'but perhaps owing a little too much to Wordsworth.'

Mary stares at her; she cannot get used to Claire as an equal, engaged with Byron in the discussion of her lover's poetry.

Deep in their excitement of having finally met the great man together they do not notice the small gathering of people staring at them from the terrace of the hotel until they are almost amongst them. Several women raise their lorgnettes as the three of them approach, staring unashamedly at them. The men shade their eyes against the sun to see the two women better.

'Who are they?' asks one.

'Sir Percy Shelley and Lord Byron, blasphemer and sodomite!' says another as the three of them come closer.

'I wonder which one of the girls is the child of the prostitute,' says a woman. Mary blushes, fighting to hold her head high, refusing to allow it to drop and hide her face.

'And that,' says Bysshe loudly in response, 'is why we believe in educating the masses!' He goes on as though the three of them are talking quite normally. 'To release them from their misapprehension and prejudice!'

Mary clutches his hand and he holds on tight as they continue walking. They are in amongst the crowd now, and must walk right through them to get to the door of the hotel. 'Shameful!' declares one woman, jostling Claire slightly.

'But it is not shameful to block someone's way,' Bysshe asks her, 'simply to satisfy your unquestioning curiosity?'

Claire stares the woman in the eye as they walk past, pleased that she is not the first to look away. Finally they reach the entrance to the hotel and safety. They do not look back but sense the crowd turn to keep watching.

'It is as if we are being hunted,' says Claire indignantly, 'and they have us in their sights.'

Mary says nothing. Is this how she will be remembered? she asks herself. As the daughter of a prostitute and the lover of a blasphemer?

Mary tries to wait up, anxious to know how Bysshe's evening with Lord Byron has gone. But he doesn't return until deep in the night, tiptoeing into their room. The candle has burned down and Mary is fast asleep propped up on her pillow, until he trips in the darkness. 'Bysshe?' she asks.

'Oh, I thought you were asleep.'

'I was.'

'Sorry.'

'How was it?'

He lands next to her. 'It was wonderful,' he sighs. 'We spoke of so many things, and he has read *Alastor* and thinks it worthwhile.'

'Oh, Bysshe!' she cries. 'What did he say of it?'

'Mary, I am so sorry,' he yawns, 'but I am . . . the wine was very . . .'

Mary smiles, for he has fallen asleep.

The five of them meet together in the hotel dining room the following day. There are whispers as Byron and Polidori enter but the two men barely seem to notice. The noise increases as they approach the table where Mary, Bysshe and Claire sit together. Bysshe stands as they approach. The men kiss Claire and Mary's hands. 'It is an honour, Miss Godwin!' Polidori says to Mary, whilst merely grazing the back of Claire's hand with his lips. Surely, thinks Claire, smiling to herself, he knows that with Bysshe here it is not me who is his competition!

'Does such interest follow you everywhere?' Mary asks when they are seated.

'It does,' Byron sighs. 'It is why we have been driven from London, and yet, as you see,' he says with a twinkle in his eye, 'the English find they need me far more than I do them! Why else would they follow me here?' He makes no attempt to lower his voice and seems entirely at ease with the attention, whilst the three of them have to work hard to resist turning their heads to see what the crowd are doing.

'Indeed,' laughs Shelley equally loudly, 'it seems they still hang upon your every word!' He turns to look at a woman who is quite clearly leaning backwards upon her chair, which she rights as Bysshe smiles at her. The two men grin at each other. Mary blushes, and Byron is immediately solicitous.

'I am sorry if it discomforts you,' he says quietly, 'but I find if better if one does not shrink away from the attention, for it only makes the baying of the pack louder. They sense one's vulnerability, the possibility of a kill.'

'It is terrible,' Mary whispers. 'Such interest might be worthwhile if it brought their attention to what we are saying, but they turn every noble idea into something salacious.'

Byron laughs out loud. It is a deep, ringing hearty laugh with a note of pure ribaldry in it. Claire cannot help but respond to the freedom in it. 'Well, it may be that they have a point!' he says, surprising Mary. 'So many noble ideas are at heart simply ways of getting what one wants. Yes, they might have it right at times but generally I find it best to pay no attention at all to them,' he says, his voice rising. 'For the mob are a fucking fickle rabble,' he finishes, glaring around the room, forcing heads to turn back to their plates.

'But how can one pay no attention when they stare at us so?' asks Mary, and yet she finds that as the conversation deepens the five of them do forget, becoming intent upon only each other. They do not notice the female guests who linger over their meal, continuing to cast surreptitious glances at the five whilst their men become impatient to leave. The women note how Bysshe lightly touches Mary's arm as he speaks, how Mary and Claire lean forward and talk as earnestly and intently as the men – and are listened to in return.

Later, in the privacy of their expensive rooms, the women express shock at the girls' behaviour, speculating upon whether they are shared between the men. They stand at their bedroom windows expressing a sudden desire to go out whenever the five of them are walking or when they spy Byron and Shelley sailing their new craft together, taking it in turns to man the sail. The breeze lifts the poets' hair as the women whisper to each other of how appalling they are, even whilst several of them know that at night, beside their sleeping husbands, they imagine the wind in Shelley's hair replaced by their fingers, or their words, like Claire's, commanding Byron's laughter.

'This is ridiculous,' cries Mary one morning, when she opens her bedroom window to find a man with a telescope trained upon her from a boat upon the lake. 'I cannot write when every time I walk or open a window, they are there staring back at me! What pleasure can it possibly give them?'

'We can never know because we do not think like them!' Bysshe says, drawing her away from the window.

'They malign my mother,' she says, 'and we can never escape them. In London they ignore us and here they plague us, yet I fear they will never accept us – or our thinking.'

'Perhaps not these particular people, but their children, or their children's children,' he says easily.

'I heard one of them say yesterday that you had signed yourself "A Democrat, Philosopher and Atheist" in the hotel register at Chamonix!' says Mary.

'I did!' he admits, blushing slightly.

'You bait them,' she says coldly, 'you and Byron, and it only encourages them in their curiosity!'

'What would you have us do?' he asks. 'Agree to be ashamed?'

'No! Of course not.'

'And yet that is what happens if we are not allowed to fight back.'

'We should fight as my parents did – in writing, in books, in describing justice. Not by scribbling in hotel registers.'

'We can do both,' he says mildly, for despite the unwanted attention Shelley is happy; he and Byron spend long hours in the afternoon sailing, and so he does not understand Mary's frustration at being trapped in the hotel.

'We must rent somewhere else,' she says, 'as soon as Will and Elise arrive. Will you start searching so that we are ready to go when they come?'

'Yes,' he agrees, 'and I think Albe might agree to stay by the lake for a while with us.' He lingers over Byron's pet name.

'Not in the same house?' she asks.

'No,' agrees Bysshe, 'but perhaps somewhere nearby.' The two men have become friends, tied together by their love of poetry and experience of being scorned by society.

1ST JUNE 1816: HOTEL D'ANGLETERRE

Mary and Claire wait anxiously for Elise to arrive with William. Mary paces her room, occasionally stopping to glance out of the window, whilst Claire remains with her ears wide open for the sound of the wheels arriving as she transcribes Byron's poetry. The women no longer enjoy being in the garden or promenading around the lake.

Claire lifts her pen from the page so that the ink does not drip or smudge her clear transcription. He has begun the long-awaited third canto of his poem and Claire feels a thrill each time she receives a sheaf of his papers, knowing that hers are the first eyes apart from his own to read his poetry. She likes transcribing, working through the alterations and crossings out, making sense of the final choice of words and writing them down in her neat, clear hand. The orderliness of it calms her and makes her feel useful. The poetry itself, so new and fresh, speaks of a different Albe to the one she knows, a man she might be proud to have as the father of her child.

She is aware that he no longer particularly cares for her, and yet she loves him for the way he writes and the moments when he is able to be tender. And most of all for when he makes her laugh. That is enough. Bysshe is becoming his friend, and assures her he will, in time, persuade Byron that the child is most definitely his. Claire sighs. It must work. It must, for this time there is no alternative. She cannot lose another child.

The thought of holding Will in her arms makes Mary's heart beat with equal amounts of excitement and fear. It is far easier to love William in his absence; the reality of his presence creates within her an anxiety so great that she cannot be at ease with him, and like a vicious, infectious disease the boy senses her fear, and it makes him uneasy. And now she has not seen him for several weeks, will he remember her? Will she be able to love him again, as easily as she did when he was first born? And if she cannot, what then? Is his destiny to die for lack of her love, as Everina has died?

The sound of wheels turning into the stable yard distracts her from her thoughts. It must be Elise and William. Feet run past her room and she opens her door to see Claire disappearing down the stairs ahead of her. Mary begins to run. She cannot allow Claire to be the first to greet William – what if he should think that Claire is his mother? He has been away so long. But Claire, realising Mary is not already there, stands back waiting for her to go first. There he is, her little man. Sitting up in Elise's arms, and looking around. Mary feels suddenly shy; he looks so at ease in his nurse's arms.

'Hello!' she says, her arms reaching out for her child, only to fall back as he turns to Elise, burying his face in her chest.

'He's tired,' says Elise. 'Let's take him up for a sleep.' She is efficient and makes Mary feel inadequate as she directs the hotel staff to take up her cases, all the while holding Will easily upon her hip.

Feeling unnecessary and unwanted Mary takes up a case. Claire comes up just as they are about to set off into the hotel. 'Will!' she calls, and the child turns at the sound of his name. 'Let me take him,' she says briskly, 'so you can have a free hand, Elise!' And without asking she scoops beneath the child's arms, lifting him away. Mary notes the sour look on Elise's face but says nothing. Claire holds Will at arm's length with ease. 'Did you miss us, Will, did you?' Her voice trills up and down the register, soothing and warm, and with a dreadful inevitability Mary watches as Will smiles up at her in delight.

Mary and Elise stalk ahead. Once they are in the room

Elise snatches Will back. 'He needs to rest, you shouldn't overexcite him!'

'He's fine!' Claire says. 'Talking to a child won't keep him awake!'

Mary thinks of her father, of his stern kindness and unbending rules. There was never any silliness, only sober thoughtfulness and the reward of a smile or an awkward pat on the shoulder whenever she demonstrated an ability to override her feelings, subjecting them to the power of reason. Only Bysshe has ever treated her as Claire so naturally treats Will, with an easy, happy abandon. No wonder I love him, she thinks, with a stab of pain beneath her breast, but I do not have that capacity. It is only my reason that he admires, my ability to calm him when he is too wild, and keep him sane when he is tired and ill, or scared.

'The child needs quiet now,' says Elise, dismissing them.

'He's your child,' says Claire as they leave Will's room. 'You could give her the rest of the day off if you would like to be with him.'

'But he's used to her,' Mary says, her heart aching, 'and routines are important for a child.'

Claire says nothing. She will never have a nurse for her own child, she decides. She will be with it always. For ever.

2ND JUNE 1816: TOWARDS MONTALEGRE, LAKE GENEVA

The move away from the hotel and across the lake is a relief for everyone. The three of them pile into a carriage with their luggage and rattle along. The road climbs up out of Secheron, leaving the curious rabble far behind, the lake disappears and reappears through the trees to their right before the road straightens out upon a ridge, and the deep blue water comes clearly into view beneath them.

As they unload, all three of them stop to look out over the lake. Bysshe and Byron's new boat bobs below them in the tiny harbour at the foot of their garden; from the house they can hear the rub of the halyard against the mast in the sudden breeze as the lake is whipped up into tiny white peaks. The breeze lifts the hair from their brows as each of them is filled with a sudden sense of freedom from the endless peering faces.

'I can read in the garden!' says Mary.

'And Will can play there!' says Claire.

Mary's heart sinks. Why wasn't that her own first thought? Why is she such an unnatural mother?

'And we can walk through the vineyards, in total privacy, all the way up to Albe's villa!' Claire adds.

They throw open all the doors and shutters of the tiny cottage, shouting and exclaiming to one another. The biggest bedroom, with windows facing out over the lake and another pair looking back towards the vineyards will be Bysshe and Mary's, the small attic room Claire's – and the room at the end of the corridor on the same floor as Mary is for Will and Elise. The shutters bang as they learn how to fasten them properly and begin to rearrange furniture, making a desk for Mary, so that she can write in their bedroom. She has been trying to turn some of those early remembered days with Bysshe into poetry. A shutter pulls loose and bangs again; the wind picking up.

Bysshe stands alone in front of the house looking out over the lake. He has a feeling, a sense of something. Perhaps it is simply the storm that is coming but it feels far deeper and stranger than that; it feels as though all of his longings, all the things he and Mary once spoke of so eagerly as they fell in love, hover in the air above him; he stands staring until he no longer sees the lake, or the sky or the vineyards stretching away from him, but feels only the delight of possibility. Of his dreams about to come true.

'Bysshe!' shouts Claire from her tiny window, but he does not respond. She leans out further and watches him, lost to everything around him, standing and staring at something that no one else can see.

When they are finished unpacking, the three of them race each other through the vineyard and up to the villa that Byron has rented; the sound of their laughter straying up through Byron's bedroom window as he exercises, forcing his arms up and down, strengthening the muscles of his upper body in an attempt to compensate for his withered limb.

Polidori opens the front door to them, master for a moment of the grand house. The three of them pause on the threshold; the grandeur of the entrance halting them before they step into the hallway. 'Come in!' Polidori gestures.

They stare at the wide staircase and polished floors; he leads them into the drawing room with its tall shuttered windows looking out over the lake. 'It's beautiful!' whispers Mary, thinking of all the dingy rooms they have rented and fled from, unpaid, in London.

The sound of Byron clumping down the stairs warns them of his arrival. 'Hello!' They each turn towards him and he spreads his arms out to the house. 'They say that Milton stayed here!' he says proudly.

'I would,' quotes Shelley, *'that thou and I, led by some strong enchantment, might ascend a magic ship, whose charmed sails should fly with winds at will, wherever our thoughts may wend.'* They are silent for a moment the words hanging in the air. 'Dante, translated by Milton,' Bysshe explains.

'I know that,' snaps Byron. 'It is that you capture so exactly the feel of the place. The enchantment of it!'

'It does feel like a ship,' gasps Claire. 'But one that hovers above the lake.'

'Who knows where it might take us,' laughs Polidori, 'should we entrust ourselves to its sails?'

'Well, it can't take us too far,' says Mary practically, 'because we have to get back soon – Elise is bringing Will up to the cottage.'

'Well, at least look around,' says Byron, 'and perhaps have a drink!'

They stand in the drawing room looking out of its grand windows, exclaiming over the modesty of their own cottage sitting so neatly beneath them. A paddleboat steams across the lake below and Shelley steps closer to the window, framing his face to block out the light.

'See there!' he says, and they all peer out. 'Look. On that boat below, there's a woman with a telescope aimed right at us.'

'No!' wails Mary, stepping back. 'We've only been here a few hours.'

'It's that M'sieur Dejean at the hotel, he hires them out,' says Byron, laughing, 'now that he no longer has us as his customers!'

'But are we to have no privacy at all?' Mary asks.

'It's the price we pay – for daring to be different.'

They all watch as the boat disappears, the woman moving the scope to keep them in sight for as long as possible.

'What is it that they hope to see?' asks Mary. 'What could possibly be so interesting?'

'Perhaps,' says Claire suddenly, 'they are all keeping an eye on us, waiting for the moment that God should choose to strike us down!' The men laugh.

'We should go now,' Mary says, 'before the next boat arrives and the weather gets worse.' She is upset. Her fame is not because she has written a novel, or a poem – but only due to the fact that she dares not to marry, and is considered to share herself between the men. The thought that anyone might believe that to be true brings a hot unwelcome flush to her cheeks. She must write. She *must*. She should be known for more than this.

As they run down the hillside through the vineyards a brief flash of summer lightning sparks above the mountains beyond the lake; the air seems to solidify around them suddenly – damp and hot. Bysshe and Claire disappear inside the cottage but Mary sits on the grass waiting for Elise and Will to arrive. She watches the clouds coming closer over the ridge of mountains, turning the lake a dark grey. A storm is rising; sure enough another flash of lightning arrives followed by a single fat drop of rain. As she watches, the flat surface of the lake roughens into ripples and the sky darkens. She feels the air change and the wind lift. She stands anxiously staring into the growing fog for the sound of a carriage and Will arriving – longing for him to be here, and safe.

The rain begins to gather pace upon her shoulders and she lifts her face up to it, welcoming it, each fierce little drop an explosion upon her skin. She will wait until Will comes; if she stays in the rain, if she makes this small sacrifice, then he will be fine.

'Mary!' Claire runs out into the storm, carrying a cloak. 'Come in!' she cries, the wind whipping at her hair.

'No! I'm waiting until Will comes.'

'Well, at least take your cloak!'

'I don't need it.' She stares into the mist, immobile in the rain.

'She won't come in until Will is here,' says Claire, rushing into the kitchen. Bysshe stands immediately. 'Bysshe,' she says rapidly before he leaves, 'you will talk to Albe soon, won't you – about the baby?'

He comes to her, taking her hands. 'I will,' he promises, 'as soon as the time is right.' Claire nods and lets go, pushing him towards Mary.

Mary has not moved and seems not to notice the rain pouring over her face and falling from her shoulders.

'Mary?' Bysshe says. 'The carriage may have stopped in the fog if it is unsafe to continue. Will does not need you to be ill, come inside!' She shakes her head; he places the cloak over her shoulders and wraps his arms around her until eventually she turns.

'Go in!' she demands. 'Your chest is still weak; you cannot stand outside in the rain.'

'And yet here I stand,' he replies, 'until you come in with me.'

Thankfully the sound of wheels comes at them through the mist and rain and Mary runs down the garden to the road. 'Elise! Elise!'

'What on earth is the matter?' asks the practical young woman, covering Will in her cloak as she gets down from the carriage.

'I thought the carriage might tip in the rain and fall down the hillside—' Mary stops. The sight of her child covered in a cloak to ward off the rain, just as Everina was the day before her death, fills her with a sudden fear. 'Take him in!' she cries. 'Quickly!'

'I am trying to,' snaps Elise, 'but you are in my way.' Mary stands aside and they rush indoors, Mary following. She reaches out for Will but Elise pulls him away. 'You are sodden,' she says, 'and will make him cold!'

Mary blinks at the words as she goes up the stairs, changing quickly so that she can go back down to Will. '*You are sodden. You are sodden.*' They are the exact words Bysshe said, when she arrived at Arabella Road. Is it a sign? Is William to die?

When she comes down Bysshe is alone with Will in the small kitchen. He throws him high into the air and catches him. 'Oh no! Not too high!' gasps Mary.

'But listen,' says Bysshe, doing it again, 'he loves it!' And it is true. William laughs aloud with pleasure.

That night Mary dreams of Everina and wakes in the night reaching for her, longing for her small warm body and imagining that she is about to hold her between them in the wide bed, feeding her back to sleep. When her hand falls upon the emptiness where her child should be, she is confused for a moment, cannot understand.

'Mary?' Bysshe asks half asleep.

'I was dreaming,' she whispers, her voice so wrenched by grief that he places a palm upon her hair.

'Of Everina?' he asks. She nods beneath his hand. 'Oh, Mary,' he says hopelessly.

She sinks into his side. 'Why?' she mutters. 'Why must children die?'

He says nothing, for there is no answer.

16TH JUNE 1816: LAKE GENEVA

The weather worsens as the weeks pass, each day dawning grey and heavy, the darkness clinging to the windows of the cottage; the fog so thick that the garden falling away below is invisible, the blue lake an impossible dream.

Claire paces through the small rooms, unable to settle. 'Do you think it will clear later?' she asks. Mary does not answer. Bysshe has gone to check the boat is secure. 'At least we cannot be seen by the leisure boats now,' Claire rattles on, staring into the fog beyond the sheets of rain, waiting for Bysshe to appear. From above them Will lets out a yelp and Mary half rises before he subsides. Again Claire opens the door, hoping the rain might seem lighter.

'Close it!' snaps Mary. 'And read something, or go upstairs, I'm trying to work!'

'I'm waiting for a gap in the weather.'

'To go up to the villa?' asks Mary.

'I can at least transcribe something, anything rather than sit here and wait for the rain to end!'

'Byron will barely be awake.'

'I know,' Claire bites back.

'You should stay there,' says Mary, knowing that Claire has not been invited to stay with Byron, 'if you prefer it.'

17TH JUNE 1816: VILLA DIODATI, LAKE GENEVA

They are all relieved when six o'clock arrives and they can finally make their way out of the cottage and up to the villa. 'Do not wrap Will up too tight when I am gone!' Mary instructs Elise.

'But it's cold!' Elise argues. 'And if he is not properly wrapped it might wake him.'

Mary is not sure if Elise will obey her, suspecting she will do exactly as she likes as soon as Mary is gone. 'He must not get too hot!' she insists, remembering Everina and her swaddled body broken free of its bands.

'I will be coming back to check, Elise, so make sure you

do as Mary says!' Bysshe threatens, anxious to reassure Mary and be off.

Claire, desperate to escape the confines of the house, has already gone ahead, leaping easily from tussock to tussock up through the vines, illuminated by the odd flash of lightning. They follow her, slipping and sliding, Mary clinging to Bysshe's elbow and laughing as they almost pull each other over, relieved to be outside even in the thunder and drenching rain. Claire turns and waits for them under the protection of the porch door; behind her the lit windows of the villa gleam warm and inviting.

'Quick! Quick!' says Mary, as they reach the paved terrace. 'Knock on the door.'

From behind the windows, Poli hears her and rushes to the hallway to let them in. 'Come in from the storm, we didn't know if you would come. It might as well be night it's been so dark all day!' he says, peering into the sky.

They run into the warmth of the drawing room, the red velvet curtains drawn tight and the light of the fire and candles making the walls draw closer, womb-like and warm. Bysshe sits close to the fire, the flames making spiky shadows of his long lashes against the wall. A sudden gust of rain flies against the windows, rattling the shutters so hard it seems for a moment that they might shake loose.

'Quite a night!' says Byron, standing beside the fire, one arm resting lightly upon the mantelpiece as the fire flickers and fights to stay alive against the breeze drifting down the chimney. A sudden bolt of lightning strikes beyond the window, illuminating the room in a brief white glow.

'Oh!' Mary cries out in surprise, before laughing at her fear. 'It is silly to be scared,' she says, collecting herself, 'and yet it feels so alive, the storm – doesn't it? – as though it were a thing in itself and not merely some natural phenomenon.'

361

As she speaks, the wind moans around the house like a live thing. Byron moves from the mantelpiece towards the window, drawing back a curtain to peer out. A sudden gust of wind drives the rain against its panes. Beyond lies the distant sound of rolling thunder.

'What a start to a tale this would be,' he says. 'The five of us trapped together by the storm.'

'And my tale would begin with you standing exactly as you are,' Polidori replies, 'standing beside the window, your body framed for a moment by a shaft of lightning!' His voice lit up with adoration for Byron.

'And would I be real,' asks Byron, 'or some spirit newly returned from the dead, a mere shadow of my former self?'

'I think,' says Polidori slowly, 'that you might be one of the living dead, a vampire.'

'There is no such thing!' laughs Byron, but the others shudder at the image.

'Well then, the lightning might turn you into ash,' says Mary, 'for vampires are creatures of the night, aren't they, and dissolve in the daylight?'

'They are not only creatures of the night,' says Byron, 'but of passion too!' He eyes Polidori as he speaks. 'It is passion that ties them to the human world. Beyond death.'

Mary shivers at his words; did her mother not have enough passion to return from the dead, nor Everina? Or perhaps they are already here, hovering above her – unknown to her – watching.

'As a doctor,' Mary asks Polidori, 'do you believe in an afterlife, or an elixir that might create life? Or in any of the things that so fascinate the storytellers and scientists?'

'I know only that we are all born and that one day we will die!' he answers soberly. 'I do not know what animates us, or drives our desires.'

'And yet you have watched the spirit leave the body?' she asks. Polidori nods soberly. 'What happens?' asks Mary. 'Do you feel there is separation, that a soul departs?'

Shelley stands up and moves next to her, knowing that Mary is thinking of their lost daughter. He sits beside her, holding her hand beneath the cover of her skirts. Beyond them the curtain remains open, the clouds racing across the sky, the light of an early moon silvering their edges.

'Death is a strange thing to witness,' says Polidori. 'Most often, at the end there is a struggle, whether it is between the soul and the body or between life and death itself, I do not know, but only can tell you what I see.' The four of them lean closer, unaware of how rapt they are, or of what pleasure it gives Polidori to witness them each so intent upon him. 'At first the breath persists in fighting for life,' he says, 'but finally it fades – and there comes a moment of such stillness, such peace.'

'A passing!' says Mary.

'Yes!' he agrees. 'But to where we can only imagine.'

Mary would like to think it was as gentle for Everina as Mrs Knapp described it was for her mother – a slipping away – and yet she does not believe it was so.

'And will we ever defeat death?' she goes on. 'Are the things that some scientists claim truly possible?'

'What do they claim?' Byron asks.

'That the lightning that we witness falling from the sky is the very thing that animates us!' announces Claire in sepulchral tones, her words accompanied by a loud crash of thunder and a white flash that makes all five of them jump in shock, before laughing together in embarrassment – ridiculing their fear.

'The storm is directly overhead,' says Byron matter-of-factly. 'That is why it sounds so loud! More wine!' he calls, and a servant enters and fills their glasses, silently withdrawing as soon as he is done. 'Bring the rest of the decanter,' he instructs, 'and do not disturb us again, for we will manage for ourselves now.'

'On a night such as this it is easy to see why people might believe that a storm is in fact God's anger directed at us,' says Claire.

'It is not God who sends lightning from the heavens,' scoffs Bysshe. 'That is no more believable than the story that it might be Thor.'

'And yet it is believable to some, even some who are scientists,' says Poli mildly. 'We cannot know if it is God who sends bolts of electricity to frighten us with – but we are close to being sure that electricity plays some vital part in our being.'

'How?' asks Mary, her chin in her hand and her mind full of questions.

'Because of two brilliant men,' he replies, 'both Italian, of course!' They laugh at his patriotic pride and he nods his head in recognition. 'The story is a little gory,' he warns them, enjoying playing to the crowd. 'Would you like me to continue?'

'Oh, get on with it, Poli!' laughs Byron.

'Well, a man called Galvani, a scientist of course, applied an electric current to the nerve of a frog's leg – and although it was incontrovertibly dead, yet the frog's leg moved.'

'How?' asks Claire.

Mary imagines the frog laid out upon a table, its limbs stretched and immobile. In her imagination a lit taper burns feebly in the background – all that illuminates the scientist's bench; she sees the tip of some implement draw closer to the small leg, the application, the touch of electricity and then the spark – and the sudden movement. The sudden movement of a dead limb – and the horror.

'It moved of its own accord?' she asks.

'That is the right question,' says Polidori, 'but we do not know the answer, for the two scientists disagree. Galvani believes

364

that it is God who resides in that current – that when the leg moves it is God's power we witness, conferring momentary life upon the dead.'

'As though it were God's own breath,' whispers Mary, 'bringing life to the poor dead animal!' She remembers her own attempt to hold Everina to her breast, as though the life force of her own milk might restore her child to life. What a gift it would truly be. What magic!

'Galvani *would* believe that,' scoffs Bysshe. 'He is a Catholic, after all!'

'And I heard they made the same experiment with a man,' says Claire, 'in London.'

'And did they make our dead bodies move?' exclaims Byron, lifting his arms as though manipulating a puppet. There is something monstrous in the movement, his shadow playing on the wall behind him, hunched over and grotesque.

'They did,' says Polidori. In the short silence that follows his words they notice that the rain has stopped, and yet even as they take note it begins again, a slow pattering like a crackling of dry leaves that gathers pace until it is beating steadily again against the windows.

'How?' they each say.

'By the same method, by applying a current.'

'And to which part of his anatomy did they apply it?' asks Byron with a raised eyebrow. Polidori, Byron and Claire laugh together but Mary and Shelley are too intrigued by Polidori's words to notice.

'Was it the man's leg?' asks Shelley seriously.

'Did he sit up!' asks Mary, imagining it.

'Did his eyes open?' asks Claire.

'Or perhaps he stood up and said a few words to the company,' sneers Byron. They each turn to him, too dazed and intrigued by the story to allow his cynicism entrance.

'Ridiculous!' he sighs. 'Just think, if lightning had the capacity to bring us all back to life then surely we would have learned by now to simply lay our dead out on the ground in a storm and have them restored to us.'

Mary remembers her dream in the days after Everina's death, of her child's cold white marble body slowly flushing with a pink rosy glow, of her eyes opening and her breathing restored. She would happily have lain naked all night in the fiercest of storms if there was even the slightest chance that it might have brought her daughter back.

'You are a cynic, my lord,' says Polidori, 'as is the other Italian scientist. A man called Volta of Pavia – who claims that electricity is but an external force that comes from outside the body and yet still has the capacity to make it move.' Both Byron and Shelley nod in agreement.

'But who is right?' asks Claire.

'How can we know?' replies Polidori.

'Do you think that one day,' asks Mary, her eyes glinting in the firelight and her face full of wonder, 'we might truly bring someone back from the dead?'

'At times,' whispers Polidori, 'anything feels possible. We are on the brink of a scientific revolution as big as Copernicus's discovery. We no longer believe that God or the church rule over us –' he nods at Shelley, recognising his part in the change – 'and so the bonds of marriage become unnecessary, and perhaps soon we will also discover that death itself is also unnecessary!'

Mary rises and walks over to the windows where she gazes out into the darkness, transfixed by the ideas Polidori spins so easily, needing to think.

The fog has cleared but the lake remains a distant gleam behind the curtain of rain, its drops lit up by the odd flash of lightning. Her thoughts shifting as rapidly as the clouds above her. Anything might happen, she thinks, if all the wild energy of such a night were to strike a dead frog lying silently by the road. Who knows? It might bring it to life. Her thoughts swirl and she would like to lie alone and follow them to some conclusion.

'We should go,' she says suddenly. 'Elise will be waiting.'

They gather their belongings, but as soon as they step outside the door a sudden crash of thunder and deluge of rain causes all three of them to retreat; sheet lightning illuminates the mountains beyond the lake and the image appears burned on Mary's retinas, the tops of each pine clearly delineated before being plunged back into darkness. The thunder and lightning come in brief consistent bursts one after the other, framing the lake, the clouds, and again the mountains. The rain is relentless.

'You cannot go home in this,' says Byron.

'But we must!' says Mary. 'We cannot leave William alone all night.'

'He is not alone; he has a nursemaid, doesn't he?'

'Yes, of course but—'

'Mary, the lightning is almost constant,' says Shelley, 'and it does not only confer life but can also take it. William will be asleep – it will not hurt him for us to remain here a night.' Unsure, Mary agrees, for what if she were to step into the night, to insist upon going home, and it were the wrong decision, leading them all into tragedy. No, she should let others decide.

'And tomorrow we shall each write a ghost story!' says Byron. 'There's little else to do in this vicious weather. It will take up the afternoons.' He glances at Bysshe as he says it, thinking of the long afternoons they have spent in the boat together, lost to them now with the change in the weather. 'We'll each read them all when they're done, shall we? – and decide whichever we like best!'

Claire groans inwardly. She doesn't want to write a ghost

story; we each have ghosts enough of our own, she thinks; both living and dead. 'Well, I am tired,' she sighs, 'and must sleep if about to embark upon a story tomorrow.'

They all stand and in a burst of enthusiastic chatter make their way to the stairs. A manservant appears, guiding the guests to their rapidly prepared rooms, the fires in each of them already lit.

'Goodnight,' says Claire.

'Do you know what you will write?' Mary asks.

'Nothing!' says Claire. 'But I understand Polidori is writing about vampires. Perhaps that is not so surprising for he loves Byron, and Albe is a man who sucks people dry and discards their dead bodies!'

'Bysshe?' asks Mary as soon as they lie down together.

'Mmm.'

'If a man, a man like Dippel, who owned that castle on the Rhine, and gathered up dead bodies . . .'

'Mmm.' Bysshe strips off his shirt and leaps into the bed. It's cold. 'Hurry, Mary!'

She lies down fully clothed and he sighs. 'Well, if he did manage to confer life upon a dead body, then what might happen, do you think?'

Bysshe settles his arm beneath the weight of her head as he thinks. 'I imagine it might be quite a surprise to find oneself alive again!' he says.

'But it is not life as we know it, is it?' she persists. 'Not really, for it is only movement.' He waits, knowing that her thoughts have not unwound, that there is more to come. Sure enough, after a few moments she begins again. 'I mean, a charge of electricity might animate the body, but what of the soul? What of the very thing that makes you Bysshe or Poli Polidori?

Would electricity bring that back to life too? Or would we have lost the essence of ourselves and be like children once more, all unknowing?'

'There is no answer,' he says. She can hear the smile in his voice; the delight he still has in her thinking. 'We can but imagine what might happen.' Her thoughts revolve as she closes her eyes, losing herself in the warmth of his body, revelling in the knowledge that they are alive together – not dead, the warm blood flowing through their veins.

Bysshe waits until her breathing slows and she is sleeping, her eyes moving lightly to the images behind them. He slips his arm from beneath her head and stands – slipping out into the corridor where he fumbles with a candle, trying to light it quietly in the dark. He walks lightly along the landing and down the stairs towards Byron's study. He must talk to him and there is a strong chance that he will still be awake and writing. He carefully looks around the open door to see Byron staring back at him.

'You look as though you've come to rob me!' he laughs. 'Is there anything you particularly wish to steal?'

Bysshe blushes. 'I simply hoped we might talk privately.'

Byron stands. 'Come in.' He stands from his desk. 'More wine?'

Shelley shakes his head, sits back and waits for Byron to place himself in his usual position by the fire, as though he might be posing for a painting. Bysshe stands opposite him. 'It is awkward . . .' he begins.

'Yes,' says Byron, scratching an ear. 'I imagine it is when you are not used to it.'

Bysshe frowns; does Byron already know why he is here, and if so how? 'And yet it must be discussed between us,'

Bysshe suggests. Byron merely nods again, forcing him to go on, as though amused by his discomfort. 'Claire is distressed,' Bysshe says. 'She tells me you still do not believe that her child is yours.'

Byron demonstrates neither his surprise nor disappointment that Shelley is not here to declare a passion for him. 'Is she?' he asks. 'She appears quite content to my eyes.'

'But she is not,' says Bysshe. 'She is unhappy that you deny you are the father of her child.'

'And you are here to tell me that I am, is that it?'

'Yes.'

'And are you sure?' Byron persists.

Bysshe is surprised to find a slight blush rising in his cheeks. 'I am,' he declares, perhaps a little too vehemently.

'I do not think so!' Byron smiles at him.

'I do not understand what you mean.'

'No?' Byron asks, reaching across to stroke Bysshe's cheek. 'Perhaps you do not, for I believe you are one of those rare men who is truly blind to his own beauty. But you cannot also be blind to Claire's love for you, can you?'

'I think you mistake a deep affection. We have been through much together.'

'I am neither blind nor stupid enough to believe that with your beliefs your love for each other has not been consummated.'

'It has,' says Bysshe with a quiet dignity, 'but it was too long ago for it to be of any consequence here.' He does not like lying, but his aim is to find a father for Claire's baby.

'She came to me freely,' says Byron, 'claiming that she would expect nothing but pleasure for each of us.'

'Do you claim that you have no responsibility at all for the natural consequence of what has occurred between you?' asks Bysshe. 'Or do you suggest it to be the woman's responsibility alone?'

'It is her body,' Byron says simply. 'And it is also a consequence of free love! So what is your solution?'

'I would not desert any child of mine,' Bysshe claims, 'without the agreement of the woman concerned.'

'And Claire wants this brat, does she?'

'She wants a father for her child. You must know her story – she has never had a father herself and so it means much to her that her child be acknowledged.'

'And you are not simply palming a brat of your own upon me?'

'No!' Shelley shakes his head and is utterly convincing, for in that moment he has convinced himself.

'And your own dalliance produced no child?'

'It did,' says Shelley, 'but Claire decided that she would not keep it.'

Byron is shocked by the truthfulness of his admission. 'And what changes her mind this time?'

'Perhaps it is the loss of our child. It was more shocking than she imagined it might be. She has sacrificed so much to her belief that we might build a different world.' Bysshe falls silent.

'And what place do I have in your world, Shi'loh?' Byron whispers.

'Why do you call me that?'

'Because despite being an atheist you persist in believing that you might find heaven upon earth, that we might love and not feel envy or jealousy, but each share and be happy, as did the angel Shi'loh believe in such perfection – but it is a dangerous philosophy, my Shi'loh.'

'Why is it?' asks Bysshe, drawn close by the rough gleam in Byron's eye. He watches, hypnotised, as Byron's hand comes closer, holding his jaw, until with a profound inevitability he feels Byron's face come so close that his lips brush against his own. He is intrigued by the soft fleshiness of them, closing his eyes to concentrate better.

They stand together in the firelight, unmoving.

'Should not this be equal too?' whispers Byron. 'Is there room in your dream of a perfect world for the sodomite, poet, my Shi'loh?' he asks.

Unable to speak, Bysshe merely nods.

'You are right, as ever,' says Byron. 'It is a love that cannot be spoken, and yet we must find the words, and the courage to speak them. Tell Claire I will acknowledge her child and that I know the truth of it.'

'Thank you,' whispers Bysshe.

The next morning Mary looks anxiously through the windows hoping for a break in the weather, but it only settles deeper, a heavy drenching mist drifting up the hill to hover at the edge of the villa's terrace, making the inhabitants feel strangely cut off from the rest of the world – suspended from reality.

'Byron was up late,' explains Poli as they eat breakfast, 'starting his story. And I too have made a beginning. And you?'

'No! I cannot think of anything at all,' says Mary, irritated by the fact that they all seem to find it so effortless. 'What about you, Claire?'

'I have given up on writing tales!' Claire says. 'I am better at letters and perhaps . . .' She was going to say 'journals', but stops herself. The girls avoid each other's glance and Polidori is curious for a moment, sensing something. They are a strange trio: Mary, Claire and Shelley.

'Bysshe is writing of a haunted wood; it is a tale he used to tell his sisters, when they were children together!' says Mary. 'Did you study long to become a doctor?' she asks Poli, hoping to change the subject.

'A while,' he answers, buttering his bread and lifting jam from a jar.

'I do not think I could do it,' says Mary quietly. 'I have heard you must study the dead, cutting up their bodies as though they have never had life flow through them.'

'But we cannot learn in any other way,' Polidori says gently. 'If we are to heal what lies beneath the surface then we must know how each joint is formed, how it moves and where each organ lies. And I at least always treated each body with the utmost respect – although, I am afraid, a fellow student spent much of his time pulling tendons and making the cadavers wave!' Mary shudders as she imagines it.

Afterwards they each disappear as Mary paces through the empty rooms and hallways, a ghost herself, in search of an idea. She stops and sits, staring into the rain for a while, picks up a volume of ghost stories hoping they might inspire her, but nothing comes. She feels a faint sense of dread as the evening approaches – anxious that she alone has failed to begin.

As they gather in the drawing room they ask her again: 'Have you made a start yet, Mary?'

'Nothing!' she says, frustrated. 'I spent the entire afternoon reading ghost stories and yet not a single one inspired me!'

'Perhaps,' says Byron, 'we can read some together, after supper as the witching hour approaches?'

Byron reads well, acting the words as he speaks, inhabiting the characters in the story – he transforms himself easily from a young girl terrified of a portrait whose eyes seem to follow her, into a man who returns after his death, desperate for revenge. He brings the stories alive in the flickering firelight, the pictures he paints floating behind their closed eyes.

In the midst of the story Mary rises, once more unable to sit, too consumed by the memory of her own mother's portrait and her childhood belief that her mother was always silently alive behind her picture, watching her daughter go about her everyday life – approving of her. She cannot stay still but needs to look out at the rain falling and allow her thoughts to rise.

After a while Polidori comes up behind her. They are alone by the wide window. Byron has stopped reading and he and Bysshe and Claire are deep in a quiet conversation around the fire. Polidori says nothing but she can feel his affection for her.

'What do you think remains of us,' she whispers eventually, 'when we are gone?'

'Do you mean of the body?'

'No, beyond the body.'

'I think perhaps that it is only love,' he answers, 'that remains beyond death.'

'And the spirit?' she asks. 'What of that? I understand that if Bysshe died my own love would remain, but what of the dead one's love? Will Bysshe's love for me simply dissolve when he dies? I cannot believe it. It must remain *somewhere*.'

'What troubles you, Mary?' Polidori asks gently. And she almost speaks; indeed she would speak, if she but knew the answer to his question. 'Perhaps after death our love is somehow reborn?' he suggests. 'For that is what some eastern religions would have us believe.'

'You mean that we inhabit a new body?'

'Or many bodies,' he replies, 'over and over until we learn to be free of our passions. And so perhaps you are right, Mary, it is our passion that remains after death, only it is not a blessing, but a curse.' He glances rapidly at Byron. He looks sad, realises Mary, as though he is speaking of himself. She nods in agreement. Polidori may be young but she can see why Byron has chosen him as his companion. His thoughts run so easily alongside one's own. He talks of love with ease. Is he

Byron's lover? The thought makes her shiver with fear for them. If it is so, then they can never return to England without facing terrible danger.

She rests her hand gently upon his forearm. 'We talk of everything and nothing,' she says; he understands at once.

'There are things we cannot speak of freely,' he replies.

'It should not be so,' she says passionately.

Touched, Polidori clasps her hand. 'Perhaps one day such love will not be consigned to the dark.' He smiles lightly but his heart is heavy, the darkness coming not only from the hidden nature of his love, but also from Byron's failing interest in him. Poli has replaced Claire and now will be replaced himself. 'Come,' he says, 'we should join the others.'

Claire looks up as they return. 'We were just wondering,' she says lightly. 'If you were to return from the dead, what would it be that draws you back?'

'A time when I was happy,' says Poli, touching Byron's arm, but Byron does not notice for he is gazing at Bysshe.

'Meeting Mary,' says Bysshe. He makes shadows on the wall as he speaks, his long supple fingers slipping from birds to sails in the wind. 'Or a longing to write the things that death has robbed from me!'

They each turn to Mary. 'I do not know!' she says, stumbling, for there are so many longings within her; the longing for her mother and Everina to have lived; for Bysshe to be hers and hers alone, and beyond it all there lies the longing that she feels she has carried from birth; the need to have written something that might set the world alight and make her name not only as the child of Mary Wollstonecraft and William Godwin, or as the lover of Shelley, but as Mary Wollstonecraft Godwin in her own right. A woman attached to no one but herself and her own fame. 'I think,' she says eventually, 'that I would rather not die at all.' Making everyone laugh as they agree with her.

Mary falls asleep easily that night, breathing lightly in Bysshe's arms to the accompaniment of the rain against windows; a sound that has become comforting and expected. As she sleeps, her thoughts writhe within her, gathering themselves together into an image that slowly forms behind her sleeping lids. She sees her lover's face hovering over a table in the flickering candlelight, haunted and pale with the effort of creation, lost as he so often is in his attempt to bring to life an idea or a piece of poetry. She turns in her bed and the dream vision deepens. Bysshe is no longer writing but standing over a table that is hidden from her sight, the shadow of what lies upon it thrown against the wall. She cannot see it. In the dream she peers but cannot make out what form the thing takes.

As she dreams, the storm throws a bright lance of lightning through the window, illuminating her sleeping face. The shaft of light crosses the barrier between sleeping and life, entering her dream, where it falls across the face of her lover, lighting up each feature, accentuating the hollow of his eyes intent upon the table, staring in horror at something she cannot see. Beneath the covers of her bed her heart begins to pick up its beat. She is afraid. She does not want to look down, to see what lies there on the table, and yet against all desire she finds her eyes inevitably begin to drift downward.

It is a body! Her heart stops in fear. A body, and yet not a body: a thing of parts, a thing that has been gathered together from charnel houses and graveyards. Visions flicker fast across her brain – splintered empty coffins, her father pulling her away from the graveyard, the face of her lifeless child – and above them all the repeated bright white flash of electricity until as she watches in horror the thing on the table, at once both monstrous and magnificent, begins to rise.

'No!' she calls out in her sleep, and sits bolt upright in the darkness, her heart racing. The image threatens to fade but she clings to it, despite the fear it brings her, for her heart is racing not only with fear but also with excitement.

It has happened! She has had her idea. She stares at Bysshe as he sleeps on, unaware. Quietly she rises from the bed and sits by the window. The rain has stopped; the storm abated. The lake lies silver under the moon and her thoughts rise within her, tumbling one after the other, so fast that she can barely catch them.

'This,' she mutters to herself, 'is what I shall write of . . . a man in the grip of an idea, a man as intent as Bysshe; a man haunted by the magnificence of an idea, caught in the grip of it, as she is now. An idea that does not only question the world's thinking but challenges its very foundation. A man who wishes to create a world in which death is finally defeated.' It is a wonderful idea. A glorious, breathtaking idea; even the sight of her beloved's gently sleeping face fades before her as his imaginary self takes hold of her. Slowly the words begin to come and she whispers them to herself, committing them to memory, ready to write in the morning.

'Do you have an idea?' they ask her the next morning.

'Yes,' she says. 'I do. It came to me in a dream, a dream of all the things we have been talking about, and how they— Oh, I cannot talk too much about it!' she says happily, eating rapidly before disappearing upstairs, the pen in her hand and the others forgotten as she writes. She had always dreamed it might be like this; the ideas simply rising up ready for expression. In creating a character she realises she must give him a family, and at once the Baxters come to mind, their easy love and joy

377

in each other flowing on to the page, surrounding this haunted scientist of a man, whom she has decided she might call Frankenstein, in honour of the castle upon the lonely crag by the Rhine, where she once imagined living alone with her lover.

She leans back, stretching her arms; her wrists ache almost constantly, cramped from clutching her pen. She writes for so long that she does not hear the ticking of the clock in the hall and only vaguely remarks upon the sun finally breaking through the clouds for an hour or two. She does hear Bysshe shout up to Claire: 'Don't disturb her, don't call, she'll join us when the muse tires of her.' But her muse, so hard to find, does not desert her and they flow together into another dimension, where she is at peace. She does not notice Bysshe standing by their bedroom door, or hear him. It is only when he touches her arm that she jumps and turns away from the page.

'The storm is over, Mary,' he says gently, 'and we can go back to Will.'

'Oh yes, yes!' she cries, appalled that as she wrote she had entirely forgotten her child.

'She is happy!' says Claire, as she and Bysshe leave the house to walk along the banks of the lake in the rain. 'I do not think I have ever seen Mary so happy, except when she was falling in love with you!'

'It is like that,' he agrees, 'when the muse has a hold of you.'

'I used to think that only poets could love a person with such intensity, but now I wonder if it is truly the person they love or the idea of love itself.'

'I have spoken with Byron,' says Bysshe when they are no longer within earshot, 'and he has agreed to acknowledge that he is the father of your child.'

'Truly?' she asks, trying to take the words in, to allow herself to believe them. 'He will acknowledge the child?'

'Yes!' Bysshe says, holding her elbows.

She begins to shake. 'You are sure?'

'Yes, he will give the child his name and agrees to acknowledge it openly.'

'Why?' she asks sharply. 'What has changed his mind?'

'I told him the truth, Claire.'

'What, that you might be the child's father!'

'No! That we have had a child, and I have assured him that I will continue to support you even to beyond my death should you or the child ever need it.'

'What do you mean?' she asks. 'Why should that be necessary?'

'It is my own acknowledgment of our relationship,' he says, 'and I should have done it long before now. Forgive me.'

'Done what?' she asks, exasperated.

'I have included you in my will. I will show you the document!' He laughs, mistaking her silence for disbelief.

'No! No! It is not that I did not understand you . . . it is . . . a shock,' she says. 'It means that I will never have to consider marriage without wishing to, or have to become somebody's servant should you die. Oh, Bysshe, it means that my child will be secure and my freedom to live as I choose complete. I have hoped that this child would have a father's name upon her birth, and feared so much it would not be so. So now we can tell Mary,' she says happily, 'that I am with child? And we can live with you and Will – they will be like brother and sister as l hoped . . .' Her words begin to fall over themselves in relief and happiness.

'Yes! But only once we have agreed the details with Byron.'

'Yes. Yes, of course. Oh, Bysshe . . . I . . .' She looks up at him. She has entrusted all her hopes to him, lived daily with the fear that he might fail or desert her, but here he is, standing beside her, unaware of the rain running over his face or of how wet they both are – jubilant at her happiness.

'Claire,' he cries, 'whatever happens to me, or Byron, you and your child will be free. You are no longer dependent upon anyone!'

'Thank you,' she whispers. 'And my child will have an acknowledged father!'

'Miss Clairmont.' He bows. 'I declare you a woman who is free never to marry, but shall live independent of any man.'

She bows in return. 'I am for ever in your debt!'

'No!' he replies with delight. 'Although I have promised you the money, you are not! That is the whole point of the exercise!'

They laugh, Bysshe with joy and Claire with relief.

22ND JUNE 1816: THE SHELLEY HOUSEHOLD, LAKE GENEVA

'I think,' says Shelley, 'that Byron and I might go sailing tomorrow.'

'Mmmm!' says Mary. 'You should go whilst the weather is good.'

'We might go for a day or two, or even a week if the weather holds. We want to sail to Chillon and to the spot where Rousseau wrote of Heloise.'

'Yes,' she says again, 'you should,' thinking that it will give her yet more time to write. Byron has finished his canto and Claire spends her time at the villa, transcribing. The thought of a house empty of everyone except her and Will feels like bliss. Shelley is amused by how her writing seems to have freed her of her possessive need of him; even now he is expecting some objection or suspicion at his departure, but there is none, only thoughts of her story.

'We will never truly be able to recreate man, will we?' she asks.

'We might, we do not know,' he answers.

'I think,' she says slowly, 'that to create a being we must also recreate that moment of separation when we are born. Without it we are born from nothing, and if a man came back from death as ignorant as a child, and without the love of a parent, or creator, then what would life offer him?' She falls silent.

Yes, thinks Shelley, the writing is filling her, taking my place. She will barely miss me at all whilst I am with Albe.

'May I read you something?' she asks. He nods and she says, 'This is where the monster thinks of his own hate:

'*I am malicious because I am miserable. Am I not shunned and hated by all mankind, even you, my creator, would tear me to pieces. You would not call it murder if you could destroy my frame, the work of your own hands. Shall I respect man when he condemns me? If I cannot inspire love, I will cause fear, and chiefly towards you, my arch-enemy, because to my creator do I swear inextinguishable hatred. I will work at your destruction until I desolate your heart, so that you shall curse the hour of your birth.*'

She is surprised – on hearing the words aloud – by the powerful venom in them – but she will not change them. For this, she thinks, is how it felt to be abandoned by her father, to be powerless and voiceless, and to have no say in the course of their relationship.

Bysshe understands immediately. 'It describes exactly how I feel when I think of how they treated us in London, or when your father refused to see me. You have it exactly, Mary. Promise me you will continue!'

'I shall. I will. I can do nothing else!' she says happily. 'And Bysshe?

'Yes.'

'We do monstrous things when we are hurt, don't we?'

'You are thinking of Claire,' he says simply.

She nods and he opens his arms to her. 'I was scared,' she goes on, 'that only one of us could have a healthy child. I did not—'

'It is in the past,' he whispers into her hair, 'and Claire has her own life now. She will tell you soon how happy she is.'

'She is?' Mary pulls back to see him better. He nods. 'Then I am glad!' exclaims Mary.

When he is gone she goes to the nursery, anxious to see Will.

'He's sleeping!' says Elise sharply. 'Best not to disturb him!'

Mary does not turn away as she normally would, chastised and overwhelmed by her fear that she is a poor mother. 'I know,' she says. 'I just want to look at him.' Elise turns. Mary sees the surprise on her face and its immediate softening at Mary's admission.

'I do that too sometimes,' Elise whispers. 'They are so beautiful when they sleep, aren't they?'

Mary nods; they are, she is thinking, but I had not allowed myself to remember that for fear of losing him. She bends over the cot, looking down upon her son. He is beautiful, the drift of his eyelids the very shape of Bysshe's as he sleeps – a perfect miniature rendition. Perhaps, she thinks to herself, I can do it differently now. She reaches out a finger, running it lightly across William's sleeping cheek. He stirs and settles. 'Will,' she whispers, and again, 'Will.' His name a talisman. He turns on to his stomach, his tiny arms a spread half-rectangle, his breathing regular and relaxed. Above him Mary smiles, unaware that her own breath matches her son's, her chest rising and falling alongside his in an unconscious rhythm.

What if she were to die in her next childbirth and Will was

left with a new sister who grew up and deserted him? Her heart goes out to Fanny, for that is what Mary has done to her. Filled with such thoughts she turns from the nursery and writes Fanny into her story, imagining what a pleasure it will be to show it to her one day – Mary's apology to her.

She makes Fanny a maid, for Mary cannot prevent a little of her contempt for Fanny's sweet, docile nature stealing into her imagination, but Justine, as she calls the character, is as sweet-natured and kind as Fanny, as eager to please, and will become as wronged – as misunderstood.

23rd June, Lake Geneva

D*ear Fanny,* writes Mary,

We are in a small village called Coligny, in a small cottage with a garden that ends with a tiny harbour. Lord George Byron, who we call Albe, has taken a very much grander villa upon the hill above us. Now that the weather is better he and Bysshe have set sail to the other end of the lake together, travelling in the footsteps of Rousseau's La Nouvelle Héloïse.

Albe has challenged each of us to write a story, a story of horror and terror, a story of the type we might read in a storm with the wind in our ears and the rain against the window. Finally, after a while of not knowing how to begin, a tale has come upon me, and it is strange, but in the telling of it I have understood more than I ever dreamed possible of myself.

Dear, sweet Fanny, I hardly know where to begin, except that it must be with an apology, I have been unkind and cut you out of my life – when you are all that remains of a blood connection to our true mamma. I have learned much since I left, and understand now that a part of me has always been jealous of you, has always longed to have had more of our dear mamma than the ten days after my birth, to have had Mr Lamb tell me tales (not you) of how I sat on her knee, or to have a book just like the one she wrote you when your teeth started showing. But I have only had Papa, whom I have loved too excessively, and who made me his own creature so completely that when I defied him he could no longer bear to be near me, but must destroy our love completely – consumed by a rage that meant I would not – indeed, Fanny, I could not – concur with his wishes. I am writing now of such a monster, a man who when his own creation does not meet his expectation abandons him. And that abandonment will make a monster of his creature. As it has, in part, of me. I have done some terrible things, things I cannot speak of but yet appear unbidden in my fiction. I believe, Fanny, that we commit the most terrible crimes when we despair – perhaps that is why it is named a sin?

But enough of me, it has always been that you sit quietly and listen to others, faithfully doing their bidding – so that even as I write with thoughts of you, yet I speak of myself. The house is quiet now and I have time to write and consider many things. Claire is content to stay at the villa, transcribing for Byron. They are no longer joined together so do not listen to the gossips, and do not believe what they say about us, we are not shared. I remain faithful to Bysshe and he to me. Yet again I digress. It is because what I wish to tell you is so difficult, and I cannot be with you, or see your dear face as I speak and so hesitate, take up my pen, hesitate, stop and start again. But I have made this decision a thousand times, and I know now that I must share your history with you. Our father is a man I admire, but he has cost us both very dear: me in his rejection of me, and you because he has lied. All of your life he has told you that you are his child when you are not. There, it is said. You are the child of the man our mother loved more than any man in the world. Her love of Father was *real and true, but it was a twilight love, not the full passionate love of youth. She loved a man called Imlay, and she loved him so completely that she had his child, as we have William, out of wedlock. You are born of a great passion, Fanny, and she loved you with all her heart.*

I am guilty of so much, Fanny, but I hope to redeem myself. Please forgive me for not writing sooner. Write to me soon, or visit us if you can. I do not know when we return, if ever. Lord Byron claims he is done with England, and for us too Italy might beckon as the weather turns colder. We have not decided.

With my love, your true sister,
Mary

27TH JUNE 1816: 41 SKINNER STREET

Fanny is returning from an afternoon walk when she is given the letter. She takes it upstairs; any letter is precious, any break in her routine a delight. She saves it until bedtime. After reading it her first thought is to reach for her father, to reassure herself that he loves her and that her life spent pleasing him is worthwhile – but she cannot. She cannot move. The shock of seeing the truth written down, rather than dug deep into a recess of her mind where she does not have to think about it – makes her shake. She feels the ground beneath her feet begin to tremble. She stares at the floor; it remains steady and in place, but nonetheless she can feel it shaking. 'He is my papa,' she whispers, 'whether or not by birth.' He is the man she has spent a lifetime trying – and failing – to please, and Mary in her kindness is cruel to remind her of the fact that he has always preferred her.

'Mr Imlay is not my father,' she says to herself firmly.

'He is a monster who deserted us both and—' Fanny stops there, for beyond the fact of Mr Imlay, her birth father, lies the thing she cannot face and truly does not wish to think about. Why has Mary assumed it is a gift of knowledge that she has given and not a curse?

Slowly Fanny begins to rock herself, backwards and forwards. Backwards and forwards. 'You are loved,' she begins to whisper, but the words do not convince her.

27th June, Lake Geneva

Dear Izy,

I am writing to you again because I cannot believe that you would not want to know that I am engaged upon a novel, not fitfully, but fully and committed to a single story. It started as a small thing, but Bysshe has said it should have a proper life of its own and become a novel.

I think often of my time in Scotland, and you and your family inform my writing every day. In my book, I have transformed our own friendship into the friendship between a man called Victor Frankenstein and his closest friend, Clerval, and your family is at the heart of the happy family that I imagine. It is strange how people one has known in life, with just a small twist, become the characters in a novel, unhampered by their gender. But perhaps more alarming is how one exposes one's own history. Even as I write I notice that which I have fought hard not to see.

Without any conscious will of my own it is become a story of my own feelings; of rejection, of hate, of revenge and all attributed to different aspects of different characters. I understand more and more each day, and I long to finish so that I can step back and see the whole of it. In truth I both long for and dread that day, for it will be yet another loss when I have already had so many, not the least of them being you.

As I write, I come to understand that in my heart of hearts I am not made for free love; much as my reason demands I acknowledge its value, so equally my heart revolts at it. Much like the men in my novel, I long for a partnership that I share alone with someone in the wilderness, and yet it is my misfortune to love a man who, whilst I understand I am his rock and anchor, the person to whom he will always return, yet loves others.

Izy, I know of no one, not even Shelley, with whom I could share such thoughts. They lie at the core of me, and I do not doubt that, as you read, you will sense what an agony it is for me to be alone with them. I feel, as my protagonist, that I have destroyed the lives of those around me, that I am a curse, and that those I love best are destined to desert me. Whether this is because my birth destroyed my mother I do not know. I only know that like my protagonist, I lived like a child, so sure of the sunshine, so full of a belief in my own omnipotence, that the rejection by my father, when it came, awoke a hate so deep that I think I have been almost entirely in the grip of it, and that I practised it upon others, most especially Claire.

She did not behave well, but I behaved worse, and now I feel I have settled my fate. If ever I could have escaped the curse of my birth my own envy has stuck me to it. And my own bitterness and desperation to wrest Shelley from her made me run into the rain with a child who was not able to bear such treatment, and so I am doubly ashamed. Whatever I do, it seems I merely increase the curse upon those I love. It is in that knowledge that I joy in your rejection of me, for it places you far from my harm, and frees me to imagine sharing my innermost self with you. What a sad thing, it seems to me, my journals are. I have directed them all towards making it appear that our life and love is perfect, even now I cannot give it up. I have taken from Harriet, his first wife, what Claire has taken from me. I did not know what my father told me was true, that I am not one of those, like Shelley and Claire, who can share themselves. It destroys me, it tears my soul in two and shreds it and it turns me into a monster no better than my own creation.

Pity me, Izy, pity me even as I imagine you in your life. A life that shines in my imagination as proof that such simple joy can be found.

Mary

28TH JUNE 1816: VILLA DIODATI

Claire is woken by a rare ray of sunlight breaking through the crack in the thick velvet curtains. The words of Bysshe's Last Will and Testament running through her mind: *To Claire Clairmont I leave the sum of six thousand pounds, along with a further six thousand pounds to any beneficiary upon whom she chooses to confer it.*

She feels a rare sense of ease and joy as she lies awake, her hands resting lightly across her belly as she takes a deep breath before sinking into the luxurious pillows to bathe her face in the thin strip of sunlight. 'You have a father,' she whispers to her child. 'And I have everything that I need from Bysshe.' She revels in the feeling for a few minutes. 'Except one thing,' she acknowledges, 'that I would like.'

With that thought she forces herself out of bed, and dresses. Missing a slipper, she decides to walk down through the vines in her bare feet, imagining the mud damp between her toes. The rain arrives in odd squalls now rather than the steady, beating endless storm. The grape harvest has been ruined, and as she walks down a man stands in amongst the vines, staring at the mouldy, ruined grapes. Claire waves gaily. '*Bonjour!*' she calls, and he nods dryly, a bare acknowledgement. For a moment she is tempted to stop and kiss his cheek, to witness his surprise and confusion, but she resists; the Swiss she has found are not, on the whole, the joking kind.

'The sun's out!' she calls as she enters the cottage. Mary does not answer. 'Mary?'

Claire searches through the cottage. Elise is not in her room, and Will is gone. The house feels empty and silent. She goes out again. At the side of the house, sitting in the sun, is Mary. Will sits on a blanket beside the desk she has set up. Claire notices how she sits very straight even as she writes. Mary has not seen her, lost in the words as they come. Claire watches, feeling a wave of unexpected affection. As she turns away, not wishing to disturb them, Mary looks up.

'Oh!' she says. 'Claire!'

'Yes,' says Claire, 'it's me. Can I make you some tea?'

'Mmm,' says Mary. 'I'll just . . .'

'It's all right, I'll go and do it now!' She turns and goes inside, humming as she stokes the fire that has been built beneath the stove, fills the kettle and reaches for the precious tea. There is a joy in performing simple tasks, she thinks, when one feels secure and happy. This perhaps is what both Bysshe and Mary's mother longed for everyone to feel; that they have a place in the world and money enough to feel secure. She takes up the teapot and two cups, placing them on a tray, taking them into the garden. Mary continues to write and Claire waits a while, pours the tea, does not, as she might usually do, disturb Mary by playing with Will, who is contentedly rocking himself back and forth, his filthy fingers in his mouth.

'There!' says Mary eventually, sitting up. Claire pours her some tea.

They sit together faces up to the sunshine.

'This is nice,' says Claire.

'Isn't it?' says Mary.

'Mary?'

'Yes?' Mary keeps her face tipped up to the sun, eyes closed.

'I have some news.'

'Mmmm?'

'I am carrying Byron's child.'

Slowly Mary's head tips forward and her eyes open. 'Really?' she asks.

'Really,' replies Claire, hesitant, watching.

'How many months are you? How long have you known?'

'A while, but at first he would not acknowledge it as his own.'

Mary sighs aloud. 'That does not surprise me at all; he does not really like women, does he?'

'Not as much as he likes men!' says Claire.

They smile, and then they laugh. They laugh until their hands clasp. Passengers out on the lake lift up their telescopes and stare, but the two girls no longer notice, having long since stopped caring.

'But he will acknowledge it now?' asks Mary. Claire nods. Mary closes her eyes, offering up a short prayer of thanks; for the chance to redeem herself, for the opportunity to make reparation.

'Yes, he will acknowledge it as his own,' says Claire, awaiting a volley of accusation that the child might belong to Bysshe.

'Claire,' Mary says slowly, 'that is wonderful! When, when do you think . . .?'

Wisely Claire blushes and says, 'I am not sure! I thought you might be angry?'

'No! No! I am glad, I am so very, very glad.' They clasp

each other, each remembering the closeness they once shared, the loss of it and the possibility for renewal.

From below them comes a sound. They both turn. Will looks up at them both, squinting in the sun. 'Mamma!' he says.

30TH JUNE 1816: LAKE GENEVA

Both girls are waiting when Shelley's boat docks on his return. He waves from the bow, and they run down to the harbour. He jumps up and wraps his arms around them, reminded of the three of them standing in the churchyard, embracing, capturing that same feeling of joy in each other.

'It's working!' says Mary, her eyes shining. 'The story. It's stretching itself out, growing.'

'As am I!' laughs Claire.

Ah! She has told her, he thinks – and it has worked.

Shelley turns back to help Byron dock, but he waves him away. 'I think Poli has seen the boat from the terrace, he's on his way down,' he says. 'We'll see you after supper.'

He watches as the three of them move away, all talking at once, Shelley's hand resting now on Mary's head, his lips in her hair, his arm circling Claire's waist. Byron turns away, looking up at the Jura Mountains, shadows against sunshine. His Shi'loh has let him go as easily as a fish returning to water, with no knowledge of the longing that remains in Byron's breast, a stone lodged there that will pain him, not constantly, but suddenly and sharply whenever the memory of this week returns. The three of them have entered the house now, the door still open, and the sound of Shelley shouting his son's name audible on the clean air.

'Will!' he shouts. 'William!'

'Shhh,' laughs Elise, coming to the top of the stairs. 'He's only just fallen asleep.'

'But I want to see him!' declares Bysshe, running up and clattering into the nursery where Will remains asleep, despite the noise. He touches his son's cheek, lightly straightens a few silken curls. 'I'm here,' he whispers. He does not yet want to tell Mary of how close they came to death in a sudden storm upon the lake. His son stirs slightly, before turning and sucking his thumb, returning to the world of sleep.

'Claire's with Byron's child,' says Mary, standing framed by the bedroom door.

'I know,' says Bysshe.

'How long have you known?'

'She told me as soon as we set off from England.'

'But why?'

'Because she knew she might need me to intercede with him.'

'She told me he has agreed to be a father to the child!'

'He has, but he has now told me he no longer wishes to have any relationship with Claire.'

'Because?'

'He fears she only wanted a child from him.'

'Ha,' sneers Mary, 'and what did he want from all the women he has bedded? Does he not stop to think of the way that he has treated them? Oh, Bysshe! And she was so happy to have a father for her child!' she cries.

'Shhh, Mary, I will tell her later.'

'I will tell her myself,' decides Mary, 'and I will tell Lord Byron that he must learn to sow his seed more carefully if he is to take umbrage every time the consequences of his love-making become apparent.'

'Mary! You cannot. He does not wish you to know.'

'Because he is ashamed, as he should be.'

Claire appears at the door. 'I heard your voices,' she says, her face pale. 'I do not mind him abandoning me, if he will only acknowledge our child.'

'He will!' cries Bysshe. 'But he says we must negotiate his rights over the child, if he is to put his name to it.'

'But the child will live with me, as its mother. He cannot take it from me, can he?' Will begins to cry at the sound of Claire's distress. Mary picks him up. 'Oh!' whispers Claire. 'I cannot lose another child!'

'You will not!' says Mary. 'Will she, Bysshe?' The two women glare at him.

'I will talk to him.'

21ST JULY 1816: CHAMONIX, FRANCE

A few weeks after this return, Bysshe finally arranges their longed-for trip to the Sea of Ice. It will take days and they must ride the last miles by mule before they can approach the glacier.

Bysshe rides ahead of Mary and a guide ahead of him. Claire rides behind, silently concerned for her child, followed by yet another guide. They are pulled forward by the pace of the man in front and harried by the man behind. The mules struggle to keep their footing and Bysshe has already fallen once, rapidly grasping the animal's leg and saving himself from the precipice. Since then Mary has stopped looking up at the surrounding mountains, staring doggedly only at Bysshe's back, full of the knowledge that she could so easily lose him – longing only to arrive.

It is only when the mules slow and stop that she looks up. The mountains rise all around her, their sides white with snow, at the base of them a field of ice. No, thinks Mary, it is not a field – but a true sea; the motion of the waves caught and held in stasis, their curling sides a clear deep blue, and the tops a flume of white curves. All around her, waves reach and turn, suspended in the air, prevented from tumbling to the earth. The field stretches into the distance surrounded by mountains – at the valley's end stands a mountain that rises above them all, proud and alone, its steep sides rising to a snow-covered peak. The scene appears desolate beyond words, overpowering Mary, whispering to her of her own desolation, of the parts of her own sorrow for ever buried beneath such ice.

She watches as both Bysshe and Claire leap off their mules, striding fearlessly forward – already they are climbing the base of that first wave, running their hands along its icy blue sides and exclaiming at the cold; the colour, the sheer terrifying beauty of the landscape.

Mary cannot move, is held mesmerised, whilst within her thoughts move as deeply as the hidden water flowing beneath the earthbound ice. My own heart once lay so buried, she thinks. There it ticked, waiting for Bysshe to release it. She feels drawn to the ice then, cautiously climbing the base of its hills and peaks, holding tight to Bysshe's hands and staring silently, not exclaiming with the rest. 'You are spellbound!' he laughs as she remains silent throughout their open-air meal.

'I am,' she replies, falling silent again, eyeing the landscape, committing it to memory, connecting with the nature of its untouched glory. 'It is not lovable!' she manages to say. 'It exists alone and separate.' Even as she tries and fails to describe it, she senses that she speaks not only of the ice but also of herself – of the child in her torn from its mother – whose heart ticked, silent and slow, frozen and alone, longing for reconnection. 'It is such a desolate place!' she cries, and Bysshe reaches for her hand.

'But beautiful nonetheless,' he says.

Only he, thinks Mary, has pierced the surface of the ice and made my heart feel warm and alive. It is no wonder that I cling to him, wanting him only for myself.

As they begin the ride back she has an idea. What if the creature brought so suddenly to life on the table of a scientist, abandoned by its horrified creator like a child neither loved nor understood, were to become lost in such frozen wastes, longing for the love of another? It is as though, she thinks, the world itself conspires with me in the writing of this story, offering itself up to its creation.

As soon as they reach the hotel she continues to write. Yes, she is thinking, the creature will wake and in the very moment of its creation will face abandonment – as she did, not only from her mother but from her father too, and the whole of London. What rage she feels now, when she stops to think of it. How she would like to strike and smite and share the freedom Claire has always had to lash out, allowing her rage an existence.

She lifts her pen and bends her body to the task, unaware of Bysshe who stands watching. It is strange for him to witness his own passion alive in his lover, to note the intense concentration, her face moving through the emotions as she creates them on the page. A fleeting glance of horror consumes her features followed by a sigh of relief as the pen stops and she reads what she has written, a smile on her face followed by a frown and a change rapidly made. It is, thinks Bysshe, as though it is no longer me, but she, who has another lover.

Mary reads the words that she has written:

'I saw the dull yellow eye of the monster open, it breathed hard, and a convulsive motion agitated its limbs. I had worked

hard for nearly two years for the sole purpose of instilling life. For this I had deprived myself of rest and health; but now the beauty of the dream vanished, and breathless horror and disgust filled my heart, unable to endure the aspect of the being I had created, I rushed out of the room, and continued to traverse my bedchamber. At length I threw myself upon the bed, endeavouring to sleep, but wild dreams consumed me. I thought that I held the dead corpse of my mother in my arms, a shroud enveloped her form, the grave worms crawling in the folds of flannel . . .'

She is stunned by it. 'Would you read this?' she asks Bysshe.

He reads the words she has written. 'It is good,' he says, 'in fact, it is wonderful, Mary!'

'But why,' she asks him, 'would he dream of his dead mother?'

'Because he loved her!' declares Bysshe. 'And he has defiled her right to remain dead and untouched.'

'And it is not my own vision rather than Frankenstein's?'

'It is both,' he says, reassuring her.

Mary smiles, but the writing troubles her; it cracks her ice and swims beneath it. When she sleeps she dreams of her mother wrapped in her shroud, always just ahead of her, untouchable as she races after her through tunnels bored deep into the earth. She knows she must catch her for if she does not then her heart will tick for ever, lost and alone. When she wakes she is troubled. 'Do you think,' she asks Bysshe, 'that my mother ran from my birth, welcoming the arms of death?'

'I do not think,' he answers, 'that we choose either the hour of our death or of our creation.'

'But if we are not made of God then where do we come from, Bysshe?'

'Love,' he says simply. 'Do you doubt it, when you look at Will?

'And without that?' she asks, insistent, the dream hanging over her. 'If we are not loved, but only abandoned, as I was?'

'You *were* loved, Mary – you have been told how much your mother fought to stay alive for you.'

'And yet I was newborn and could not know it.'

'It is not your mother who abandoned you, Mary, but your father.'

'No!' she cries. 'He loved me when she could not!'

'He did,' Bysshe agrees, 'as long as you were his creation. You were his pride and joy – and he displayed you to the world as evidence of his philosophy, of what he believed a woman should be – but then you became yourself and it was not at all what he wanted and so you must no longer exist.'

His words are harsh and for once Mary does not disagree or beg that he remain in favour with her father, for the words she has written come to her, and she whispers them to herself: '. . . perhaps my father was *unable to endure the aspect of the being he had created.*'

'Yes,' says Bysshe. 'The part of you that loved another.'

'So I am writing of myself?' she says.

Bysshe knows it is a question that does not require an answer, so simply watches as she picks up her cup and disappears.

2ND AUGUST 1816: VILLA DIODATI

Byron watches from his window as Bysshe and Claire walk up through the vineyards together. Is the brat his? It is possible, he thinks, even probable, but he doubts it. He will not be fooled, however beautiful his Shi'loh may look with the wind in his hair. He will not go down and let them in himself. He has had enough of Claire; if it were not for Shi'loh's attachment to her, he would simply leave her behind, as he has every other woman. He makes them wait for a while in the drawing room; its windows wide open now to the sunshine, so different to the wind and the rain.

'Has he told you of his plans?' whispers Claire. Bysshe shakes his head. They hear his feet on the stairs.

'So!' he says. 'You are both come.'

'You asked us here,' snaps Claire.

'We need to agree a course of action,' says Shelley, Mary's words clear in his mind that he must do whatever is necessary to preserve Claire's right to keep her child.

'If,' Byron says, 'the brat is mine, then I suggest we offer it to my sister Augusta, to be brought up with her child. They are much the same age and will be playmates for one another.'

'No! The child is mine!' cries Claire.

'That is unquestionable,' laughs Byron, 'where its paternity lies, however, is doubtful. I am prepared to agree it is mine, but I must have some rights of ownership! I wish my child to understand its heritage, not to be sequestered in some strange community of equals!'

'But Claire must be allowed to give birth to her child where she is comfortable,' says Shelley calmly.

'And I am to pay for her right to such comfort?'

'It is not a question of money!' says Shelley angrily. 'I will happily support Claire and the child—'

'And we know why, do we not?' interjects Byron.

'I have been honest with you, and that is my failing,' declares Shelley. 'Claire and I have loved each other in the past, and yet you doubt my integrity.'

'I do when you offer to support a brat not yours.'

'And yet I love the child's mother, and I am not ashamed to answer a woman's need, whether her child be mine or not.'

'Then you are fool, Shi'loh,' Byron sneers, 'living in a heaven that will take you for whatever you are prepared to give.'

'A willing fool. I shall support Claire until the baby is born. We will leave here at the end of the month.'

'And what of my child afterwards?' asks Byron. 'Am I to have any rights at all, or am I merely needed to provide a name for the little bastard?'

'You know,' says Claire quietly, 'how likely this child is to be yours.'

'I would be sad,' says Shelley, 'if this matter were to threaten our friendship. Surely we can resolve it.'

'If you are prepared to support them both then you may go wherever you wish to have the child,' Byron says suddenly. 'But you must bring the child to my household eventually, to be brought up properly.'

Shelley glances at Claire, who nods. Once they are away from here he will forget; she is sure of it.

'We shall leave at the end of the month,' says Bysshe.

'I do not wish to see you except in the company of others,' declares Byron to Claire.

'And I,' says Claire, 'am in complete agreement with that, although I am sad you do not wish to know your child's mother.' She nods at him and holds her arm out for Shelley, who takes it.

'You, my dear Shil'oh,' says Byron to his back, 'may come alone as often as you wish.'

PART
FIVE

10th September 1816, 5 Abbey Churchyard, Bath

D_{ear} *Izy,*

Yet again I have taken another journey home. If I can call it home. I can mark my life by this journey: England, France, Holland, Germany, Switzerland, and again in reverse. This same journey forms the backbone of my novel, holding the story in place, it is the skeleton my life has taken place against. We have decided to live in Bath, for Claire is with child and we need to protect her. It is Byron's child. He has acknowledged it as such, but Claire still does not wish her mother to know. For these reasons we will no longer live in London but will stay here in Bath until Claire is delivered, and then we hope that we can find a way for her to be with her child until it is old enough to be educated – or perhaps live in Byron's household. Neither of us wish to think of that time, for although he is a wonderful poet he is not a man whom any of us would trust with a child.

I hope my novel will be finished this year; should you happen to read it then you, more than anyone else, will understand the journey I have made. Two visions, dear Izy, haunt me; the first is running up Law hill with you. I see us, breathless and laughing, so full of hope and dreams. I wish that time had stopped and kept us there; and then I remember that soon the dream of being a published writer (the dream I first expressed that day) might be realised, and I hug the knowledge to myself in secret joy. The second vision is much stranger and more troubling. I see the Frenchman in the Polygon leaning over me repeating his words, 'Live well, young lady, for the clock ticks for you.' I shiver every time this vision arises. I feel time changing its pace, becoming faster, heading inevitably towards a climax that I can neither stop nor foresee, and I feel helpless, as helpless as a mole above ground, blind and vulnerable. It is a terrible feeling; I cannot explain it but it fills me with fear and drives me to write each day; harder and longer. To hug William tight and to forgive Claire, to love Shelley and all his foibles, even when it is hard. And it can be.

Oh lord, I hate boats, I have no idea why I have made one central to my story – but of course – it is in honour of Coleridge, the ice-bound boat that gives one time for reflection, and reflects also perhaps the ice-bound heart that cannot feel, but ticks on hopefully beneath the frozen ice, deep in that blue water, waiting to be allowed to rise one day – and feel. Just as I was encased, until he came and cracked my carapace – releasing a flood of feeling. Enough! Enough! This is what happens when the words come too easily, they speak their own sense and will not stop!

Your grateful,
Mary

15TH SEPTEMBER 1816: 5 ABBEY CHURCHYARD, BATH

When Mary is stuck and the words will not come, she steps out of the door in the row of neat Georgian houses and turns right. Before her stands the abbey, a monument to all that Bysshe despises, and yet the building is beautiful. On sunny days the light seems to sink into the stone, lighting it from within. England feels small to her now, its streets narrow and dark, its people as cramped as its cities and as downtrodden. Despite Mary's best efforts to accept Claire's constant presence, she remains an irritation, which leaves Mary feeling guilty once more. Why, she wonders, and how, has she ended up living alone with Claire, whilst Bysshe is in London again, sorting out his finances?

The sight of the abbey calms her, and unbeknownst to either Claire or Bysshe she sometimes slips inside and sits quietly in a pew, thinking about her writing and allowing her mind to drift up into the beautiful rafters of the building. She decides, as she sits there, that Frankenstein, creator of the creature, will marry the woman he loves after all. She wonders if the public will notice he is in love with his stepsister, and that she has carefully made it so in defiance of the way the public has treated Byron, for he did not grow up with his sister, as Frankenstein did, and so, thinks Mary, was more of a stranger to him. She has been trying to find a way for the couple to remain unmarried, some other way in which the love that both Frankenstein and his monster crave might find expression; in a lover, perhaps, as Bysshe has suggested, but as she sits in the abbey enjoying the peace of its hushed noise, she acknowledges that a single, true love is all that she has ever wanted.

With that recognition comes a sense of peace. I would like, just as Frankenstein does, to be married, she thinks. She slips easily to her knees; above her she imagines her mother – perhaps she is smiling at her or perhaps she is horrified. Perhaps she is nowhere and cannot, and has never been able to, look down and watch as Mary grows; it does not matter now. As Mary lands on her knees she thinks, I have accused my own sister of existing merely to please others, whilst I aped my father's beliefs and tried too hard to live out Bysshe's philosophy. But I am not them. *I am not them*, she whispers as she prays. I am Mary Wollstonecraft Godwin, and I would like, more than anything, to be Mary Shelley. It is said. She rises from her knees and walks quickly away from the church.

Back at the house Claire is resting; she hears Mary enter and run immediately up the stairs.

'Mary!' calls Claire.

'Not now!' she shouts back, and Claire falls silent, knowing she is rushing to her notebooks.

I will never, thinks Mary, have what I most desire, and neither can Victor Frankenstein. He might have his victory over the act of creation but he will never find that love which is the true creation of life. And neither will his creature. She can see it all now, the story resting clearly in her imagination; the longing for love that lies at the heart of it; the belief that knowledge is not enough to overcome life's pain and loss, just as reason and learning could not prevent her falling in love and leaving her father, or allow her mother to live as long as she desired.

Alone at night the dreams come. The devastation and corpses; the bloodied parts of suspended bodies suddenly animated that cause her to wake bolt upright, breathing hard, until she is driven from her bed to gaze out at the sleeping street, or to light a lamp and read. The fear will not leave her that she is responsible for the death of her mother and child, that like Victor Frankenstein she too plays with life and death, but unwittingly, never knowing when she might do something that results in the loss of yet another loved one. What have I done? The phrase repeats itself at strange moments throughout the day. Haunting her. Behind the question lies the unspoken fear – that it is she who is monstrous.

27TH SEPTEMBER 1816: 2 NORFOLK STREET

Shelley is glad to be back. London, despite its grime and stink, still lies at his centre. Walking the streets he feels the beginning of an uprising in the air, of revolution. The people are angry and it fires him. Byron has introduced him to a radical journalist called Leigh Hunt and in his home he sees the life he longs to build for himself. Leigh is a man who draws radical poets and writers to gather around him and has offered to publish Bysshe's poem, *Alastor*, in the hope it might receive a better reception a second time around.

There is a lightness in his step as he walks through London, retracing the paths he once took with Mary and Claire, haunting parks and doing his best to avoid Godwin who writes almost constantly and has started to send Fanny to Norfolk Street to request yet another loan. She is often on his doorstep when he arrives home each evening.

'Hello, Fanny!'

'I'm sorry!' she says immediately.

'For what?' he answers lightly. 'You are not here of your own accord, are you?'

'Well then, I am sorry on my father's behalf,' she says, blushing. The truth is that recently she has begun to visit the house without her father knowing, the thought of seeing Bysshe filling her with a delighted terror. If only she did not have to ask him for money, what might they speak of then?

The knowledge that Mary and Bysshe have returned and decided to live in Bath, away from Godwin, has given her hope – and an idea. This evening she has taken especial care, trying to rouge her cheeks and wearing a dress that best shows off her figure; her anxiety has made her so slender that she has barely any curves at all. She has to walk the block a few times before she spots him turning into the street. She will not blush this time, she will not – but as soon as he talks to her she feels the familiar heat spread across her cheeks and lowers her head, hoping to hide it. She is determined to do what she has set out to do. She has thought about it and thought about it, and sees that there is no other way. She has chosen this evening to ask if she can join them in Bath, for to remain where she is with Godwin no longer feels possible.

'Perhaps you do not understand the extent of Father's financial need?' she hears herself saying whilst her thoughts fly wildly within her.

'I think,' says Bysshe gently, 'the truth might be that he does not understand the extent of my own finances. We do not have the money, Fanny. If I did I would offer it, as I hope you understand. I have a duty to Harriet, and your father has treated Mary unkindly.'

She nods. 'Mary sent me a letter,' she blurts.

'And I'm sure she explained our situation. The courts have decided that to sell an annuity in exchange for one's inheritance is not legal, and yet my father will do it, for he is not happy that I go on taking loans. But he will not do it so that I can lend your father money.'

'No she did not write to me about that but about . . . something else.' He waits, watching as she fights to find the words. 'She has told me that Godwin is . . . he is . . . not my father.'

Bysshe rises and sits next to her, wrapping an arm around her shoulders. Even in her distress she notes the feel of his arm, appreciates the deliciousness of allowing herself to relax against his chest. For a moment she shuts her eyes, listening to the sound of his heart against her ear.

'And yet Godwin has always treated you as his daughter,' he says eventually. 'He loved your mother, and he loves you.' He feels her nod her head against him.

'He always loved Mary best,' she says after a while, 'and as a young child I never knew why.'

'Yet he has not abandoned you as he has Mary.'

'That is because I have never found the courage to disagree with him,' she says, finally pushing herself away and sitting up, 'as Mary did.'

'She did not find it easy,' he says slowly, 'and I suspect, at times, that she might regret it.'

'No, she does not regret it,' Fanny says firmly. 'How could she!' Then blushes, for her adoration is, as ever, too naked. 'I . . . have been thinking,' she says, her voice shaking. 'And I have been reading, and I have come to a decision.' Again he simply listens, forcing her to continue.

'I cannot live like this.' Unbeknownst to her his head lifts. 'I too am Mary Wollstonecraft's daughter, and I would like to be a part of your community.' She takes a breath.

'Fanny, I—'

'Oh!'

'I—'

'Please . . .' she says, 'at least think about it! Cannot anyone who desires it join you?'

'It is not that,' he says gently. 'It is that we are in a difficult position – there is someone we must protect and you would be giving up your family. I wonder if that is truly—'

'You do not want me!'

'It is not that!'

'*Mary* does not want me.' She has hit upon the truth.

'Mary has to manage Claire and she finds that difficult, perhaps we can think about it.' Bysshe longs to tell her about Claire's coming child but he cannot: Mary and Claire do not trust Fanny; she is too torn in her loyalty and so he cannot take that risk. And yet she is so vulnerable, sitting before him with her heart wide open. He must do something – so he takes her in his arms. 'Fanny,' he whispers into her hair.

'Will you refuse me too?' she asks.

He kisses her, lightly at first, and then deeply, drawn by the innocence and longing of her before he pulls away. 'I am not refusing you,' he says, 'but it would not be right if I cannot offer you support and a home. And I cannot. Not without discussing it with Mary.'

Fanny gathers herself together. 'I should leave,' she says, her eyes glistening.

'You do not need to leave!'

'But I *should* leave, and I always do what I *should*, do I not? My words, my thoughts this evening, are an aberration. Forgive me.'

'There is nothing to forgive. You are brave,' he says, 'and honest.'

'No,' she says truthfully, 'I am only desperate.'

'Fanny!' He stops her at the door. 'Your mother was once desperate too, but she found the will to live. I will talk to Mary, do not doubt us!'

Bysshe stands watching her leave. A vision of her remains framed within the door, her lip quivering against her fight for dignity and self-possession. He is troubled by her but has much to do. He must find Harriet, and taken up with that task he turns to his desk and writes to Hookham, hoping that once they locate her he can solve his financial difficulties and then think about Fanny.

Fanny walks along Norfolk Street. She will not cry. In fact, she discovers that she does not want or need to cry; tears already feel as though they are part of another world, a world where feelings might matter. She no longer lives in such a place, has slipped beyond it into nothingness. It is a familiar place, and makes sense to her now. I am not wanted. Not wanted. Not loved. Marguerite was wrong. Her mother's sisters do not want her, for she is tainted by association with Mary.

410

Her father has never loved her as he does Mary – even the strength of his hatred speaks of the depth of his passion for Mary, where Fanny is merely a conduit to her. Her own mother is long gone.

Mary will not want her to live with them; she is sure of it. If even Bysshe, who is gentle and kind and believes in free love, does not want her then she has nothing. Her thoughts revolve endlessly, holding her captive. She does not want to go home for it no longer feels a place where she belongs. She sees herself a spinster, the despised sister of Mary Godwin. A failure. 'I have nothing and no one,' she whispers.

At home Fanny writes to Mary, a brief, business-like letter, questioning whether she understands the magnitude of Godwin's debts, and the consequent stress they live under in Skinner Street. This is what I can do, she tells herself; if I am to be a conduit between them then I must try to be a successful one. Mary picks up the letter late one afternoon, reads it rapidly and drops it to the table.

'From Fanny,' she says to Claire.

'Oh! How is she?'

'Begging on behalf of Father again. A stupid letter – she cannot understand that we don't yet have the money for ourselves, let alone my father.'

Claire says nothing and the letter lies abandoned on the drawing-room table, serving as a reminder that her father remains as intransigent as ever; if they were to know of Claire's pregnancy then Mrs Clairmont would heap yet more hatred upon Mary. She will show her father. She will finish her novel, and when it is published it will stand as evidence that her decision to elope has cost her nothing in terms of success. Perhaps then he will be forced to receive them.

*

When Bysshe returns, suggesting that perhaps Fanny might live with them, Mary is dismissive. 'How can we have her here?' she asks angrily. 'She will see Claire and she will be unable to resist their questioning. If she tells my stepmother then my father will never be reconciled to us. I cannot. We cannot.' Bysshe nods. 'You must see that,' she insists. He nods again. 'You are disappointed in me?' she asks.

'No,' he says. 'We cannot help her and yet it feels wrong. We have strayed so far from our beginnings.'

'Yes,' she says, 'we have.'

'There is something so . . . lost about her.' He tries to express the fear he feels.

'It is hard,' Mary says more gently, 'to live out our beliefs in a world so decided against them, and the consequences for women – for Claire and for Fanny – they are incalculable. We did not know how much pain it might cause.'

'That is true,' he says, and turns away.

'Bysshe!'

'Yes?'

'I am right, aren't I?' she asks, filled with a feeling of anxiety. 'It is not that we would not have her, but that we cannot.'

He nods again; already the lightness he felt on arriving back in England is beginning to leak away as the constraints of living near Godwin press down upon him. It is a small country, he thinks, not only in its geography but also in its philosophy. Once more he is forced to go against his instincts, and Fanny's face as she left haunts him. He would like to have said yes; to witness the smile that he is sure would light up her face.

Fanny waits for a reply to her letter that does not come. She waits for word from Bysshe, or Mary, or Claire that they have discussed her situation. There is nothing. The evenings begin to close in and become dark; the days inside the house grow longer and Godwin's fury at Bysshe deeper. 'You must write again!' he tells her. Fanny nods, knowing that she cannot. 'I will do it now,' she whispers, knowing that she will not. 'And stand up straight!' her stepmother shouts after her. Fanny straightens her back, obeying instinctively as she has always done.

In the dusk of her room that evening she makes a decision. It is not a difficult decision, and once it is made a sense of ease floods her whole being. She has always known that the road she is about to take has been waiting for her: to resist it has become too difficult, to relent easy. She will follow her mother. She will emulate the heroine of her mother's novel, *Maria*, by taking laudanum. But she must not, as her mother was, be found and revived. She must go away to do it to be sure. She can no longer wait; she picks up a pen and writes. The words come easily:

. . . I have long determined that the best thing I could do was to put an end to the existence of a being whose birth was unfortunate, and whose life has only been a series of pain to those persons who have hurt their health in endeavouring to promote her welfare. Perhaps to hear of my death will give you pain, but you will soon have the blessing of forgetting that such a creature ever existed as . . .

Fanny Wollstonecraft Imlay

She stares at the words. She will go by post to Bath and from there to Bristol. It will be nice to see the sea once more and it is but a short ferry ride from there to Swansea. She will stay in the Mackworth Arms; she has heard it is very grand and she would like to die somewhere smart. The next day she dresses carefully before leaving, choosing a white and blue striped skirt. She wears her mother's bodice next to her skin with her initials printed on it, MW, and her favourite fur-lined brown pelisse with its matching hat. She leaves, ostensibly to visit Shelley.

Mrs Godwin notes the high colour in her cheeks. 'You must make them understand how desperate we are!' she says.

Fanny nods.

As she walks away from the house she remembers watching her beloved Marguerite walk across the Polygon away from her. She will not stop and look back; she will not wave at the tall thin ugly house on Skinner Street that has become her prison. Perhaps one day the world Bysshe and her mother imagined will really exist; a world where women might be more than either wives or spinsters, but that world is not now and so for women like her there is no alternative. It is not a long walk, a mere half an hour past the charterhouse, then on to Cheapside and the Two Swans Inn from where the post leaves. She feels intrepid as she mounts the steps; she feels – for the first time in her life – a sense of purpose. She is following in her mother's footsteps; and she will succeed where her mother failed. Soon she will be free.

At Bath, where she has to change coach, she hesitates; perhaps she should go and see them, ask again if they might have room for her . . . but no – her decision is made and she can see quite clearly how easily she might become the same encumbrance in a different house. She must not stop, she must go on. At Bristol she posts her note to both her father and Bysshe. That evening she leaves Bristol for Swansea.

'Another letter from Fanny,' says Mary, 'but addressed to you this time, Bysshe.' She raises her eyebrow, Fanny's desire for him a gentle joke between them.

Bysshe takes it from her; the note is short, and as soon as he has read it he turns back to the envelope, searching for the postmark. 'It is from Bristol,' he says, a pale shock upon his face.

Mary takes it from his hand examining the envelope. 'What?' she asks him. 'What does she say?' Her heart clenching in fear. *What have I done? What have I done?* The phrase echoes inside of her.

' *"I depart immediately to the spot from which I hope never to remove,"* ' Mary reads. 'Go!' she says. 'Go at once, Bysshe, and find her! Bring her back to us!'

He stops only to find himself a warm coat before running to catch the post to Bristol. He has no idea how he might search for her, or where, only senses – as Mary does – that he must find her.

The coach she must have taken arrives at the Bush Inn and Tavern, in Corn Street. The area is awash with people and horses as the coaches deliver the mail to the post office opposite. People step down to be met by friends and family, the inn is still busy, even at night, and Bysshe asks the drivers if they remember a young girl. 'Pretty,' he says, 'with dark hair and very slender.' They look at him askance; he cuts a strange figure in his distress, unaware of the impression he makes. He is annoyed by their refusal to stop and consider whether they might remember such a girl. Determined to find her, he carries on into the inn and asks to talk to the innkeeper.

'And how am I meant to be able to remember every miss that decides to stop here?' the man says. 'There was one, but then there was also more than one, so who's to know which one's your one!' He laughs at his own wit but Bysshe barely notices.

'She'd be hesitant,' he says, 'and perhaps a little shy, well dressed and with the demeanour of a lady.'

'None like that.'

'She is important to me!'

'Come back with a bit more,' he says, 'like what she was wearing or at least some sense of her looks.'

'There *was* a woman,' says a waiter in passing, 'wore a blue striped skirt and a matching coat and hat. She seemed sad.'

The innkeeper flaps at him. 'Another one of your stories,' he says, but Bysshe is arrested and holds out a hand. 'Did she look slender and did she have dark hair?'

'Might be her,' says the boy, still holding a tray full of food. 'She ate in her room and left on the post to Swansea, leaves every day, at eight.'

'And is there another post today?'

'Not till tomorrow!' says the boy, moving away.

Bysshe does not know what to do – he is frustrated that he cannot describe her for he sees her so clearly standing before him, her head lifted and her words ringing in his ears: '*It was an aberration to ask you.*'

He had not listened, nor allowed himself to feel her desperation. He eats at the inn, watching the people come and go with the coaches, sensing that if he fails to find her in time the consequences may be tragic. He walks, stalking through the city, hoping against hope for a glimpse of her.

THAT SAME EVENING: SWANSEA, WALES

Fanny does not go to the Mackworth Arms immediately after arriving, but walks alone through the city. People note her and move past; there is something about her that captures their brief attention. In the small room at the inn, after a dinner that she manages to enjoy, the chambermaid asks her when she would like her candle put out.

'I can take it up and see to it myself,' Fanny says calmly, 'for I am very tired.' The words express a deep truth; she is so tired that she is ready to sleep for ever.

Alone in her room she drinks the laudanum quickly and with determination. She arranges herself elegantly and then quietly, and without a fuss, she dies.

Bysshe catches the last post home. At two o'clock in the morning, he walks through the streets of Bath, to Mary. She is waiting, a candle burning in the window as he walks up to the door.

'You did not find her?' she says, her face hollow with shadows in the flickering light.

'I could not describe her, or what she was wearing.'

'I have already sent to Father for a description of Fanny's clothes!'

Godwin's reply arrives the following day.

11TH OCTOBER 1816: BRISTOL AND SWANSEA

Bysshe sets off at once for Bristol, pacing the streets as he waits for the post to Swansea. He cannot rid himself of the vision of Fanny as she stood in the doorway, her voice quivering with distress. He turned her down, he did not do what felt right and he did not respond to their mutual desire and hold her in his arms; he refused her. What a small thing it would have been for him to comfort her further, what joy it might have brought them both – and yet he could not – for the consequences of such love are too evident to him now.

He arrives in Swansea and walks immediately to the Mackworth Arms; it is the type of place he would expect her to go, where he would go himself. He calls for the innkeeper as he enters, unable to wait.

'Steady up!' says the man. 'How can I help you?'

'I am looking for my sister-in-law,' says Bysshe. 'She is dark-haired and very respectable. She may have arrived a few days ago from Bristol. She is in distress and wearing a blue and white skirt with a brown pelisse and—'

'I think perhaps,' says the man, holding up his arm to halt the flow of Bysshe's words, 'you might want to read this, sir.' He hands him a newspaper.

Bysshe's heart drops at the sudden change in the man's tone. He holds the print close and begins to read:

The *Cambrian*: Friday 11th October, 1816:

'A melancholy discovery was made in Swansea yesterday: a most respectable-looking female arrived at the Mackworth Arms on Wednesday night by the Cambrian coach from Bristol: she took tea and retired to rest, telling the chambermaid she was exceedingly fatigued and would take care of the candle herself. Much agitation was created in the house by her non-appearance yesterday morning, and on forcing her chamber door, she was found a corpse with the remains of a bottle of laudanum on the table and a note.'

'Sir?' asks the innkeeper. 'Are you all right, sir.' He calls for a glass of brandy to be brought.

'It is her,' says Bysshe. 'Can you remember what she was wearing, or may I see her?'

'I'm afraid she's gone, sir. It was only yesterday she was found, and the—'

'What was she wearing?'

'Why, I don't know, but the chambermaid will be able to tell you.'

'Please, call her.' His voice is high and cracked with fear; the man leaves, immediately returning with a young girl with mousey hair and extraordinary green eyes. 'She hadn't changed, sir, she was wearing her clothes, a blue and white striped skirt and a brown pelisse was resting on the chair.

It is her then. He turns and walks away; he does not hear the patter of her feet following him, does not notice her at all until she clasps his sleeve.

'Sir,' she whispers. 'Sir!' He turns. 'Was her name Fanny?' He nods, the tears blurring his vision. She holds out her hand. Inside it is a scrap of paper.

'What?' he asks.

'It is her name, sir. I took it from the note, because she . . . I mean her family might not . . . but I kept it by me in case anybody came!'

Bysshe takes it, unfolds the scrap of paper. *Fanny Wollstonecraft Imlay*, it says. 'Thank you.'

'I'm very sorry, sir.'

'Thank you.' He turns away, blinded, knowing only that he longs to be near Mary, yet dreading the telling of his tale.

5 ABBEY CHURCHYARD, BATH

Bysshe is talking to her, Mary knows that, but the words appear and disappear.

'Yes, it is definitely her,' he is saying. 'Definitely Fanny. She took laudanum. The maid described her clothing.'

His words struggle to get past the chant inside of her: *what have I done? What have I done?* Things are happening almost exactly as she writes them; her family is dying even as she

419

destroys her creator, Victor's family. She tries to tell herself that it is nonsense but it is not. It is real. It is happening.

She pushes the manuscript on the desk away from her, horrified by the words she has written for she believes now that they will undoubtedly become true. She knows now what it is that she has unwittingly caused to happen. *She* refused Fanny. It was *she* who insisted, against Bysshe's better instinct that she should not be allowed to live with them, *she* who did not write to explain why, but put it off, telling herself she was too busy, too caught up in the writing of her story to stop and think of Fanny: her only sister, her mother's first child.

The words keep coming from Bysshe's mouth. 'She was wearing the brown coat you sometimes wore, and its matching hat.'

'I have done something terrible,' Mary whispers.

'No,' says Claire, 'it was not you, Mary. Fanny has always suffered, always been frail in her mind.'

'It was you too,' says Mary bitterly. 'How often must we refuse her because of you! Or make our lives fit yours, Jane?'

'I am not—'

'You may have changed your name but you are still your mother's daughter. You are a succubus and you stick to us, causing us shame and grief! It was because of *you* we could not take her in!' Mary turns and runs up the stairs, stops and runs back down again. 'Sorry,' she says coldly, 'do not listen to me. I am angry, I do not want my words to cause another tragedy.'

Claire stares at her. 'She was my sister too,' she says, 'and I loved her also.'

Bysshe takes Mary's arm. 'Put a coat on,' he says. 'Let's walk.'

They go past the abbey, taking a path out of the city up towards the hills. Mary is grateful that he chooses a long route. They do not speak until the city lies far beneath them.

'Did you see her?' asks Mary. 'Her body?'

420

'No.'

'It is definitely her?'

'Yes.'

'Then she is gone?'

'Yes.' He holds Mary as she weeps.

'And even now,' she says eventually, bitterly, 'my tears are for myself, for fear of my own life and how her loss affects it.'

'What do you mean?'

'I write of how selfishness, rejection and lack of love lead to rage and envy, to hatred and death, or vengeance. We tell ourselves that I am writing about the need for a decent society and how without that, as humans, we are lost; but I am proof of what can happen when one is abandoned at birth.'

'What do you mean?' He is lost, appalled by her self-lacerating fury.

'Was I abandoned,' she asks, 'just as the creature I write of was abandoned in his moment of birth – or was it me who killed my mother? I wrote about Fanny as Justine. I killed her in the story, and now Fanny is dead. That is incontrovertible, isn't it?' she asks, her tear-stained face staring intently as she asks the question.

'Mary, Fanny died by her own hand, and your mother died of a fever and because she lost blood. It could not be helped.'

'But there is another world, is there not, where other things are true? Where we believe in life after death, where we dream as we sleep, where the unknown exists deep within us and I fear that if we touch upon it in our work then we *make* things happen!'

She seems wild to him now, and fey, entirely unlike the Mary he knows and most needs to tie him to the earth, to help them manage their grief.

'We cannot know all things, but I know that you are not responsible for the death of Fanny,' he says stoutly.

'No?' she asks.

'No.' He tries a smile but she remains solemn.

'Come with me,' she says, taking him by the hand. She does not speak as they rush down the hill back towards the house. Once there she pulls him up the stairs to her room, where she flicks through the manuscript, searching for the terrible words she has written. 'Look!' she says. 'Look at what I have done.' She shows him how she has given their own son's name to a child who is killed by the monster, strangled with the thumbprint visible on his tiny neck.

'What mother could write this,' she asks, 'even as she is in the grip of a terror that it might come true and yet never stopping for the drive to write, to succeed, to be as great as my mother or father, and as you, Bysshe, burns deeper in me than the care for my own child?'

A terror of his own grips Bysshe at her words and only his own sense of what it has cost her to write it prevents him tearing the manuscript from her hands and ripping it to shreds.

'If we believe the act of creation connects with some unknown force deep within the universe, then how can we be sure we do not evoke some terrible tragedy of our own in the writing of it? And if so then what have I done? What am I doing?' begs Mary.

For a wild moment he is taken up by her words, flailing himself before catching at her hands. 'You are doing what you were born to do,' he says calmly, knowing this is what she would say to him. It is what she has taught him.

'I am so frightened,' she whispers, 'that what I write I bring to life, and now Fanny has died I fear I am right.'

'And will you let that stop you? Did your mother allow her fear to stop her? Perhaps Fanny was inspired to this dreadful act by your mother's writing, not your own.' Mary shakes her head. 'We cannot know,' he says, 'and even if we did I am not sure that we could stop it. Tell me, could you stop now?'

She thinks for a while, before shaking her head. She will finish her story; she knows that beyond all else – her fears will not stop her.

'Then there is no choice.'

'No,' she agrees.

'And all you can do is continue until it is finished.'

'But perhaps I should rename the child?' she asks.

'It is done now,' he says gently, and she knows that he is right. What is written is written and cannot be undone.

'Bysshe?' she asks.

'Yes?'

'Why can't we find Harriet? Where is she? I am frightened for Claire and for her child. And for Harriet. We must help Harriet whilst we can.'

He is touched by her concern, and writes to Hookham, Harriet's solicitor, again.

13TH DECEMBER 1816: 5 ABBEY CHURCHYARD

Solicitor's letter to Shelley:

My dear sir,

It is several weeks since I had the pleasure of receiving a letter from you and you have no doubt felt surprised that I did not reply to it sooner. It was my intention to do so; but on enquiry found the utmost difficulty in obtaining information you desired relative to Mrs Shelley and your children.

Whilst I was yet endeavouring to discover Mrs Shelley's address, information was brought to me that she was dead – that she had destroyed herself. You will believe that I did not credit the report. I called at the house of a friend of Mr Westbrook. My doubt led to conviction. I was informed that she was taken from the Serpentine river on Tuesday last, apparently in an advanced state of pregnancy. Little or no information was laid before the jury which sat on the body. She was called Harriet Smith, and the verdict was – found drowned.

Your children are well, and are both, I believe, in London. This shocking communication must stand single and alone in the letter which I now address to you: I have no inclination to fill it with subjects comparatively trifling: you will judge of my feelings and excuse the brevity of this communication.

Yours very truly,
T. Hookham Jnr.
Old Bond St

Unaware of what he is doing, Bysshe's hands instinctively fold the paper over into a boat. He bends forward, the air knocked out of him and the earth receding as his lungs struggle for air. The words repeat themselves, fighting for an understanding that he cannot yet offer them. Harriet. Harriet, Harriet. Dead. Dead. Dead.

He sees her as she was when he first met her, hears her voice as she read to him. Remembers her standing at a customs post in Ireland with pamphlets in her skirts, humming at him, her smile as wide and unfrightened as a child's. How brave she was then, her blue eyes shining with excitement. She came to Ireland with Ianthe curled up inside of her like a promise and his love for her felt endless – that it would never unfurl,

424

becoming that dead weight that he dragged in his wake, longing to sever himself from her.

'I could not love you any more,' he whispers. 'I could not.' When he can stand, he goes to Mary. She is writing, her head bent over and her pen flying easily across the page. She does not see him, too engrossed in the story as she creates it. He stands in the doorway and watches her. There is a peace in knowing that she remains free of the knowledge he holds in his hands, that in her world as she writes Harriet yet lives and they might still find her.

He is tempted to leave her, but just as he turns away she comes to a stop, sits back and sighs, lifting her arms up and stretching. She catches sight of him, knows at once that something terrible has happened.

'Bysshe?'

'Harriet.' The sound of her name on his lips brings a fresh wave of grief.

'No!' She takes him to the manuscript, and there on the page he reads of a woman's death, at the very moment of her marriage.

'She was not strangled as I have written?' begs Mary.

'No,' he says, 'she was found in the Serpentine.' He sits on the bed, the letter fluttering to the floor.

Mary picks it up, unfolds the boat and reads. 'She was with child – again?' she whispers. He nods. Mary sighs, yet does a quick calculation; it could not have been Bysshe.

'Ianthe and Charles, I do not know where they are,' he says.

'We must have them with us,' Mary says rapidly before he can speak. 'We will do everything we can. We must write at once to her father and offer to have them!'

'Ianthe,' he whispers, 'she has blue eyes, just like her mother's.'

Mary holds his face in her hands. 'Bysshe,' she says, 'look

at me.' He looks into her eyes, sees strength there and determination. 'We will find them and look after them. They can live with us. Perhaps we will return to Windsor, to the Great Park. We were happy there, Bysshe, we will find a garden for them to play in.' Her words wind their way around him, wrapping him in her kindness. 'And we will never ever send them away to school, but only keep them with us for ever until they find their own love, and long to leave us.'

He rests his head against her shoulder. 'Mary.'

She gently unfolds him on to the bed where she lies beside him until he sleeps.

Letter received by Harriet Shelley's sister, Eliza, and parents, written before her death:

7th December 1816

To you, my dear sister, I leave all my things as they more properly belong to you more than anyone, and you will preserve them for Ianthe, God bless you both. My dearest and much beloved sister, when you read this letter I shall no more be an inhabitant of this miserable world. Do not regret the loss of one who could never be anything but a source of vexation and misery to all belonging to me. Too wretched to exert myself, and lowered in the opinion of everyone, why should I drag on a miserable existence, embittered by past recollections and not one ray of hope to rest on for the future. The remembrance of all your kindness, which I have so unworthily repaid, has often made my heart ache. I know you will forgive me because it is not in your nature to be unkind or severe to any; dear amiable woman that I had never left you, oh! That I had always taken your advice. I might have lived long and happy, but weak and unsteady,

have rushed on my own destruction. I have not written to Bysshe.
Oh no, what would it avail, my wishes or my prayers would not be
attended by him and yet should he see this perhaps he might grant
my last request to let Ianthe remain with you always, dear lovely
child; with you she will enjoy much happiness, with him, none.

My dear Bysshe, let me conjure you by the remembrance of our
days of happiness to grant my last wish – do not take your innocent
child from Eliza, who has been more than I have, who has watched
over her with such unceasing care. Do not refuse my last request –
I never could refuse you and if you had never left me I might have
lived; as it is, I freely forgive you and may you enjoy that happiness
which you have deprived me of. There is your beautiful boy. Oh!
Be careful of him and his love may prove one day a rich reward.
As you form his infant mind so you will reap the fruits hereafter.

Now comes the sad task of saying farewell – oh, I must be
quick. God bless and watch over you all . . . you, dear Bysshe. And
you, dear Eliza. May all happiness attend ye both is the last wish
of her who loved you more than all others. My children; I dare
not trust myself there. They are too young to regret me and you
will be kind to them for their own sakes more than for mine. My
parents, do not regret me. I was unworthy of your love and care.
Be happy, all of you. So shall my spirit find rest and forgiveness.
God bless you all is the last prayer of the unfortunate,

Harriet S

14TH DECEMBER 1816: 5 ABBEY CHURCHYARD
When they wake, Mary and Bysshe are resolved.

'You must go to London, and speak to Harriet's father,'
Mary says. 'We must let them know at once that we will take
the children.'

'Will you come with me?'

'No, I am so close to finishing now, I must carry on, but I will come as soon as I can.'

Bysshe goes to see his lawyer, Longdill, immediately.

'The Westbrooks, Harriet's parents, intend to contest your right to custody, and have employed a very able lawyer,' he tells him.

'But why?' asks Bysshe, bemused. 'I am their father!'

'And yet in the eyes of the world you have abandoned them,' he says, 'and you remain both unmarried, an advocate of free love. Do you believe any judge will find that acceptable?'

'What must I do?' he asks.

'Perhaps you might respect your wife's final request, which was that you abandon any attempt of custody of Ianthe, who has come to love her aunt Eliza – and remain content with custody of your son.'

'They are my children,' he says again, angry now.

'Bad temper will not help you,' says Longdill smoothly. 'It is a fact that you sired them; it is also a fact that every aspect of your life appears to any reasonable person to prove you unfit to keep them.'

'I am to lose everything then?' he asks.

'Except your principles. They, it seems, might remain intact,' says the lawyer drily.

'Then tell me what am I to do?'

'You can accept the facts as they are,' he says, 'and desist from any and all types of accusation. Be aware, Sir Percy, that they have hired an excellent lawyer and intend to make the most of your . . . unusual way of living. They have a dying woman's request upon their side. She has asked that you do not have charge of Ianthe, only of Charles.'

'I will write to them at once.'

'Do so. There are other things that might aid your case.'

'Anything.'

'If you were to . . . legalise your union with Miss Godwin, then they would have less cause to act against you. Without marriage and a secure home we must proceed with the utmost caution, for we might find ourselves faced not only with a custody case, but with a criminal prosecution.'

'They would prosecute me?'

'You've returned from an extended summer with Lord Byron, who is rumoured to be a sodomite, and you persist in making public your views on free love and the non-existence of God.'

'That is not illegal.'

'But inciting a revolution may well be.'

'This is ridiculous, Longdill!'

'But it remains the case. You are an avowed revolutionist, not a supporter of the status quo, and you would be bringing your children into a godless union.'

'So you are suggesting I should marry,' cries Bysshe. 'But that is the very thing that has caused this terrible situation! I should never have married Harriet.'

'And if you had not you would now have no right at all to your children,' says Longdill, gathering his papers together. 'I suggest you think about it and discuss it with Miss Godwin.'

'We are of the same mind on marriage; it is a commitment made necessary only for the advantage of men.'

The lawyer merely nods at him as he ushers him out of the room.

5 ABBEY CHURCHYARD

Mary writes, the words coming fast and furious, the images playing through her sleep and on into the day. She is careful to spend some time each day with William, but it is the writing that fills her mind and captures her attention. In her heart she is with Victor Frankenstein as his story spins out over the familiar mountains and lakes of Geneva, or in the ice-bound ship. She longs for a break – for both herself and her characters – from the string of tragedies which has been visited upon all of them.

She picks up Bysshe's letter on her way out of the door; she has begun to write at a small coffee house away from William and Elise, she enjoys being in her imaginary world amongst the noise of humanity. The letter is a snag in her routine and she opens it impatiently:

I have had yet another meeting with Longdill, the lawyer, and have told him that I was under contract of marriage to you; and he said that in such an event all pretences by Harriet's parents to retain the children would cease. Hunt said very delicately that this news might be a soothing intelligence for you.

She reads it again. And again. She carries it, alongside her manuscript out of the front door and into the abbey, where she sits in the same pew where she once acknowledged how much she longed for such an event. As she sits silently in the abbey, she wonders at the terrible cost of her desire to be married.

The death of Harriet.

She would not have chosen it and yet she bows her head, expressing gratefulness to whatever deity has granted her wish. And she vows to look after Harriet's children well.

In the coffee house she orders her papers and begins to write.

She decides that the stubbornness of the captain, who has insisted that he will make his journey north whatever the cost to his crew, will begin to soften, just as her own beliefs have been called into question and made to bend in the face of tragedy, so in her novel the ice begins to melt and break up, offering passage to the men, back home to their families.

She is close now, so close to finishing her story. Months of revision might remain, but the story itself is coming to an end. She looks at the manuscript, at the words she has written. '*I have murdered the lovely and the innocent.*' It is true, in her writing she has found a place for her fury at her creator, and the misery his rejection has caused her, but she is tired of it now, and longs for it to end. '*I think on the heart in which the imagination of it was conceived . . . and I long for the moment when that imagination will haunt my thoughts no more.*' She sits back and smiles before leaning forward and taking up her pen again. '*Fear not that I shall be the instrument of further mischief, my work is nearly complete,*' she writes. '*Soon these burning miseries will be extinct . . . I shall ascend my funeral pile triumphantly, and exult in the agony of the torturing flames. The light of that conflagration will fade away; my ashes will be swept into the sea by the winds. My spirit will sleep in peace.*' She sees her monster leaping from the ship into the sea: '*He was soon borne away,*' she writes, '*by the waves, and lost in the darkness and distance.*'

Gone. She takes a sip of coffee. It is cold and unpleasant. She looks out of the window over the street where people rush past under an already darkening sky. What sorrow our love has caused, she thinks. And what tragedy we invite when we try to make the world perfect.

She picks up her papers and straightens them.

It is done. She must edit and work upon it, but the story itself is finished.

Mr Godwin to Shelley:

It will not have escaped your notice that two of the women who have loved you have gone to their deaths; you have two motherless children and the courts are unlikely to award you your children when you are known as a practitioner and supporter of free love. It cannot, I repeat, have escaped your notice that now is the time to retract your determination and to marry my daughter. Should you choose to do so, we might be reconciled. You once spoke of me as your mentor, as your father, I speak now in this capacity.

William Godwin

29TH DECEMBER 1816: 41 SKINNER STREET

Today Mary and Bysshe will finally see her father again. They will lunch in the old dining room together as they once used to, only this time neither Fanny nor Claire will be there. Mary will see her mother's portrait again. It is strange, but that is what she is most looking forward to.

The thought of seeing her father after these two long years fills her with equal amounts of excitement and fury. As she steps into Skinner Street, Mary has the strange sensation that she has never really left, that a part of her has remained here and that she might look up and meet her young self running down the stairs or coming in from the bookshop.

And then he is there, Papa, standing outside his study and waiting for her as he so often has.

'Papa.' He seems smaller; Bysshe towers above him.

'Mary.' He nods at her. 'Sir Percy.' He inclines his head at Bysshe. 'I am glad to see that you have both come to your senses.'

They say nothing.

'Welcome, welcome!' Papa continues, as though nothing at all has happened. 'We are all looking forward to tomorrow.'

'I cannot truly claim that I am,' says Bysshe, and Mary tugs at his wrist.

They sit around the table. 'Hello, William,' says Mary to her younger brother. She can see herself in his quiet, serious demeanour, his anxiety to demonstrate his cleverness.

Bysshe kicks her under the table. 'Miss Godwin,' he says, recalling that those were his first words to her.

'Sir Percy!' she responds.

'It is true you both met at this very table?' her brother asks.

'Yes, and also that I too have a child called William!' She looks up at Bysshe and he winks; she feels her heart turn over. Instinctively she looks to Fanny to see if she has noticed, but her chair lies empty. Being in Skinner Street has brought that loss home more deeply; if only Fanny had waited just a few more months she could have lived with them – a married couple – without shame. Mary says nothing. Beneath the table Bysshe rubs his shoe against her ankle.

'So,' Mrs Godwin is saying, 'we shall gather at St Mildred's at noon tomorrow. Is Claire really so very ill that she cannot attend?'

'She has a very bad fever,' says Bysshe. 'We should visit her as soon as we are able after the deed is done.'

'Yes, we should!' agrees Mary.

'And you have decided what to wear?'

'Yes, a dress of my mother's.'

'Oh!'

'Neither my mother nor I believed in marriage and yet we both succumbed, so it feels appropriate.'

'I have no doubt that she would give you her blessing!' says Papa happily.

You always attributed your own thoughts to her, thinks Mary. 'I hope so,' she replies. She finds she does not feel anything at all when she looks at her father. It has been too long, she thinks, and I can never go back, no longer love or believe in him as I once did.

Bysshe is tired; he accepts their congratulations and celebratory comments with a pained expression, relieved when Mary asks if they might look at her mother's portrait.

'Of course,' her father says, standing.

Together they stand beaeath the picture of Mary Wollstonecraft Godwin. 'I used to think she watched over me,' says Mary quietly, not wanting her father to hear, 'and that she was always with me.'

'And now?' he asks in response.

'And now I do not know any more,' she says quietly.

William appears at the door. 'She is not my mother,' he says matter-of-factly, looking up at the portrait, 'but only Fanny's.'

'And mine,' says Mary.

'Where is Fanny?' her half-brother asks them.

They clasp each other's hands tight. 'Where does Papa say she is?' asks Mary.

'He says that she had very bad flu and died of it, but I am worried for I have not seen her body and do not know where she is buried!'

Mary rests a hand upon his head. 'She is dead, William; I am afraid that is true.'

'I miss her,' says the boy.

'I'm sure you do. She was kind,' she agrees, angry with her father for not being truthful with the child. Yet more lies she thinks, in a house that prides itself on truthfulness.

'You are sure?' she asks Bysshe before they part that night.

He nods his head against her shoulder.

'Let me hear you say it,' she asks.

'I am sure,' he whispers.

'We will move to Windsor when it is done,' she whispers back, 'where the woods make you happy.'

He nods again, and thinks of Claire alone in her rooms in Bath, awaiting the birth of her child.

12TH JANUARY 1817: 12 NEW BOND STREET, BATH

Claire sits. She does not want to read and she does not want to look out of the window. It is a grey day, the sky lacking all light, the city at its worst. She shifts in her chair; she is uncomfortable, and very close to giving birth now. She holds her belly from beneath, taking the weight of it in her hands for a while, easing the pressure upon her bladder and sighing in relief. She would like this baby to be born, to emerge and be separate from her. Her back aches and when she walks she finds herself breathless.

'Let us hope she is not born on your wedding day!' she had joked to Bysshe, gratified by the darkening of his expression. On the day of their wedding he sent her a letter:

Dearest Claire,

Thank you, my kind girl for not expressing so much of what you must feel – the loneliness and low spirits, which arise from being entirely left. Nothing could be more provoking than to find all this necessary. However, they will now be satisfied and quiet. The ceremony, so magical in its effects, was undergone this morning at St Mildred's church in the city. Mrs G and G were both present, and appeared to feel no little satisfaction. Indeed Godwin throughout has shown the most polished and cautious attentions to Mary and me. He seems to think no kindness too great in compensation for what has passed. I confess I am not entirely deceived by this, although I cannot make my vanity entirely insensible to certain attentions paid in a manner so studiously flattering. Mrs G presents herself to me in her real attributes of affection, prejudice and heartless pride.

Yours,
Bysshe

On the morning of the wedding Claire had listened for the sound of the clocks striking noon. 'Hear that, Alba?' she whispered to her unborn child. 'That bell tolls for Sir Percy Bysshe Shelley. It tolls for the death of his belief, and the birth of his compromise.' The baby shifted as if in answer.

'I wonder who I am the disciple of now?' she asked aloud.

But now it is a fortnight since it was done, and still Claire cannot get used to the idea. Lady Mary Shelley. Her mother must have been beside herself with excitement and pleasure. Claire shifts again, uncomfortable. 'I hope,' she says firmly to her child, 'that you will never feel the need to be married!'

The baby stills and Claire smiles, rises and takes to her bed. Mary has returned to be near for the birth of the baby. Claire draws the bedclothes up to her neck, placing a pillow between her knees to ease the pain in her hips and, finally closing her eyes, whispers: 'You and me.'

A few hours later she feels her waters break, and the birth begin. 'Elise!' calls Claire, her voice high and clear. 'It's begun!'

Elise runs down the stairs. 'I shall send for Mary.'

'And Bysshe,' says Claire.

But it is Mary who comes. She sits with Claire through her

labour, holding her hand and promising her that the child will be safe. As the head of Claire's child crowns, they clasp hands in excitement and hope, the memories pouring between them.

'Oh, A girl!' cries Mary. They stare at her. Her dark eyes searching up at them.

'Alba!' cries Claire.

'A new dawn,' smiles Mary.

By the time Bysshe arrives, Claire is sitting in bed, her child wrapped and in her arms, feeding.

Bysshe laughs aloud with delight in her and Claire remembers that very same laugh lighting up the house at Skinner Street. She remembers conjugating the verb 'to love' in their Latin lessons. She remembers how much she loves him. Alba stirs at the sound and opens one eye, her face pressed to Claire's breast.

'She is beautiful,' he says. 'You both are!'

Claire does not answer. She does not turn away from her child as Bysshe stands to leave.

'Goodbye,' he says, 'Claire and Alba.'

She looks up then and smiles a brief, happy smile before turning to her child again. 'Your name is Alba Claire Byron,' she says, 'and you are all mine.' Alba opens both eyes wide and gazes up at her mother. Claire gazes back, unaware that Bysshe has gone and that Elise has left the room. Her eyes lost in her child's dark blue gaze.

Dear Izy

I am married! I never thought that I would write those words. And I have finished my novel. It will not be published under the name *Mary Shelley*, not yet, but I hope that it might one day sit next to *Shelley* on a bookshelf. The practical reasons for our union are many, principal among them the hope that Shelley's children will come to us. The court will decide soon. Harriet's family fight for custody, and Harriet also did not wish Shelley to have Ianthe; it is a sad tale. There are rumours that she had sunk so low as to become a prostitute; but Claire insists that she was more likely to be hiding a new pregnancy from her parents.

But, dear Izy, despite my determination to make as little of my marriage as possible, I'm afraid it is true that my heart leaped up as we spoke the vows to each other, using words repeated for centuries and feeling myself sanctified by something bigger than myself. Bysshe was uneasy and spoke the words as though each one might be a link in a chain that unwillingly binds him, but I hope that in time he too might feel the ancient strength in that commitment before a community; if only it could be done outside of a religious context, then I believe he might have no objection at all, alas that is not possible. Claire, of course, could not come; for the very specific reason you already know of.

The best thing, the very best thing, Izy, is that there is no longer any reason for David to object to our communication? I think of us both, our backs to Law hill and the sun upon our faces, and I remember so well my words to you then: I cannot marry, because my mother does not believe in it. *Like her I have come full circle, I have understood the need of such external bonds and rituals, to reflect the internal bond between two lovers. I am sending this with all my letters, for I have never stopped writing to you. When my life has felt too much to bear you were the only person I could turn to in my mind, and unburden myself.*

Please write, Your loving
Mary

Dear Mary,

David received a letter from Mrs Godwin, Claire's mother. She writes exactly as you have always described her, in an hysterical tone and with much drama. She writes unkindly that your father threatened suicide to force you into marrying; fortunately we remember that she told the same story of Shelley, inducing David to believe that he threatened to take laudanum in an attempt to persuade you to elope with him. This alone has convinced David that not all we hear from your parents is true and has alleviated some of his concern. Enough, at least, for him to feel ease at my writing.

Let us not speak of our separation and the reasons I have abided by it until we meet, it is enough that I have read your letters, and that you know I will soon be sending you several of my own, for I too have so often sat and written to you. Even deep in Scotland we heard tell of you, and the stories seem, perhaps, to be as full of envy as they are of hate. How, I ask myself, can Rousseau's novel La Nouvelle Héloïse *remain a bestseller, and yet those few who dare to live it remain so vilified?*

Tell me more, and more and more, of your finished novel, and your hopes for it. I too think of the times we spent together as girls, we who now have a boy and a girl between us. We used to imagine our children playing together, and perhaps now our imaginings can be made real – and I might finally meet your infamous poet for myself. David sends his congratulations. And I, of course – send my love.

Your,
Izy

1ST JANUARY 1818: ST PANCRAS CHURCHYARD

Mary enters the churchyard alone. In her hand she carries a manuscript, the pages loosely held together. Last night, at the dawning of the New Year, her novel was published anonymously. The fronds of the willow tree hang in strands of bright yellow, as she approaches her mother's grave. It is cold and the cemetery empty. She kneels before the stone and lifts her fingers to its damp surface, allowing them to fall into the familiar shape of the letters of her mother's name, the closest she has ever come to her caress.

'Mamma,' she whispers. 'I am a writer.'

There is a silence. The fronds of willow brush against her face. Mary rests her head against the cold stone, the pages in her hands fluttering upon the cold earth. 'I have brought it for you, Mamma,' she whispers.

The manuscript she holds in her hand is not anonymous. It has her own name written clearly across it. She holds it pressed against the stone. The wind lifts the willow, catching it in her hair, brushing her brow.

She sits on the damp earth in the cold, waiting. 'I have written my name upon it, Mamma,' she whispers.

'And what is your name?' the stone asks her.

'I am Mary Wollstonecraft Godwin Shelley,' she says aloud. 'I am each of those names. And I am myself.'

And with those words she is suffused with love. Slowly she places her manuscript beneath the tree. Upon the earth. Beside her mother.

Mary Shelley

Frankenstein was published, anonymously, on New Year's Day in 1818. It was felt that such a groundbreaking, daring novel could not be published under a woman's name. Mary's claim (in later editions) that she dreamed the novel neatly circumvents taking full conscious responsibility for the creation of a monster whose existence defied the natural godly order of the day. Whether she really did dream it or not we will never know. Initially, sales were slow, and there was no hint that it would become the book that has inspired generations of writers and artists. I hope that from somewhere up in the ether Mary knows that she not only matched, but superseded her parents. That Mary Wollstonecraft is having a bit of a revival would please Mary immensely. In death, Mary never forgave her stepmother Mrs Godwin. She had her mother's and father's bodies removed to Portsmouth, where they are buried with her. It seems that Hate, the name of her first-ever attempt at a novel, lasted.

One of the saddest and most difficult pieces of research for this novel was learning of the deaths of Mary's babies. In 1818, Mary, Bysshe, Claire, Wilmouse, Clara (Mary's second daughter) and Allegra (Alba) all moved to Italy. Byron still refused to see Claire, whilst insisting he had care of Allegra. In mid-August 1818 Elise contacted Claire, expressing grave concern about Byron's debauchery whilst caring for Allegra.

Shelley and Claire left immediately for Venice, leaving Mary with Wilmouse (aged two) and Clara (fifteen months). Clara became hot and feverish as the temperature in Italy soared. Terrified, Mary contacted a friend who tried to help, but Clara got no better. Meanwhile, Shelley arrived in Venice and, finding Byron viciously determined to refuse Claire the care of her daughter, lied to him, saying that it was Mary waiting to collect Allegra – not Claire. He then instructed Mary to arrive as rapidly as possible. So Mary, with her desperately ill daughter, made the four-day journey (much as she had to Arabella Road) with both Wilmouse and Clara. In the heat Clara deteriorated rapidly, probably becoming dehydrated, and upon arrival in Venice they frantically tried doctors, but to no avail. Clara Everina died on 24th September. Yet again, the fate of Claire and Mary's children was inextricably linked.

On 2nd June, a year later, as a friend painted his portrait, Wilmouse became ill with a stomach complaint. A doctor diagnosed worms, but three days later he developed a fever. Shelley remained by his bedside without moving as Mary tried her best to save him, but on 7th June 1819, their beloved Wilmouse also died.

Mary entered a deep and lasting depression, from which it is questionable she ever truly recovered. '*My dearest Mary, wherefore hast thou gone/ And left me in this dreary world alone?*' wrote Bysshe. And to William: '*My lost William, thou in whom/ Some bright sprite lived,*' the beginning of a poem he would never finish.

Mary had one final son, Percy, who did survive.

Life was not kind to Mary Shelley. She was born to famous parents with an immense talent, which she put to good use. She was gifted both the intense love affair and the fame she craved, but I suspect that in the end she would have happily traded it all for a life like the Baxters', a life in which her beloved Bysshe and their children survived.

Upon Shelley's death his father, Sir Timothy, offered to support Mary, as long as she refrained from discussing or popularising her dead husband. She refused, and spent the remainder of her life not only writing her own novels, but also editing and promoting Shelley's work. In the end, his father gave in. She never remarried, although she did become religious. She died of a brain tumour aged fifty-three, survived by her son, who with his wife continued to promote his parents' work, if in a highly romanticised and sanitised version of history. It may well be that the torn pages of the diaries (writer's gold!) were actually removed by Mary's daughter-in-law, Jane, who felt that they were too racy to remain as potential evidence of Mary's brief journey into polyamory.

Percy Bysshe Shelley died whilst sailing in the Mediterranean Sea in Italy on 8th July 1822. He had already written the poems that were to make him so firmly a part of the Romantic English canon. Writing about Shelley was perhaps the most difficult part of this novel – I both loved and hated him. He was undoubtedly a part of the romantic tradition that believed in poetry as a force for political change: '*Men of England wherefore plough/For the lords who lay ye low/Wherefore weave with toil and care/The rich robes your tyrants wear?*' – and described poets as: '*the unacknowledged legislators of the world.*'

He was wonderfully eccentric and unbelievably gifted – as well as beautiful. He was capable of profound instinctive understanding. He was full of love and integrity, but he also demonstrated an equally powerful lack of compassion or understanding. He ignored Clara's illness when he called Mary to Venice, and seemed entirely unaware of Mary's dilemma in loving him – a polyamorous man, who too often put his own ideas before her feelings.

But perhaps this gives us the clue to the powerful unconscious connection behind their mutual love; for didn't Mary's own father display exactly the same pattern, both adoring her and yet failing, ultimately, to allow her the expression of her own feeling? On hearing of William's death, Godwin wrote to Mary of her grief that although she may at first be pitied for it: '*When they see you fixed in selfishness and ill-humour, regardless of the happiness of everyone else, they will finally cease to love you, and scarcely learn to endure you.*' I find it hard to forgive him for offering his wonderful daughter such a comfortless condolence.

Claire Clairmont

In his biography of Shelley, Richard Holmes claims that he was perhaps a little unkind to Mary, partly because he fell under the spell of Claire Clairmont. I fear I may have done the same. Claire, with her dark eyes and her capacity to undercut the sometimes precious nature of Mary and Bysshe's thinking, stole my heart from the very beginning.

I did not want to paint her as 'second best' or a burden that Mary and Bysshe simply had to endure. Her letters demonstrate a vivid intelligence and a gift for self-parody. What happened to her next is as heartbreaking and difficult as what happened to Mary.

After Allegra's birth, she went to live with Mary and Bysshe in Windsor. They pretended that Allegra was one of their friend's (Leigh Hunt's) children. It was, by all accounts, an idyllic summer. Mary and Bysshe were finally part of a community of politically active and poetically creative people through Leigh Hunt's circle, which included a young poet named Keats (my first ever crush!). They rented Albion House in Windsor where everyone gathered.

Eventually however, the agreement made with Byron in Geneva that fateful summer had to be enacted, and Byron called for Allegra to be brought to him. Claire had avoided it for as long as possible but now (with Mary, Shelley and all the children) took the journey to Italy. Needless to say, their parting devastated Claire.

She wrote: '*I send you my child, because I love her too well to keep her. With you who are powerful and noble and have the admiration of the world she will be happy, but I am a miserable and neglected dependant.*'

Claire had no choice, no rights, and fighting for her child would almost certainly have resulted in her losing any rights of visitation. She had to succumb. When Allegra was to be collected (by a servant of Byron), Claire claimed Allegra was too ill to travel. Mary, realising that to refuse might mean Byron would react by refusing her visitation rights, offered to provide for Elise to go with Allegra. Weeping, Claire agreed. On 28th April, she wrote: '*I love Allegra with a passion that almost destroys my being as she goes from me. My dear Lord Byron, I most truly love my child . . . She loves me . . . She stretches out her arms for me . . . and coos for joy when I take her. I assure you I have wept so much tonight that now my eyes seem to drop hot and burning blood.*'

Byron did not respond to Claire's letter.

On 14th and 16th August, letters arrived from Elise, saying that Claire must come and save her and Allegra from Byron. We know the consequences of that journey for Mary – she lost a child. Meanwhile, Claire was allowed to spend the rest of that summer with Allegra in Este, whilst Mary watched and grieved for Clara. In the autumn, Allegra was returned to Byron, who placed her in the care of the British Consul.

After Wilmouse's death, Claire cancelled a trip to visit Allegra, too concerned for Mary's ill health. On 12th November 1819, Mary had a new baby. The winter was freezing and Mary remained in bed with little Percy, whilst Claire sang to them both. Meanwhile Shelley, true to form, flirted with a young cousin visiting Florence. The group met Mrs Mason, a radical woman who persuaded Claire that she should leave Shelley and Mary in the interests of her own independence, and find work. Claire became a governess in Florence.

When Allegra was four, Claire heard that Byron had placed her child in a convent near Ravenna. She wrote Byron a furious note: '*You promised me . . . That my child, whatever its sex, should never be away from its parents.*' Claire understood that what Byron had done represented '*a serious and deep affliction*' for a child so young. Her powerlessness and pain was such that Shelley and Mary invited her back to stay, and the sisters got on well, Claire delighting in little Percy. She left them on 1st November 1820, the day Byron arrived for a visit.

In the spring of 1821, Mary received desperate letters from Claire, saying that she had dreamed Allegra was dead. Knowing that Byron, Shelley and Mary were spending the summer in La Spezia together, Claire wrote to Shelley, begging him to intervene, and hoping Allegra would be removed from the convent. So desperate and full of dread was Claire that she asked Mary and Shelley to help her kidnap Allegra. They refused. Perhaps they felt Allegra was safer away from Byron, or that once Byron left Italy, Claire might visit Allegra freely?

Shelley did speak to Byron, but his hatred of Claire was absolute and he claimed he wanted to protect Allegra from her mother, and bring her up 'a Christian and married woman'. What a ridiculous irony, given Byron's appalling treatment of women.

The triangle of Shelley, Claire and Byron is fascinating, and Byron's deliberate cruelty and furious dismissal of Claire is suggestive, but of what? Was he envious of Shelley's love and commitment to Claire? Why was he so disgusted by free love and atheism when his own behaviour was so clearly godless? Was his physical insecurity so deep that he could not bear to question the social hierarchy that offered him his wealth and privilege? Or did he realise, perhaps, that Claire had successfully played him for a fool, and taken his name for a child that was Shelley's? We can only speculate.

Claire arrived to join Mary for the summer. Mary was

pregnant again, and the sisters happy to see one another. On 23rd April Claire went to find a place for them all to rent on the coast, near Lerici. Whilst she was away, the news arrived that Allegra was dead. Claire's dreams proved prophetic. Fearful that Claire might attack Byron, who was nearby, they did not tell her Allegra was dead, but decided to wait until they had taken summer lodgings.

Mary and Claire left on the 26th. Everyone arrived at Casa Magni, a desolate villa on a rocky coast, three miles from the nearest settlement. No one could bear to tell Claire that Allegra was dead. Finally, on 2nd May, as they were discussing the situation, Claire came searching for everyone and overheard that her daughter was gone. Claire, who was known for her volatility, did not react as anyone expected. She became silent and withdrawn. She grieved in her deepest self for her child. Byron, at Shelley's request, sent her a lock of Allegra's hair and offered her the right to arrange the funeral. Far too little, and much too late. Claire could not do it; she was too grief-stricken. Byron arranged for Allegra to be buried at Harrow, the vicar named her a bastard and had her interred in the courtyard outside of the cemetery, with no stone.

After Shelley's death that summer, Claire and Mary lived apart. Claire became a governess in Russia, she lived independently and never married. In her old age she denounced the free love ethic, claiming Byron and Shelley were: '*monsters of lying meanness, cruelty and treachery . . . Lord B became a tiger slaking his thirst for inflicting pain upon defenceless women who under the influence of free love, loved him.*' Hence the title of this book – *Monsters*.

The final summer 1822

In La Spezia that summer, Mary and Shelley slept apart. Mary was suffused with dread but Shelley refused to take her fears seriously. They were estranged in their grief for their lost children, Shelley (as ever) finding distraction in falling in love, and Mary no longer finding the sexual love that results in procreation – and the loss of children – desirable. She was depressed, cut off and fearful for Percy, her remaining child.

She did not like Bysshe sailing, but he adored his new boat. When Byron sailed into their bay with a bigger and better boat, Shelley increased the length of his own masts. He did not realise the sails were too tall for his boat, making it dangerous. Mary begged Shelley to return to Pisa, he refused. She punished him by withdrawing.

On 16th June, the pregnant Mary began to bleed. She bled unstoppably for seven hours and began to lose consciousness. She was dying. The doctor failed to arrive. Shelley sent for ice and when it arrived, despite Claire and Jane Williams begging him to stop, he filled a bath and plunged Mary in. He undoubtedly saved her life, but when she recovered she could only grieve for the lost pregnancy. A week later, Shelley woke her in the midst of a terrible nightmare. He dreamed the sea was flooding the house, and he must strangle Mary.

When his friend Leigh Hunt arrived across the bay, Shelley longed to sail in his boat to greet him. Mary begged him not to go. At first he relented, but eventually he could no longer resist and left. When Mary learned he had arrived safely she sent him a note begging him to return. He enjoyed a week where he was reportedly in wonderful spirits, planning his new magazine and laughing with his friends. He promised Mary he would return and, despite a storm brewing, he set off on Monday 8th July.

Mary waited. He did not arrive. She went to Livorno and Lerici and heard of two bodies washed up. She drove twenty miles to Byron's house; he had no news but described her as:

'More like a ghost than woman. I have seen nothing in tragedy or upon the stage . . . So affecting.'

On 19th July it was finally confirmed that Shelley was dead. His body identifiable by his trousers, and a copy of Keats' poetry tucked safely into the inside of his jacket pocket. He was twenty-nine. Their earthly love affair was over.

ACKNOWLEDGEMENTS

Writing a book may look solitary from the outside, but it is peopled with imaginary characters on the inside and so never feels lonely – at least not for the writer. But it does take you away from your family and friends. So my first and greatest thanks are to my family. Alastair, for living with me as I write. I often forget he exists – or when I remember that he does, sometimes wish he'd go away again so that I can continue imagining. Thank you for not going away. To our children: Jem, Xa and Ela, each of you far more engrossing than any story I could ever write. Thank you for having far more faith in my capacity as a writer than I do – and telling me so. Special thanks to Ela for work with the copyedit. To Sarah Eastaff and Becca Burney – more wonderful women for our family.

Thank you to Blackbird Leys and Oxford city libraries and Blackwell's children's bookshop (now defunct). In these places (undisturbed by sensitive librarians and booksellers) I read endlessly, and so entirely unconsciously began to learn how to write. Libraries are irreplaceable resources; without them there would be fewer writers like me, from working-class immigrant backgrounds.

To Ro Turan for your support and sensitivity, reading each manuscript whether published or unpublished and talking it through with unfailing care and (often enough) enthusiasm. I am deeply grateful for the time you give me.

To Barbara Bradshaw, as ever, for your friendship. Martin Jennings, helpful, self-deprecating and with a profound understanding of the process. Natasha Narayan and Paul Rutman for explaining the particular fear that is commission anxiety. Who knew? Bruce Cockburn, Scots advisor, and Tess Belnkinsop, for knowing about sailing. To Nick Hicks, Helen and Tony Nolan, and Ian and Felicity Blair for their incredible generosity in offering their homes as places to write. Paula Barry and Danny Lee, legal eagles. Lucy-Jean, colleague and friend. The lovely receptionist, Victoria, at Hotel Angleterre, Geneva. The staff at the New Weston library, Oxford. Invaluable.

Joe's café, for never throwing me out, although the coffee's gone cold the place is heaving – and it would be really good to have that extra table.

To the remarkable historians who do all the heavy research so that I can learn on the back of their extensive efforts – yet wilfully ignore the occasional fact – in the interests of the story. Especially Richard Holmes, Charlotte Gordon and Daisy Hay.

To all at Andersen Press – Charlie Sheppard, for commissioning me and sticking with it through the endless revisions in such a limited time; Chloe Sackur, editor, Kate Grove for the lovely cover, Paul Black for publicity and Sue Cook, copyeditor. Any mistakes must, ultimately, be my own. There will certainly be some, but I hope not too many.

To you, the reader – for reading.